REDWINE HILL

The Secrets at Primevil Asylum

Chris,
To my gifted
Nephew, Your Aunt
L.L. Stolmeier

L.L Stolmeier

CONTENTS

Redwine hill

1

Primevil

The day Charlotte C. Carrion turned sixteen, she was in a bread shop near a blighted area of Boston where lost souls would congregate begging for scraps of bread. Although the exact time she turned sixteen is unclear, the moment she stepped out of Mrs. Longley's bread shop, she was greeted by a throng of outstretched arms and begging cries, and she dropped her sack of bread and staggered down the street toward Boston's town square holding the sides of her skull in the palms of her hands, and with an ear-piercing shrill screamed, "It's not my time!"

In a glassy-eyed, pitiful catatonic-like state, Charlotte roamed the streets of Boston for at least a week before one of the Collectors came upon her and wrestled her to the ground. Charlotte yelled and clawed at the man and his two sidekicks. "No, don't do this. Please—you can't take me to one of the asylums. Get your slimy hands off me."

The Collector smacked Charlotte across the face. "Shut up!" He looked her up and down. "There doesn't seem to be anything you can barter with, for better accommodations."

Charlotte screamed, "Yes, I have something."

The Collector was unshaven, and smelled of filthy cheap rum and spoiled cheese. He wore garments, she thought, that he'd stolen from one or more of his previous encounters, teens whom he believed to be insane. One of the gangsters was noticeably ravaged by polio and had a hard time with his gait. The other presented with a quarter-inch-size reddish-purple lesion under his left eye oozing yellow puss that settled in a cavern of his emaciated cheek. Charlotte knew this to be an early sign of scurvy.

The Collector motioned toward the one with the hideous sore on his face. "Let go of her arm. I want to see what she thinks would be worth making the long trip over to a 'good' asylum."

He got close to Charlotte, and she thought about spitting in his face, but that would put an immediate end to her situation, and not an acceptable one for her. The Collector would surely kill her for any small infraction. She reached in her pocket, and after digging to the bottom, where lint would normally gather, she grabbed hold of the only thing that had any material or emotional meaning. She lifted something into the air, held between her thumb and index finger. "Here, this was my mother's ring." Her eyes swelled with tears. "It's the only thing I have left besides the clothes I'm wearing."

The teen with the sore on his face grinned an almost toothless smile. "We've tortured a teen for less."

The Collector ripped the ring from Charlotte's fingers and held it up to the dim light that was coming from a nearby store. "It's not much of a ring, and since we're so close to Redwine Hill, that's where we'll be taking you."

Charlotte kicked and screamed. "Please, I beg you—not Redwine Hill." She saw a shop owner look out at her, but she quickly pulled the curtains and turned and walked away. "No one is going to help you. You've had a sixteenth birthday, whether you want to admit it or not—that's up to you—but no one is going to step in and help an insane teenager."

With a length of rope he'd undoubtedly stolen off a nearby merchant ship, he bound Charlotte's hands together and with the remaining length dragged her like a sickened mule to slaughter. "Sorry, lass, but I'm tired, and it's been a long day. But most importantly, I don't give a crab where you end up." He held up Charlotte's mother's ring. "This little bobble isn't going to buy me anything. We'll see what we can get for you at Redwine Hill." He put the ring in his pocket and once again jerked on the rope, causing it to dig into her skin.

Charlotte knew that one of the asylums on Redwine Hill was known by the inmates as Prime-evil because of its dark and damp brick-lined rooms and the bands of rats that scurried across its floors scavenging specks of dried, putrid cheese. It was also rumored that they did experimental surgeries on their inmates. At the time, when Charlotte's friend told her this several years ago, she didn't believe it, but now she would find out firsthand whether Prime-evil was as horrific as she'd heard. The name had been shortened just a few years ago to Primevil.

As the Collector pulled Charlotte up toward the pinnacle of Redwine Hill, the two rat-like adolescents pawed at her golden-fleece-colored hair and scurried back and forth under the taut length of rope that joined her and the Collector, giggling and chanting, "A half penny for us and two for Collector . . . a whole penny for us, and four for Collector."

The Collector yelled, "Shut up, you fools. She'll bring a lot more than just a few pennies."

Unknown to the Collector (but not to those who would soon be the benefactor of Charlotte C. Carrion), like the others, deep inside her brain lived a glow of sanity, but not enough to penetrate the confusion that cloaked the inner core. Charlotte knew she was near somewhere but to her it wasn't a place she wanted to be. Her brain was cloudy, and she was having trouble concentrating, due to the pain that resided far below the surface of her skull.

She could feel the undoing of something deep inside her brain. She tried to grab her head, but the Collector yanked her hands away. "Stop stalling. I need to collect my fee and visit the pubs. I don't want to spend any more time on teenage lunatics tonight. I don't need to know the reason for the sixteenth birthday curse; all's I need to know is I get paid for ridding the town of teenage squalor."

Charlotte's wrists began to bleed from the taut rope she was struggling to pull off. "I know everyone must say this, but it's true—I'm not sixteen yet. Look—I lost all my identification a few months back. You'll just have to take my word for it."

The repulsive sidekicks burst into wild laughter, and one wiped his oozing sore on his shirtsleeve, which left a streak of puss across his face from his open facial wound.

Charlotte shivered as the Collector forced her down on an empty overturned bucket, at the back door of Primevil. The dark, dank alley that smelled of rotting garbage was vacant. She didn't think anyone would come to her rescue. The Collector pounded on the back door of the asylum, while his sidekicks chanted, "Pennies and coins enough for three. We'll be rich when we get our fee."

The Collector yelled, "Keep your trap shut. I can't hear if anyone's coming."

He pounded on the door again, and it slowly opened. The woman at the door said in a disgruntled voice, "Its past midnight, and we've been closed for an hour. Come back tomorrow."

The Collector pushed the door open. "Listen, Nurse, I'm weary, and I'm not coming back in the morning. We'll split the fee with you."

His two freaky comrades circled around him, and the one with the open wound on his face said, "She ain't getting any of our fees."

The Collector pushed him back. "Get out of my face, you derelict." He landed on the cobblestone alleyway. "Splitting the money four ways is better than no money at all."

The one with the compromised gait put his hand out and helped his friend up. "Thanks, Polo."

The nurse grimaced. "How original. Did he get his name from his affliction, polio?" Polo nodded and held his hand out for his portion of the fee.

The Collector seemed irritated. "Just go get the money."

The three men were looking inside Primevil waiting for their payoff. Charlotte saw this as the time to get away. She slid off the bucket and tried to crawl away, which was almost impossible with her hands tied together. It didn't matter though; the Collector heard her and picked her up by the back of her hair. It felt as if a huge part of her scalp was being torn off. She was trying to push her head toward the Collector's hand, to relieve the pressure. She let out a scream and went limp. The only thing keeping her from hitting the stone ground was the Collector holding her up by her hair. She could hear the lady come back and count the paper money into the Collector's free hand as he held tight to the back of her head.

The nurse finished counting the money. "That's forty-five dollars for you and fifteen for me. Nice doing business with you."

The Collector held the money in the palm of his hand as the nurse put a wad of ones in her pocket. He then pushed Charlotte into the building, and she hit her head. The next thing she heard was the Collector saying, "You each get two dollars. Now get the hell out of here before I change my mind and give you each a buck."

The nurse was disgusted. "You can't leave her on the ground. Bring her in, and put her on the exam table."

Charlotte could feel her arms being picked up, and she could feel her body being dragged across the stone alleyway, over the threshold, and onto a cool smooth floor. She could feel the pain in her back, and she suspected that it was covered with abrasions. Charlotte didn't weigh but a hundred pounds, but the Collector was breathing heavy as if he had done an enormous amount of work.

The lady in the white uniform sneered. "Here, I'll help you get her on the table. You seem to be out of shape for a Collector."

As the Collector grabbed Charlotte's upper body and the nurse took her feet, the Collector let out a loud moan and grabbed his back. Charlotte's head hit the table, sending waves of pain throughout her brain. She heard the nurse. "For God's sake, pick up your end."

The very last thing she remembered was the woman in white jabbing a needle into her neck, and everything went black.

Charlotte was out, but her mind still raced in the silence of her skull. She remembered her mother saying that suspicions had arisen nearly ten years ago, when she was about six years old. Something about a virus spreading across the area, catapulting otherwise normal boys and girls into lunacy, although some guessed it was more sinister than that. Something had to have caused the epidemic that now covered large areas of the population throughout the world. Charlotte's mother would say, "You know, Charlotte, some say there's a pattern to this madness. Infected teens are born with God-given sanity, but on their sixteenth birthday, it's thought that neurons in the brain explode, casting the teens into an abyss of confusion they never recover from."

Darkness weighed heavy on Charlotte, and she felt as if the room were closing in on her. She couldn't move, and her breaths were coming slow and steady. She felt movement to her body, but couldn't tell what or who was doing it. The pain in her head became so intense, she went into a netherworld. She knew she was doomed.

Redwine hill

2

What the Tides Washed Ashore

As Charlotte C. Carrion dug her nine stubby toes into the cool dense sand, she looked back at the asylum that she now called home. She helplessly looked at the moon and wished it would blink out and put her in total darkness. Just a few months ago she was still living in one of the few pockets of normalcy the big city of old Boston had left to offer. Asylums dotted the Massachusetts coast—and for that matter, hundreds lined the Atlantic coastline. Once-abandoned buildings now housed the truly insane, as defined by the Collectors and their gangs of juvenile hoodlums and derelicts who roamed the streets of New England, who captured those they believe to be crazy and delivered them to one of the notorious asylums for a fee.

As Charlotte sat on the beach, she saw a flicker of light against a towering wall, and knew she had little time before she would be dragged inside. They'd come looking for her, but there were no attack dogs like she'd heard were in some of the institutions. Rumor was, if inhabitants of Primevil found any four-legged creatures on its property, the animals would be added to the evening stew. It was no secret that during mealtime Charlotte guarded against eating anything that resembled meat.

The lights flickered again. "Oh, no, they've sent someone for me."

She could tell by the outline of the approaching guard that it was Jared. He was handsome on all accounts. Muscular, tan, and in a different world she would have thought him a great catch for her, but others would have said he was beyond her reach. He had been at Primevil for only a short time, but quickly worked himself up to become one of its guards. Asylum patients, or prisoners, as Charlotte called them—no one really cared—were all on the lower floors of the seven-floor facility, while so-called trusted patients were housed on the top floor. They had special privileges, and since Jared was a guard, that's where his room was located.

Jared turned out to be one of two friends Charlotte had at Primevil. The other was Serenity, who was older than she, but more severely debilitated by deterioration of her mind.

Jared, Serenity, and Charlotte did everything together: meals, recreational activities, any academic programs, which the teens were forced to go to, even though, in their current situation, there was no need for such knowledge. They spent every free minute together as well. Although new patients such as Charlotte couldn't be assigned a roommate until later, they did spend hours on the beach talking. There were tall rock walls with coiled barbed wire on either side of Primevil. The walls extended into the ocean, and disappeared some distance out. There were security cameras and sirens located everywhere. Escaping was not an option; it would be suicidal.

Serenity and Charlotte had similar upbringings. They'd both had had loving parents. Fathers both dying before they hit their teen years. Serenity's mother died several years ago, and Charlotte's mother had died just recently. The big difference was in how they died. Charlotte's parents both died in some type of accident. Her mother had been in a car accident just a few months earlier and died instantly, while her father died when she was just ten years old. He was climbing an apple tree for fresh fruit and fell and broke his neck. He lingered in the hospital for several days before passing. Charlotte's mother had been a free spirit, and didn't set any household rules or chores for her. Her father had been the disciplinarian. Once her mother died, she lost interest in school and her friends. She didn't even take Jamie with her the day she went insane at the bread store. Jamie just sat on the front porch as Charlotte looked back at her beloved dog sitting and wagging her tail. Just waiting for her to return, but she never did.

The death of Serenity's parents was a different story. They both died under suspicious circumstances. They'd worked for the government and told Serenity that they were getting close to finding out what was happening to the young people of the world. They were supposed to be doing research on a cancer drug, but in their spare time they worked on the question everyone was asking but no one was doing anything about: What was happening to all the teenagers to make them go crazy?

Charlotte turned and looked back; she could see Jared had stopped to talk to another guard.

She thought, *I wish Serenity was here tonight. I haven't heard how she was doing since I dropped her off at the infirmary yesterday. Jared will want me to come in, but I can't. I haven't gotten to talk with my therapist, Serenity, tonight.* Serenity wasn't Charlotte's therapist, but conversing with someone her same age was very therapeutic.

Charlotte leaned back on her elbows and let her face feel the cool breeze as she watched something floating in the water—nothing significant, probably a stick. Since being dragged here by the Collector, she wondered what had happened to her dog. She worried if her dog, Jamie, had been forced to become an attack dog or had been ground up for someone's meal. Tears came to her eyes. She couldn't think of the past. Somehow, the past was special and not to be brought up by her or anyone. The world could never be the same. She remembered sitting for hours while throwing a stick for her beloved dog, and watching her retrieve and return it each time. Jamie had been a loyal companion up to the day Charlotte's brain went screaming mad outside the bread store. Jamie would've gone after that stick in the ocean, and Charlotte would've laughed during their carefree day, but there was no longer any laughter.

Charlotte remembered her mother saying, "We no longer have to worry about wars to destroy us. We now can destroy our world one step at a time. One wrong move, one greedy or heartless person, or one unchecked virus is all it takes to extinguish our precious existence."

She thought about how different she and her mother had been. "Charlotte C. Carrion," her mother would say, "the C stands for cantankerous, which you know means hard to deal with, and our last name, Carrion, I'm afraid to say, means dead and decaying flesh. Sorry, Charlotte, you don't have a lot to work with." Charlotte's mother had approached every day as if something good was going to happen, but it seldom had. Her mother loved the ocean and the soft salt mist that covered her entire body, even on her eyelids. She might have liked this asylum, where one of the privileges allowed was to sit on the sand facing the ocean, as Charlotte often did. The bay seemed to be the outer wall of this prison.

Charlotte felt herself drifting off to sleep and nearing a dream of her and Jamie playing, when the tide belched up an unexpected surprise. She sat upright to get a look at what the waters had deposited at her feet.

It wasn't a stick. She let out a scream that set off a siren from the facility, prompting Jared to come running toward her. She recognized the thing as an arm, but not from its decomposing appearance. From the elbow down, the arm was bloated and stretched like a balloon ready to pop, and the fingernails bore a bleached-out orange color. Earlier yesterday she had painted Serenity's fingernails with bright orange Monarch Butterfly polish, just before Serenity went to the infirmary complaining of stomach cramps.

Jared reached her as she pointed to the almost unrecognizable appendage. "It's Serenity!" She sobbed.

Jared gently turned and eased Charlotte's face into his chest. "We need to go. The Collectors are coming."

Charlotte knew the Collectors had a lot of power. They were appointed by the head of security for each continent. Each colony had several head Collectors that mainly sat around and did paperwork, but the majority of the street Collectors were given a lot of leeway to do as they pleased. Who they choose for their sidekicks, to help round up the insane teens, was up to the Collectors themselves. This was the government's solution to manage the epidemic of teens going berserk. Lock them away until they could find the reason behind the outbreak.

Charlotte watched as a few Collectors came down the hill. She thought Jared seemed to be taking in the gruesome sight too casually. "What's happening?" she screamed into Jared's chest.

The Collectors were now at the waterline scanning the surface. One of the men picked up a waterlogged object and put it in a burlap bag. "Anyone find any other pieces?"

Charlotte whispered, "Pieces. What do they mean by pieces?"

That was more than Charlotte could handle. Her last sight was Jared's face in a torturous grim look before she went into a dark place and went limp in his arms. She could still hear what was happening around her, but she couldn't move.

The Collectors walked toward them. The one carrying the burlap bag stopped right in front of them. The bag was still dripping; Charlotte guessed the saltwater and some bodily fluids from Serenity's arm were making a puddle next to the Collector's feet. Charlotte could hear the dripping and cringed with every drop. The Collector blurted out, "I need to talk with this patient."

Jared held on to Charlotte's waist. "Perhaps tomorrow would be better. You can't exactly interrogate an unconscious person."

The lead Collector came over and lifted one of Charlotte's eyelids. "Yep, she's out for the night. Wrap it up, boys. It's getting cold, and I'm losing my patience. This is the fourth time this week that body parts have washed ashore."

.

3

Mystery Meat

As Charlotte was coming out of her stupor, Jared carried her to her room on the first floor, laid her on the bed, and rested her head gently on a pillow covered with a stained light-brown fabric. Charlotte could feel her brain starting to work. She had no roommates; she would remain alone until the three-month evaluation. The guards protected Charlotte, as they did any new patient, while she slept apart from the mentally ill residents who roamed the halls in the late night looking for patients to rob of their belongings. Until she could fend for herself, Charlotte would be confined to segregation, a world unto herself. This suited Charlotte just fine. She even thought of blowing the evaluation so they would think she was crazed and not give her a roommate. She enjoyed her privacy.

When Charlotte sat up, she cupped her hands to the sides of her head; her fingertips could feel the blood pulsate through the arteries leading to her brain. "It feels like my head is going to explode. What happened?" she asked Jared.

Charlotte couldn't tell for sure, but it was either one of the patients or a member of the Collector's gang peering in at her through the pane of glass on the door to her room. He had a crooked grin on his face caused by his top row of teeth jetting outward into his lip. He was singing, "The girl is causing trouble, trouble, trouble.

You're going to be locked away." She could see his blurred figure dancing outside her room like some kind of gruesome ballerina.

Charlotte yelled, "Get out! Get out before I hack you into little pieces."

Jared held Charlotte's hand. "It's talk like that that'll get you thrown into solitary confinement."

"I don't care. I'm tired of being poked and prodded, stared at by degenerates, and having my privacy violated. What is it with this place that they're always spying on me?"

Charlotte could hear one of the patients in the hallway. "We Willy Wanda, crippled and deformed, you count your sanity while I count mine."

Charlotte got up and ran for the door, opened it, and screamed, "Leave! Get away!"

The man had a putrid smell and left an oily brown film on the window where he'd pressed his face against it. He had stained mismatched clothes on, and filthy bare feet. He danced in front of her door. "You be Wanda?"

"No, I'm not Wanda. I'm not anybody you know. Get out of here." She grimaced. "Would it kill you to use a toothbrush every now and then?" He slinked down the hallway and looked into the next room.

Charlotte shivered and went back to Jared. "I hate this place."

Jared tried to sound comforting. "Charlotte, you seem a bit paranoid this evening, but after finding Serenity's arm floating in on the tide, I guess it's justified." He sat on the edge of the bed, and his weight tore the threadbare sheets. "Charlotte, do you know how fortunate you are that I was able to come to your rescue this night?"

She stammered, "Rescue! Are you insane?"

Before she could say anything, Jared said, "Yes, Yes, I am a bit insane, but that doesn't detract from what I did for you."

"Okay, Jared, bad choice of words, but didn't you also see Serenity chopped up and floating in the froth from the ocean? Did I really see that?"

She looked at Jared with searching eyes, wanting him to say it was all a bad dream. "Charlotte, I'll tell you this once, and after tonight we'll never speak of it again."

She was almost yelling now. "What do you mean 'it'? That was Serenity! She was, besides you, my only friend in this dungeon."

14

He picked up Charlotte's hand and brushed his lips against her soft, thin fingers. "I've been here longer than you have, and seen things, but if you ever want to get out of here you need to play by their rules. Why do you think I rose through the ranks and became a guard?"

She was quieter now. "Whose rules?"

He ran his fingers the length of her hair and put it behind her shoulder. "This is all going to sound like I'm a bit crazier than you thought, but I feel it's time you should know. There is a way to get out of here and it's not by escaping."

Tears came to her eyes once again. "Yes, I know—it's by getting sliced up, and used for our next meal." She put her head down and sobbed.

Jared was firm this time and took hold of her shoulders. "Listen to me. That's not what I meant. If you don't want a needle in your arm or a canvas jacket that has no beginning and no end as your daily ensemble, I suggest you start listening."

Charlotte crossed her legs and sat up straighter. "All right, Jared, what do you know that I don't?"

"First of all, I don't believe that Primevil Asylum would ever use cannibalism to their advantage. If Serenity is gone, it's because she died of natural causes."

"No, I don't believe you. She was just feeling a little down; nothing physical was wrong with her." She became hysterical. "They're butchers, and I'm next because I know they killed Serenity."

"Charlotte, you don't know that for a fact. Serenity could've had a virus, or something could have ruptured inside her body. Or maybe, God forbid, she took her own life."

Charlotte screamed, "You don't know what you're talking about. Get out! Serenity would never take her own life."

Jared kissed Charlotte on the forehead. "When you're ready, I'll tell you what you want to know, but for now, you need to rest."

He pushed the button that would summon a nurse to give Charlotte a sedative. She could tell by the look on his face that he felt bad, but that didn't stop her from shouting obscenities at him. As he turned to go, he said softly, "Charlotte, you better get your emotions in check."

Screaming at the top of her lungs, every insult that had been locked in her mind for the past few months was now escaping her lips. "I hate this place. Lowlife degenerates squirming around chanting stupid songs and picking at themselves; you all stay away from me. You hear me, stay away. I hate all of you. Dirty, filthy, lunatics, I'm nothing like any of you! Most of you belong behind bars in prison and not running around in your underwear, dancing with imaginary friends. At least I have friends."

She thought about Serenity, and Jared. "Well, at least I did have friends." Charlotte put her head down and sobbed. Jared stood in Charlotte's room with his arms crossed leaning against the wall and staring at her.

She thought about the life she'd had outside of Primevil. It hadn't been a good life, but she had her dog, Jamie, and she tried to attend school as much as she could. Since her mother's death she'd lived at home by herself with a halfway house counselor making frequent visits. She never told anyone her true birth date. She barely remembered it herself. The halfway house counselor provided her with some clothing and little food, but she had to beg and scrounge for food for her dog. Charlotte had to smile when she thought of her dog, how she would gobble the food scrounged from the garbage as if it were something special. She hoped her four-legged companion remembered how to find food without her.

Not every teenager went insane when they hit their sixteenth birthday, but the majority of them did, so the high school population dropped to nearly nothing for the junior and senior classes. No one seemed to care that the teenage population was dwindling, or if they did care, nothing was being done. Some parts of the world were worse than others. Charlotte had watched many of her friends that had birthdays before hers go insane, but she had been helpless to do anything for them. She never believed in the virus explanation, and when she voiced her concerns with her friend Serenity, she too confirmed that her parents were on to something more sinister than a naturally caused virus.

Once again she thought of her now-deceased friend and started screaming. She bent down and picked up her shoes and threw them at the door. "You killed her. You all killed my friend, Serenity."

Two nursing assistances walked into the room. They were called cadets, and lacked any kind of bedside manners. They were usually in their early twenties and had escaped the curse of the sixteenth birthday, which you'd think would make them sympathetic to the teens' plight, but it was just a job to them.

One of the cadets said, "Well, young lady, if you're not going to behave, we'll just have to stick you—and by the way, wasn't that your friend's arm they found this evening?"

Charlotte went ballistic, and she thrashed around to escape the two men and the long probing needle. Her sheets were torn to shreds. It took two full syringes of sedation to finally calm her down.

One cadet said to the other, "Write down that she destroyed the bed-sheets. That will be an additional charge she'll have to work off. She'll never get out of here."

The other cadet shrugged. "Does it really matter? She's insane. They're all insane."

Jared had been standing just outside Charlotte's door and heard what was going on. He walked up to the seven flights of stairs with a heavy heart. He had suspicions about Serenity's death, and hated ordering that Charlotte be sedated. Would she forgive him? Would they still be friends after tonight? He doubted it. As he stripped his clothes off and crawled under the sheets, his mind was still on Charlotte. He wished he could have a sedative, but knew it would delay his progress back, but isn't that what he had just done to Charlotte? To be a guard he had to follow all the rules, not receive any demerits or fines, and could take no sedatives or any meds of any kind.

Jared got a sick feeling in the pit of his stomach when he wondered where they got the meat for the cafeteria, but he had an acquaintance that worked in the kitchen who told him the asylum drew the line after dogs and cats. No humans used in any of the kitchens recipes. "Don't want the insanity to spread," he had said laughingly. Even the thought of eating domestic animals was enough to make Jared shudder, but he needed meat to be able to build muscle and keep fit.

Jared had reached his first goal at Primevil. He had been there for almost six months and been promoted to guard status. He complied with every rule whether he believed in it or not. He wished Charlotte would start following the rules. She was building up quite a repetition for being outspoken and combative. Once the doctors and the head Collectors found a patient competent and trustworthy, they promoted from within each of the asylums—thus giving them more freedom and movement outside the asylum. They treated it like some type of gang mentality where, given a chance, even under horrific circumstances, a teen will do what is expected of them and not what is best for them. It was like a peer-pressure thing that Charlotte didn't seem to get or understand, or maybe she just was self-righteous and didn't play by the rules, no matter what the cost. She would be an easy target for a tragedy to happen to her. *I need to watch her more closely, and try to protect her.* He ran his hand through his hair and thought, Why does she have to be so stubborn?

He finally fell asleep around two a.m., but it was a restless sleep. He'd try to make things right between Charlotte and himself. He liked her, but it was more than just a friendship, at least in his mind.

4

The Infirmary

In the morning, Jared went to Charlotte's room, but she was gone. A different shade of filthy sheets lay across her bed on top of the strips of the old torn ones. Jared ran out and found a cadet. "Where's Charlotte?"

"Who?"

They no longer went by names at Primevil. "Case number 3737—where is she?"

"Dr. Oracle came and took her before the sun came out this morning."

"Took her where? And how'd she look?"

"Don't know, sir. She was under a blanket of sedation."

Jared ran down a flight of stairs into the basement, where Dr. Oracle's office was.

The cultivating smell that assaulted his nostrils was making his nose run. The air was thick with formaldehyde and the decomposing of some life form that had been extinguished days ago. He wondered if it was Serenity's decaying body he smelled.

Jared yelled, "Dr. Oracle!" He yelled it several more times, and from a closet in the lab out stepped the tall, thin, wiry man with uncontrollable hair follicles. Dr. Oracle had a beaker in his hand. "What is it? Do we have another runaway that's perished?"

"What! No. Where is case number 3737?"

"Oh, I finished with her about thirty minutes ago. She had no knowledge of how number 5426 died. As a matter of fact, she was quite the basket case. She begged me not to turn her in for her odd behavior."

"What odd behavior are you referring to, Dr. Oracle?" Jared thought the death of Serenity might be the cause of her demise.

"Just that she had such an attachment to a girl she barely knew. I was going to summon the cadet or nurse to give her a jab with something, but she said she would be fine and not cause any more trouble. I let her go."

Jared got in the doctor's space. "Where did she go?"

"That I don't know, but you'd better keep your patients under your thumb or you'll be demoted."

Jared clenched his fists and his jaw tightened. "I'll keep that in my thoughts, Doctor."

Meanwhile, Charlotte went to the infirmary. She wanted to see what had happened to Serenity. No one was in, so she tried the knob. It was unlocked, but she thought for sure this was a mistake. Maybe it was a trap, but she needed to find out something about her friend. There were a few patients in canvas jackets. The population at the asylums ranged mainly from age sixteen to twenty-six, since the epidemic started ten years ago, but there were some older patients that had naturally gone insane who were housed there also. Two men were spinning in circles and rolling their heads. Their tongues were hanging out of their mouths, almost as if their tongues were too big to fit behind their lips. Charlotte tiptoed past the first imprisoned soul and was making her way past the second. She opened the nurse's desk drawer, and one of the men reached out and grabbed her arm.

His canvas jacket fell away. "Hello, my name is Billy Thomas the Third, and I'm a patient here at this fine establishment. My friends just call me BT. What are you looking for? Snooping?" BT looked to be in his early to mid-twenties, but it was hard to tell. With such little grooming, and the weird movements he made with his body, he could be older or younger than her estimation.

"No, no, I'm just looking for someone."

"Looks like you're snooping to me."

"Listen, Mr. Billy Thomas the Third, my head hurts, and I wanted to find the district nurse to give me something."

Jared waved his arm in the air. "Wait!" He looked at Charlotte, and his pleading eyes urged her to come up with a reasonable excuse for this argument. "Let her speak."

Charlotte glanced hurriedly around the food room. "I . . . I can't eat in there, with the patients from cell block B."

The lady turned to look at the patients. "They're just about finished."

"I know. I can see that by the food all over the floor and their clothes. It's just that I have a weak stomach, and I don't think I can keep the food down with an image of these patients with their heads slumped in their food trays."

"My dear, they're just people—the same as you and I."

Jared looked around the two ladies and got Charlotte's point. "You lovely ladies may be used to this and don't think anything about it, but I'll have to agree with this patient. It's a bit disturbing to some." Jared winked at Charlotte as the frustrated ladies walked away, and he said, "Charlotte, that was a close one. Quick thinking."

She stepped out of the lunchroom. "It was the truth. My stomach's upset. I never get to lunch early. I don't like the looks of the patients on cell block B. They have the least hygiene in the entire asylum."

Jared changed the subject. "How was your visit to the infirmary?"

"Nothing productive, but I think I know what job I want to get, to work off my fees."

"I'm scared to ask, but what is it?"

"I'm going to apply to be an assistant in the infirmary."

"Charlotte, let's just talk about his." He went and grabbed some fruit and crackers off a tray. "Let's go to my room. I want to show you something anyway."

"Fine." Charlotte opened a pack of crackers with her teeth and started eating.

Gretchen, a guard friend of Jared's, walked by. "No eating in the hallways. Jared, you know the rules."

He whispered to Charlotte, "Please, just don't do anything until we get to my room."

The patients were filing out of their rooms and heading for the lunchroom. Their eyes were blank saucers, just there to catch the light and nothing else. They walked, drooled, picked every orifice on their body known to man, and made guttural sounds.

Charlotte squeezed as close to Jared as she could. At one point she stepped on his foot. "Hey, watch what you're doing. The patients aren't going to hurt you."

She shrugged as a group of patients passed and said together, "There is Wanda." They started chanting, "We Willy Wanda, crippled and deformed, you count your sanity while I count mine."

Charlotte was too scared to say anything to the group of patients or even make eye contact. She just squeezed Jared's arm as hard as she could.

They walked the many flights of stairs in almost complete silence, but once they reached Jared's bedroom Charlotte said, "I was just trying to settle my stomach with the crackers, and Jared, why didn't you say anything to those idiots when they called me Wanda and chanted that stupid song?"

He placed a finger over Charlotte's lips to quiet her; a surge of energy went through her body. Jared said very softly, "I have a surprise for you. Besides, you know as well as I do that Block B patients say that to everyone."

"No they don't, Jared. You're just saying that so I won't turn into a raving lunatic."

No one knew the reason why some sixteen-year-olds were so severely affected and others barely fazed. There was a wide range of mental incapacitation with the teens.

Charlotte remembered back to a time when she was about six. Her elders had thought the root of all evil was due to one reason only—teenagers—but things were so much worse now. No longer were there first-time employees doing jobs their elders wouldn't or couldn't do. The summer jobs were no longer being filled by teenagers. Life-guard and amusement park positions, and internships, were being filled by those with little enthusiasm for these jobs.

Jared pulled Charlotte out of her thoughts and tipped her head up and kissed her. The kiss was warm and gentle. Her insides swooned, and she had to lock her knees to stay upright.

The lights flickered, and a siren blew a screeching melody. Jared quickly pulled away from the kiss. "Charlotte, I need you to

stay here. Promise me. I can't have you getting any more demerits."
He grabbed both her shoulders. "Do you understand?"

"Yes, but what's going on?"

"I don't know—could be a patient escaping, a power surge or
outage. Once, a rodent ate through the wires of a transformer. It was
fried, but I'm sure that thing was put into our soup the next day. "

Charlotte grimaced, "Now, you've got my stomach rolling
again."

Jared immediately pushed a button on his wrist, and his hand lit
up like a flashlight. "I mean it, Charlotte—wait here."

"I can't see anything in the dark anyway," Charlotte shot back.
She didn't want to run into any patients. She whispered, "They're
scary enough in the light." Jared took off to find the reason for the
blackout.

Charlotte felt her way to Jared's bed and put her weary body on
his mattress. He had a nice, soft comforter, and she thought, *I
wonder how many hours he's had to work to get this.*

This is what she had wanted the other night. To be bathed in
darkness, but instead, Serenity's arm had washed ashore. She shut
her eyes, and could see little bits of color bouncing and forming
shapes under her eyelids. She started drifting out of her conscious
mind and fell asleep, but not before she felt the warmth come over
her when she thought of Jared. Sure, he was out of her league in
looks and also in seniority at Primevil Asylum, but then, she wasn't
really looking for a mate. She fell asleep whispering. "We Willy
Wanda, crippled and deformed, you count your sanity while I count
mine."

She went deep inside her mind and started thinking about her
previous life. She wondered why she hadn't seen any of her
classmates. A lot of them had parents that were still alive. Maybe
they hid their sixteen-year-olds so they wouldn't be taken away.
Maybe they bargained or paid to have their teens placed in a better
asylum. After all, the dozen asylums on Redwine Hill were the worst
of the worst. Only the truly misfortunate had to come to these run-
down, rat-infested buildings. The asylums on Redwine Hill were
known as the slums—previously condemned. Every patient who was
dropped here usually had no family to complain or protest about the
conditions for the teenager. Charlotte had a lot of restless dreams as
she slept.

Redwine hill

5

Great-Great-Grandfather's Legacy

Jared and a few other guards found the source of the problem. Dr. Oracle had been doing an experiment and blew the entire transformer. Dr. Oracle hurriedly shuffled around his office. "Go back to what you were doing. Just a miscalculation on the energy needed. Nothing here."

Jared didn't think much of Dr. Oracle. There were other doctors at the asylum that deserved respect, but Dr. Oracle wasn't one of them. He was basically harmless though. Jared replied, "Try not to blow anything up." And then in a whisper, "He must have gotten his degree through a vending machine. He knows nothing about physics."

Jared made his way up to his room, in which, by this time, the lights were flickering, trying to stay on. He could see Charlotte lying on his bed. "Taking a nap?"

Charlotte stretched and wiped her eyes. "I guess I was tired." He went slowly over to the bed and lay next to her when she cooed, "Are you sure I won't get another demerit for this?"

Jared whispered in Charlotte's ear, "With so many demerits already, are you really going to pick this time to object?"

"No, my head still feels like it's going to explode."

Jared was beginning to think there was more to Charlotte's headache than what she was saying. "Charlotte, let me take you down to the infirmary."

"No, I just want to lie here for a while. You'd think this place would be free of stress. Everything is done for you, but my skin crawls with all the oddities of this place. It's creeping me out."

Jared gently whispered, "Yes, I know." He started rubbing her neck and listened to the pleasing sounds coming from her throat.

"That's just what I needed." She was soon asleep, but Jared had an intense feeling that he couldn't fall asleep being so close to her.

Jared woke several hours later to her movement. "Everything all right?"

"Yeah, I'm fine. I was just thinking—how did I wind up at Primevil?"

"The Collectors brought you here when you had the teenage breakdown outside a bread store. You know you had to have turned sixteen. And you obviously had very few assets to your name, so you ended up at one of the asylums on Redwine Hill."

Charlotte cuddled into Jared. "Sounds simple enough, but I mean, how did 'my family' end up like this? I mean insane. It's more than the usual 'turn sixteen and ward off the goonies in your mind.'" She paused for just a minute and rubbed the back of her neck. "You know, my great-great-grandfather was in the war. He called it the 'big one.' "

Jared hugged Charlotte. "Does this story have a plausible ending?"

"I'm not sure what you mean by that, but it's a true story. My great-great-grandfather only told me this one time, right after he'd had one of his surgeries. He was still under sedation and slightly out of his mind. During the war he was in a battle for his life, and his comrades had all perished from gunfire and grenades. Most of their bodies had blown to bits in the foxhole. He had plenty of ammunition from the dead soldiers, but there was no food."

Charlotte stretched. "This is uncomfortable for me to tell you this. I've never shared this with anyone but my parents."

"Charlotte, it can't be that bad." But he pulled her close to him.

She continued. "As the days went by, he had no choice; he ate some of the friends he had come to know and trust as his brothers. He said there was an unconditional bond between soldiers. Closer than any group of people he ever saw. He ate mostly the parts that were unrecognizable—the parts that had blown away from the actual bodies themselves. He had to eat them raw."

"Charlotte, is that why you're a vegetarian?"

She nodded. "That's a big part of it." She pursed her lips and blew slowly out. "When he was finally rescued, his mind was too far gone for them to save him. He went into a mental institution. They didn't have many back then, not like they do now. He had to have many surgeries to remove the inanimate objects he'd eat. He'd complain of stomach pain, and they'd do an X-ray and find all kinds of metal objects buried in his GI tract: nails, a metal cross, a belt buckle, even a metal bracelet. No one knew, at the asylum, where he got the stuff, because after the first surgery they kept all metal things away from him. No one knew why he only ate metal, but my mother said it was because when they found my great-great-grandfather, he had swallowed all the dog tags of his soldier friends. She said he didn't want the enemy to know their identities, but my father thought that he had probably started eating the dog tags before eating his friends. Either way, it made him go insane. I think that's where it all started—the insane gene that runs in our family."

Charlotte tensed her entire body. Jared said, "I don't think you have to have a gene to make you go insane. That situation would make the most stable person lose their mind. For what he went through, I think the outcome was obvious. Besides, you got here by way of your sixteenth birthday."

Charlotte said, "I think I got a double dose of craziness. Even though I burst into tirades, I feel they are justified."

Jared gave a little laugh. "I concur."

She snuggled down into Jared's chest. "I wake up at night sometimes being chased by body parts. I've had that same dream as long as I can remember. So when Serenity's arm washed ashore, I almost went to the dark side never to return. Dr. Oracle thinks I'm unstable because I showed a severe attachment to a friend I barely knew. He told me that was the beginning of a breakdown."

"Charlotte, don't listen to Dr. Oracle. He got his degree from a mail-order catalog. I heard he barely passed his boards. I've been meaning to ask to see his degree, but I've heard he doesn't want anyone getting their grubby fingers all over it. If that doesn't say something about him, I don't know what does."

Jared waited to see if there was more to the story, but when Charlotte said nothing, he asked, "Would you like to see the surprise I was telling you about?"

She sat up just like a kid at Christmas. "Yes, what is it?"

Jared got up and crossed the room, bent down, and pulled open his bottom dresser drawer. He then pulled out two small kittens. Charlotte let out a squeal. By the sounds of her excitement, you'd never know she was sixteen years old. She jumped out of bed so fast that she caught her foot on the corner of the footboard, and went tumbling to the floor and landed right at Jared's feet. "Let me see," she said, holding her knee in pain. "Where did you get them?"

Jared handed Charlotte the little black one while he stroked the larger gray one. "I was outside checking the perimeter on my rounds a few nights ago, and I found these two in the dumpster."

Charlotte cuddled the small black kitten. "Where is their mother?"

"Don't know. I don't want to think about what happened to the mother cat. She probably ended up in the stew, and the only reason these two survived was because they were too small to extract any meat from their small bodies."

"Why didn't you tell me about them sooner?"

"I think you were a bit preoccupied with Serenity's arm floating in on the tide." He looked down immediately.

"Jared, why'd you have to bring up Serenity's name?" Charlotte felt taken aback, but the kitten was pulling at her heartstrings to play. The little fur ball was chewing her fingers. "I think she's hungry."

Jared said, "Yeah, I think they're old enough to eat regular food. No cat food around, but I did get them some stew meat. I hate to say this but I think the kittens may be eating their own mother."

"Jared, please, don't talk like that. I don't want to think about how Primevil gets their meat." Charlotte put a few pieces of meat down that Jared had brought from the cafeteria, and the little black cat ate it without hesitation. "She really likes this. Are you going to keep them?"

Jared said softly, "Charlotte, we'll both care for them. You can have the tiny black one. You know if they were dogs we couldn't hide them. They'd become too big and start to bark. With cats, it's different."

Charlotte thought about her abandoned dog, Jamie. "You know I had a dog, Jared. She was my best friend." Tears came to Charlotte's lashes.

The tiny black kitten purred in her arms, and she kissed it on its forehead. Charlotte, for the first time since coming here a few months ago, felt a glimmer of hope. She kissed the kitten several more times. "I'll call you Midnight, and Jared, yours can be Noon."

They watched as the two precious kittens finished their meal, before Charlotte put them back safely in the dresser drawer. As Jared turned off the light to his room, she quickly pressed her lips on his. "Thank you, Jared."

He was taken off guard, and gave her a puzzled look. He watched as she happily bounced and skipped her way down the hallway. "You might want to curb your enthusiasm or they'll really think you're insane."

She glanced back. "No one is going to spoil my good mood. Not even you, Jared."

Redwine hill

6

No Time for Self-Pity

By the next morning, Charlotte felt not great, but so much better. Just the thought of Jared and her secret kittens made her smile. She was going to apply for a job in the infirmary. Jared was against it, but it was the one place where she knew she could find information on Serenity's death. The only other place was Dr. Oracle's lab, and he never let anyone but himself in there.

As she made herself presentable and headed for the infirmary, she saw a line forming out the door of the clinic. "Is everyone sick today?" She decided to ask one of the patients who didn't look so frightening. "Are you all sick?"

The lady said, "No, we're here for the job, Wanda."

Charlotte said with a firm tone in her voice, "I'm not Wanda. You have mistaken me for someone else."

Charlotte never thought she'd have competition for a position at the infirmary. Maybe they wanted to work here to steal some medication, she thought. Charlotte whispered, "I'm terrible on interviews, I'm terrible on interviews. I'm terrible on interviews."

She bumped right into the district nurse and said, "Oh, excuse me."

"That's quite all right, 3737. Have you come to apply for the position?"

"Yes, but I see so has everyone else on my floor."

The nurse came close and whispered, "Don't worry, Charlotte, and don't look so startled. Yes, I know your name. A nice young man, who I believe is a guard, put in a good word for you earlier this morning. I remember when I first met you, with that ridiculous piece of bedsheet tied around your head. I was a little leery of you, but your guard friend said you'd make a great nursing assistant."

Charlotte held her breath and said, "So, do you think I've a chance at the job?"

"Honey, look at this line and tell me—does anyone look sane enough to have a job besides you?"

Charlotte looked at the transfigured human beings in line; some were barely standing upright. A few still had on their cumbersome jackets, which hid their hands and arms, and others were talking to themselves, which wasn't bad, but they were also answering their own questions. Still, most disturbing were the ones that kept hitting themselves in the head or biting their arms, or pounding the wall with their fists and making their knuckles bleed.

"I see what you mean."

"Well, if you want the job it's yours, but I've got to run it through Dr. Oracle first. If you could just disburse these patients while I go ask."

Charlotte had a sinking feeling. Dr. Oracle would never agree that she have the position as assistant to the district nurse. He hated her. He thought she was insane for liking Serenity too much.

As Charlotte was redirecting the patients back to their rooms, the nurse came back smiling. "All set. You can begin right now if you like."

"Dr. Oracle gave me the all clear?" said Charlotte.

"Oh no. Dr. Oracle had left for an emergency at another institution. Dr. Farrow came in to take his place for the day."

"Thank you. What do you want me to do first Mrs. . . . .?"

"The name is Mrs. Bellow. Mrs. Sylvia Bellow. My husband died many years ago, and I never remarried."

"All right, Mrs. Bellow, where can I start?"

"Charlotte, based on our encounter the other day, I suggest you leave the bedsheets in one piece and let me do anything that entails bandaging or any other nursing procedure."

Mrs. Bellow pointed directly in back of her. "Charlotte, I hope you don't mind if I call you that." Charlotte shook her head no.

"Take this set of keys and go through that door there, and take a right. The large door with the glass panel that always seems to be steamed up. Start in there."

"What do I do in there?"

"That's where we keep all the supplies. We keep the room at a low temperature. I want the entire room organized."

"Yes, Mrs. Bellow."

"Oh, Charlotte—just a few things. You don't have the key to the narcotics, so don't even try. Not that you have any intention of taking any, but that's why most patients want this position—to get access to the narcotics and sedatives."

"Yes ma'am."

"And one more thing. I don't want you quitting the first day. Don't take a left instead of a right or you'll end up in the morgue. My last assistant quit for that very reason."

"I'll not make that mistake." Charlotte wondered if Mrs. Bellow, this seemingly harmless woman, knew something about the morgue and the dismemberment of a body.

Charlotte didn't want to get fired her first day, but what if Dr. Oracle came back and let her go? This was her opportunity to find something out about Serenity, and any other patients that had disappeared.

She could hear Mrs. Bellow humming in the nurse's office. Charlotte thought, What is there to be happy about?

Charlotte didn't know if the cold storage room she was in had an automatic door lock, so she used a roll of gauze to hold the door open just an inch. She slowly made her way past where Mrs. Bellow could see her, and turned the handle on the morgue door. If she hadn't been shaking so badly she could've opened it a lot easier, but she was fumbling with it as it clicked and then sprang open. She was still holding on to the doorknob as she was thrust into the morgue.

"Oh my God . . ." The putrid scent brought tears to Charlotte's eyes. It reeked of anything and everything rotting in a warm environment even though the temperature was in the low fifties in the room. She rubbed her eyes so hard she thought she was going to tear them from their eye sockets. As she wiped her nose and eyes on her shirt for the umpteenth time, she slowly looked around.

What she saw made her repeat a sentence. "I'm okay. I'm okay. I'm okay." But she really didn't think she was. The sight in front of her was just the type of thing to push her over the edge and make her go totally insane. Not temporarily but for the rest of her life.

There, hanging in the back of the room over a large drain, were body parts. It looked like some kind of horrific art gallery. She felt tenuous, as if her legs could no longer support her. Something caught her eye to drag her consciousness out of its frozen state of fear. There was half of an arm hanging among the guts, and appendages dripping who-knew-what on the floor, only to have the fluids swirl and mix together and gurgle down the drain, bubbling and foaming as they disappeared.

Charlotte whispered, "That's Serenity's arm." She walked over and stood just inches from the bloated arm. It looked worse than it had the day it washed up on shore. The smell was more than she could take now, and she remembered she had a few mints in her pocket that Jared had given to her. She'd put them there when she was nauseated the other day. She reached in her back pocket and tore open a few, and she also tried breathing through her mouth instead of her nose. This did little to cover the smell, but the mints were helping her stomach.

She looked to the right and saw small hooks holding smaller body parts such as eyes, fingers, a few ears, and a nose. Charlotte didn't want to think it, but she did anyway. Are those Serenity's?

Charlotte hung to the table for support and cautiously walked on the slippery floor. The dead-body drawers were nickel-plated tombs. The morgue had been updated compared to the rest of the asylum. She pulled the handle on the first one she came to. She let out a slow sigh; it wasn't Serenity. It was a very old man, who might or might not have died from natural causes.

The second one held a pregnant lady—there were two deaths in this tomb. The third and fourth drawers had two male teenagers. And then she yanked open the fifth and final drawer, and there was her friend Serenity.

She jumped backward into the standard morgue table and hurt her back. Then she walked over to her friend, who barely resembled the worried seventeen-year-old girl she had left at the infirmary that day.

There was nothing special that had been done for Serenity after death. Charlotte remembered going to her great-great-grandfather's funeral, and he'd looked like a mannequin with so much makeup on.

Not Serenity. She was deteriorating, and her skin was so thin in some areas that Charlotte could see her organs underneath.

Charlotte quickly slammed the door. She heard Mrs. Bellow humming.

Charlotte said with disgust in her voice, "What could she possibly be happy about? She's coming in here!" She quickly slid under the table as Mrs. Bellow entered the room.

Mrs. Bellow took one of the keys hanging around her neck and opened the file cabinet. "Where's that file? I bet the night nurse misfiled it again."

There was a loud bang in her office. "Now what have those idiots done?"

Charlotte shrank down and mouthed, *Mrs. Bellows isn't as nice as she wants everyone to think—idiots?*

Charlotte could hear Mrs. Bellow in her office. "Gentlemen, stop this fighting at once. All three of you are ill kept. Is this the way the nurse on block J lets her patients look? I'll have to speak with her; this is unacceptable."

One of the men repeated, "Unacceptable," and then there was loud, shrill laughing.

"Once again, gentlemen, what do you want? Make it quick. I've got work to do, and the smell of you three is enough to make me sick."

Charlotte said, "The smell of patients makes her sick, but the smell of formaldehyde and rotten flesh she's all right with."

She peeked out from under the table and realized the file drawer was still open. This was her chance to get Serenity's file. She quickly went to the Cs for Serenity Cinder, and immediately her fingers trembled so severely that she could barely pull out the file. She tucked it under her shirt and opened the door to the morgue.

She could hear Mrs. Bellow forcing the patients out of her office. "I'm not the least bit humored by your request. You tell your nurse that the next time she sends someone to my office for soap, it will be her last day."

The one man repeated, "Last day," and the other two went into an animallike laugh.

Charlotte made her way over to the cold storage area and quickly stowed the file on the back shelves of the room, then picked up a broom. She could hear Mrs. Bellow go into the morgue and quickly come out. She opened the door to the storage. "My word, Charlotte, it's freezing in here. Why didn't you tell me? I'd have given you a sweater. Look at you. You're absolutely bloodless. Come, let's get you warmed up."

Charlotte wanted to take Serenity's file with her, but she was lucky she had hid it behind some restraints and boxes of tongue depressors.

Mrs. Bellow started rubbing Charlotte's shoulders. "Do you like coffee, my dear?"

She didn't like coffee, but she just nodded her head.

The nurse said, "I don't want to leave my office unattended. I'll call ahead and have the ladies in the meal room prepare you some coffee."

Charlotte hated the ladies in the cafeteria, and they hated her, but surely they wouldn't think ill of the nurse. Mrs. Bellow carried a lot of weight even if she'd only been there a short time.

Mrs. Bellow yelled after Charlotte, "Remember a sweater tomorrow, and I'll set the thermostat warmer. Can't let my help freeze to death."

Charlotte was hesitant to go into the lunchroom. One of the ladies saw her and said, "Come in, my dear. Mrs. Bellow called us. Said she had half-frozen her new assistant. Are you her?"

"Yes, I started today."

She wrapped a huge arm around Charlotte. "I've got your coffee all ready. Can't disappoint Mrs. Bellow; cream or sugar?"

"Both please." Charlotte could see Dr. Oracle standing with a few nurses by the freezer. I thought *Mrs. Bellow told me that Dr. Oracle wasn't here today.*

Charlotte stayed out of sight and drank her bitter coffee. The lunch lady said, "Can we expect you every day, or is this a onetime occasion?"

Charlotte said, "I'm sorry for the inconvenience, but this coffee is just for today. Some rooms off of the clinic were cold, and I didn't bring a wrap to wear."

The lady got close to Charlotte. "Were you working in the morgue?"

She shook her head. "No, just the supply room. Mrs. Bellow wants it straightened out, that's all."

The rotund lunch lady turned toward Dr. Oracle and said, "Dr. Oracle, have you met Mrs. Bellow's assistant? What is your number, dear?"

Charlotte ducked out into the hallway. "Excuse me, but I have to go. I'll meet him some other time." Her heart was pounding, and she began getting an enormous headache. *Why would the lunch lady care if I met Dr. Oracle? Maybe she was trying to be nice.* She slipped into the bathroom, and there was a knock at the door. She pretended to be a man; it was a universal bathroom.

She said in a deep voice, "I'll be in here a while. Better find another toilet to use." She didn't know who was on other side of the door, but she thought it might be Dr. Oracle. She waited a few minutes and opened the door; the coast was clear. She ran up to Jared's room, and pulled Midnight and Noon out of the dresser drawer. She put the kittens on Jared's bed and fell asleep with the little balls of fur cradled in the crooks of her elbows.

Redwine hill

7

No More Demerits

Jared met up with Charlotte after his shift was over. He'd remain on call when off duty. Charlotte whispered, "I found Serenity and her chart."

"Wait! What! Charlotte, you're lucky you didn't get caught. I told you to try to stay out of trouble. And, what do you mean, you found Serenity?"

Charlotte put her hand on his arm. "Relax, will you? I didn't get caught. I have the same amount of demerits as I had when I woke up this morning. Not a single additional one. Pretty good, huh?"

"Yeah, that's terrific. You're a regular cat burglar; Now, what did the file state was the cause of death?"

"I don't know. I had to leave it in the storage room. I couldn't get the file out without Mrs. Bellow seeing it. I'll get it tomorrow though."

Jared said, "Charlotte, just be careful. At the rate you're going, you'll never be given special privileges for good behavior. Anyway, it's time for dinner, but I know how you don't like the ladies in the meal room—"

Before he could finish Charlotte said, "No, I'm fine really. I was half frozen today in the clinic, and Mrs. Bellow called ahead for some hot coffee. The meal ladies were very thoughtful. Just so we don't get there early." *And, hopefully, Dr. Oracle will be gone.*

The meal room was crowded, but Jared managed to find a two-top table deep in the corner of the room. "Now, Charlotte, tell me where you saw Serenity."

She told him about the grim sight she had seen in the morgue, not leaving anything out. She couldn't eat afterward, but Jared was in charge of his faculties, and closely listened to every word Charlotte said.

"I think the file is our only answer," she said. Jared was consuming his meal as if Charlotte were talking about the weather.

She was watching a disorderly patient out of the corner of her eye. She was about to tell Jared, when the patient got up pulled the intravenous tubing from the bag on the pole and started twirling it around in the air like a lasso. Blood started splattering on everyone around him. The faster he twirled the tubing in the air, the more the blood spattered. No one was spared the blood.

Charlotte got a big blob on her cheek, and as she wiped it off with her shirtsleeve, she said, "I'm never eating in here again. This place is a madhouse. Food fights are one thing, but this just reaches a whole new level of grossness."

The man screaming obscenities was wearing a hospital gown. He should have never been in the meal room. Over the loudspeaker, a voice announced, "Request help in main meal room. Infraction in progress."

The man was tearing at the windows and saying, "You can't keep me in here. I'm not insane. I'm a drunk, not crazy."

Jared pointed to another patient. "Get a nurse or Collector! Any nurse with a hypodermic needle. I think this man is going through withdrawals."

The man started screaming and pulling at his skin. "Get them off me. They're eating me alive. Someone, help me! Don't just stand there staring at me; help get these things off. They're crawling into my ears."

Jared had blood spattered on his shirt and neck. "I'll take care of this. Charlotte, you go back to the room. Midnight and Noon are up there."

Charlotte had forgotten about the two kittens, "Okay by me. Try not to get too much blood on you." The only bright spot of her entire day was waiting for her in a small dresser drawer in Jared's room.

She grabbed the meat off her tray and ran out of the lunchroom. She could hear the commotion behind her, and a patient yelled, "Wanda, run, run after your sanity. I'll find you and take what's left."

Charlotte ran all the way to Jared's room and slammed the door. She opened the drawer and began to feel almost normal again. She loved cats. Charlotte's mother had told her that when she was about two years old, they drove down a street and saw a dead cat in the middle of the intersection. Whenever they went down that street, Charlotte would say "dead cat." Ever since then, she'd tried to save every cat she found.

She picked the two kittens up and let their soft fur melt her anxiety away. She closed her eyes and for just a second forgot where she was. She'd loved her dog, Jamie, but cats would sit on her lap for hours and relieve her stress. They couldn't fetch or run on the beach, but cats were comforting without knowing it.

Charlotte cuddled with the two kittens and fell asleep in a restful, peaceful dream. She was awakened by a tickle on her face. She grabbed for the kitten, but it was a hand.

It was Jared stroking Charlotte's cheek. "Wake up. You have to return to your room."

Her eyes were glazed with sleep. "Why?" was all she managed to say.

"I was informed this evening after my shift that you can visit my room but you can't spend the night."

She easily sat up. "What time is it? Did you know this policy?"

He nodded his head yes and looked down. "I received ten demerits for the infraction. It's almost three thirty in the morning."

"Jared, I'm sorry. What did I receive—a hundred demerits?"

"No, Charlotte, you got off with a warning. It was either you or me, and I know your paper list is as long as my arm. You couldn't afford any more violations."

Jared helped Charlotte to stand, and she looked him in his beautiful brown eyes. "I didn't know. I'd never have slept over if I knew you'd be penalized."

He looked deep into her eyes and lowered his head. She could feel the brute strength of his arms around her small waist. He bent down and found her lips in the half-darkened room. She was frozen with fear, but her insides were burning and bubbling in a way she'd never felt before. The kiss was brief, but it was warm and pleasant. She was glad for the shadow of the darkness. From the neck up she must have resembled a red popsicle. Jared started to walk her to her room with his one arm still around her waist.

She wiggled out of his gentle hold and said in a cracked voice, "No, Jared, I'll be fine. I don't want you, or me, getting anymore demerits." That was the furthest thing from her mind after the kiss, but it was the only reasonable explanation Jared would agree with.

Charlotte was tiptoeing as fast as she could down the hallway; she felt like a theatrical dancer on caffeine. She got to her room on the first floor and silently closed her door. She quickly slipped under her sheets and thin blanket and fell asleep dreaming a sweet dream about Jared.

Charlotte heard her door open. She thought it might be Jared. But as she listened intently to the sounds the intruder made, she knew it wasn't. She lay back down, and several times throughout the night she heard someone enter her room.

"Who's there? Get out of my room, you lunatics. If I catch you, I'll pound you into dust." She knew she had to talk tough so the other patients would leave her alone. But the last time caused her to bolt upright. "What the . . ."

She heard a splatter. Something hit the floor, and then there were footsteps running out of her room.

The intruder said, "Wanda, I'm taking your sanity. Join me in the loony bin."

Charlotte quickly got out of bed and ran to turn on her bedroom light, only to step in the pile of mush someone had so generously left in her room. The floor was slippery with a liquid substance mixed with semi-formed objects. She stumbled into the wall and clicked the light on. "Oh," she said as she clutched her stomach, ready to add to the pile on the floor.

Someone was out to scare her, because on the floor was a bag that had been ripped open with the innards of someone or something, which had splattered everywhere—even up on the walls. She lifted her foot. Something stuck between her toes, and her foot was dripping sticky semi-bloody fluid onto the floor. She skated out of her room as best she could on the slippery substance and took the stairs as many at a time as her legs would allow. She reached Jared's room out of breath and out of the sanity that she had clung to.

She screamed in Jared's ear, "Wake up! Jared, wake up."

He rolled over. "Charlotte, what is it? Did you get in trouble? Another demerit?"

She was hysterical. "No, Jared. No, listen to me. Someone threw a bag of guts in my room just now, and said something about joining him in the loony bin."

Jared sat up. "What!"

She didn't have to convince him; he was already throwing on a pair of jeans. Charlotte looked away since he wasn't wearing any clothes under his comforter. She was shocked, but not in the same way she'd been from the gruesome present someone had just left her.

Jared took the stairs three at a time, almost falling once. He didn't look back to see if Charlotte was following; she figured Jared wanted to catch whoever had brought her to the brink of insanity.

He pushed the door open and it hit the wall. The light was still on, and there were no guts or innards on the floor. Charlotte came running in and knocked into Jared. "Where . . . I mean, what happened to the entrails that were on the floor?"

Jared said, "Charlotte, I know you weren't hallucinating or making this up. I see the futile attempt made to clean the floor and walls." There were little bits of tissue left from a hasty cleanup job. Charlotte was crying silently. Her shoulders were shaking, and tears were flowing, but no sound was coming out.

Jared scooped up Charlotte's petite frame. "I don't care about demerits—you're sleeping in my room tonight."

He carried her to his room and put her under the comforter. She knew she must look like a scared, caged animal. Jared unzipped his jeans and saw Charlotte staring at him. He got the hint. "I think I'll just sleep in my pants tonight."

He got under the covers and cradled the emotionally drained Charlotte in his arms.

"I'm going to make some inquires tomorrow. There are only a few people who have access to body parts, and I plan to interrogate all of them."

Charlotte said in a small voice, "Jared, why do the young teenagers keep coming, but Primevil never gets to full capacity? Are they being transferred to better accommodations, while we unlucky, misfortunate ones with little to no family get stuck here in this horrific place?"

Jared hugged Charlotte. "I don't know the answer to that. When I came here, my mother was still alive, Charlotte."

"Was she a good mother? Why hasn't she come to see you?"

"In other asylums they let family in to see their sons or daughters but not here at Primevil. The twelve asylums on Redwine Hill have their own agenda, and there are no visitors allowed or luxuries of any kind."

"Gee, Jared, I hadn't noticed. You really think the other asylums are more liberal with their policies and procedures?"

"Sure. We were just unlucky to be dumped here. My parents were very loving before this all started happening, but by the time I turned sixteen, they had already gone through this with my older sister and brother, watching them go insane. Actually, Charlotte, you and I are fairly normal compared to some. My father stopped visiting my siblings, but my strong-willed mother kept going. Both my sister and brother died in the asylums shortly after they got there. My dad was fairly young when he took his life. I guess he couldn't bear to see me institutionalized when I turned sixteen, but my mother, God love her, tried to hide me. We were poor so I guess that's why I ended up here.

"My sister was three years older than me, and my brother was just a year older. They both were severely incapacitated on their sixteenth birthdays. My sister was put in diapers. My parents tried to hide my sister, but it was no use. I think they found her by some type of tracking device that lets the head Collector know where the insane are located. My mother said they try to keep birth records accurate and up-to-date, so the minute a teenager turns sixteen, they're ready for them.

"My brother wasn't as bad off as my sister, but my parents still tried to hide him in our attic. My mother would visit my brother and sister every day, for the few months they remained alive at the asylum, but when I turned sixteen, I was brought here, and I never saw my mom again."

Jared stretched his arm that was on top of Charlotte, and with a shaky tone said, "It's time for sleep. I'm exhausted."

Charlotte could feel Jared's heartbeat. It was strong and powerful—not like hers, which was weak and sporadic. She felt sorry for Jared. He had a loving mom, who was still alive somewhere outside the asylum but was never permitted to visit him.

She fell asleep in his arms. It was the only place she felt safe in this bottomless pit of anguish.

Redwine hill

8

A Roommate for Charlotte

Jared gently tapped Charlotte's shoulder. "Time for work. I've fed Midnight and Noon. We're going to have to let them roam free around the room. They're getting too big for the drawer."

Charlotte expected to hear a knock on Jared's door and someone handing her a stack of demerits, but there was only silence from the hallway. Jared threw her an apple. She got up and stretched. "I don't think I can go back to my room."

Charlotte felt uneasy and blushed when she caught him staring at her. "We'll talk about that later today, after I ask around."

Charlotte shimmied past him and started eating her apple on the way to the clinic. Jared yelled after her, "You're going to get another infraction on your already long list."

She quickly took seven or eight bites and threw the remainder of the apple in the trash. She could barely speak with her mouth full. "I'll see you later."

She made it down to the infirmary with a few minutes left on the hall clock. Mrs. Bellow was just walking down the long hall. "Well hello, Charlotte. Did you bring a sweater today?"

"No, I guess I forgot."

"Honey, that's okay. You can use mine, and we'll keep the door propped open to circulate the cold air. Did you have a good night's sleep, dear?"

"No, not really. I had an unexpected surprise last night."

Mrs. Bellow handed Charlotte her sweater and unlocked the door. "That young man you have your eye on is exceptionally nice. It was thoughtful of him to surprise you with a gift."

Charlotte was going to explain that it wasn't Jared who had given her the unexpected surprise, but she decided to keep that bit of information to herself.

Mrs. Bellow said, "Well, I also have a surprise for you today."

"A surprise for me?"

"Yes, Charlotte, you will be getting your roommate today."

"But I thought I wouldn't get one until my three-month evaluation." Charlotte was actually thrilled she wouldn't spend one more night alone in her room. "When will she be here?"

"She's probably headed for the room as we speak. I told her to come here when she's finished getting settled."

Mrs. Bellow went and propped open the supply room door. "If it gets too cold in there, just come sit with me, in my office, for a while. I'll check on you throughout the day to make sure you haven't turned into an icicle."

She was grateful for this job. It not only kept her busy but gave her access to the medical files.

Things were stacked on the supply room floor, but she managed to find room for every item on the shelves. Mrs. Bellow looked in on Charlotte and scared her.

Charlotte let out a scream and grabbed her chest. "You scared me. I didn't hear you come in."

"I'm very quiet with my rubber-soled nursing shoes. The place is looking nice. What were you doing in the back?"

Charlotte couldn't possible tell her the truth—that she was trying to read Serenity's file. She didn't know what some of the words meant, but she bet Jared would know. "I . . . I was just refolding the hospital gowns."

"Oh, my dear, you don't have to be that precise. No one here cares if the gowns have wrinkles. Now, it's almost time for lunch, and I see Brooklyn has not showed up, so why don't you go to your room and walk her to the cafeteria? That will be good for you two to bond."

"Okay. Her name is Brooklyn?"

"Yes, I'm not sure if that was her given name or not. She came here with nothing. I think she was a street rat. I was told, due to the filth the nurse and guard had to scrape off of her, that she'd been on the streets for a very long time. But they said she seemed harmless to herself and anyone else. So it looks like you have a roommate. Charlotte, you can't be too picky in an asylum on Redwine Hill. I guess the head Collector is making an exception with both of you, forgoing the three-month rule for roommates. I'll see you after lunch, and you can tell me all about her. She just turned sixteen years old."

"Mrs. Bellow, have you ever seen the head Collector?"

"Dearie, the only thing I know about him is he's known for being cold-blooded. He's not just the head Collector; he's called the Validator. I'm not privy to his family name. I believe I heard it once, but I've forgotten it. You see, Charlotte, I'm just a peon also—no grandiose blood running through my family. At least I had the forethought to go to college, but the teens nowadays don't have a chance. Something goes haywire in their brains and they end up in an asylum."

Charlotte nodded. She thought she saw a contemptuous sneer cross Mrs. Bellow's face. She left the clinic and headed for her room. As she looked back, she could see Mrs. Bellow locking the clinic. *How am I going to get Serenity's folder out of there?* She patted her chest with her hand when she thought about how close she came to getting caught with the file.

As Charlotte walked into her room, she saw her roommate painting her toenails with Serenity's bright orange nail polish. She was in a pretzel-like form on the bed, humming and painting her toes, but Charlotte could tell she was lanky, and a lot taller than she. Her skin was pinked. *Probably due to the soap scrubbing she received earlier.* Her hair was mousey brown in color and just hung down over the sides of her face. *I wonder how she can even see her toes to paint them.*

The minute her roommate twisted the cap back on the polish, she held it in the air saying, "I wonder whose crappy color of polish this is?"

Charlotte went off. She attacked Brooklyn without warning. They went tumbling down, each pulling the other's hair and clothing.

Charlotte yelled, "You have no right to touch my things!"

Brooklyn was a street fighter and was getting the best of Charlotte. "It's only polish. I didn't think you'd mind." Brooklyn had Charlotte in a choke hold, but Charlotte would not let go of Brooklyn's hair. She was dragging Brooklyn down to the ground.

Jared walked in. "Charlotte, you ready for lunch? What's going on?" He immediately picked up one girl in each arm. They looked like two battering rams. He deposited them on their beds without a care.

He had to yell "Stop!" several times and physically restrain one or the other, or both of them, before he had any kind of control. He took the uncomfortable straight-backed flimsy chair that sat propping the door open and positioned it between the two beds. He sat with his legs stretched out in front of him and his arms crossed. "Charlotte, can you tell me what's going on?"

Brooklyn spoke up. "I see you have a boyfriend. You want to share him as well as your lousy nail polish?"

Charlotte yelled, "He's not my boyfriend," and lunged at her new roommate.

Jared said, "Charlotte, if I'm not your boyfriend, what am I?" She was getting the worst of it because of the size difference. Charlotte's lip started bleeding as he grabbed them both. This time he sat on Brooklyn's bed staring at Charlotte. He had hold of Brooklyn's arm so she couldn't jump across the bed at Charlotte.

Brooklyn gave a victorious grin and stuck her tongue out at Charlotte.

Charlotte felt tears coming on, not because of her lip but because Jared chose Brooklyn over her. She snapped. "She was using Serenity's Monarch Butterfly nail polish. It's the only thing I have left of her."

Brooklyn had a twinge of pain on her face. "Did your sister die?"

Charlotte said with disgust in her voice, "She was my best friend in this crap hole, and friends are hard to come by. You'll find that out soon enough though."

Brooklyn bowed her head and said in a whisper, "I'm sorry. I lost everyone in my family, and I don't have any friends."

Charlotte wiped the blood from her lip on her sleeve. "Well, I can see why. You can't go around taking or using other people's things without asking."

Jared released Brooklyn's wrist and she said, "I know. I just don't have anything. I'm sorry I looked in your drawer. You have several items, and I don't have any. I wasn't jealous. I'm not that kind of person. Although, you did get a little upset when I said I'd take your boyfriend."

This time Charlotte didn't say anything. She looked at Brooklyn and could tell she'd had a hard life. The sparkle was gone from her eyes.

Charlotte got up, and Jared was ready to separate the two once again, but Charlotte took Serenity's nail polish and went over and opened Brooklyn's dresser drawer. "You weren't kidding that you have nothing."

Charlotte placed the polish in the drawer and closed it. "Now you have something. Did you know that Mrs. Bellow, the nurse, has an entire closet full of clothes? She keeps it stocked for any patients who need clean clothes or just want to look better than when they were brought in. I work for the nurse, you know?"

"No, I didn't know that. You must be pretty high up in the rankings."

Charlotte didn't say anything. "Let's go to lunch, and then when I get back to work, you can rummage through the closet for a few things, for your dresser. Since you don't have anything, I'll give you my friendship. You can't put it in a drawer, but it'll come in handy around here."

Brooklyn's eyes were moist. "I've never had a friend before. Kind of nice. Sure, I've had people who used me, but never a friend who thought of me and what I needed."

Jared said, "Now that you two are best friends, let's say we eat."

Charlotte and Brooklyn walked to the lunchroom talking about the clothes closet and Charlotte's supposed seniority position. "So, Charlotte, do you get paid for working at the clinic?"

"Yes. I'm not sure how much though. I forgot to ask Mrs. Bellow that, but I'm sure it's quite a bit."

Brooklyn said, "Do you think the clothes closet has clothes in my size?"

"I'm sure of it, and if not, we can alter them. I'm not the best seamstress in this place, but I think I can adjust the length of pants and things. You know, they have a sewing class here at Primevil. You could sign up for that. But this place doesn't have many educational classes. They don't believe academics are for the insane."

Brooklyn said, "At a certain point, I think they're right not to have schooling. I believe I turned out okay, and I stopped going to school when my parents died. I think I was around seven years old."

Charlotte put her hand on Brooklyn's arm. "I'm sorry you lost both your parents at such a young age. Have you been out on the street since then?"

Brooklyn scratched the back of her head. "Can you see if I have head lice? They soaped me up pretty good this morning, but it feels like something is in my hair."

Charlotte grimaced. "I don't know what head lice look like." She looked at Jared.

"Okay, Charlotte, but you owe me one."

"I don't owe you anything, Jared. Brooklyn does."

"Whatever. Let's step into this room. It will only take a second. Head lice can spread like wildfire in a place like this. I'd rather have just one patient with lice than an entire floor." He got his comb out of his back pocket. "This is not one of my favorite duties as a guard, but since you are Charlotte's good friend now, I don't see how I can say no to my girlfriend's request to check your head. Brooklyn, tip your head down."

He took his comb and separated some of the hair strands. He meticulously went over each strand of hair, and then checked the nape of her neck and the sides for any nits. "You're all clean of lice, but you might want to catch up on your bathing and take a couple of baths a day. Looks like you have dirt imbedded in your scalp."

Brooklyn scratched her head again. "Thanks, Jared. I think it's been several years since my last encounter with a tub or shower."

They continued walking toward the lunchroom. "I used to live off and on with my aunt, but she only needed me for free labor and beatings. I guess I was her punching bag when she was stressed. She always said she felt so much better once she whacked me around for a while."

A male patient came running down the hall. He looked to be in his late teens or early twenties. He had on a plaid long-sleeve shirt with an ugly sleeveless Christmas sweater over the shirt. He said, "You stole my watch."

The three turned to look at the crazed man running toward them. He stopped in front of Brooklyn. "You stole my watch, and I want it back. I saw you three exit my room." He pointed to Brooklyn. "I saw you put something in your pocket when you came out of my room."

Charlotte looked at Brooklyn. Had she stolen this man's watch? Was she a kleptomaniac?

Brooklyn yelled at the man. "You're crazy. I didn't take anything."

Brooklyn clenched her fists, ready for a fight. "Come on. You want to take this outside, so no one can see me pummel you?"

Charlotte said in a calm voice, "Brooklyn, just show him your pockets."

"No, I won't."

"Please, I already have too many fines and demerits. Somehow they'll think I'm involved and throw another fee my way."

"All right, just for my friend." She pulled all her pockets out. "See, nothing."

The man went to feel the out-turned pocket, and Charlotte gasped. "Is the watch on your wrist, the one that you claim was stolen?"

The man looked at his long-sleeve shirt, and a glistening silver wristband was peeking out from under the sleeve. "By cracky, there it is." He turned and skipped down the hall and disappeared into his room.

Brooklyn tucked her pockets back into her jeans. "I hate this place."

Jared said, "Get in line."

Charlotte sighed. "Look at the bright side. You didn't end up in a second fight today."

"It was close. I thought I'd have to pound him into mulch."

Jared laughed. "I take it by your positive words you could have taken him easily."

"I'm not proud of much, but when it comes to fighting, I think I'm pretty good."

Charlotte said, "Yeah, you cheat."

"I didn't know there were any rules to street fighting. Anything goes, if you know what I mean. Anything."

The lunch ladies interrupted Charlotte and Brooklyn's chatter. "Come on in. I see we have a new patient today. I think you'll find our selection of food acceptable, and we have a nice rump roast today."

Charlotte whispered in Brooklyn's ear. "Stay clear of the meat. Don't know where it came from."

With that said, they both got a salad, but Jared still needed his protein. Jared said to the lunch lady, "I'll have my usual full helping of meat and any extra you can spare."

Charlotte just looked at Jared. "How can you eat that stuff?"

He flexed his arm. "Need to build muscle, and can't do that on a salad."

Charlotte caught Brooklyn transfixed on Jared's bulging muscles, but this time she didn't mind—even the lunch ladies were drooling all over themselves trying to serve Jared his meal.

Brooklyn said, "Ladies, this man is spoken for. Pull yourselves together."

Charlotte laughed hard. It was the first time she had laughed since she turned sixteen and was deposited at Primevil. "Thanks, Brooklyn, for putting those women in their place." She poked Jared. "You never know. Jared might have been tempted to go after one of them."

They had a relaxing lunch, and Jared walked them both back to the clinic.

Charlotte said in her sweetest voice, "See you after work, Jared."

He was caught off guard. "Yeah, okay. I'll see you both after work." He pulled Charlotte aside so Brooklyn couldn't hear. "By the way, no one knows anything about the bag of innards that was thrown in your room last night."

She whispered so Brooklyn wouldn't hear. "Thanks for asking around, but I knew no one would talk." She waved to Jared and then turned her attention to Mrs. Bellow.

Charlotte asked, "Mrs. Bellow, would it be all right to let Brooklyn take a few things from the clothes closet? She has absolutely nothing in her dresser drawers."

"Well, of course. Brooklyn, you can have whatever you want, my dear. All these things have been donated, so take what you want."

Charlotte tried to read more of Serenity's file, but every time she brought the folder out of its concealed place, Brooklyn would pop in with a different outfit, wanting Charlotte's approval. By the end of the workday, Brooklyn had an armful of clothes, and Charlotte wasn't any closer to finding out what had happened to Serenity.

As the two girls were leaving the clinic Mrs. Bellow said, "Girls, don't forget to get a nice dress for the dance this weekend."

Charlotte looked at Brooklyn as she said, "What dance?"

Charlotte shrugged her shoulders. "I don't know. I've never been to one."

Mrs. Bellow said, "Nothing special, girls. Just that all the patients get together every few months for a dance. Brings everybody closer together, if you know what I mean. I'm new to Primevil, but that's what they did at the other asylums I worked at. Besides, I saw it on my monthly calendar this morning."

Charlotte said, "I don't think I'll be going. I've seen all the patients, and I don't care to be close to any of them."

Mrs. Bellow started sifting through the clothes. "Charlotte, it's not up to you, my dear. The dances are mandatory."

Brooklyn was already trying on a dress she had found. Charlotte took the dress Mrs. Bellow was holding in her hand. "I'll go, but I'm not dancing."

Mrs. Bellow shook her head. "Did you know that is not your choice either? For every dance you dance with another patient, you get a demerit knocked off your list." She smiled at Charlotte. "See, there's a silver lining in everything."

Charlotte said, "Wait, Mrs. Bellow—I forgot your sweater back in the supply room."

"I'll get it, Charlotte. You and Brooklyn can run along."

Charlotte snatched the keys off Mrs. Bellow's desk and ran to the supply room carrying her dress. "That's fine, Mrs. Bellow. I'll get it." She opened the door and quickly got the sweater, then ran to the back of the supply room and picked up Serenity's file. She slipped it under the dress she was carrying. She handed Mrs. Bellow the sweater and keys. "See you tomorrow, Mrs. Bellow."

"Have a good night," she answered.

The two girls walked back to their room carrying their dresses. Brooklyn said, "Charlotte, I can't believe how many clothes I got."

"Brooklyn, some of them have holes in them and are stained."

"I know, but they're my clothes, no one else's."

As soon as they got back to their room Jared was standing there. "Nice to see you two getting along."

Brooklyn said, "Look at all my new clothes, and this beautiful dress for the dance."

Jared watched as Brooklyn opened her dresser drawer and fussed over each item as she put it away. He said, "Oh yeah, the dance."

Charlotte said, "You knew about the dance?" She flung her dress across her bed along with Serenity's file.

"Yes, but I didn't want to tell you about it. I was afraid you'd have a fit and end up in a tantrum."

Brooklyn said, "Mrs. Bellow said that for every dance that Charlotte dances, a demerit will come off her file."

Charlotte corrected Brooklyn. "For every dance with a patient, that is."

Brooklyn looked at Jared as she held up her dress. "Do you get to dance, Jared?"

He was reluctant to answer. "Only with the female guards. No patients though."

Charlotte said, "Let's go show Brooklyn Midnight and Noon."

Jared paused. "I don't know if that's such a good idea."

"Oh, come on, Jared." She tucked her arm in his. "No harm. We have some time to kill before the evening meal."

Brooklyn patted her thin indented stomach. "I don't mind meeting your friends with the weird names, but can we eat first? I'm so hungry I could chew my own arm off."

Charlotte wrinkled her nose. "All right, but no more sayings like the one you just said." She shivered when she remembered Serenity's arm, the body parts hanging in the morgue, and the bag of innards that was thrown onto her bedroom floor.

Charlotte despised the lunchroom. It was always dark and dank. It smelled like stagnant river water. The walls were dirty and could use a new coat of paint, or at least a good cleaning. There were mice and rats that would occasionally visit, but they didn't stick around for long. The lunch ladies would go running after the rodents like they were shopping at a meat market. A lot of the old laminate flooring was missing, and most of the veneer had been peeled off the tables and chairs. Charlotte had to concentrate hard on Jared, and now Brooklyn, so she could eat without getting an upset stomach.

As they entered the cafeteria, it was dark. The lights were off, and the light shining through the many reinforced windows was nonexistent. There seemed to be some type of commotion in the food line. Over the loudspeaker came, "Infraction in progress with number 2581; request assistance."

Charlotte could see Mr. BT in the front of the line. He said, "What the hell is this crap you're serving me today? You might be able to fool some of the patients, but not me. There are innards in this soup, and I think I see an eyeball staring at me, and a portion of a lip."

The lunch lady fired back, "You better sit down before I call a nurse. There's nothing in your food that I wouldn't eat."

Mr. BT didn't back down. "By the looks of you, I believe you'd eat just about anything, moving or otherwise."

The lunch lady yelled at Jared. "Guard! Guard, get over here and restrain this patient. He's going to cause a riot if he's not subdued."

Charlotte said, "I know that patient. He's a little eccentric, but otherwise harmless."

Jared left Charlotte and Brooklyn and went over to patient number 2581. He had his number written in big, bold letters on the back of his shirt.

Jared, with a steady calming voice, said, "I see you have your number on your shirt."

"Yeah, I've written my number on all my clothes. I got tired of everyone asking my number. My name is Billy Thomas the Third, but no one seems to care about that."

Jared said, "Well, Mr. Billy Thomas the Third, what's the problem with your meal?"

"Take a look for yourself. There're body parts in my soup."

Jared lowered his voice. He didn't want a confrontation in front of all the other patients, especially Charlotte. "Let me get you a fresh bowl."

Jared looked at the soup, and there was an eye floating in it. He didn't see the portion of lip, but he thought it must be there also.

Mr. BT said, "I don't want any more of that doggone soup. Just get me a salad and crackers—they can't destroy that."

Jared found Charlotte and Brooklyn sitting at a crowded table. "Is this the only table?"

Charlotte said, "Pretty much. We should have called ahead for reservations."

Brooklyn said, "Were there really body parts in his soup?"

Jared lied. "No, he just thought he saw something floating. It was just a piece of potato with a rotten spot on it." As Jared looked to the patient next to him, he could see body parts in his soup also. "Let's hurry up and get out of here. I think the patients are restless today."

He didn't want to alarm Charlotte or Brooklyn, but he now knew that Primevil was using body parts as their meat products. Just how many people have I eaten? Jared put his hand to his stomach as his insides were churning.

9

Serenity

As soon as the three finished the evening meal, Charlotte went and got the file out from under her dress that was lying on the bed. She handed the file to Jared. "I snuck Serenity's file out of the clinic." Charlotte looked at Jared. "Jared, you look ill. Are you okay?"

"Yeah, I'm fine."

Charlotte pulled out a mint from her pocket and handed it to him. "Helps with an upset stomach."

"I'm just thinking about what I've eaten lately. That's all."

"What do you mean? What have you eaten? I know the cafeteria food is bad, but at least you haven't died."

He gave a weak smile. "At least not yet."

Charlotte hated this time of night. The patients had free time after dinner, and there was a large group of them wandering the hallway by her doorway. During the day, there were always activities, like cooking, sewing, woodworking, and handyman classes. The asylums wanted all the patients to learn a trade so they could help. No idle patients allowed, sane or insane.

They stepped into the hallway, and before Charlotte could say anything, Brooklyn said, "Hey, creeps, get away from our bedroom door. I don't want you touching any of my new things. If I see any of your greasy paw marks on my dress, I'll make you the next day's meal. Comprehend what I'm saying?"

Several of the patients got in Charlotte's space as Jared moved the patients back. "Give the ladies some room."

The patient closest to Brooklyn pointed to her and said, "She ain't no lady. She's a street rat; can tell by her eyes and her smell."

Brooklyn punched the man in the stomach, and he doubled over with a groan.

Several of the more deformed patients pointed at Charlotte. "There's Wanda."

Charlotte screamed, "I'm not Wanda, and get away from my door!"

Jared grabbed Charlotte's waist and steered her away from the patients and down the hall. He looked back at Brooklyn, who seemed content with talking to a few of the male patients. "Brooklyn, you can choose a boyfriend later. We've got some reading to do."

She went running after them. "Jared, very funny. I wasn't picking out a boyfriend, at least not here. I'll wait until the dance, when they won't be able to resist me in my new dress."

Charlotte sighed. "You really can't be serious about dating any of these patients."

Brooklyn shrugged. "Charlotte, just because you have someone who could stop traffic with his looks doesn't mean there are any other good-looking guards. I got to take them where I can get them. I'm not picky."

"Yes, I know."

They made it up to Jared's room, which didn't have a lock on the door, but he was allowed to shut it without anyone saying anything. Jared leaned a chair under the doorknob and said, "Charlotte, let's see the file."

Charlotte sat next to Jared on the floor. "Hey, Brooklyn, go pull Jared's bottom dresser drawer open and meet our friends Midnight and Noon.

"Is this some kind of joke? Is there something weird in there?"

"I promise it's a good thing."

Brooklyn slowly opened the dresser and yelled. "Kittens, oh my God, kittens! Oh Charlotte, can I have one?"

Charlotte looked at Jared with pleading eyes. Jared said, "Sure, Brooklyn, you can have the little gray one."

A tear rolled down Brooklyn's cheek. "Thank you." She played quietly with the little bundles of fur while Charlotte's hand trembled as she slowly opened Serenity's file.

Jared took the lead and started reading the information out loud. "Serenity Cinder, age seventeen, diagnosis paranoid schizophrenic."

Charlotte said, "Jared, what does that mean?"

Brooklyn said, "I don't know what *schizophrenic* means, but paranoid means she didn't trust anyone. Your friend thought somebody was out to get her."

Charlotte said, "She wasn't paranoid; obviously someone was after her. They killed her, and they're covering something. She got confused about how old she was, but I don't find that so strange. She was supposed to be my age—sixteen."

Jared said, "A lot of people forget their actual age once they get here. Every day is the same. Nothing changes, and there are no celebrations for birthdays or any other special days. Schizophrenic means disease of the mind."

Charlotte said, "I'm still not clear on what she had."

Brooklyn said, "She was a nitwit who was suspicious of everyone."

Charlotte said, "Don't say that about Serenity."

"I didn't say it. That's what the doctors said about her."

Jared said, "I guess when we are dragged here, they have to give us a diagnosis of some kind. But the real reason we're all here is because something happens to us when we turn sixteen."

Jared put his hand on Charlotte's arm. "Let's just keep reading. It says she had no family, and she's had mental problems most of her life. Bounced around from asylum to asylum, and that she had violent outbursts."

Charlotte looked at Jared. "I suppose you think that since I've had several tantrums that I have violent tendencies."

Jared said, "No, Charlotte, I don't think you're a violent person."

Brooklyn held Midnight up to her lips. "I think you're violent. But I don't see anything wrong with that." Brooklyn winked at Charlotte.

Charlotte asked, "So she wasn't one of the teens that came here because of going insane on her sixteenth birthday?"

Jared shrugged his shoulders.

Charlotte said, "Jared, find the part that tells when Serenity went to the infirmary."

He thumbed through the pages and started reading the nurse's notes. "It states that she was escorted to the clinic in the late afternoon by another patient."

"That was me," Charlotte said.

Jared said, "It doesn't give your name, but we know it was you. Anyway, it says Serenity had a low-grade fever and complained of stomach pains."

Charlotte grimaced. "Yeah, I told her not to eat the meat that day, but she did anyway."

Brooklyn said, "Charlotte, you're never going to find out what happened to Serenity unless you stop commenting on each thing your boyfriend says."

Charlotte stuck her tongue out at Brooklyn. "Sorry. Jared, go on."

"Serenity's temperature kept rising, and the night nurse called Mrs. Bellow for instructions. She was advised to call Dr. Oracle."

Charlotte started to say something but quickly clamped her hand over her mouth.

"They had given her medication to keep the fever down, but it wasn't working. They tried a tepid bath, and alternating the meds, but her fever was close to one hundred and seven degrees. It says the nurse was worried about brain damage if they couldn't bring her fever down. Dr. Oracle ordered a round of blood tests to see if she had an infection. Her levels came back off the charts, diagnosis sepsis."

Charlotte blurted out, "Jared, What's that?"

"I believe it's some type of blood infection. Few people survive with that diagnosis, and if they do they could be brain damaged."

"What would cause that?"

Jared rearranged his position on the floor. "Charlotte, I'm not a doctor. I know more than most, but not enough to know how Serenity got the blood infection."

He started skimming the notes. "This is where it gets weird. It says that when the nurse was on the phone with Dr. Oracle, Serenity went missing."

Brooklyn was playing with the kittens with a string she had torn off her jeans. "A person just doesn't go missing. Sounds like foul play."

Charlotte got excited. "See, Jared, I told you—foul play."

Jared shook his head. "The Collectors were called in, and a full-blown search was launched. The nurse wrote that she thought Serenity was a runaway."

Midnight came over to Charlotte, and as she picked up the soft purring kitten she said, "Serenity wouldn't run away. She'd already been in half the asylums around here. There was no place for her to go, and she had no family, no friends."

"The nurse stated Serenity was talking out of her head."

Brooklyn said, "Imagine that, in an asylum."

"Here's an incident report stating Serenity went missing, and they did all they could to find her. After looking for hours inside, the Collectors went outside to look."

Brooklyn was getting upset. "Why would she be outside the building? Aren't the doors locked at night? Aren't they? Do I need to hide all the nice things that I got from Mrs. Bellow? What if they do some kind of panty raid, and steal my stuff?"

Charlotte tried to comfort Brooklyn. "Don't worry, Brooklyn, no one would want to come into Primevil, even if the doors were wide open and they had an invitation."

There was a knock on the door. "Hey, Jared, you in there?"

It was a female voice. Charlotte and Brooklyn looked at Jared, and Brooklyn said, "Hey, Charlotte, I guess you're already sharing your boyfriend."

Jared said, "She's just a friend. Not now, Gretchen, I'm busy. I'll get with you later."

"What are you busy with—or should I say who?"

Jared shook his head. "Gretchen, I promise I'll get with you later. Can whatever is bothering you wait?"

"I guess. Come find me when you're done."

Charlotte said, "Who's Gretchen?

"She's just another guard. Let's get back to what we were doing."

Charlotte got quiet and Brooklyn said, "I guess you don't like sharing your boyfriend."

"He's not my boyfriend." Charlotte sat there with her arms crossed. "Jared, what else does Serenity's file say?"

He cleared his throat. "Two of the Collectors found Serenity hanging over the north fence. When she fell, she landed on the sharp edge, which serrated her arm at the elbow. There was a large puddle of blood that had pooled under her."

Charlotte started to cry and Brooklyn said, "Charlotte, you crying because of Serenity or because Jared has another girlfriend?"

That was more than Charlotte could take. She launched at Brooklyn, and the fists went flying. It was a full-blown catfight. Jared immediately got up and started pulling the two apart.

Gretchen was pounding on the door. "Jared, what's going on? Jared, are you all right? Gretchen shoved the door open with her shoulder, screeching the chair and spilling it to the floor.

She ran over and grabbed Brooklyn. "Jared, who are these girls?"

As he held Charlotte with both hands around her waist he said, "They're patients."

Brooklyn saw the hurt in Charlotte eyes and yelled at Gretchen, "Get off me, you beast."

Nobody in the room was prepared for what Gretchen did. She smacked Brooklyn in the face as hard as she could. The entire room hung with the silence of a bad surprise. Brooklyn's face started to swell, and her lip was bleeding where her tooth had cut into it.

Jared yelled, "Gretchen, stop!" She turned to face him and saw the file scattered on the floor. As she bent down to pick it up, Charlotte lunged at Gretchen's legs. Gretchen fell hard on the floor, and Jared picked up Serenity's file.

"Gretchen, this is none of your business."

She fired back. "And what makes you think a patient's file is your business?"

Charlotte let go of Gretchen's legs. "That's my file, Gretchen. I asked Jared to interpret it for me, but I've not given you permission. So take a hike."

She air-kicked Charlotte. "I'm writing you both up. What's your number?"

Jared walked over to Gretchen. "If you write them up, I'm going to have to write you up for abusing a patient."

Gretchen smirked. "You think anyone cares if the patients are abused?"

"Some do, and I know who they are. You had no business forcing yourself into my room."

Gretchen started for the door. "I believe I'm going to look at Primevil's handbook on patients in the guards' rooms."

Charlotte blurted out. "I already know, Gretchen. I can be in Jared's room. I just can't spend the night with him."

This threw Gretchen off guard, and with a surprised look she said, "I'm sure there's something in the handbook about putting a chair against the door. Jared, if they wanted you to be able to secure your door, they would have given you a lock. You know the patients' rooms, including the guards', have lockless doors."

Jared went over and held the door open for Gretchen, and as she left he said, "Next time have the fortitude to knock."

Brooklyn yelled, "Yeah, were you born in a barn?"

Jared lowered his voice. "Charlotte, you need to get this file back to the clinic. Do you believe Serenity's death happened the way it states in these notes?"

"I don't know. There's a lot to think about. Some things don't add up. Is there anything else, like a death certificate?"

Jared looked for the certificate. "It just states the date, her name and number, etc. And, the cause of death: accidental fall."

Brooklyn said, "We're lucky the kittens ran and hid from the beast or she would have reported that also."

Jared said, "I've a little seniority over Gretchen, so I think I could persuade her to do just about anything."

Charlotte was deep in thought. "Jared, do you think Serenity's death was accidental? I thought they said she had that blood thing."

"I don't know. It doesn't hurt to keep checking. She did have sepsis, but that's not what killed her."

Brooklyn said, "What else we got to do in this place? You can count me in."

Charlotte took the file from Jared. "I'll take this back tomorrow." The file didn't have the answers she thought it would. "Those weren't all Serenity's body parts in the morgue."

Brooklyn said, "Charlotte, you've been in the morgue? And what body parts are you talking about?"

"Yeah, I've been in the morgue, and there is something horribly creepy about Primevil, if you haven't noticed. Like I said—just don't eat the meat in the cafeteria. I found Serenity's arm hanging over a drain, along with other patients' body parts."

Brooklyn gave a look of disbelief as Charlotte looked under the dresser and pulled the terrified kittens out. "Charlotte, that's even terrifying for a street rat like me." They petted the fur balls until they were calm and purring again, then tucked them back in the dresser for a relaxing nap. As they left Jared's room, Charlotte had Serenity's file under her shirt.

Gretchen was standing in the hallway smacking her gum. "Looks like you've got a growth on your chest, Charlotte."

Brooklyn said, "Well, at least she has something there, Gretchen."

Charlotte said in a whisper, "You know, Brooklyn, sometimes when you try to make things better, it just doesn't sound quite right."

Jared put his arms around both girls and looked back at Gretchen. "Stay out of my room, Gretchen. I'll know if you've been in there."

She smirked and walked away.

Brooklyn said, "Do either of you want to see me in the dress I'm wearing to the dance?"

They both shouted, "No!"

Jared walked them to their room. "See you later. I've got work to do. Charlotte, try to stay out of trouble."

"Yeah, Jared, Brooklyn and I are just going to keep to ourselves tonight." Charlotte opened her dresser and pulled out her hairbrush. "Let me fix your hair, Brooklyn."

Charlotte sat on her bed and patted the stained sheets. Brooklyn smiled and jumped on the bed. "First time I've had my hair done."

Charlotte looked around the room and somehow it didn't seem as depressing as every other night. The furniture was the same—the dark brick walls were gloomy, the light was dim, the flooring was chipped, and the two dressers and bedside tables were falling apart—but now she had a roommate. This reminded Charlotte of the times she had a friend spend the night when she was younger. This was filthier, by far, and her parents weren't around, but at least she had a girlfriend. Her thoughts weren't as scary, and Primevil was more tolerable with a roommate to share everything with. The good, the bad, and the ugly—the good being her friends, and Primevil was full of the bad and ugly. You didn't have to go looking for that—just open your eyes and there it was.

Brooklyn turned and smiled at Charlotte. "You think Mrs. Bellow has an extra hairbrush for me, just lying around the clinic?"

Charlotte shrugged her shoulders. "You can always use mine." She brushed and did a French braid on Brooklyn's mousey brown hair.

"Thanks, Charlotte. Do you want me to try something with your hair?"

"No, it's pretty late, and I've got work tomorrow. Maybe tomorrow night. "

They both finished brushing their teeth and removing their shoes, and then dove straight under the covers. "Charlotte, do you think anyone will dance with me?"

"Sure. It's not like the patients are picky or anything."

"Thanks a lot."

"No, I'm sorry. I didn't mean that. I meant you'll probably dance every song. You'll be exhausted when the night ends."

"You think? Wouldn't that be great?"

Charlotte yawned. "Get some sleep, Brooklyn."

Redwine hill

10

The Monkey Dance

The next day Charlotte had an opportunity to put Serenity's file back. Not exactly in the correct spot, but close enough to make Mrs. Bellow think the night nurse filed it wrong.

Mrs. Bellow came out of the morgue. "It's just so hard to find good help nowadays.. Charlotte, that night nurse knows nothing about the alphabet. No wonder so many patients die on the night shift. She is the most incompetent nurse I have, with the exception of that idiot on J floor, Mrs. Rogers."

That sentence about patients dying on the night shift grabbed Charlotte's attention. She asked, "Why do you think that, Mrs. Bellow?"

"Who knows? Maybe she didn't go to an accredited nursing school."

"No, I didn't mean her academics. I'm talking about why more deaths on her night shift."

"Oh, well, who knows? Could be the same reason. I think she's slipping into the narcotics cabinet also, but that's between you and me, Charlotte."

"Yes, Mrs. Bellow."

"I think I'll request a camera be put in here to monitor things when I'm not in. These walls aren't going to talk and neither are the patients on this floor. There have been too many deaths at this institution, as well as at others, and it's being investigated. I hope they find out something soon. I don't want to be a nurse at Primevil for much longer."

Charlotte looked at Mrs. Bellow. "You really think something is going on at Primevil?"

"I'd bet my life on it. I'm just not sure what's going on. I was hoping to retire this year, but then the Validator sent me over here." She sighed and went back to her paperwork.

Charlotte said. "You must be pretty high up, if you know the Validator personally."

"Well, I have my connections." She tapped her pen on her lips. "Even though he's known for being uncaring and ruthless, I find him just the opposite. Oh, and, Charlotte." She didn't wait for a response. "I want you to tell me if you see or hear anything strange at Primevil."

She didn't know if she should tell Mrs. Bellow about her suspicions about Primevil's exotic meats served in the meals, so she just nodded.

Three o'clock came and Mrs. Bellow said, "Charlotte, I see Brooklyn is peeking into the clinic again. Why don't you take the rest of the day off and get ready for the dance."

Brooklyn had heard and came running into the clinic jumping up and down and screaming. "Come on, Charlotte, I can't wait."

She held up her hand, which she had painted with the Monarch Butterfly nail polish. "Charlotte, I hope you don't mind. You did give me this, but I hope you haven't changed your mind."

Charlotte looked at Brooklyn's hand. "No, I don't mind." She was thinking, *I hope this isn't the last day I see you.* She had almost thought the nail polish was a link to death. *Is that why I so easily gave it to her?*

Charlotte said as they entered their room, "Brooklyn, let me fix your hair."

Brooklyn said, "You know how to fix my hair for the dance? Not a braid, something nice. My father, Lord rest his soul, would say you're a jack of all trades."

Charlotte said, "Yeah, that's me. I can do everything a little, but nothing great to elevate my standing." Before Brooklyn could rattle off all the reasons Charlotte should feel good about herself, Charlotte went to her dresser and took out the old torn sheet.

"What are you going to do with that thin, bare sheet? I don't need a ghost costume; this is a formal dance."

Charlotte had to smile at Brooklyn. "Wait and see." Charlotte took the sheet and tore about twenty-five strips. "Now, trust me on this. My mother use to artfully wrap my hair in strips of material when I was young."

Brooklyn sat patiently staring at her nails. "Do you think I should put on a second coat?"

"No, looks nice the way it is."

"Do you think there'll be any good-looking patients at the dance?"

Charlotte didn't want to destroy any hope of Brooklyn having a good time. "Maybe. You know, we haven't seen all the floors. Could be that Primevil is hiding their best for the dance."

When Charlotte was through with Brooklyn's hair, it looked like two dozen flower buds perched on her head. "Now, Brooklyn, come into the bathroom with me."

Brooklyn saw her reflection in the mirror. "You can't be serious. I look like a Saturday morning cartoon."

Charlotte laughed out loud. "You're so funny. This is to curl your hair." She put her hands under the running water and sprinkled the tight knots with just a small amount of water. "Now when the water dries, you'll have a nice light curl in your hair. If you want it really curly, you have to leave the knots in overnight."

Brooklyn started to say something but Charlotte stopped her. "Please don't tell me I'm so smart for knowing this little trick. It was just something my mother used to do for me before Sunday church."

"All I was going to say was it must have been nice to have a mother."

Charlotte paused for a moment. "My mother was a hard worker. I could always count on her to say the right thing. I miss her a lot."

Brooklyn said, "I'm sorry I said anything. Now you're sad."

"It's okay. It's not the thinking about my mom that's hard; it's knowing I'll never see her again that gets me upset. I don't think I'd be here at Primevil if my mother were still alive. She would have tried to hide me as long as possible, and then when the Collectors came she'd have seen to it that I got put in a better asylum. I know she'd have visited me every day."

Tears splashed down on Charlotte's cheek, and as she brushed them away Brooklyn said, "Aren't you going to fix your hair?"

"No, I'm just going to wear it in a high ponytail. Don't want any patients getting the wrong idea, that I like dances."

There was a knock at the door, "Can I come in?"

Charlotte recognized the voice. "Sure, Mrs. Bellow."

"My, my, Brooklyn, what an interesting hairdo. I've come to help with your makeup."

Charlotte protested. "Really, Mrs. Bellow, I don't think that's necessary."

Brooklyn was already looking through the items Mrs. Bellow had brought in. "Yes, please, Mrs. Bellow, make me look gorgeous."

Charlotte laughed at Brooklyn. "You've been so deprived your whole life, you're ready for anything."

"Charlotte, you're too serious all the time. Are you going to let Mrs. Bellow decorate your face?"

"Yes, that would be nice, but not too much."

Mrs. Bellow went to work on Charlotte's face. "Charlotte, you have a perfect nose, my dear." She looked over at Brooklyn, who wanted to do her own face, "Easy on the lipstick, Brooklyn. You don't want to look like a clown."

"Mrs. Bellow, I want to accent my lips since my teeth are crooked."

"But, honey, that's just the opposite of what you should be doing; you need to tone down the bright shades on your lips so not to attract attention to your flaws." She turned and said in a whisper, "Of which she has many." She turned back and smiled at Brooklyn.

Mrs. Bellow handed Charlotte a hand mirror. "What do you think?"

"I look like one of those porcelain dolls I'd see in the window of the antique shop, just down the street from where I lived."

Mrs. Bellow blew out a long sigh. "Now let me turn my attention to Brooklyn."

"I think I've done a pretty fair job." She turned to face Mrs. Bellow and Charlotte.

Charlotte jumped a little and grimaced while Mrs. Bellow grabbed a dozen tissues and said, "For a minute there I thought it was Halloween."

It took a while, but Mrs. Bellow finally got most of the makeup off Brooklyn's face and hands. "Honey, you must have thought this was a finger-painting class." She turned Brooklyn to face the mirror. "What do you think?"

"I liked mine better, but I guess this will do."

"Now, girls, I've got to run home and change and be back here by seven o'clock."

Charlotte said, "Are you one of the chaperones?"

"No, actually I'm the one who keeps track of removing the demerits. So put on your dancing shoes, Charlotte. I hope you have a busy night. Oh, I almost forgot—I saw Jared in the hallway. He said not to worry, that he would be late."

Brooklyn was admiring herself in the mirror. "Doesn't matter, Mrs. Bellow. Charlotte can't dance with him anyway."

"You're right. Now, I'm going to let you girls keep my old makeup. That is, if you want it."

Brooklyn spoke up. "Are you kidding, Mrs. B?" She scooped up all the small containers and quickly put them in her top dresser drawer. She saw Charlotte staring at her. "I'm sorry, Charlotte—did you want any?"

She shook her head no, and Mrs. Bellow said, "Brooklyn, I'd appreciate it if you'd call me Mrs. Bellow."

She was looking down into her drawer. "Okay. Thanks for all this stuff."

Mrs. Bellow waved and said, "See you girls in a few hours."

They went to eat the evening meal before putting on their dresses. Some patients were already dressed for the dance, but Brooklyn noticed everyone was staring at her. "Look, Charlotte, I think everyone thinks I'm pretty; they're all staring."

Charlotte looked at Brooklyn, with her hair in two dozen knots and still looking a little garish with the makeup. "Yes, I can see why. You look very special this evening."

After supper Brooklyn went running back to their room. She was half dressed when Charlotte came in. "Hurry, Charlotte, so you can do my hair."

They were finally ready, and as they looked in the mirror Charlotte couldn't help but think she was understated elegance and Brooklyn was overstated something. Charlotte knew if Serenity were here that she'd look just as plain as she did.

They walked arm in arm to the huge cafeteria, which was now decorated, and the chairs and tables had all been pushed to the perimeter of the room. "Charlotte, how'd they get this decorated so fast?"

Charlotte saw Mrs. Bellow waving at them. "Yoo-hoo, Charlotte, I've got the perfect patient to dance with you."

Brooklyn was already scanning the scenery for victims. The cafeteria-turned-ballroom was filled with anxious patients, mostly in their teens to mid-twenties. There were a few older patients, but not many. There seemed to be at least a hundred patients all milling around waiting for the music to start up again. Most of the decorations were paper cutouts, streamers, and balloons taped to the tables. The lighting was set low with just a few sparkles of light coming from the side sconces. It was hard to tell if the men outnumbered the women or vice versa. The smell in the cafeteria was better than normal. It was a combination of soap, shampoo, and gallons of fragrances all mixing together.

Mrs. Bellow dragged Charlotte across the room and introduced her to a man wearing shackles and a pair of shiny handcuffs.

"Charlotte, this is Martin. Quickly, my dear, the music is going to start up again."

Charlotte thought, *Mrs. Bellow must be testing me.* "You're kidding, of course."

"No, my dear, there are very few patients who want to dance with you. They seem to think you resemble Wanda."

"Who's Wanda?"

"She's just a ghost that roams the hallways of Primevil. Now, Charlotte, this young man isn't going to wait forever. We can talk about Wanda later."

He was a tall man with greased-down hair. He didn't smell too bad, and at least he had okay teeth. Charlotte smiled at Mrs. Bellow and said under her breath, "How bad could this be?"

Mrs. Bellow said, "You kids go have fun."

Charlotte looked back over her shoulder. "Don't forget to mark off a demerit."

The music came on once again and it was a slow song. Charlotte started to walk off the dance floor, but Mrs. Bellow held up one finger for the first demerit coming off her long list.

The man grabbed Charlotte's hands in his. They were sticky and she started to pull away, but the man held on tight. He said, "Do you know what I did today?"

Charlotte shook her head no. She really didn't care what this man's daily routine was; she just wanted the dance to be over.

The next sentence he said paralyzed her. He said, "I pleasured myself."

Charlotte twisted her hands free of the man's grip and stormed off the dance floor.

Mrs. Bellow said, "Charlotte, you have to dance the entire dance with the patient. I don't think that counts as a full demerit."

Charlotte ran to the bathroom, and when Mrs. Bellow came in Charlotte was scrubbing her hands under hot water with soap.

"Charlotte, what's the matter? Brooklyn seems to be enjoying herself, but she's not the one who needs the credit for dancing."

Charlotte washed her hands twice more, and when she was drying them off she asked, "Why did you have me dance with that patient?"

"I guess it's because no one ever dances with him. I thought since you needed to clear some demerits, you wouldn't mind a sympathy dance."

Charlotte bit down hard on her lower lip to keep from losing control. "I suggest, Mrs. Bellow, that you not inflict this patient on anyone else, and least of all on me."

"Charlotte, what are you talking about? He couldn't have harmed you physically. He's in restraints, and he doesn't talk much. What could have happened in the twenty seconds you were out on the floor?"

"His hands were sticky, and he said he just got finished pleasuring himself. That's what happened."

"Oh, Charlotte, I didn't know. From now on, just fast dancing, nothing slow. You don't have to touch any of the patients. Don't give up now, dear. I'll take off one full demerit."

Charlotte looked at Mrs. Bellow. "Are you sure you didn't know this patient would do that?"

"No, of course not. Please, just go back out there. I saw Jared come in when you ran off the dance floor. I thought you had a lover's tiff and when you saw him you ran into the bathroom. I had no idea what happened."

"Mrs. Bellow, Jared and I didn't have a tiff. We're fine. Now if you'll excuse me, I've some demerits to work off." Charlotte felt safe now that Jared would be observing the event. She had to laugh when she saw Brooklyn on the dance floor. She had found a patient who looked as ridiculous as she did. They were doing some kind of monkey dance. It was hysterical and everyone was watching them, but she then realized she had seen Brooklyn's dancing partner someplace else.

She let out a small gasp. Billy Thomas the Third was dancing like he was peeling a banana, and Brooklyn was pretending to climb a tree.

Charlotte was laughing so hard she jumped when Jared tapped her on the shoulder. "How's the dancing going?"

"Kind of sticky. Why?"

"Work off any demerits yet?"

"Yes, I have. One, as a matter of fact."

"Charlotte you don't mind if I dance with Gretchen, do you?"

She smiled. "No, go right ahead. If I have to endure this torture I think it's only right that you do too."

Charlotte looked at Jared dancing with Gretchen, but not an ounce of jealously wisped over her body. How could she be jealous? The nickname for Gretchen was Rat Teeth.

The dance ended, and Brooklyn and Mr. BT came over to Charlotte, and she said, "Mr. Billy Thomas the Third, you clean up nicely. Where's your nice jacket?"

He was almost handsome in his suit and nicely combed hair. His teeth were nice and straight, and he had deep-set brown eyes. "Didn't have to wear it this evening; anyone wearing a blazer wasn't allowed at the dance. So I was on my best behavior this week." He gave Charlotte a huge grin.

Brooklyn said, "What are you talking about? There are a lot of patients with just blazers on and not a suit."

Mr. BT grabbed Brooklyn by the waist and said, "It's a special blazer. Now, let's go do the Monkey Dance."

He then took a small step toward Charlotte and whispered, "I need to meet with you later. It's about Serenity."

Charlotte shook her head and just stood there as he walked away. *He knows something about Serenity's death. I knew someone had to know something at Primevil.*

As the dance was winding down, Brooklyn came up to Charlotte. "Mrs. Bellow should've had us wear gloves; that guy in the shackles has something on his hands. I guess he doesn't know how to use a napkin when he eats."

Charlotte said, "You danced with him?"

"Sure, I danced with everyone. I had a great time. How many demerits did you manage to get removed?"

"Well, Mrs. Bellow officially marked me off for twelve demerits. She said that was about a third. I've got to work the rest of them off some other way. I hate this dance thing."

Jared, Charlotte, and Brooklyn headed back to the girls' room. Brooklyn said, "Charlotte, that was a great night. I wish I could've worked off some of your demerits for dancing with the patients. Then Primevil would've ended up crediting your account." They walked and talked on their way back to their room, dancing and skipping in the hallways.

Jared could barely keep up with them. "Wait up."

As Charlotte looked back at Jared, she could see some of the other patients coming down the hallway. She saw Brooklyn staring at the other women. "Brooklyn don't say a word. I can tell by the look on your face that you're going to say something hurtful. Let's just enjoy this evening. Besides, you don't want to get your pretty dress torn."

Brooklyn moved close to Charlotte. "I was only going to say that the male patients didn't have a lot to choose from, if you know what I mean."

Jared said, "Here we are, ladies." As Brooklyn went into the room, Charlotte hung around hoping for a good-night kiss.

Charlotte looked deep into Jared powerful brown eyes. "What an unusual evening."

Jared leaned into Charlotte. "It was a shame I didn't get to dance with you."

The closeness made Charlotte stammer. "Yeah, I'd have liked that."

Redwine hill

11

Mass Exiting

Brooklyn was inside the room admiring herself in the mirror when Jared gently pushed Charlotte back into the wall and leaned over and kissed her. It would have been the perfect kiss. She wasn't shy, and she could feel her face didn't flush with warmth. His lips fit perfectly with hers. They were soft, and she wondered if all guys' lips were soft.

The kiss ended abruptly when the sirens and lights began flashing. This wasn't like anything Charlotte had ever heard before.

Brooklyn tore herself away from the mirror. "What the hell is that?"

Jared said, "It's either a mass exiting of patients or there's a major riot. You two go up to my room and place whatever you can in front of the door. Don't worry about demerits. Just do it. I've got to go."

Charlotte said, "Won't the noise and lights be just as intrusive up there?"

"At least you'll be safe. The only place that's fairly quiet is the basement because nothing is down there with the exception of Dr. Oracle's lab. Charlotte, don't argue with me; just go."

Jared took off running, and Brooklyn grabbed Charlotte's arm and squeezed it. "Charlotte, get your head out of your assssss."

They ran for Jared's room and saw Gretchen running down the hall, trying to load her gun. Brooklyn yelled, "Hey, Snaggle Teeth, watch what you're doing."

Charlotte broke out into laughter. "It's not Snaggle Teeth, it's Rat Teeth."

Brooklyn said, "Whatever. She's still horrible to look at."

Gretchen pointed her gun at the two just as they slipped into Jared's room. They heard a shot above the sirens and saw a piece of the door frame fly up in the air. Gretchen screamed, "Shut up, Brooklyn. The next shot will be in your backside."

Brooklyn didn't bother answering; she just helped Charlotte move the bed in front of the door. They then piled anything that had some weight to it. They could hear Gretchen yelling, "I'll deal with you two idiots later."

Charlotte said, "Do you think she means it?"

"Of course she does. We now officially have our first enemy. Don't worry, Charlotte, I've had plenty of nemeses throughout my life. They outnumber my friends, which means, counting Jared and you, I've got exactly two."

Charlotte was breathing heavy from moving the cumbersome furnishings. "I'm not exactly rolling in friends, as you can see."

Brooklyn sat and pulled out the drawer and picked up Noon, then handed Midnight to Charlotte.

"Brooklyn, I think the chaos is too much for the kittens."

They were clawing and trying to break free. "Just put them back. No reason for them to go insane."

Brooklyn put the cats away. "Can cats actually go insane?"

Charlotte didn't answer; she was looking out Jared's window.

"Charlotte, what's wrong?"

"All the asylums are defecting or rioting. Primevil isn't the only one." It looked like all twelve of the asylums on Redwine Hill were having their share of problems this evening. Patients, mostly in their teens, were running out of the asylums in droves. Some were dressed, and others had just their underwear on, but they were all trying to hold their heads with their hands. Some were screaming out in pain and rolling around on the sand, resisting the guards and Collectors who were trying to corral them back into the asylums. Charlotte could hear sirens and see lights blazing throughout many of the other areas, not just on Redwine Hill.

Brooklyn was jumping up and down, getting hysterical. "What do the patients want? Where are they going? The Collectors will just round them up and put them in prison."

"Look, Brooklyn, some are headed for the ocean. Are they going to try to swim to freedom?"

They watched for several minutes. "Crap, Charlotte, they're just walking in and not coming out. This is a mass suicide, or some kind of revolt."

Charlotte looked on in fear. "The Collectors are beating the patients, and it looks like the guards are shooting them."

Brooklyn grabbed Charlotte's arm in a not-so-gingerly grasp. "Charlotte, we need to hide. Gretchen will come back and shoot us."

"What about the kittens?"

"She doesn't even know they're here. They'll be fine. Shake a leg."

They moved the furniture, and Brooklyn slammed open the door, putting a dent in the wall behind it. Charlotte said, "Take it easy. Tread with a light foot. You want people to notice us? Let's go to the clinic—Mrs. Bellow will hide us."

They crept down the stairs, but when they got to the first floor they saw the clinic was crawling with injured patients, guards, and Collectors. The patients outnumbered any other group. They were wandering the halls with the gore of their lifeblood drained out of their pale withered bodies. There were both men and women in shackles running amuck with a deranged gaze in their eyes. The patients had their hands pressed to their heads, and they were screaming and yelling, "My head is going to explode."

They were tearing at their eyes and banging their heads on the wall trying to relieve the pain inside their brains.

Charlotte said, "Brooklyn, does your head feel funny?"

"Just a slight buzzing. Does yours?

"I can feel something deep inside my brain, more like an irritation—like an itch you desperately want to scratch, but you can't."

The patients were still fighting as they looked down the hallway. "Charlotte, where's the basement?"

"No, Brooklyn, we can't leave Mrs. Bellow in the clinic. They could kill her if they haven't already."

The debate was over the minute they heard Mrs. Bellow let out a full-throated scream. The two went running, dodging the chairs and trash that was being thrown. They pushed the bloody individuals out of the way and reached Mrs. Bellow.

She was on the ground with a gash to her shoulder and head. "Charlotte!" she screamed. "Help me!"

Brooklyn got hit in the head with a flying clipboard. "I don't care who threw it, someone is going to pay for this indiscretion." She turned and punched the first person who was the closest. The man doubled over with a groan, and Brooklyn smiled and said, "That'll teach you to keep your hands to yourself."

Charlotte was helping Mrs. Bellow to her feet, when Brooklyn yelled, "Charlotte, watch out!"

The patients had gotten into the clothes closet and were putting on the clothes and throwing the shoes and whipping the belts around in the air. The end of a belt buckle hit Charlotte in the left eye. Blood immediately filled the white part. Brooklyn grabbed Charlotte and Mrs. Bellow and yanked them through the mob that was forming in the clinic.

Mrs. Bellow said, "They're after the drugs."

Brooklyn said, "Who cares? Let them have them."

Charlotte blotted at her left eye with the sleeve of her dance dress. "They're already insane—what difference will the meds make?"

Mrs. Bellow was becoming hysterical. "Where do we go?"

Charlotte dodged a trash bin. "Where's the basement?"

"Yes, yes, the basement. You need a key to be allowed access." She reached for the chain. "My keys! Someone must have torn them from my neck."

Charlotte ran back, weaving in and out of the bodies, slipping on the red slippery floor. She was having a hard time focusing with her good eye.

In the clinic, she saw the keys on the floor where the patient had thrown them. He had just opened the narcotics cabinet with them.

The leg of a stool hit the back of her head, and she went down hard. She slithered on the floor and grabbed the keys as a Collector stepped on her back and hand. He fell backward, and she crawled out of the clinic.

Charlotte's burgundy dress was covered in blood, which was soaked through to her undergarments and skin. When she reached Brooklyn and Mrs. Bellow, they didn't hesitate—all three went running for the basement. Charlotte and Brooklyn followed Mrs. Bellow as they watched her plump hand try to unlock the door.

Charlotte took the key from her and unlocked the door. There was a man in a strait jacket and another man—the one with the shackles who had pleasured himself at the dance.

Charlotte yelled, "Mrs. Bellow, Brooklyn, hurry up."

She shut the door so it caught the full skirt of Brooklyn's dress. "Charlotte, open the door," she whimpered.

The two men were right outside the door. Charlotte could see them through the glass panel inlay. "No, just pull your dress out."

"I tried; it's stuck."

Mrs. Bellow walked over with a pair of nursing scissors and cut the dress. "Now you're free. But under no circumstance will that door be opened—especially when there are two patients standing on the other side."

Brooklyn looked at her dress and said quietly, "That was the prettiest thing I'd ever owned."

Mrs. Bellow was examining her gash on her shoulder. "Well, Brooklyn, perhaps you may want to wear it in your coffin at your funeral."

"I think I could've gotten it out by pulling on it a few more times."

Charlotte said, "No time for that. Let's find a safe place to hide before someone else gets the bright idea to hide down here." She looked at the man she had danced with earlier. He was now placing his face against the glass. It looked like he was kissing the glass. The man in the armless jacket pushed him aside with his shoulder.

Brooklyn looked back as the satin light-blue swatch that was hanging from the door. "What a waste."

"I'll get you a new one, dear. Now, you both follow me and don't make a peep."

Charlotte said, "I hear someone or something coming." They ducked into the lab. It was so much worse than the morgue.

There were at least twenty-five bodies squeezed into the room, some stacked two to three feet high. Brooklyn said, "Gross! What is this place?"

Charlotte said, "It's got to be Dr. Oracle's lab." The temperature was around eighty degrees in the room, and the smell literally hung in the air and on the walls. Brooklyn leaned against the wall and quickly pulled away. Her hand was covered with a thick film of slime and brownish-red residue.

Body parts covered the floor. Charlotte put her hand over her mouth. "This must be where the bag of innards came from."

Mrs. Bellow said in a somewhat calm voice, "I think I know some of these bodies."

Brooklyn pinched Charlotte. "I don't know any of them, and I know I haven't met any of their innards, so let's just get out of here."

Charlotte figured it was the gash on Mrs. Bellow's forehead that made her seem like she had no emotions for what was presented in front of them.

Charlotte opened the door and suddenly shut it. "Dr. Oracle is out there talking to . . . I think it's a man."

Mrs. Bellow asked, "What do you mean, you think it's a man? It's either a man or a woman. What's the gender?"

Brooklyn said, "Who cares? Stop quibbling."

Charlotte said, "Follow me." There was no way to avoid stepping on the body parts and squeezing the liquid out of the insides.

Charlotte spotted something. "Wait. I see the clothing they must have removed from the dead. They've got to be easier to move around in, instead of these ball gowns. How about your fancy dress, Mrs. Bellow—you want to get into something more accommodating for the surroundings we're in?"

Mrs. Bellow rubbed her forehead and pulled a bloodstained hand away from her face. "I suppose."

Brooklyn was going to protest, but she looked at her shredded dress with blood smears.

Mrs. Bellow was changing slowly, and Brooklyn said, "Hurry up, Mrs. B. We need to get moving."

"Brooklyn, it's Mrs. Bellow, and I think the hit to my head has given me a concussion. I won't be able to go very far—just enough to get out of this room."

As soon as they were dressed, Charlotte and Brooklyn each grabbed one of Mrs. Bellow's arms. Charlotte pointed to a distressed door off to the left. As Charlotte passed a two-tier body tower, she noticed a saw sticking out of the man's arm. It was wedged in his bone. Charlotte's shoulder bumped the saw, and the man let out an agonizing moan. The saw went clanking to the floor and splattered some bloody liquid. Charlotte grimaced. "Is he alive?"

Charlotte was waiting for Mrs. Bellow to reassure her with her nursing opinion, but she was holding her wound on her head. Brooklyn said, "Probably just some knee-jerk reaction. Now, let's go before Mrs. B. faints."

Charlotte propped Mrs. Bellow up against Brooklyn as she worked on the bulky wooden door with embellished ironwork. The door was heavy and swollen from the humid conditions in the lab.

Brooklyn tried to ease Mrs. Bellow to the floor, but she landed with a thud. She helped Charlotte pull on the iron ring, and together they eased the door open. They could hear commotion on the other side of the lab door where Dr. Oracle had been. Charlotte said, "Brooklyn, help me get Mrs. Bellow up and through the door." It was quite a struggle, and with the temperature being around eighty degrees, they were working up a sweat.

Once on the other side of the door, it was just as hard to close due to the snug fit. They sat Mrs. Bellow down once again and did their best at closing the door. They were in some type of corridor. It was stuffy and rancid-smelling. The flooring was made out of rocks stuck together, and water oozed between the rocks, making them slippery.

Meanwhile, they could hear Dr. Oracle arguing with the man in the manacles. The man was saying, "My girlfriend, Wanda, is in there. I need to go after her."

Dr. Oracle was yelling at the man. "Your friend is not in here, I quite assure you. Unless she's dead—no one alive is in my lab. Now, go away before I call a Collector for you. I mean it—go. You've worn my patience. I need you to take your sorry self away from my lab."

It was quiet for a moment, then Dr. Oracle yelled, "Good, and if I see you again around my lab, you will find yourself in a horrific accident."

Charlotte drew in the musty odor that hung in the confined area. She could hardly swallow. Her tongue was plastered to the roof of her mouth, even though the stone tunnel was humid.

As he opened the door to the lab, a piece of blue satin material fell to the floor. "So, that patient wasn't talking out of his head." He walked in and started searching the lab. "Nothing out of place, but it's hard to tell with all these corpses in here." He saw the dresses and the nurse uniform on the floor. "There are only two places they could've gone: out the door they came in or . . ." He made his way to the heavy wood door and pulled on the ring. "Seems tight enough. Doesn't matter—if they decided to take this route, they'll perish soon enough." He ran his fingers through his scalp, which left streaks of blood running though his unruly hair.

He counted the bodies and began to cackle. "This is the most I've ever had at one time."

12

No Turning Back

Charlotte said, "We can't carry Mrs. Bellow around with us. We need to find a hiding place for her." The narrow musty enclosed hallway looked like it had been dug out of an underground rock quarry.

About a hundred yards later, Mrs. Bellow threw her hands in the air. "Girls, I must sit. I can't go any farther. Please just let me be. My head is throbbing, and I'm seeing two of everything, and I believe I'm going to regurgitate the contents of my stomach. You go on without me."

Charlotte said, "Wait here. I'll look up ahead for someplace for you to hide."

Brooklyn looked at Mrs. Bellow. "Charlotte, it's going to have to be a fairly big space."

About forty yards ahead Charlotte spotted a sizable boulder, and above it a ledge protruded. Charlotte went back and helped Brooklyn get Mrs. Bellow to a standing position, and they forced her to walk, but she was having a hard time on the slimy rocks underfoot. After a lot of grunting and groaning, they pushed Mrs. Bellow up the slight incline and onto the rock ledge.

Charlotte wiped the sweat from her forehead. "Now, please, Mrs. Bellow, just stay put until we come back."

Brooklyn added, "And don't roll off the ledge, Mrs. B."

This time Mrs. Bellow didn't correct Brooklyn about abbreviating her name. She was holding her head between her hands. "Girls, I need to lie still for a while. I feel like I've got a bad hangover."

Charlotte and Brooklyn took off in the dimly lit corridor. There were small pin lights lining the primitive stale, damp passageway.

Charlotte wiped her neck, which was covered with dirt rows. "Brooklyn, we need to get out of here and find Jared."

They trudged on, and Charlotte wished her eyes would become more accustomed to the light or lack thereof. Brooklyn touched Charlotte's arm. "Do you think Jared is out there shooting patients?"

"I don't know. I hope not, but I haven't known Jared long enough to know that answer."

Charlotte thought about the kiss she'd had with him and got a grin on her face. He was truly a handsome man. Then she slipped, which knocked her out of her daydream.

The rock path was covered with algae and was slippery even with their rubber-soled shoes. Charlotte put her hand on the ceiling. "The rocks are cool but not wet. The water is coming from some other place."

"Charlotte, should we go back and check on Mrs. B?"

"No, Brooklyn, she'll be fine. Hopefully this rock hallway will lead us someplace."

The little round pin lights on the side walls were covered in a greenish film, and the water behind the glass looked at them like a bunch of lazy eyes. It was extremely humid and hard to breathe.

Charlotte said, "Brooklyn, let's get out of here. You can tell by the waterline how high the water is going to get, and I'm not the best swimmer under those circumstances."

Brooklyn took off running, passing Charlotte. "I can't swim at all, or hold my breath. Never had anyone who liked me enough to take the time to teach me."

Charlotte took off too. "The holding-your-breath part is easy. Every kid does it at one time or another, when showing their parents who's the boss. Just hold your breath."

There was a warm, light breeze. "It's not the holding my breath I'd mind. It's the drowning part that I object to."

Charlotte said, "Shhh. Listen, I think that's the ocean."

They made it to the mouth of the cavern and quietly looked out. Patients were walking into the ocean, some holding their heads, others rolling around on the sandy beach. The tides kept lapping at the patients, as if calling them into the ocean. Charlotte scanned the scenery, looking for something or someone familiar.

Brooklyn said, "Charlotte, let's go back. We can't do anything for these patients."

"We didn't come through that tunnel to help the patients. We did it to find a way to get away from Dr. Oracle."

"Are we going to leave Mrs. Bellow back in the corridor?"

"Of course not, but I don't know if we can carry her all this way. Just let me think for a minute." Charlotte scanned the beach as she thought. She shrieked. "Oh my God! The patients have Jared pinned down and are pummeling him."

Several patients stood over guards that were writhing on the ground and were beating them with their fists, and hitting them with rocks and sticks—using anything that had washed up on the shore for a weapon. The Collectors were trying to separate and get control of the fighting. It was hard to tell some of the Collectors and their sidekicks from the patients.

Charlotte didn't hesitate or think of a plan; she just took off—screaming like the wild person the Collectors thought she was several months back when they secured her on the streets of Boston. Charlotte looked over her shoulder and saw Brooklyn running with her hands up in the air, and her face in some kind of contorted scream.

The patients were beating him senseless. Charlotte yelled, "Stop! Stop!" She grabbed the first one around the neck and started choking him. Brooklyn was right behind, and ran toward a man who stood at least six feet tall. She lit in to him, taking her right leg and swinging it backward, then bringing it forward with all her might. She made contact with his privates, and he immediately doubled over and rolled around in the sand.

Brooklyn said, "Learned that on the downtown streets of old Boston."

Charlotte wasn't faring as well. She scratched and kicked as hard as she could, but then the man she was unsuccessfully subduing turned toward her as she shot the palm of her hand up and slammed it into his nose. Blood went everywhere. It came out fast like a faucet, and the man fled toward the ocean. Charlotte watched as he frantically tried to wash the blood away, but it wouldn't stop.

Jared slowly got to his feet and tackled one of the remaining men, while Charlotte and Brooklyn did what every girl does best: scratch, bite, pull hair, and kick. Charlotte took both her hands and slammed them against one man's ears. He looked inebriated and kept hitting the sides of his head. Charlotte figured she had ruptured his eardrums, and he was no longer able to keep his balance.

She turned to Brooklyn. "Only one left."

Jared wasn't doing all that well; he had been beaten badly. He had a black eye and a cut over his left eyebrow that kept dripping blood, and as he tried to wipe it away, more gushed out. He had a deep gash on his left deltoid and a chunk missing from his right leg. The patients were acting like rabid animals, cutting, slicing, and tearing off each other's limbs.

Charlotte saw Jared's gun half buried in the sand and picked it up. "Can't be that hard to shoot." She took aim, and the first round hit the sand and buried itself. The man pummeling Jared looked directly at Charlotte and staggered back, with Brooklyn still wrapped around the man's shoulders. Charlotte yelled, "Brooklyn, get off!"

Brooklyn saw the gun and jumped off, landing in the soft water-soaked sand. Charlotte tried to aim, but found it a bit difficult with her eyes closed. She fired in the general direction and heard Jared yell, but it was too late. She fired again—this time hitting her target. The man fell back into the ocean as the water lapped at his blood.

Brooklyn said, "For freaking sake, Charlotte! You hit Jared in the leg."

"Oh my God, I'm sorry. Jared, I'm sorry."

As he grimaced, he took her hand. "All right, Charlotte, just find me a tourniquet or something." He didn't sound mad—just in severe pain. "The bullet caught the outside of my thigh muscle."

Charlotte quickly took off the belt she had on, and Jared pulled it tight around his leg. She looked up to see a never-ending flow of patients coming toward them. "Brooklyn, grab under Jared's arm." The girls hoisted him up, and Charlotte said, "This is one time where I wished you didn't have muscles, and you were some scrawny shell of a person. It's not doing us any good right now, and you're heavy."

Jared had a pained look on his face. "I think I'd have been more help if you hadn't shot me."

Charlotte stammered. "I'm sorry. I was just trying to help you."

Brooklyn said, "Quit arguing. We need to get out of here."

Charlotte caught Jared looking at her, and she mouthed the word sorry. "We'll go back through the tunnel, the way Brooklyn and I came."

Jared smiled at Charlotte. "Remind me, later, to show you how to shoot."

Brooklyn said, "Hey, she'll pass on that, big guy, if you're the one who showed Gretchen how to shoot."

They could hear the reinforcements coming. Jared said, "The Collectors have been pulled off the streets from their regular duties, and now they're trying to get the patients back in line by using their clubs, or a poke of a needle, or whatever means they need to use. Charlotte, don't look at me that way. I didn't say I agreed with their behavior."

They were in the tunnel and hopefully safe when Jared said, "I don't know what the hell has gotten into the patients."

Charlotte wiped some blood off Jared's left eye. "It's not just Primevil; it's all the institutions."

Brooklyn said, "Can you two talk later? The water seems to be coming up between the rocks, and my shoes are getting wet."

The three of them limped down the corridor, and as the water rose, it bathed the open wounds in cold saltwater, which was painful. Jared was covered in sweat, even though the water was now up to his waist. Charlotte was doing her best to help Jared stay upright. Finally, they made it to the ledge.

Brooklyn said, "Hey, Mrs. B.—it's time to get up."

Jared said out of breath, "Brooklyn, I'll boost you up. I'm going to have to take a rest."

Brooklyn squeezed onto the ledge. "Mrs. B., you're going to have to sit up. We all can't fit if you're going to sprawl all out like a beached whale."

Mrs. Bellow held her head in her hands. "What? Oh, you're back."

"Yeah, we need you to move your *tuchus* over."

Jared, even with his injuries, got up with little problem. Charlotte saw shadows coming down with the flow of water from the corridor. He reached down for Charlotte's arm as bodies began floating by. She let out a faint scream.

Brooklyn said, "So that's how Dr. Oracle disposes of the bodies."

Jared was already in the water when the second bloated gangrene body got tangled in Charlotte's hair. "Charlotte, grab my arm."

The current started dragging Charlotte downstream toward the ocean. She could swim, but this dead body was dragging her under. Before she could swallow her second mouthful of water, Jared had his arm around her. Using his other hand, he did a quick karate chop to the entangled extremity caught in Charlotte's hair. It broke from the body, filling the area with toxic fumes. The arm was still caught, and Charlotte fought with the appendage. Jared grabbed hold of the arm, and it literally fell apart in his hand—tissue, veins, arteries, and muscle going everywhere.

Charlotte let out another scream and went limp against Jared's arm.

"Charlotte!" Jared shook her. "Charlotte, hang on. I can't hold on to the slimy rock much longer."

She could feel Jared's muscles tense and his strong fingers digging into the rocks. He inched his way over to the ledge. He handed Charlotte up to Brooklyn, and then lifted himself up, his arms shaking from the effort.

Charlotte was fully awake now, coughing, and a bit embarrassed. "I can swim, you know. That dead body was dragging me down."

Jared smoothed her hair away from her face and looked at her injured eye. "No wonder you couldn't swim; you couldn't see."

Charlotte said in a stern voice, "I was swimming, and I can see out of my eye just fine. You didn't see me on the bottom, did you?"

Brooklyn said, "Okay, Charlotte. There must be some other reason you looked like a one-legged duck."

Charlotte stuck her tongue out at Brooklyn. "At least I resembled something of a good swimmer."

The three of them watched as the bodies, appendages, parts, and innards floated by. Mrs. Bellow was sound asleep; not even the putrid smell was enough to wake her. Brooklyn covered her mouth with her hand. "I think I'm going to be sick."

Charlotte jabbed Brooklyn with her finger. "Just look away, and try not to breathe through your nose."

As Charlotte leaned her head against Jared's shoulder he said, "How many bodies do you think there are?"

Charlotte said, "At least fifty; Dr. Oracle must have gotten some from the morgue."

Brooklyn said, "More like sixty or seventy, plus body parts."

Jared looked down at Charlotte. "Let's see if we can rest for a while, at least until the show is over." The rock corridor was hot and humid, but the cold water had put the sweltering heat out of Charlotte's mind. The smell hung heavily, as the putrid green-brown whiffs of air circled the top half of the cavern.

Mrs. Bellow looked comfortable enough, and Brooklyn tucked her long legs under the thin opening at the back of the ledge. "There's plenty of room if your legs are thin enough, Charlotte; stretch them out."

"No thanks. I've found a good spot to rest my head."

Jared was leaning against the ledge wall with his legs outstretched in front of him. Charlotte was between his legs with her head resting on his chest.

Jared kissed her forehead and whispered, "Are you sure you can see out of your eye?"

Charlotte looked directly at Jared, "I can see everything I want to see just fine."

Jared smoothed Charlotte's hair. "Try to get some rest. We can't go anywhere until the bodies pass."

Mrs. Bellow was in a deep sleep, snoring. Brooklyn and Jared nodded off, but Charlotte tossed and turned. She needed to figure out why the patients went berserk. The patients were acting suicidal. How could they benefit from killing themselves and others? What was Dr. Oracle's reason for killing the patients and then disposing their bodies down this tunnel? The only thing making Charlotte's mind go numb was Jared's body under her head, as she rested on his pectoral muscle. As he slept, she would occasionally pat his chest with her hand or run her fingers up and down his chest or rest her hand on his abdomen. This alone lulled Charlotte into a deep sleep.

13

The Lobotomy

Charlotte woke to Jared's heartbeat. As she looked over the small ledge, Jared quickly grabbed her. "Whoa, you're not going anywhere."

Charlotte covered her mouth. "I wish I hadn't looked." The small lights lining the rock corridor were still on, but the bodies and water were no longer there. The odor still loomed heavy in the air. There was no getting away from it. There were entrails hanging off the rocks.

He gave her a quick soft kiss, and tipped his head so he could see. He didn't say a word—just quickly leaned back.

Brooklyn said, "I'm hungry and I have to use the toilet."

The fumes were stifling in the enclosed cavern. Jared coughed and rubbed his eyes. "Lead the way, Brooklyn. We'll follow you."

Brooklyn poked Mrs. Bellow. "Time to get up, Mrs. B.—unless, you want to get left behind. How's your head?"

She sat up slowly. "What's that smell? Where are we? Brooklyn, I told you—its Mrs. Bellow."

Brooklyn yawned and stretched her arms above her head. "Come on, Mrs. Bellow. I'll help you down. You slept through all the fun."

Mrs. Bellow noticed Charlotte eye and Jared's wounds. "What happened to all of us?"

Jared smiled. "A wild night of partying?"

"Dear boy, my party days expired many years ago. Brooklyn, help me down." She looked at the unfamiliar clothes she had on. "I'm not even going to ask whose clothes I've got on, or who put them on me. I need a fresh outfit—one that belongs to me—and something to eat."

Brooklyn helped Mrs. Bellow down. She almost ended up falling from the rocks that were covered in nasty viscous liquid. She grabbed the sides of the rock wall to stabilize herself.

"What is that putrid smell?"

Brooklyn jumped down. "Mrs. B., just don't put your hands near your mouth."

"You talk nonsense, Brooklyn."

She raised her voice. "Well, you were sleeping like a baby when the rest of us saw a gruesome dead body buffet floating by. My back hurts, my eyes are burning, and my stomach is doing flips, so excuse me for being subtle."

"Brooklyn, I have no idea what you're talking about. I just want to get out of here and get something for my head pain."

Jared tried to jump but landed on his side. He was covered in the foul-smelling stuff and tried to scrape off as much as he could. He then lifted his hands to help Charlotte.

"No offensive, Jared, but I think I'll get down on my own," she said.

They made their way back to the huge wooden door. Mrs. Bellow pushed everyone aside. "Let me try one of my keys."

Charlotte patted Mrs. Bellow's arm. "That won't work. We need brute force to open it, and we better hope Dr. Oracle isn't on the other side."

Brooklyn looked at Jared. "Just lean with your good shoulder, and put your back into it."

Charlotte shook her head at Brooklyn. "I think we can all push."

Mrs. Bellow protested. "I don't feel well enough to go around straining my muscles."

Brooklyn snickered. "What muscles?"

"Brooklyn, never you mind. I'll have you know I was quite the bodybuilder in my day."

As Mrs. Bellow was reminiscing about the good old days, Jared forced the door open with his shoulder. "Ladies, after you."

Mrs. Bellow nudged past the other three. "I'll show you a picture sometime if you don't believe me."

Charlotte gave Brooklyn a dirty look. "That won't be necessary, Mrs. Bellow; we believe you."

Brooklyn said, "Yeah, Mrs. B. It's kind of like we believe in the tooth fairy and Santa Claus too."

As the four entered Dr. Oracle's lab, it was spick-and-span. Charlotte looked at Brooklyn. "I know where the bodies went, but how'd it get so spotless?"

Brooklyn squirmed. "Yeah, no innards or eyeballs anywhere."

Charlotte said, "Dr. Oracle must have had help."

They made their way to the first floor and deposited Mrs. Bellow at her clinic. There was only a slight hint of what had happened the day before. Several holes had been knocked in the wall. Blood spatterings that had not been completely washed away marred the floor, and a pile of broken furniture lay at the end of the hallway. "Mrs. Bellow, you're going to find everything missing in the narcotics cabinet."

"Charlotte, why would anything be missing? Do you know something?"

"I know as much as you do. Don't you remember the patients rioting yesterday? They went mad, stealing and throwing anything that wasn't bolted down." Charlotte pointed to Brooklyn and herself. "We found you injured in the clinic, with the patients going berserk all around you. You don't recall any of this?"

Mrs. Bellow touched her forehead and felt the gash. "The patients did this to me?"

Brooklyn looked at Mrs. Bellow with compassion. "Mrs. B., the patients went nuts yesterday, and you got hit in the head, pretty hard. You don't remember?"

Mrs. Bellow shook her head. "No, I don't remember anything."

Two guards came running toward Jared. Charlotte and Brooklyn were propping him up as best they could.

As Mrs. Bellow leaned against the wall in the clinic she said, "Charlotte, the hospital part of Primevil will check out all your injuries. The hospital is attached to the residential housing. The infirmary here is for smaller things, but the hospital is used for emergencies or anything life-threatening. All twelve of the asylums on Redwine Hill are connected to the hospital. For every dozen or so asylums there will be a hospital to oversee the serious patients. I'm going to rest here. The guards will show you where to go. I'm sure Jared knows, but he's not in any kind of condition to show you."

Brooklyn only had superficial cuts and abrasions; Charlotte's worst injury was her eye, which looked worse than it actually was. Jared was a mess, not just from the flesh wound where he'd lost a lot of blood but from the beating he had taken at the hands of the patients. He was confined to a hospital bed, but Charlotte and Brooklyn were treated and released. Mrs. Bellow had a concussion, and the doctor on staff ordered at-home bed rest.

Charlotte didn't want to leave, but the nurse physically pushed her out the door. "You can see him tomorrow, honey, if he's feeling better. It's been quite a night."

Charlotte said, "Does this kind of thing happen often?"

"Some of the nurses who've been here a long time tell me it happens once or twice a year."

"Why? What's wrong with the patients that they run amuck?"

"No one knows the answer to that question," the nurse replied.

As Charlotte and Brooklyn left the hospital and made their way down the hallway toward Primevil, Charlotte said, "Brooklyn, when the rioting was going on, did you feel something strange happening in your head?"

"Yeah, it started when we were upstairs in Jared's room. A constant whirring sound, deep in my brain, but nothing that would make me hold my head and go ballistic."

"Same here. I felt something happening, like my brain was being invaded by bugs and they were working their way around in my head, but it didn't hurt. It was a weird sensation, but nothing that would make me kill myself or harm others."

The two went to their room and changed out of their sour-smelling clothes. Then they went to see their kittens.

They passed Gretchen in the hallway. "You two are lucky I'm in a good mood or I'd put some lead in your rear end, but I'm going to see Jared, so get out of my way."

Brooklyn said, "You're such a buffoon, Gretchen. No one can see him."

"Well, maybe you two peons can't, but I already called the nurse who's taking care of him, and she said it would boost his spirits to have a visitor."

Charlotte started to go after Gretchen, when Brooklyn grabbed Charlotte's arm. "Charlotte, don't waste your time on Rat Teeth."

Gretchen walked over to Charlotte and looked down at her. "What was that your friend called me? Rat Teeth? What does that mean?"

Charlotte could tell her face was turning red. *How could they let her see Jared and not let me see him*? "I'd think it was self-explanatory. Perhaps you haven't looked in a mirror lately."

Gretchen bent down and got within inches of Charlotte's face. "Why, you little nine-toed toad . . ."

The nurse was coming down the hall and yelled, "Gretchen, if you expect to see Jared when he's awake, you'd best come soon. I just filled him up with something to make him sleep."

Gretchen turned, and Charlotte ran up to Jared's room with Brooklyn close behind. Brooklyn slammed the door as Charlotte was opening the drawer to the kittens. Charlotte's hands were trembling. "I hate her. I think she's scheming to go after Jared."

Brooklyn took Noon out of the drawer and kissed him on his head. "What do you mean? Go after, like a boyfriend?"

"Yeah, something like that."

Brooklyn burst into laughter. "You can't be talking about Gretchen. Jared wouldn't look at her even if she saved him from a dreaded disease. She's just another guard, that's all."

Charlotte cuddled with Midnight. "I think they're hungry. Let's go to the dining hall and bring them back a bunch of stuff."

Charlotte rearranged one of Jared's old shirts in the drawer and put the kittens snuggly into the nest she had made for them. "See you in a bit," she said to them.

As Charlotte opened the door, Gretchen was standing there. "See who in a bit?"

"None of your business," Charlotte barked in Gretchen's face.

Brooklyn held on to Charlotte's elbow in case Charlotte decided to lunge for Gretchen. "I guess you didn't get to see Jared after all."

"Yes I did. He fell asleep about a minute after I entered his room. The nurse said I could come back anytime."

Charlotte twisted out of the light hold Brooklyn had on her. "Bully for you, Gretchen."

As they reached the cafeteria, Charlotte had watery eyes. Brooklyn told her, "Charlotte, don't be upset over Rat Teeth. She's just a guard—that's why she gets privileges we don't."

Charlotte wiped her eyes on her shirtsleeve. "It's not that—it's just my eye hurts, that's all."

Brooklyn said, "I didn't know you injured both eyes."

"Let's just go eat."

They ate with little conversation. As Charlotte wrapped her meat in a napkin she said, "I'm going to see Jared tomorrow. I'll get Mrs. Bellow to write a note for me. She's the nurse in charge of this entire hellhole."

Brooklyn said, "I don't know how to tell you this, but Mrs. B. is at home for the next week. She's resting due to her concussion."

"I'll think of something," she said, and ran into Jared's room.

Gretchen was bent down stroking the kittens and spouting baby talk to them as Charlotte and Brooklyn ran in. Charlotte pushed Gretchen away. "You have no right." Her face was warming, she could feel her blood pulsating in her neck. "Get out! Get out! Get out!"

Gretchen immediately stood up. "I just came in to get some overnight things for Jared. I wasn't doing anything wrong. Jared's nurse phoned me and said it would make him feel better. He's in a lot of pain, and he might be in the hospital for a while."

Charlotte noticed a softness in Gretchen she hadn't seen before. She didn't know if that was because of the kittens or because she was becoming one of the few people allowed in to see Jared.

"I don't care what your reason, you need to ask permission."

Gretchen knelt and picked up Midnight. "Ask who? Jared is sound asleep. His nurse asked me to do this for him. Was I supposed to ask you? This is Jared's room."

Charlotte went over and, as gently as her anger would allow, took Midnight. "No, not me."

Gretchen grabbed an armful of Jared's personal possessions she had collected. "Then, Charlotte, whose permission was I to get?"

Charlotte didn't say anything, but Gretchen wasn't finished. "Oh, and girls—no pets are allowed at Primevil."

Charlotte and Brooklyn pleaded for the life of their kittens. "No. Please, Gretchen."

Gretchen walked toward the open door. "Don't worry, I love animals. Why do you think I don't eat any of the Primevil's meat dishes?"

Charlotte was too mad to even cry. She just carried Midnight and slipped under Jared's comforter. Brooklyn picked up Noon and sat on the bed, then fed the two kittens. Charlotte was crying so hard her shoulders were bouncing. She wished Brooklyn could say something to make the pain go away, but she knew her friend was a street rat and comfort wasn't one of her strong points. So, she tried to calm her sobs and pretend to fall asleep.

The following morning Charlotte and Brooklyn went to eat, but they didn't see Gretchen. Charlotte said, "I bet she's with Jared. I can also bet you, Brooklyn, that we get demerits for sleeping in Jared's room last night."

Brooklyn could tell by the tone in Charlotte's voice that she was mad. "Charlotte, keep your temper under control. I'm going to feed the kittens our leftovers. Even if Gretchen is in with Jared, maybe you could talk her into taking you with her the next time she visits. Just be nice."

"You're one to talk about being nice. I didn't think 'street rats' were ever pleasant." She hissed, "I'll try, Brooklyn, but Gretchen just gets under my skin."

The two went their separate directions, and when Charlotte got to Jared's hospital room Gretchen wasn't there; only a guard stood outside his door. Charlotte dug deep for as much courage as she could. "I'm here to see Jared."

"Are you a patient?"

"Uh, yes."

"You seem normal enough."

Charlotte said, "Thank you. I consider myself normal."

The guard said, "I can't see the harm in it, and anyway, I need to use the latrine. If you could just stay in the room until I return. It might be a while. I had broccoli earlier and it tears my stomach up, but I love it."

"Yeah, I'll stay. Why are you guarding Jared's door anyway?"

"After what happened to him on the beach, and him being so weak and incapacitated, we need to keep him safe."

Charlotte was a bit upset. "I don't understand. Do you think that the patients would harm Jared again? Are they still crazed and dangerous?"

The guard was fiddling with his belt. "Seems likely, since they went berserk the other day, but we guards stick together. I really got to go."

"Yeah, okay."

As soon as she saw Jared, she forgot about everything else. She ran to his bedside as he was opening his eyes. He put his arms out. "Hello, beautiful."

Charlotte got embarrassed and looked behind her to make sure Jared was talking to her. No one was there.

"Hi, Jared. How are you feeling?"

"Come, Charlotte, sit next to me." As Charlotte sat, Jared moaned. "No, don't get up. Please sit."

Jared sat up and gave Charlotte a hug and a light kiss on the lips. "I've missed you."

"Jared, I've only been away from you for a day." She was growing warm from his closeness. "So, what's wrong with you?" She held up her finger to his lips. "And don't tell me that you're insane; we both are. Do you have anything broken?"

"You want to know?" Charlotte nodded. "Well, let's see: I have three cracked ribs, two broken bones in my foot, internal bruising, several broken fingers, a black eye, a chunk of my lower leg gone, and a gunshot wound to my leg." Charlotte looked away and Jared grabbed her hand. "Charlotte, it's okay. I'm fine."

"Are you in pain?"

He looked at Charlotte. "A little."

Charlotte figured he was lying. His face looked strained from the pain.

The nurse came in. "Where's the guard?"

Charlotte said, "He had to use the bathroom."

The nurse said, "Don't leave Jared alone."

"I won't."

The nurse rolled her eyes. "That guard is a piece of work. Jared, would you like something for the pain?"

"No, I'm fine; maybe later."

The nurse walked out mumbling something about bad help.

Someone entered the room and Charlotte turned, expecting to see the nurse again, but it wasn't her. It was one of the male patients. Charlotte stood up and grew nervous. "Can I help you?"

He was a tall, husky man with a semi-shaved head. He looked like someone left over from the barbarian era. Before Charlotte could say anything, he advanced on her and choked out, "You're a nice little girl, aren't you?"

Before she could answer, Jared struggled to sit up. "What do you want?"

Once again, the patient stepped closer to Charlotte. "You're a nice little girl, aren't you?" He kept repeating those same words over and over.

Charlotte backed up toward the window. "I . . . I don't know what you're talking about."

The patient's hands were enormous, and he wrapped them around Charlotte's neck. Gently at first, he then started squeezing, all the while saying, "You're a nice little girl, aren't you, Wanda?"

Charlotte couldn't scream, and her hands were flailing. Jared came up behind the man. He punched him once in the lower right side of his back. Immediately the patient turned his attention to Jared, and Charlotte fell to the floor. Jared's gunshot wound tore open, and blood began running down his leg.

As Charlotte crawled toward the door on her belly to get help, Jared was wrestling the patient to the ground. The patient had Jared on his back and was trying to dig out his eyes. Jared hit the man directly in the nose, and blood squirted out in all directions. Through the blood, the man noticed Charlotte almost at the door. He lunged at her feet and started pulling her backward.

Charlotte was screaming at the top of her lungs. "Help! Help, nurse! Anybody—we're being attacked by a lunatic. Help!"

Jared grabbed the man's lower legs and flipped him around so he was on his back, and started pelting the man with his fists. Charlotte wiggled out from the man's grip, and crawled out the door just as a nurse and several guards came running.

The patient kicked Jared in the throat, causing him to fall backward onto the floor. The nurse jammed a needle into the thigh of the patient as the guards wrestled with him.

Jared was gasping for breath and holding his throat as Charlotte ran out of the room to get Dr. Oracle. She hated the doctor, and at the very least he was unstable, but he wouldn't kill Jared in front of all those witnesses. Besides, she thought Jared was dying.

She pounded on the door to the basement. "Dr. Oracle! Dr. Oracle, it's an emergency."

Dr. Farrow came and unlocked the door. "What is it?"

"A patient has gone nuts."

"Yes, they're all nuts in here. What's your number, my dear?"

"No, Dr. Farrow, you don't understand. A patient has attacked one of the guards."

Dr. Farrow immediately said, "Is the guard dead?"

Charlotte ran up the stairs with Dr. Farrow following her. "No, he just needs some medical attention."

"Oh," was all he said.

Charlotte sensed a slight disappointment in his voice, and he seemed to slow down.

"Hurry, Doctor." His feet were like lead as he slowly trudged forward.

Charlotte was now pleading and dragging the doctor to Jared's room.

As they entered, the nurse had things under control, temporarily. The guards were dragging the half-comatose patient to a jail cell in Primevil's prison, but Jared was still on the floor having a hard time breathing.

The nurse stepped away to let Dr. Farrow examine Jared, but he took his sweet time crossing the floor. "Put him on the bed."

Dr. Farrow looked at Charlotte, who was demanding he do something. "Nurse, get me a suture kit and an auto injector of epinephrine."

The nurse came back with the items, and the room was filled with the heaviness of silence, with the exception of Jared's labored breathing.

The nurse handed the suture kit to Dr. Farrow and injected Jared with the epinephrine. The nurse got a weird look on her face. "You know, Doctor, that patient who attacked this guard is the same one who attacked one of my nurses last week. I think he needs a lobotomy."

Dr. Farrow worked on Jared's open wound as Charlotte sat on the edge of the bed holding Jared's hand. Dr. Farrow shot a look at the nurse. "Mrs. Rogers, if I needed your opinion, I'd have asked for it. Besides, he's already had a lobotomy. Many of these patients already have had the procedure done."

Charlotte turned toward Dr. Farrow. "What's a lobotomy?"

Dr. Farrow didn't answer, so Mrs. Rogers said, "It's done to help decrease the violent behavior in the patients."

Charlotte squeezed Jared's hand and said, "I don't think it worked."

Dr. Farrow snapped his attention to Charlotte. "Are you telling me how to run things around here?" He didn't wait for a response. "Since Dr. Oracle and I perform the procedure, would you like to be put on the list? I could do a lobotomy on you the day after next. How does that sound?"

Jared was clearly in a lot of pain since Dr. Farrow didn't use the lidocaine in the suture kit. Through gritted teeth he said, "Doc, she was just kidding. I personally know Charlotte, and she doesn't need a lobotomy."

Mrs. Rogers added, "Doctor Farrow, you really shouldn't go throwing threats around to scare the patients."

The doctor gave the nurse a dirty look. "All finished, Jared, and I have my suspicions that number 3737 does need the procedure. Dr. Oracle has checked her file and found that she has a long list of infractions. Don't look so surprised. I know who you are."

Charlotte's eyes were bugging out of her head. "No. Please, Dr. Farrow, I have a job now. I'm following the rules."

Mrs. Rogers said, "I hear she's working for Mrs. Bellow; 3737 can't be all bad. That woman is a beast to work for, so this girl must be a saint."

Dr. Farrow stood. "Jared, you need to keep that one on a short rope."

Charlotte thought of the rope that the Collector and his two vagrant sidekicks had used to drag her to Primevil. Jared patted Charlotte's hand. "She's as normal as you and me, Dr. Farrow."

"I doubt that. Sometimes a person is too close to an individual to see the amount of real damage that's been done to their brain. Patient 3737, haven't you still been complaining of head pain?"

"Uh . . . no. I feel fine, Dr. Farrow. I've no physical problems to speak of."

"Well, I also heard from one of the lunch attendants that you had some kind of mental breakdown at lunch, but thanks to Jared she didn't write you up?"

Jared said, "That was all a misunderstanding. Thank you for your medical skills, but I believe everything is fine here."

Dr. Farrow was so busy staring at Charlotte that he knocked the table and sent the suture tray to the floor. Dr. Farrow yelled, "Nurse, pick that up, and 3737—I'd watch yourself if I were you because I know Dr. Oracle and I are watching you." He stormed out of the room.

Charlotte said, "Jared, oh my God, they're watching me."

Mrs. Rogers bent down and picked up the mess on the floor. "Don't worry, honey. He says that to every patient in here."

Charlotte's voice was strangled. "How many patients have had a lobotomy?"

"I'd say about seventy-five percent of them, but those are the truly disturbed patients."

The nurse walked out, and Charlotte was shaking so hard the bed was rattling.

Jared said, "Lie down with me, Charlotte." He gently pulled her into his arms and lightly kissed her lips. "I'm also watching over you. Everything is fine."

Charlotte said in a whisper close to Jared's ear, "How do they do a lobotomy?

Jared's voice was slight, as he was fading into sleep. "There are many methods, but Dr. Oracle and Dr. Farrow prefer to drill two holes in the forehead to reach and sever the nerves in the frontal lobe."

Jared fell asleep, but Charlotte couldn't stop thinking about what Dr. Farrow had said.

She had never even heard of this word *lobotomy*. *I'll have to ask Mrs. Bellow about this.* Charlotte had seen patients with scabs or bandages on their foreheads, but she figured it had something to do with the headaches, not a barbaric torture of the patients.

Charlotte curled up into Jared. She wondered if he had a plan to get out of Primevil, and even if he did, it seemed like it would take a very long time to pull it off. Would this plan include her and Brooklyn also? She couldn't be sure, so she would just need to come up with a plan of her own. One that wouldn't use up the next several years of her life. The way Dr. Farrow threw that word lobotomy around, the sooner she escaped, the better. Her plan would have to include Jared and Brooklyn.

She drifted off thinking about ways to escape the insufferable life at Primevil. But what would happen to the three of them once they did escape?

Redwine hill

14

The Asylum's Hidden Secrets

As things were getting back to normal at Primevil, Charlotte was not finished with asking questions and poking around the old asylum. There were so many questions that her mind was throbbing. Charlotte found Brooklyn with the kittens. "Brooklyn, you want to go with me?"

"Where?"

Charlotte picked up Midnight. "Just thought we'd take our own little tour of Primevil."

"Yeah, sure. I don't have any infractions, so if we get caught, I won't be the one in a canvas blazer. What are we looking for?"

"I don't know what it is, but something's out of sorts at Primevil."

"Right." They watched as several patients came down the hall. One patient smelled his fingers and then licked them. Another was rolling around on the floor saying, "The hunchback man is here today." Another sang a snatch of a song and hit his head on the wall.

"Charlotte, aren't you going to visit Jared?"

"Yeah, but Gretchen went to visit him this morning, and I'd rather see him without her."

"Okay, where do we go first?"

"I think if we're going to find something abnormal, it'll be in the basement or on the first floor, where it could be accessible to the so-called important people of Redwine Hill. I think there's a connection between the teenagers turning sixteen years old and all the deaths at the asylums."

"Charlotte, what do you mean? Not every sixteen-year-old goes insane on their birthday."

"Yes, I know, Brooklyn, but I would say at least eighty percent do, and that's not anything normal."

"One of the foster families I stayed with for four days told me I was worthless, and knew for sure I was one of the troubled kids that would go insane."

"Look, Brooklyn, I had a loving mother and father, and I was normal all the way up until my mother died, and even then I was what you would consider normal. It was only when I turned sixteen that my head exploded. And since you're the one who brought up foster parents, why the long stay of four days?"

"That was how long it took for them to get sick of me, and try to beat me."

Charlotte felt sorry for Brooklyn, but she didn't want her to know. "Well, it doesn't look like the beatings worked."

"Of course not. I got the hell out of there. Street fighting for food or shelter is one thing, but physically fighting with a foster parent would get me thrown in jail."

Charlotte looked over her shoulder and noticed the hallway was empty with the exception of some occupied patients twirling around way down at the other end of the hall. She pulled out a set of keys and went through a door that said "Staff Only."

"Charlotte, whose keys are those?"

"They're Mrs. Bellow's. She won't know they're missing until next week, when she comes back. Maybe not even then. She probably thinks she lost them in the skirmish."

They went through the door and walked down a half-darkened hallway. At the end of the hall was some bizarre surgical room. It had many different pods with surgery equipment in each room.

Charlotte whispered, "Is this where they do the lobotomies?"

Brooklyn squeezed Charlotte's arm. "I don't know what that means, but let's go back. It looks like they do some type of sci-fi surgeries or procedures in here."

"Brooklyn, not yet, I want to get some answers to why Serenity died, and why so many of us teens are going insane."

"Charlotte, you seem quite normal to me."

"Yes, well, you, me, and Jared seem normal enough, but the majority of the teens coming here are completely gone. Brooklyn, do you consider yourself crazy?"

"No. I think I've had a tough life, but I'm not crazy. I do remember my head felt like I had something burst a while back, which changed how I think."

"I'm sure, but I bet that was on your birthday."

"I wouldn't know. I don't know when my birthday is."

Charlotte saw several people walking down the long, dark hallway. She hoped they hadn't seen them.

She grabbed Brooklyn and pulled her into a small closet. There were four people approaching, and Dr. Oracle said, "Nurse, go back and get a stretcher. He won't be in any condition to walk back to his room after the lobotomy."

Mr. Billy Thomas the Third was begging. "No! No, Dr. Oracle—I don't need a lobotomy. I didn't sign any consent form. You can't do this."

The guard just kept dragging Mr. BT forward as he tried to dig his feet into the floor and slow the guard down. He was screaming, "Don't do this. I don't need this procedure. Please, no. I beg you."

Brooklyn lunged to push out the door, but Charlotte grabbed her arm. "Charlotte, I can't take his screaming. We've got to do something."

"Brooklyn, quick! Lie on the floor against the door to block the light. I need to flip the switch on to see if there's anything in this room we can use to help Mr. BT." Charlotte heard a thud.

"Okay, Charlotte, turn the light on."

They could hear the stretcher squeaking by the closet. "Hurry, Charlotte."

Charlotte looked around the cleaning supply closet. She didn't want Mr. BT's life dependent upon her memory of sophomore chemistry. She started reading the labels of the cleaning fluids, and then she heard a hair-raising screeching scream, "Oh, God, no!"

Charlotte said, "Brooklyn, just get up, I don't think anyone cares about the closet light. They're too busy torturing BT."

Brooklyn watched as Charlotte started frantically pouring all the cleaning liquids in a plastic pail in which wet rags were soaking. "Brooklyn, we don't really care if the room catches fire; the fumes alone will drive them away. Once I step out of this closet and throw this down the hall, we'll have very little time to retrieve BT."

They were beginning to gag from the fumes when Charlotte quickly opened the door to the closet and swung the bucket several times in the air to get good momentum. She threw it as hard as she could, and there was a horrible explosion. She whispered, "I forgot about the oxygen they'd be using for the surgery."

Dr. Oracle, the nurse, and even the guard took off running from the flames while Charlotte and Brooklyn sprinted toward BT. His hands were tied down with leather straps. The fire alarm and sprinkler system went off. The water was pouring down on the three of them as the girls worked at the restraints. Mr. BT was unconscious from the medication given to him for surgery.

Brooklyn pulled the IV out. "You won't be needing this anymore."

They were soaked to the bone with cold water, but BT was still under. The tightness in Charlotte's chest was becoming unbearable, and they were both coughing and their noses were running. There was no time to cover their mouths or wipe their noses; they needed to work fast or they'd all be dead.

Charlotte yelled over the downpour of water, "Brooklyn, get the gurney."

Brooklyn swung around and positioned the gurney as they shoved BT onto it.

People were coming in now to fight the fire and toxic fumes. As Charlotte and Brooklyn wheeled a limp Mr. BT past the others and into the hall, they gulped in the fresh air.

Charlotte ran into the first room she came to and tore the sheet off the bed. She covered Mr. BT and started wheeling him down the hall. They needed to get him outside. A guard stopped them to look under the cover. Brooklyn said, "He's dead."

The guard replied, "Then get him out of here and into the morgue."

Charlotte said, "Yes sir."

When he was out of earshot, Charlotte whispered, "Brooklyn, quick, let's get BT outside, to the fresh air."

They watched as the guard unlocked the door where they'd just come from and disappeared. The hall was empty. All the patients would be out front for the fire drill—being watched by the guards with guns pointed at them.

Charlotte and Brooklyn wheeled the gurney out the back door and as close to the beach as they could. The tires were weighted down with wet sand. "This is it, Brooklyn. We need to walk him down to the waterline and splash him until he comes out of his stupor."

He was too heavy, so the girls dragged him by the arms to the ocean. Brooklyn almost drowned BT. "Wake up. Wake up, you fool. Unless you want to have a lobotomy, wake up."

"Brooklyn, don't drown him. Take it easy. He'll wake up."

The fire trucks were now arriving. Charlotte said, "Looks like overkill for such a small fire."

Mr. BT was coming around, coughing, and his breaths were coming in spasms. "Where am I?"

Brooklyn took his face in her hands. "Are you okay? Charlotte and I saved you from Dr. Oracle. You're safe for the moment, but as soon as you can, you need to find someplace else to live."

Mr. BT coughed up some phlegm. "I need to tell you something first, and then I'm getting out of this stinking place."

Brooklyn said, "What do you need to tell us that we don't already know?"

"Listen, I was sent by the president."

Brooklyn said, "President of what?"

BT just looked at Brooklyn. "Of our country. What else? Anyway, there's something terribly wrong with the asylums. There are many spies throughout Massachusetts and elsewhere in the US and around the world. Scientists have sidestepped every other disease or illness to concentrate on the cause of the insanity. It's not what everyone thinks."

Charlotte choked on her words. "It's not a virus or some naturally occurring thing that happens?"

"No, it's much more sinister than what anybody ever suspected. You know the big chain of meat packers throughout the states?"

Brooklyn said, "We don't eat meat."

Charlotte added, "I know the one you're talking about, though. My mom used to take me to get meat for my father's evening meal every other day. It's called Blood Red Meat."

BT said, "Yeah, that's the one. It's been around forever. Where do you think they get their meat?"

Brooklyn screamed, "Where?"

BT's breath was now coming out in gasps. "The teens are killed and floated down rock corridors to a Blood Red Meat truck, then sold to the public for hamburger, steaks, ribs, whatever. By using human meat there's no transferring the cattle, no feed, no worrying about animal diseases. Just slaughter the teens and sell the meat. A simple, effective, gruesome concept.'

Brooklyn was yelling over the splash of the waves. "How do the teenagers die?"

A loud bang startled Charlotte. She looked at BT, who was holding his abdomen. He had received a shot to his back, which went all the way through. Blood covered his already-soaked clothes, and he tried to say something but blood kept spitting up through his lips.

Charlotte was scared and let out a weak scream. She ducked and looked around. She yanked at Brooklyn's sleeve. "Come on, we need to get out of here."

Brooklyn leaned over to hear what he was trying to say. Her hair immediately became a crimson red. "What, BT? Say it again."

More shots were fired, and the girls took off. They both knew where the slightly camouflaged cavern was and headed for it. They looked back at Mr. BT and saw him take his last miserable breath.

Charlotte pushed Brooklyn. "No, you can't go back to him. He's dead. We need to save on own behinds."

Tears were streaming down Brooklyn's face. "I think he actually liked me."

Charlotte and Brooklyn were running on the slippery rocks, and the water was starting to seep through the crevices. At any moment now, Charlotte figured, the dead bodies from that day would float on by and be hauled off by a truck of some sort. She said, "I know he liked you. He danced with you almost every dance, and who else would do the Monkey Dance with you?"

She let Brooklyn have her crying episode—she at least needed that. They had made it to the ledge and she said, "At least now I know the bodies aren't set adrift in the ocean."

Brooklyn was still sniffling and wiping her nose on her sleeve. "I don't think there'll be any bodies tonight with the fire department camped out front."

As they came to the oversized door that they had accessed before, Charlotte sighed. "How are we going to get this thing open?"

"We'll have to take a run at it. When I count three, we run and don't stop until the door moves."

"What if we break our shoulders?"

"Charlotte, let's worry about that later. We can make something up if we break a bone. Just don't chicken out. On the count of three: one, two, three."

They took off running and plowed into the solid door. They both bounced off it like flies hitting a pane of glass, but when they looked up, there was a quarter-inch opening with a dim light shining through.

Charlotte helped Brooklyn to her feet. "We did it."

Brooklyn grimaced in pain. "There's something wrong with my shoulder."

Charlotte looked at Brooklyn's shoulder, which hung limp and lower than the other. She then bent Brooklyn's arm. "Hold your arm with your other hand. Try not to move it. Walk nice and slow, and I'll get you some help."

Brooklyn yelled, "No, Charlotte, I can't go to Dr. Oracle. He's probably the one who shot BT."

"I understand. Let's just go to the clinic and see who's there." Charlotte held her finger to her lips. "Shhhh." She craned her neck to see into Dr. Oracle's lab. "Okay, it's clear."

She heaved the door open the rest of the way, and once they were through she pushed her hands against the door and planted her feet against the table behind her. She groaned and got the heavy door shut.

They walked silently out of Dr. Oracle's lab and up the stairs to the main floor. Brooklyn moaned whenever she moved her arm.

Charlotte was relieved to see Mrs. Rogers in the clinic. There were several patients who had hurt themselves while trying to escape the fire drill.

Mrs. Rogers took Brooklyn by the arm and said, "What on earth have you done?" Brooklyn had tears streaming down her cheeks as Mrs. Rogers led her to a chair. "I'll be right back. I've got to go to the supply room."

Brooklyn whispered to Charlotte, "It's not the physical pain, but the idea that BT was shot dead. We saved him only to be shot outside."

Charlotte nodded as Mrs. Rogers came back in. "I think this sling will fit. Come here, my dear. It looks like you've pulled your arm out of the socket."

Brooklyn yelled, "No, please don't get Dr. Oracle."

"No need for him. He's busy anyway. I can set your arm. I have the same problem; I dislocate my shoulder all the time, ever since I was about thirteen years old."

Charlotte said, "Mrs. Rogers, will this hurt her?"

"I'm not going to lie. It will hurt at first, but once Brooklyn's shoulder joint is back in place, it will be a true relief. Now, Brooklyn, I'm going to manipulate your arm, but try not to move."

Mrs. Rogers repositioned Brooklyn's arm, and before Brooklyn could finish her scream, her shoulder was back in place. "Now, let me give you something mild for the pain and swelling. How does it feel?"

"It feels pretty good."

Dr. Oracle slammed the clinic door open. "This place is truly a madhouse." He pushed past Charlotte and Brooklyn. "Get out of my way. Nurse, if anyone needs me I'll be in the morgue. Also, a male patient has escaped."

Mrs. Rogers followed Dr. Oracle. "What patient?"

He yelled back at Mrs. Rogers. "Number 2581. His given name is Billy Thomas the Third."

Mrs. Rogers seemed overly concerned. "I don't understand. What do you mean missing? How do you know it was Mr. BT?"

Brooklyn broke down and started crying. She murmured, "He's not missing; he's dead."

Charlotte put her finger to her lips and shook her head.

Mrs. Rogers said, "Brooklyn, you'll feel better once the ibuprofen starts working. Give it at least twenty to thirty minutes." Mrs. Rogers then went running after Dr. Oracle. "I thought he was scheduled for a procedure this morning. What happened?"

Charlotte put her arm around Brooklyn. "Let's go back to the room."

They walked back to their room and talked quietly among themselves. Charlotte said, "At least Dr. Oracle didn't recognize us.

If he had, we'd be dead right now, or at least yanked down to the surgery room for a lobotomy."

"Do you think what BT said was true?"

"Yes, I do. I've wondered the same thing myself."

Charlotte pulled the covers back on Brooklyn's bed. Brooklyn crawled in, and Charlotte took her roommate's shoes off. "Brooklyn, try to get some rest."

Charlotte shut their door to block out whatever action was happening out in the hallway. She wanted to go visit with Jared in the hospital, but she was just exhausted. She crawled into her own bed and pulled the thin blanket up over her head. "Night, Brooklyn."

She could hear Brooklyn sniveling. She got out of bed and went and put her arms around her friend, thinking how she couldn't have gotten through this day without Brooklyn. This day just elevated things at Primevil to a whole new level.

Redwine hill

15

Tragedy in Jared's Room

The next morning Charlotte looked over at Brooklyn, who was snoring as she slept. Charlotte wanted to visit with Jared by herself, so she got dressed and walked to his hospital room. He was sitting up.

"Charlotte, good news. I get out of this room today."

Charlotte said with trepidation in her voice, "That's great, Jared. Do you want me to gather your things and take them to your room?" Her eyes grew misty.

"Charlotte, what's wrong?"

"Nothing. I can't talk about it here. It was just something that happened yesterday."

"Don't tell me you were mixed up in that fiasco with the fire drill?"

Charlotte looked down at the floor. "Yes, but that's not what's bothering me."

"There's more? Something else happened?" Jared rubbed his forehead. "Did you get demerits?"

Charlotte's eyes were wet, and she felt as if she was going to cry. "No."

Jared patted the bed. "Come here, Charlotte, and tell me what's wrong."

Charlotte took her shoes and socks off and crawled into bed with him.

He threw the covers over her and hugged her to his chest. Her watery tears were landing on his bare chest, and she wiped them away with her hand. He gently took hold of her hand. "Charlotte, you're scaring me. You act as if someone died."

She began to cry uncontrollably, and Jared said, "Oh my God, Charlotte. Someone died yesterday."

Charlotte nodded and Jared asked, "Was it Brooklyn?"

She said in a whisper as the words stuck in her throat, "It was Billy Thomas the Third. You know—BT. The one who danced the Monkey Dance with Brooklyn."

"I don't understand. What does he have to do with the fire drill?"

Charlotte's breath escaped her mouth in a slow exhale. "I didn't mean for any of this to happen, but Brooklyn and I went exploring. I wanted to find the answers to some questions I had."

Jared held Charlotte in a tight grip. "Go ahead. I think I'm ready for the bad news."

"To make a long story short, I used Mrs. Bellow's keys, to gain entrance to a 'staff only' area. Then Brooklyn and I heard people coming; it was Dr. Oracle, a guard, and a nurse—and the guard was dragging BT to one of the surgical pods. Mr. BT was screaming that he didn't need a lobotomy. We hid in a closet, and I mixed a few chemicals together, but I forgot about the oxygen used in the surgery suite. It was like an explosion went off. As soon as Dr. Oracle and the others ran out, Brooklyn and I went and untied BT and put him on a stretcher."

Jared looked at Charlotte. "I'm not surprised about you and Brooklyn causing the fire. I had a feeling that it was you two. You did a good thing, Charlotte, by freeing BT, but how did he die if you saved him?"

"Jared, it was awful. I don't wish to see anybody die that way."

Jared sat up and looked directly into Charlotte's eyes. "It's not your fault that he died of smoke inhalation."

Charlotte brought her fist to her mouth, and Jared leaned close to hear her. "No, Jared, he died from a gunshot wound."

Jared stammered out, "Charlotte, you shot him."

"No, no, no."

"Brooklyn shot him, then."

"No, Jared. I think a guard shot BT. Probably under Dr. Oracle's orders."

"Charlotte, you need to help me understand. I've barely understood anything since you walked into my room."

"Mr. BT was unconscious, so Brooklyn and I dragged him down to the beach and splashed cold water on him. Even though we were soaked and already shivering from the sprinklers, we just needed time to wake him up."

Jared nodded. "Keep talking."

"He was telling us interesting things, when a shot was fired and it went through BT's back and out his abdomen. There was a lot of blood. He was spitting blood out of his mouth, and he was covered in it."

Jared kissed Charlotte's forehead as she shook uncontrollably. "Who was the guard?"

"We didn't see. We just took off running. We made our way back inside the semi-hidden cavern. You know the one. We traveled through it the day the patients rioted, when I shot you."

Jared grimaced and rubbed his leg where the sutures were.

"Jared, he said the big meat packing chain Blood Red Meats is using human meat in their stores, and the institutions are happily giving them their dead patients."

Jared laughed an uncomfortable laugh. "This is a lot to take in. Charlotte, did BT say if these bodies were intentionally killed for the meat or they died from natural causes?"

She shook her head. "He didn't say. The sad part was Brooklyn watched him take his last breath."

"Is she okay?"

"She was sleeping when I left this morning. I'll go back soon and check on her."

Jared said with trepidation, "Charlotte, do you think Blood Red Meats has a connection to the epidemic of sixteen-year-olds going insane?"

"I don't know. Can we talk about this later? I didn't get much sleep last night. I kept seeing BT spitting up blood and trying to talk."

Charlotte brought her knees up, and her toes scratched Jared's leg. He jumped a little. "Did I hurt you?" she asked.

"No, I'm just overprotective of my injured leg." He hugged her to his chest. "Let's start a completely different subject." There was silence for several minutes, then Jared said, "Charlotte, how did you lose your toe? Not that it bothers me—I'm fine with it."

Charlotte pulled her foot out from under the covers. "I've never been embarrassed by having nine toes. I just can't wear certain sandals. Do you really want to know how I lost my toe?"

He stretched out and said, "Absolutely."

"It happened about three years ago. I had just turned thirteen, and had received a toe ring from my mother, who was a free spirit. She believed in the mysteries of the world; she had tarot cards, did palm readings—she even had a crystal ball. Anyway, I immediately put it on my second toe on my right foot. Well, my mother had this old junk car that needed to be pushed a bit before she could turn the engine over."

Jared said, "So she ran over your foot."

"No, my mother called it a freak accident. I had to sit against a rock wall and push with my feet to get it moving. When I pushed, my toe ring got caught on a piece of bumper that hung from the back of the car. As it moved forward, I was screaming at her to stop, but she didn't hear me. When she finally stopped, I looked at my foot, and there was no skin or muscle—just blood and a bone sticking out. There wasn't much they could do for my toe, so they took me to surgery and cut the bone off. It was the only day I ever wore a toe ring."

Jared said, "Is that a true story?"

Charlotte pouted. "I would never lie to you."

She laid her head back on Jared's chest, and then jerked her head up. "Jared, I think Gretchen has something to do with BT's death."

"Charlotte, I know you don't like Gretchen, but why would she shoot BT?"

"I don't know if she actually shot BT, but I know she has something to do with this entire thing."

He pushed a strand of her hair behind her ear. "Go on. I'm listening."

"That night the patients went berserk, we got in a verbal confrontation, and she called me a nine-toed toad. She had to have read my file. She's never seen my feet, and I've never told her."

"How does that make her a part of any of this?"

"I don't know yet, but files are kept under lock and key. She would have no way of reading my file without help from someone."

"I thought you said Gretchen was a poor shot. How could she put a bullet through BT, that far away?"

"Yes, she's a terrible shot, or she may have meant to miss Brooklyn and me when we were going into your room. I don't know, Jared. I'm not thinking straight."

Mrs. Rogers walked into the hospital room. "Jared, let's get you back to your regular room. Number 3737—or should I say Charlotte?—can you help Jared make the climb to his room?"

"Yes, Mrs. Rogers. I'll get him up there."

Gretchen walked in as they were exiting the room. "Here, Charlotte, let me help." She put her shoulder under Jared's other arm.

Charlotte was skeptical of Gretchen, but she realized after a few steps that she couldn't get Jared to his room by herself. "Only to the room, Gretchen. The nurse said he needs his rest."

Jared moaned and groaned on every flight of stairs. As they entered Jared's room, Charlotte let out a scream and ran over to the window. Midnight and Noon were each hanging by one of their back legs from a thin piece of rope. They were twisting and turning and letting out cat cries.

Gretchen literally slammed Jared on the bed and went to help Charlotte. "Who would do this?"

They were frantically holding the kittens up and undoing the knots. Charlotte had tears running down her face. She yelled, "Who do you think did this, Gretchen?"

"I have no idea."

Charlotte had Midnight untied and examined her leg. All the fur was scraped off, and there was some blood around the injury. Gretchen was having trouble with the knot on Noon. Charlotte handed Midnight to Gretchen, and she feverishly worked on Noon's mangled leg. The bone snapped and the fur and skin tore clean through. Charlotte was holding Noon in one hand and his leg in the other.

"Oh my God." She felt sick. "Gretchen, what did you do?"

Gretchen was screaming back. "Charlotte, I haven't done anything. You think I did this? No way, I love animals."

Charlotte tore a strip of cloth from her shirt and wrapped Noon's leg tight.

Jared hobbled out of bed holding his hands out. "Charlotte, give him to me."

"What are you going to do with him? Jared, you're not going to put Noon out of his misery, are you?"

Jared was wavering back and forth, still weak from his injuries. "No, Charlotte, I want to see the damage to his leg."

Charlotte held onto the leg and handed Noon to Jared. Charlotte looked at Gretchen, who had tears flowing down her face and was cuddling Midnight. Charlotte thought Gretchen couldn't possibly be BT's killer.

The small kitten was breathing shallowly and was losing blood. Charlotte yelled, "Jared, do something."

Jared limped over to his bed and looked at the wound. "His leg can't be reattached, Charlotte."

"I know, but can you save him?"

Jared leaned over and took a rubber band out of his bedside dresser. He wound it around Noon's leg at the edge of the injury. The bleeding stopped, and Jared wiped the blood off the little fur ball. Charlotte came and sat on the bed, handed Jared the leg, and took Noon. Jared went over and pulled on the two small ropes that were hanging from a hook. He twisted the hook from the ceiling and looked it over.

"There's nothing special about the hook or the rope. Basically there's no clue as to who did this."

She screamed and jerked Midnight out of Gretchen's arms. "I know who did this. Gretchen did. Gretchen, you're a horrible person."

"Charlotte, I didn't do this. I swear my life on it."

Brooklyn walked in with her arm in a sling. "Mrs. Bellow is back. Hey, what's going on?" She saw blood and Charlotte holding the two kittens. "Why is Noon's leg missing?" Charlotte didn't say a word; she just pointed to Gretchen and Brooklyn went berserk.

"I hate you!" She lunged for Gretchen, and the two went tumbling on the hard floor.

Jared managed to get out of bed and did his best to separate the two. "Both of you, sit." He forced them to sit at opposite ends of the bed with him in between. "We'll work this out."

Gretchen sneered. "You idiot, I wouldn't hurt the kittens."

Brooklyn was rubbing her arm. The sling had falling off in the scuffle. Charlotte handed her the torn sling. "Brooklyn, are you all right?"

"Yeah, give me Noon." She became enraged again when she had Noon in her arms. She screeched, "Gretchen, you piece of garbage. What have you done to my kitten?"

Gretchen was in tears. "I would never hurt an animal, especially something so tiny."

Jared was holding his arms out, separating the two girls. "It could have been anybody. There are no locks on any of the doors, so anyone could have come into my room and did this. Everyone knows I was in the hospital. There was plenty of time to do this."

Charlotte yelled, "Jared, who else knew we had kittens in here besides us four? Jared, who else? Just tell me."

Gretchen stunned everyone by saying, "Shhh, I hear someone in the hallway."

Brooklyn said, "You don't tell me to shhh, Gretchen. Who do you think you are?"

Gretchen got up and walked to the door. "Brooklyn, shut up."

They all heard the noise now. Gretchen slowly opened the door. The sound grew louder, like a slurping sound. Gretchen's voice was shaking when she yelled, "Who's there?"

No one answered. She held her finger to her lips, and Jared got up creaking the bedsprings. He held on to the bedside table for support. Gretchen stuck her head out into the hallway, and something hit her in the face. Jared hobbled over and stood in the door frame. "No one's there."

Gretchen said, "Then, what the devil is this?"

Gretchen's entire face was covered with the dripping of someone's guts. She couldn't see anything; blood was mixed with the innards of something or someone. She was screaming as Jared shuffled with a moan down the hall. "Help me! Help me get this stuff off my face. I'm going to go blind."

Charlotte looked at Brooklyn, and they both almost laughed. Gretchen was getting hysterical. "Charlotte, get over here now and help me."

Charlotte handed Midnight to Brooklyn and grabbed a towel from the back of the door. "Gretchen, you're not going blind. Now, hold still."

Charlotte started wiping the goop off, and Gretchen yanked the towel away. "Give me that. I'll be eighty years old before you get this off me."

Jared came back in, rubbing his injured leg. "No sign of anybody."

Gretchen's eyelashes were all stuck together, and her hair was matted. "Well, Jared, it had to be someone. Or do you believe in the ghost that some say roams the hallways of Primevil?"

Jared said, "Gretchen, there's no need to bring that up."

"Why not? Would it scare your girlfriend?"

"Gretchen, it's just bad timing, that's all."

Brooklyn said, "Gretchen, you can't scare Charlotte and me. What little ghost story do you have to tell?"

Charlotte handed Noon back to Brooklyn, who quickly inspected his leg for any more bleeding. "Jared, why didn't you tell me about this ghost?"

"Because I don't know the entire story, and you had enough things going on to keep you awake at night."

Gretchen spit out. "I'm going to take a shower and wash this horrible-smelling stuff off." She stomped out of the room.

Jared yelled, "You know what? That's fine; we're going to go get something to eat. You do whatever you need to do to get presentable."

Charlotte grabbed Jared's arm. "We can't leave the kittens behind—especially not with Gretchen still up here."

"I doubt if Gretchen did this, but I'm not going to change your mind."

Brooklyn said. "Jared, you give Gretchen too much credit. I think she's very capable of doing something like this. Let's take them with us. Just find something to hide them in."

Noon's amputated leg was still oozing viscous blood. "Jared, since you're a guard, do you have any medical supplies?"

"Yeah, I have something. Can you get the metal box out of my top dresser and bring it to me?"

Charlotte dug through Jared's underwear, which made her feel uncomfortable, and got the box. She handed it to Jared. "Can you help Noon, or should we take him to the infirmary? Brooklyn, didn't you say Mrs. Bellow was back?"

"Yeah, she's back, but when I left her, she didn't look too well. She was complaining of head pain. I think that gash to her head is still affecting her."

Jared opened the small but heavy metal box. As he took things out, Charlotte said, "What are you looking for?" She cradled Noon in her arms.

Jared twisted the rubber band around Noon's stump tighter to act as a tourniquet. He then got the tube of antibiotic ointment and smeared a fairly large blob over the stump. He looked at Charlotte. "We'll need to put the topical antibiotic on several times a day, and keep it clean."

Brooklyn picked Noon up from Charlotte and stroked the tiny thing until it started to purr. "What a tough little guy—even when his leg has been severed, he still purrs. Let's look in Mrs. B.'s clothes closet for something to carry the kittens in. She gave me this new brightly colored sling for my arm, but thanks to Gretchen it's ruined."

As they walked to the clinic, Charlotte and Brooklyn were begging Jared to tell them the story of the Primevil ghost. "No, for the last time. I don't know the story well enough to repeat it. I've heard bits and pieces of the legend, but I don't believe in that stuff, so I never paid it much attention—and neither should you."

When they got to the clinic, Mrs. Bellow had her head in her hands, and jumped when the three of them walked in. Charlotte said, "Mrs. Bellow, good to have you back. Are you okay?"

"Yes, Charlotte, just a bit of a headache, that's all. Brooklyn, for heaven's sake—what have you done to the sling I gave you? It's torn; it's practically useless. You girls nowadays are so rough on things. In my day, we treated our belongings like they were worth something. You know, my mother would have made me pay for another one."

Brooklyn looked down. "At least you had a mother, Mrs. B."

"It's Mrs. Bellow, Brooklyn."

Mrs. Bellow went to get another sling in the supply room, and Charlotte yelled back. "Mrs. Bellow, would it be all right if we took a look in your clothes closet for a couple of purses?"

"Sure, Charlotte. You have something worth carrying in a purse, do you?"

As Mrs. Bellow handed Brooklyn the sling, she saw the kittens. "What happened to this kitten's leg?"

Jared said, "A lot has been happening since you've been away."

Charlotte found two purses and handed one to Brooklyn. "Mrs. Bellow, Jared found these two starving kittens in the garbage. Brooklyn and I have been taking care of them, and then today, when we went to get them, we found them like this."

Charlotte's eyes were filled with tears as Mrs. Bellow got a strange look on her face. "Who would do such a thing?"

Brooklyn said, "I think it was Gretchen. She's a disgusting human being."

Mrs. Bellow handed each of the girls a hand towel to put in the purse for the kitten to snuggle into. "I don't think it was Gretchen. I know her, and she loves animals. When I first got here she was the guard who showed me around, and she found a small white dog that had been beaten. She tried to nurse it back to health, but it died several days later. She cried for a long time. Me, I don't care for animals much, but I think Gretchen does. I know she has a bit of rough exterior, but she is fragile on the inside."

Brooklyn said, *"A bit* of a rough exterior? Mrs. B., she makes Genghis Khan look like a sweetheart."

Mrs. Bellow just sighed. "Brooklyn, are you ever going to address me by my name?"

"Sure, Mrs. B.—I mean, Mrs. Bellow."

The kittens were settled in their new traveling bag. Charlotte said, "Mrs. Bellow, we're headed to get something to eat. Do you want to come along?"

"No, Charlotte, but thanks anyway. I still have a problem with my balance and headaches."

"We can bring you back something."

"That's very kind, but you kids go ahead. I've already called in a replacement for me. I'm leaving early. Brooklyn, come here a minute and let me fix your sling." She adjusted Brooklyn's sling.

"Thanks, Mrs. B."

Mrs. Bellow shook her head. "See you kids tomorrow."

Charlotte and Brooklyn took the kittens back to their room, along with Jared, and after feeding and tucking them in Charlotte said, "Jared, are you sure you can make it up to your room by yourself?"

"Yeah, my leg feels fine."

Charlotte handed Midnight to Brooklyn, who was watching Noon sleep on her bed. She walked Jared to the door and put her arms around him.

"No. There's no way you're going to get me to tell you the story of the Primevil ghost. So stop trying to manipulate me."

Charlotte ignored Jared, and stood on her tiptoes and kissed him softly. "Thank you for being, like, the best boyfriend in the entire world."

Jared pulled away and looked at her. He put his hand softly on the side of her face and brought her in for a sweet kiss. "Thank you, Charlotte. That's the nicest thing anyone ever said to me."

Charlotte smiled and watched Jared limp down the hall. "Night, Jared." She then turned to Brooklyn and said, "Are the kittens asleep?"

"Yeah, why?"

"Help me move this dresser in front of the door. I don't know who tortured our kittens, but I don't want anyone entering our room while we're asleep."

They changed into their pajamas and brushed their hair. "Brooklyn, do you think Gretchen had anything to do with injuring the kittens?"

"I don't know. Mrs. B. said Gretchen wouldn't do anything like that."

They got into bed and snuggled with their kittens. "Brooklyn, you better stop calling Mrs. Bellow Mrs. B."

"Yeah, I know. I just have a problem with respecting adults. Besides Mrs. B.—I mean, Mrs. Bellows—no adult has treated me nice."

Charlotte yawned. "How's Noon doing?"

"He's sleeping. I think he's doing well for having his leg pulled off today."

"Let's get Gretchen to tell us about the Primevil ghost."

"Yeah, okay." Brooklyn yawned. "Night, Charlotte."

Charlotte rolled over and cuddled with Midnight. "Night, Brooklyn."

Redwine hill

16

Gruesome Wanda

When Charlotte and Brooklyn woke the next morning, there was only one thing strange in the room. The dresser was no longer pushed up against the door—it was back against the wall in its original position.

Charlotte stretched and gave Midnight a kiss. "Hey, Brooklyn—did you move the dresser last night?"

Brooklyn checked her kitten's leg for any additional bleeding. "No, I didn't move the dresser. I couldn't move it by myself if I wanted to."

They both sat up and looked at the door, then it swung open and hit the back wall hard.

Gretchen stood in the doorway and said, "Girls, it's time to wake up." She went over and held out her hands for Noon. Brooklyn hesitated at first, but then handed him over. "If you hurt one hair on his head, I'll kill you, Gretchen."

Gretchen kissed the kitten. "Oh, Brooklyn, you're so dramatic. Look—I brought them some meat. Come on, get up. Let's go get something to eat, and I'll tell you all about the ghost at Primevil. Jared's on duty, so he can't stop me. That is, if you still want to hear my story."

Charlotte got out of bed and handed Midnight to Gretchen. "Not too much meat, Gretchen; they might get sick."

Charlotte started getting dressed as Brooklyn said, "Yeah, we still want to hear your little ghost story. What do you take us for—sniveling kids?"

"I don't know, since Prince Charming isn't here to protect you."

Brooklyn and Charlotte dressed quickly and put the kittens in their purses. Charlotte said, "Go ahead, Gretchen, start talking. What are you waiting for?"

As they walked to the cafeteria, Gretchen kept her voice low, since there were other patients roaming the hallways.

Brooklyn said, "Gretchen, if everyone already knows about this ghost, why are you whispering?"

"I don't want to spook any of the patients. It doesn't take much to set them off. Besides, this is my own personal story."

Charlotte said, "I'm sure all the asylums have their own version of the ghost."

Gretchen said, "You'd think so, but Primevil has always been the creepiest place out of all the asylums. I've heard rumors that Dr. Oracle is mixed up in something horrific, but anyone who knows anything gets killed."

Charlotte spoke in a loud voice. "You mean, like Serenity?"

"Charlotte, you're too loud, and you're making me lose my train of thought. I don't know anything about Serenity. Now, where was I?"

Brooklyn said, "Something about Primevil being creepy. No big surprise there, Gretchen."

They got to the cafeteria, and the meal ladies were staring at Charlotte and Brooklyn. "What's in the bag, ladies?"

Charlotte said, "Nothing. Just personal things."

Brooklyn sneered. "None of your business."

One of the ladies crossed her oversized arms. "Yes, it's my business. Can't have you taking food out of the cafeteria and hoarding it in your room."

Brooklyn said, "You think we'd hoard this stuff in our room? I can barely eat it when it's fresh, let alone after a few hours."

They brought their purses in tight to their bodies and put their arms over the top. Charlotte said, "It's against Primevil's policy to check patients' personal items."

"Not if I suspect you're hiding something, which I think you might be."

Gretchen held up her hand and showed them her badge. "These two are with me. They're okay. They're not hiding anything."

"Fine," the lunch lady huffed. "As long as they're with you, and you assume all responsibility for them, go on in."

Brooklyn couldn't keep her mouth shut. "Hey, gorilla lady, why would we be sneaking food into your cafeteria? The time to check patients is when they leave."

"Great suggestion. What's your number?"

Gretchen got forceful. "Hey, I told you, they're with me. Back off. I've got bigger problems than sneaking food out of here."

They walked to a secluded table, and Brooklyn nudged Charlotte. "Did you see that, Charlotte? Maybe it wouldn't be so bad having Gretchen on our side."

"Brooklyn, there are no sides. Not the kind you're thinking of. We don't need to be flexing any muscles with the lunch ladies."

"I just thought it was kind of nice to have someone sticking up for me. It felt good for a change."

Gretchen slammed her tray down hard on the table. "Would you two stop babbling? When I tell you the story, don't do anything, like scream. If you're going to act like babies, I'll have to call a nurse to give you an injection."

Charlotte said, "Now who's overreacting?"

Gretchen looked around the room to make sure no one was looking at their table. "You two may not realize this, but besides Jared, I'm next in line for command of the guards that make up the patient population."

Charlotte shrugged. "Okay, that I didn't know."

"All right then, let me tell the story. One night when I first became a guard and moved to the top floor, I kept hearing weird sounds. I had heard them when I was a patient, but the noise seemed to intensify up there. I awoke one night, and something or someone was under my bed. I could hear the sounds of labored breathing, or so I thought that's what it was. I knew I had to look under my bed, and my gun was across the room. I actually thought that if I got up and ran across the room that something would grab my ankles and pull me under the bed. I lay there too scared to move. I said, 'Whoever is under the bed, you can come out now.' I was hoping this was some type of initiation for new guards or something. I thought a guard would roll out from under the bed, jump up, and burst into laughter. I tried to keep my cool. I didn't want the story getting out that I was scared to death. I waited for a long time, but no one came out. The noise was growing worse, so I braced myself for whatever was under my bed."

Gretchen looked up from pushing her food around on her plate. She gave a small uncomfortable laugh. "Both of your eyes are going to pop out of your head."

Charlotte said, "Was it a guard hiding under your bed?" Charlotte thought, Please let it be a guard.

"The moon was just barely shining in the room, but it gave off enough light for me to make out a figure under the bed. The fear of the other guards laughing at me is what gave me the courage to look under the bunk."

Brooklyn almost yelled. "What was under there?"

"It's not what I thought. Oh, I wish it had been another guard."

Charlotte had a hard tone in her voice. "Gretchen, what was it?"

"I knew I had to look fast or I'd lose my nerve. I bolted from the bed and bent down and looked. When I saw it, I froze."

Gretchen shut her eyes and rubbed her eyelids with her fingers. "I can still see it. It was some type of ghost. I use that word loosely, for lack of a better word. It looked to be a woman who was deteriorating. Some of her skin was missing, and a reddish liquid pooled on the floor. This is the worst part: she was eating from a bag of guts."

Charlotte jumped up and yelled, "What!"

Her chair hit the floor, and the patients looked over at her.

Gretchen grabbed Charlotte's arm and said quietly, "Shhh, sit down. What's the matter with you?"

Charlotte slowly picked up her chair and looked around the room. Everyone was staring at her. "Go back to eating. I'm just a bit clumsy today."

An elderly patient watched Charlotte sit down. The patient was making guttural sounds with her mouth, but she walked over to Charlotte and handed her a dirty napkin. "Here, sweetie—you need this more than I do. You have a piece of something on your face." She threw the napkin on the table and walked away laughing some kind of witch's laugh.

Gretchen said, "I told you to be quiet. You're attracting all kinds of attention to this table. Oh great—here come the cafeteria ladies."

Charlotte mouthed the word sorry.

The husky lady said, "Well, look here. I guess the food isn't good enough to eat."

Brooklyn's words were sweet. Each word hung in the air with the consistency of sugar. "We're not hungry, but if you kind ladies will just bend the rules this once, we'd like to take the meat with us. If you don't mind?"

Brooklyn was using her most agreeable voice; how could they object?

Charlotte looked at Brooklyn; she had never heard her talk with that tone of voice. She sounded like she was eight years old.

The woman put her hands on her hips. "I guess it wouldn't hurt since you're with one of the guards."

The three girls quickly wrapped their meat and headed out the door, when Brooklyn said with a Southern accent, "Thank you, kind ladies. We will never forget you."

Charlotte yanked Brooklyn's arm. "That's over the top." Charlotte looked back and saw the woman look confused as if trying to sort out if the girls were genuine or if she had been the butt of a bad joke.

Charlotte said, "Hurry, before she figures out you were poking fun at her."

They ran up to Gretchen's room. They'd never been in her room. It was understated but very clean and organized. Brooklyn and Charlotte took the kittens out of their bags, and Gretchen tore the meat into little pieces.

Brooklyn held up Noon. "Do you think his leg looks okay?"

Charlotte said, "I think it looks better than it did yesterday. It's starting to scab over."

Gretchen had the meat in two small piles on her bed. "Come sit down."

Charlotte said, "Finish the story, Gretchen."

"Are you sure you want to hear the rest?"

Brooklyn jumped up and looked under Gretchen's bed. "Just checking."

Charlotte looked at Gretchen. "Is this really a true story?"

"Yes, I've never been so scared in my whole life. You know the saying: truth is stranger than fiction. Well, this was one of those times. I couldn't sleep in this room for weeks afterward, and when I finally did, I had to shove a bunch of stuff under my bed so there was no room for anyone or anything else."

Charlotte said, "You had just told us the thing under your bed was eating from a bag of guts."

"Yeah, that's right. Charlotte, why did you get upset at that part?"

"I'll tell you later; just finish the story." Midnight and Noon were now done with their meal and were purring as the girls scratched and petted them. Charlotte was hoping the cuteness of the kittens would distract from the horrible images inspired by the story Gretchen was telling.

Gretchen continued. "Anyway, like I was saying, I was frozen with fear, stiff as a board. I thought I was going to die of fright. There was only one thing that I could focus on that took away from the ugliness of the whole thing and that was her hair. It was the color of yours, Charlotte, but it was a lot longer. It seemed to go down to her ankles. I tried to concentrate on her hair, and all the time I could hear the bag crinkling from her taking something else dreadful out and eating it. She wasn't pleasant to look at when she was eating, either. Drool would pool on the floor, and her lips were malformed and hideous. I was so terrified, I don't know if I said these words or just thought them: 'What do you want from me?' "

Charlotte said, "Gretchen, are you sure you weren't having a crazed moment, or maybe you had something to eat or drink that was intoxicating?"

"No, this was all very real. When she spoke, it was hard to understand her. I don't think she had much of her tongue left."

Brooklyn asked, "What did she say?"

"Her exact words were, 'You need to find my twin, Wanda, in the human form. She'll look like me, but without the deteriorating skin and bowels.'"

Brooklyn said, "Who's Wanda?"

Charlotte said in a weak voice, "I'm Wanda."

Gretchen and Brooklyn stared at Charlotte, and Gretchen said, "Tell me why you think—out of all the people she could be talking about—that you're Wanda. And don't say it's because some of the patients happen to walk by you and call you Wanda."

"It's more than that."

Gretchen said, "Well, Charlotte, you do have the same hair." She picked up a lock of Charlotte's hair. "Yep, same color, same texture."

Brooklyn said, "This is creeping me out, and how do you know it's the same texture? Did you feel the hair on that thing under your bed?"

Charlotte said, "Listen—before I knew either of you, someone threw a bag of guts in my room. I ran to get Jared, but when we got back to my room, there had been a fruitless attempt to clean up the mess. There were still remnants left over."

Brooklyn said, "Why didn't you tell me about this before?"

"I didn't want to scare you, but you can ask Jared if my story is true."

Gretchen said, "Yeah, I will. You can't be Wanda. From how the story goes, she helps with the problems of the world. You can't even get your list free of demerits."

Brooklyn yelled, "Is that why you wanted me to sleep in the bed by the door?"

Charlotte said, "Sorry, Brooklyn, but you said you were a sound sleeper. You could sleep through a murder, so I figured if you were murdered, you wouldn't feel a thing."

Brooklyn said, "Imagine that. Well, Charlotte, you might want to sleep with one eye open tonight."

Charlotte said, "What can I say? I'm sorry. Do you want to change beds?"

Brooklyn let out a long, slow sigh. "No, a couple of feet isn't going to make a difference. Besides, I think they're after you."

Charlotte half smiled at Brooklyn. "Gretchen, finish your story."

"I lay on the cold hard floor watching as she finished the entire bag. I was hoping she'd disappear when she was finished, but she didn't."

Brooklyn said, "What happened?"

She proceeded to expel the contents that she just ate. Projectile vomit went all over me, and she didn't spare herself either. Her hair was coated with the stuff, and every open orifice and wound pushed and pulsated the rest of the stuff out. It was only by the grace of God that I kept my stomach contents down."

Gretchen held her hand to her mouth as if trying to keep from getting sick. "Then she said some stupid nursery rhythm: 'We Willy

Wanda, crippled and deformed, you count your sanity while I count mine.' "

Charlotte said, "I've heard that several times before, here at Primevil, and that's not a nursery rhythm that I've ever heard of."

Brooklyn said, "Oh, my God, Charlotte. When BT was dying and spitting blood, I leaned down to hear what he was trying to tell me. He said, 'She's Wanda.' I didn't understand what he was talking about."

Charlotte said, "Do you think Billy Thomas the Third was the 'Willy' in the nursery rhyme?"

Brooklyn had tears in her eyes. "Does it really matter, Charlotte? He's dead."

Charlotte nodded in agreement and held her friend. "I know. I'm sorry, Brooklyn. I could tell you really liked him."

Jared heard the girls down the hall talking in Gretchen's room. "With all this talk about ghosts, I think they deserve a scare." The room was fairly dark with the storm raging outside, and the girls' backs were toward the door. They were all huddled together as Gretchen spoke about Wanda. Jared slithered in on his stomach doing the Army crawl, protecting his injured leg. He made it under the bed and let out some groaning, slurping noises.

The girls froze. Charlotte's leg was hanging over the bed. As she slowly pulled it up, she whispered for Gretchen to get her gun across the room.

Gretchen turned pale and shook her head. She whispered, "A gun won't work on a ghost."

Brooklyn said, "I'm not looking under the bed."

Gretchen said quietly. "Then I guess one of you will be looking under the bed. She pushed Charlotte off the bed.

Charlotte went tumbling backward and hit her head on the floor.

Jared popped his head up, hitting it on the box springs. He shimmied out and propped Charlotte's head on his lap.

Brooklyn jumped off the bed. "Jared! Just what do you think you were doing? Charlotte, Charlotte, are you okay?"

Charlotte looked at Jared. "Where am I?"

Gretchen said, "You slipped off the bed."

Charlotte rubbed her head. "Yeah, right. Was that Wanda under the bed?"

Jared brushed Charlotte's hair back. "No, Charlotte, that was me. I was trying to scare you. With all the talk of ghosts, I thought I'd play along with it."

Charlotte said in a disgusting tone. "Do you really think that was necessary?"

He gave her a beautiful smile that landed on her lips. "Charlotte, I said I was sorry. What more do you want me to say?"

Charlotte looked at Jared, who was sincere about his apology, and asked, "Do you know about Wanda?"

"I've had a few patients that jumped out a window to their death. Some say they met with Miss Wanda."

Brooklyn said, "Oh, now the ghost is Miss Wanda. Did you know Gretchen met her once under her bed?"

"No, I didn't know that. Charlotte, I'm sorry. How's your head?" He stroked her hair back. Charlotte looked as if she was enjoying the attention and was in a trance. "Are you ready to drop this Wanda thing?"

Charlotte said, "I don't think you know the entire story, Jared."

Jared said, "Fine. You want to explain to me what this is all about?"

The girls didn't hesitate; they jumped right in on the story. Gretchen just sat there saying very little, while Brooklyn and Charlotte took over telling the story and made it their own, not leaving out even the smallest detail.

When they were finished, Jared was somewhat unnerved and shivered. "Gretchen, is this true? Was the story embellished in any way?"

"No, it wasn't embellished. They told a true account of what happened. Now, once again, I won't be able to sleep in my room."

Charlotte sat up with Jared's help. "You can sleep with Brooklyn and me. I don't know how safe we'll be, but three is better than one, Gretchen."

They kept busy until it was time to turn in. Jared moved the beds together, and Charlotte stuffed some of her clothes in the crack. Gretchen said, "I get dibs on the middle."

Jared moved the two bedside tables to the head of the bed, and the dressers to the bottom. Blocking the space anyone would need to get under the bed, Jared thought, *I guess they don't realize that ghosts don't need any room; they can go through things.*

"Okay, ladies, can I do anything else for you?"

Brooklyn frowned. "You could sit in that chair and watch over us all night."

Jared laughed. "You'll be fine; they're three of you and only one ghost. Besides, just because you've heard the legend of Wanda, it doesn't mean she's going to show up now and torment you."

Charlotte was hoping for a kiss, so she climbed out of the fortress and walked Jared to the door. He patted her shoulder. "I'll see you in the morning. That is, if you survive the night."

Charlotte walked back to bed with a sad look on her face. Gretchen patted the bed. "Charlotte, you can sleep in the middle if you want."

"No, I'll be fine."

The headboard and footboard were almost as high as the dresser. Charlotte looked the situation over. "We need to sleep with our heads at the bottom of the bed."

Brooklyn shook her head. "Why would we do that? To see anyone entering the room?"

"No, now listen. The bedside tables just cover under the bed, but our heads will be exposed. If someone wanted me dead, they could just reach over with little trouble and slice my head off."

Brooklyn yelled, "That's gross, Charlotte."

Gretchen sighed. "If our feet are exposed to the footboard, then they could cut off our feet. We wouldn't be able to run away."

Charlotte rubbed her eyes. "Yes, but we would still be alive."

Brooklyn rubbed her forehead. "This conversation is officially over. I'm a street rat, and I don't think I've ever heard a conversation like this."

Charlotte rearranged Midnight and Noon. "Sorry, I'm just tired."

Brooklyn changed the subject. "Charlotte, when do you go back to work?"

"I think next week. Mrs. Bellow came to work and then had to leave. She was still having trouble with her head. Mrs. Rogers says she doesn't need any help in the clinic."

They all finally agreed that Charlotte should take the middle, and then they quickly settled in.

Gretchen fell asleep first, and Charlotte sat up and looked at her. "So much for Gretchen not being able to fall asleep. You know, when I was younger and had my friends spend the night, the first one to fall asleep got a prank played on them."

Brooklyn smiled a half-devious grin. "Like what?"

"Nothing too bad, like we'd put their underwear in the freezer, or draw flowers on their face with markers. My mother used to tell me not to do anything too drastic or my friends wouldn't come back."

"Sounds like you had a great childhood, Charlotte."

"Yeah, I did."

"Charlotte, can you roll Gretchen over? She's snoring."

"Sure." Charlotte pushed Gretchen, and she rolled over and hit her forehead on the dresser.

"Oops. Think she'll have a bump on her head in the morning?"

Brooklyn let out a snort. "If she does, we'll blame it on Wanda. You know, the grossest people I've seen, even as a street rat, were the Collectors' sidekicks that brought me to Primevil."

Charlotte shivered. "We must have had the same ones. There were three of them that brought me in, and each one was uglier than the next. My Collector was bad, and then there was the little guy with polio, and then the last one had all these open wounds, and he would scratch the scabs open and they would bleed. I think the two emaciated ones were called Polo and Seed."

"Yeah, that was them."

Charlotte was getting tired. "The thought of those two, even now, makes me want to vomit."

"Okay, Charlotte, you're grossing me out. Go to sleep."

Charlotte petted Midnight for a long time before succumbing to sleep.

Redwine hill

17

The Operative

In the morning, Jared walked into Charlotte's room. "You girls getting up today, or are you going to sleep your life away?"

Charlotte poked her head up. "Morning, Jared."

Charlotte had been up for a long time, but Brooklyn and Gretchen were just now starting to stir.

Jared leaned against the wall. "I see you're all alive. No ghosts attack you last night?"

Charlotte smirked at Jared. "No, the only thing that kept me awake last night was Gretchen's snoring."

Jared's voice turned serious. "Charlotte, I've someone I want you to meet this morning." He flipped her a muffin. "You can eat on the way."

Since she'd slept in her clothes, she just climbed over the bedside table and put her shoes on. "Where are we going?"

"You'll see."

She took a bite of the warm muffin. "Mmmm, banana. Okay, Jared, I'm ready." She walked alongside him as he made his way up to the fourth floor.

"I've never been on this floor before." She rubbed her hands along her arms as if to keep the chill away. "I've heard they're real lunatics. Have you brought me here because we were talking about the ghost of Primevil last night?"

"No, I just want you to meet someone."

She said quietly, "Is it Wanda?"

He gave her a hug and laughed. "No. You'll see."

Jared stopped in front of one of the rooms. "Go ahead, Charlotte—go in."

Charlotte saw who was in the room. "I'm not going in there. Is this some kind of joke? That man is a complete nut ball."

He put his arm around her and guided her into the room. "Charlotte, I'm staying. Everything is going to be fine. I've already talked with Martin, and he wants to talk with you."

Charlotte looked at the man as he extended his hand to shake. "No, thank you. I see you no longer have your handcuffs and shackles on." She looked at the man and then back at Jared, "Do you know, Jared, that this is the man that had pleasured himself before I danced with him?"

The man started laughing, and Charlotte stomped her feet and turned to walk out of the room. She yelled, "What's so funny?"

The man said in a very clear husky voice, "Serenity was one of us."

Charlotte spun around. "What did you say?"

"Serenity was one of us."

Charlotte was confused. "You mean, a patient?"

"No, Charlotte, she was like Billy Thomas and me. We were a team of three that came here to investigate Primevil. There's something going on in many of the asylums. We've been tracking things for a few months now. Going from place to place. And we now believe this is where the problem starts—at Primevil. This is top-of-the-line information that I'm giving you. Since BT and Serenity are both dead, I'm recruiting you, Charlotte, to help me complete my investigation. I believe Dr. Oracle is involved somehow."

Charlotte let out a moan. "Not Dr. Oracle. I can't help you. He hates me, and is already trying to schedule a lobotomy for me. From what I know, Dr. Oracle has something to do with the mystery at the asylums, but I wouldn't be of any help to anyone if he did a little slicing motion to my brain."

"Don't you want to find out what happened to your friend Serenity?"

She rubbed her forehead. "Yeah, but I don't see how I can help."

"Listen you already know more than most patients at Primevil, from the things that Jared has told me. Like all the underground corridors, and that Primevil may be serving humans in their meat dishes. You're one of the lucky ones who didn't go completely insane and still has her wits about her. Most of the patients here aren't even aware of 'person, place, or time,' let alone what's going on around them."

Now that Charlotte knew this man wasn't crazy, he actually seemed quite normal-looking. Charlotte looked at Jared. "I don't know. I still think you're a little creepy. What about that stuff on your hands at the dance?"

He got a wicked grin on his face. "That was corn syrup with a small amount of flour." He bent down and removed his bottom dresser drawer. "Here—see for yourself."

He handed Charlotte a plastic container, and she twisted the cap off and looked into the small opening. "Go ahead—stick your finger in. It's just corn syrup."

Charlotte put her index finger in, just barely touching the syrup, and licked it off. "It's sweet." She handed the container back to him. "What's your name?"

"Can't give you my real name, but the name I go by in here is Marty Keenley."

Charlotte sat quietly thinking. "I still don't understand why you had to act so disgusting at the dance."

"In this place, if you're aggressive in any way, you get the incredibly attractive canvas jacket, a lobotomy, or locked up. I need the people working at Primevil to think I'm crazy, but not enough to have a permanent surgery. I had to be able to walk around and observe things. Like when you, Brooklyn, and Mrs. Bellow disappeared behind the door to the lab."

Charlotte sat on the bed. "Yes, I remember. That was you telling Dr. Oracle that your girlfriend was in the lab."

Marty smiled. "Yeah, that was me. Pretty convincing, huh?"

Charlotte cried out, "Serenity was a member of your team?"

"I'm afraid so. She and BT are now dead."

Charlotte started to relax until he answered her next question: "Do you know who killed them?"

"I'm sure it was one of the doctors here at Primevil who killed Serenity, but I shot BT when he was talking with you on the beach."

Charlotte jumped off the bed. She snapped and lunged at Marty, pelting him with blows. "Why did you shoot him? What's wrong with you?"

Jared gently but firmly grabbed Charlotte around the waist and pulled her back. Jared was getting pummeled by Charlotte, and she didn't feel that Jared would let her go.

Marty gave a small laugh. "Jared, you can release her. Now that I know she's a wildcat, I can hold my own. It was just a little surprising, that's all."

Charlotte yelled, "Surprising!" Her rage erupted again. She landed a good one to Jared's eye as Marty dodged her fists.

"Listen, scum ball, you are so lucky that I'm not Brooklyn. She'd have had your stomach pulled out through your lips by now."

She was exhausted, and Jared loosened his grip on her. "I don't understand why. If he was one of you, why did you have to shoot him?" She sneered at him. "You must have had something to do with Serenity's death too."

"I want to explain. Please sit."

"I won't sit, and you better hurry up before I run out of here screaming at the top of my lungs."

"Number 3737 . . . or should I call you by your given name, Charlotte?

"Does it really matter to a murderer?"

Charlotte stood there with her arms crossed, and Marty sighed, "BT used to be a terrific spy, but lately he'd gotten sloppy. He loved to talk, and to the wrong people. He was his own worst enemy. It would just be a matter of time before he got himself, Serenity, and me into knee-deep trouble. It just happened to be Serenity. He didn't actually kill her, but he gave the doctors enough information that they did the dirty deed. Serenity wasn't insane—she was just a great actress."

Charlotte spoke quietly. "Was she even a teenager?"

"No, she was actually twenty-two, but looked very young for her age. It was either going to be BT or myself. Why do you think I paid somebody off at Primevil to say that BT was becoming aggressive and could hurt other patients?"

Charlotte's voice shrieked out. "Who'd you pay?"

"That's not important. BT had loose lips, which could have brought down months of investigation."

Charlotte's legs became weak, and Jared half-carried her to the bed. "Charlotte, are you okay?"

Jared could barely hear her. "Yes, Jared, but why didn't you tell me this sooner?"

"I just found this out. Martin here just came to me once he figured out you were Wanda."

"What does that have anything to do with Serenity's or BT's deaths? Are you saying I'm responsible in some way? And stop telling me I'm Wanda!"

"Wanda is just a code name that Billy made up. It's the ghost of Primevil, and Billy made that up to throw off anyone listening, but you are Charlotte C. Carrion, are you not?"

"Yes, that's my name."

"I don't want to scare you, Charlotte, but Dr. Oracle and Dr. Farrow are on to you."

"On to me. How?"

"They were getting close to my identity, thanks to BT, so I threw them off my tail and put them on to yours. I may have started a rumor stating that the patient that looked like Wanda was an operative."

"I don't even know you. I'd never seen you before the night of the dance."

"But you have. I was with BT in the nurse's office the day you came in with that ridiculous sheet tied around your head. Remember—you were looking in the drawer for something for your headache."

Charlotte stammered, "That was you?"

Marty started rolling his head around, hanging his mouth open, drooling, and making moaning sounds."

Charlotte yelled, "Okay, stop."

She rubbed the back of her neck. "Why does everyone think I look like a grotesque corpse that haunts the halls of this asylum?"

Martin massaged his eyes with his hands. "The legend that was told to me was that Wanda died here at Primevil just last year, by circumstances that could not be explained. Before she died, she snuck a letter out of the asylum addressed to the Validator. I've actually read the letter. It stated that she thought Dr. Oracle was somehow involved with making the teenagers go insane and then killing them for meat. Trust me when I say that if you saw the picture that BT, Serenity, and I saw, you'd know you were a dead ringer for her. Wanda was murdered, plain and simple."

Charlotte could hardly swallow or make a sound. She croaked out, "There's nothing simple about murder."

"That's why I started the rumor about you being an operative. The only reason you're still alive is because they think the president is looking closely at Primevil."

"Is that the reason I was brought to this dump—because I looked like Wanda?"

"No, that was just by luck."

Charlotte gave a weak smile to Jared. "Imagine that. It must have been my lucky day."

Martin continued. "You see, Charlotte, I was hoping that BT would get his lobotomy, and although he would no longer be an agent, at least my cover wouldn't be blown. You just had to rescue him. So if you want to point fingers, I guess it is kind of your fault."

Jared spoke. "Marty, don't go putting this on Charlotte. If you need someone to blame, look at yourself or BT, but not Charlotte."

Charlotte gave Jared the best forced smile she could under the circumstances that had just been relayed to her.

Jared spoke aggressively. "Why did you turn them toward Charlotte? Seems kind of cowardly to me."

Marty backed away from Jared. "Look, Jared, I don't want to get in a physical altercation with you. It's obvious you'd win, but let me ask you a question. Have you ever seen the ghost, Wanda?"

Jared sighed and tried to calm his flinching fists. "Several times, but nothing up close and personal. Why?"

"Except for the length of the hair, Charlotte and Wanda are identical, could even have been twin sisters. There's a rumor going around Primevil that the girl that looks like Wanda will expose the asylum for what it really is."

Jared crossed his arms. "Who started that rumor, Marty?"

"Yes, Jared, that'd be me, also, but I did it to buy me some time."

Charlotte said so softly it was hard for the other two to hear, "What really is Primevil, if not the worst of all the asylums in Old Boston?"

Marty rubbed the back of his neck. "What!"

"You said Wanda would expose Primevil for what it really is. What is it, Marty?"

"The problem is deeper than what we could have imagined. It's a twofold problem, and I only have the answer to the second part."

Charlotte calmly looked at Marty. "Go on."

Marty took in a long, slow breath. "The first part—why so many sixteen-year-olds are having their brains ravished on their sixteenth birthdays—I don't have the answer to that, but I'm still digging."

Jared snapped. "What's the second part, Marty?"

"Patients are dying at an alarming rate at the asylums. I've got my suspicions that the asylums are killing off the patients and then selling the parts to Blood Red Meat."

Charlotte and Jared both yelled, "What!"

Charlotte choked out the next sentence. "We saw bodies and parts floating toward the ocean. Isn't that the way they dispose of the dead corpses?"

"No, I'm afraid not. The bodies float down the ghoulish corridor to a semi-tractor truck waiting at the bottom to load them up and take them to the meat-processing plant. It's easy. No, livestock to feed or raise—just kill off these insane patients. Who's going to object? Most of them don't have families, and the ones that do never visit. Disposable patients."

Charlotte tried to stand but needed assistance from Jared. "I've got to go lie down, Jared. My head is spinning. I don't feel well."

Marty looked at Charlotte. "I'll talk with you later, when all this has time to sink in."

Jared turned and glared at Marty over his shoulder. Marty shrugged his shoulders. "Or maybe not. You come find me when you want to talk."

As they walked down the hallway, Jared said in a pleading voice, "Honest, Charlotte, I didn't think he was going to say all that."

Charlotte was too drained to make a comment or chastise Jared. As they were descending the stairs, they ran into Brooklyn and Gretchen. Brooklyn said, "Charlotte, what's wrong? You look sick."

Charlotte had a hard time making eye contact with Brooklyn. How could she keep the secret of how BT died?

Brooklyn put Charlotte's arm around her shoulder. "Charlotte, you look gravely ill. Did you see Wanda?"

Gretchen frowned. "She's as pale as a ghost."

Charlotte shook her head. "No, I just don't feel well. I need to rest."

Gretchen ran to turn down the sheets on Charlotte's bed. The beds pushed together with all the furniture around them was odd-looking in the daytime. Jared lifted Charlotte over the footboard. He looked into her eyes. "I'm sorry, Charlotte."

Brooklyn went ballistic. "What do you mean? Sorry for what? If you did anything inappropriate with her, I'll slice you up and give you to the cafeteria ladies to put in the evening meal."

Charlotte smiled. "Brooklyn, Jared didn't do anything. I just need to rest for a bit." It was comforting, though, to know Brooklyn would kill someone to protect her.

18

Charlotte's Surprise Visitor

Jared watched as Brooklyn took out the Monarch Butterfly nail polish, climbed up on the other bed with Midnight and Noon, and started polishing her toenails.

Gretchen stretched and massaged her back. "I need to get to work. I'm in the holding area today and need to log in the new patients. Charlotte, are you going to be okay?"

Brooklyn smiled. "I'm not going anywhere. I'll come and get you later today if she doesn't get any better."

Jared leaned over and stroked Charlotte's cheek. "I need to talk with someone, Brooklyn. Have me paged if you need me." Jared went to find Marty. He found him in his room putting on his canvas jacket. "Hey, Jared, can you give me a hand with this? I need to go check out Dr. Oracle's lab, and I can't do that without my nifty jacket."

"Yeah." As Jared pulled the ties tighter than were comfortable, Marty grunted out. "Hey, take it easy."

Marty was having a hard time breathing, and Jared got right in his face. "I don't want you talking to or upsetting Charlotte. You need to go through me. If I catch you talking to her, you, the last agent of the three amigos, will be dead. Do I make myself clear?"

Marty nodded as Jared threw him on the bed. "I'm glad we agree." Marty slid to the floor and gasped for air.

Brooklyn had fallen asleep, when she was startled by someone calling her name. She quickly looked at Charlotte, who was peacefully sleeping with the kittens curled up next to her. The sun was just starting to set. "It must be close to dinnertime."

She maneuvered around the furniture and stepped into the hallway. The hall was empty, and she stood very still. She heard it again.

"Brooklyn."

"Who's there? Listen, jerk! Come out of hiding and show yourself, so I can pull your tongue out."

Brooklyn listened to tell where the voice was coming from.

"Brooklyn . . ." The voice kept repeating her name with increasing volume, a crackly, withered sound.

"Gretchen, is that you? This isn't funny."

Brooklyn went into the last room on the left, and the door slammed shut behind her. "That's fine. I'm not scared." She scanned the room looking for someone. "I mean it, Gretchen, this isn't funny." She tried pulling on the door, but it wouldn't open. She figured Gretchen or someone was holding it shut from the outside.

She started to scream out, but someone was behind her. "Shut up, you weird street rat."

Brooklyn whirled around. She couldn't speak, and she felt something warm run down her leg. She had urinated on herself. "What . . . what do you want?"

As she backed up, every inch of her body was trembling. *It must be Wanda with her horrific smell and open wounds.* Wanda's lips were strange-looking. Something fell out of her mouth, and she bent down to put it back into her mouth. "Can't talk without my tongue." She started laughing and snorting. She put her fingers in her mouth to reattach her tongue. "Brooklyn, don't look so stunned; my looks are the worst thing about me. I don't need anything from you, but I do want to talk with Charlotte, alone." Wanda stepped toward Brooklyn.

"Don't come any closer," Brooklyn's voice shook with hysteria.

Wanda touched Brooklyn's arm. It didn't take much to put her out. Brooklyn's eyes were already rolling to the back of her head when Wanda walked toward her. "Now, Brooklyn, don't you go anywhere."

Wanda sealed the door as she oozed down the hallway. She entered Charlotte's room, where she was curled up with her kittens.

She floated over the makeshift fort. "Charlotte. Charlotte, wake up." Her voice was slow and slobbery-sounding. Charlotte blinked her eyes to bring into view the person talking to her. She froze stiff; she couldn't move or talk. Wanda reached her hand out and picked up Noon. "Charlotte, isn't it something how animals accept one's deformities?" She stroked both kittens. "No judgment like humans." The kittens started purring. "Charlotte, did you know you look like me?"

Charlotte was shaking, but she managed to nod her head.

"Charlotte, I looked just like you when I was alive. Now the only thing we have in common is our hair. My skin used to be alabaster like yours, and I had the perfect nose, or at least that what's everyone told me. My eyes could catch the smallest bit of light and sparkle, illuminating my straight white teeth." She handed Midnight over to Charlotte. "You don't even realize how perfect you are. Let me get to the point before there's an interruption. I was sixteen years old when something happened in my brain. I snapped and ended up at Primevil."

Charlotte closed her eyes. "I just can't look at you. Go on—I'm listening."

"Over eighty percent of the asylums are filled with patients who were dragged here by the Collectors when they turned sixteen. Charlotte, do you know why this is?"

She shook her head and squeaked, "No, I don't."

Wanda reached over and picked up Midnight. "I believe Noon wants to see his human mother now. Charlotte opened her eyes and snapped them shut. She could see Wanda's arm touching hers. Then she felt around and found the ball of fur and pulled Noon close to her chest.

"A hardened gel-like probe is implanted in all babies at every hospital in the entire world. It's calibrated to explode the day they turn sixteen. There are a few whose implanted probe malfunctions for unknown reasons. It just sits comfortably inside their brain tissue not bothering its host. I suspect your probe didn't fully burst, and that's why you still seem sane. That's why some sixteen-year-olds are exempt from this life-changing event."

The kittens were both purring, but Charlotte kept her eyelids closed tight. "I don't understand—how does this fit with everything that's been happening at Primevil? Does this have to do with Serenity's death? And, how do you know all this?"

"Isn't it obvious how I know this information?" Charlotte just kept her eyes closed and didn't move. "I can float anywhere in this place. There are no secrets to me now. And, yes, it has to do with your friend's death. You know she was an agent?"

"I was told that recently."

"Well, Charlotte, if you can get into the holding area of Primevil, and see the patients when they're dragged here, you'll note the ones that turned sixteen will have a small burn mark within their hair. It's hard to see on the girls, but easier to see on the sixteen-year-old boys. Anyway, that's the probe that has gone off, leaving a charged, blackened area on the scalp."

Charlotte opened one eye. "Who is putting these probes in and why?"

"This might scare you, but I need to tell you."

"I don't think it's possible to be more scared than I am right now. I feel I'm at some type of tragic celebration and there are only two in attendance."

Wanda patted Charlotte's arm, and this time Charlotte didn't flinch. "It's a huge organization of doctors run by a good friend of yours—Dr. Oracle. That weasel has an enormous amount of power."

She watched Charlotte for any type of negative reaction. "It gets worse. Once the sixteen-year-olds have been here for about six months, they start thinning them out. They have to wait to make sure they're not carrying anything contagious within their bodies, like tuberculosis, hepatitis, any sexually transmitted diseases—things like that. Once the patients have been tested and are cleared, they are put on a list to be executed, then sent to Blood Red Meats to be sold to customers for meat products. I use the term executed loosely. But, basically, they turn up the voltage on the gel probe in the patient's brain and, viola—the vessels in their brain burst and they're dead."

Charlotte asked, "Why do so many of them get a lobotomy?"

Wanda looked at the door. "I think someone's coming. The lobotomy is almost standard procedure now. It takes the fight out of the patients before they lead them to slaughter."

Wanda handed the kitten to Charlotte just as Gretchen entered the room. "Hey, Charlotte."

That's all Gretchen got out before Wanda turned around and with a gruesome smile slobbered out the words, "Surprise, Gretchen."

Gretchen landed on the floor with a loud thud. Wanda looked at Charlotte. "Sorry about your friend. Oh, Charlotte, I left your other friend down the hall in one of the rooms. You might want to go and see if she's all right."

Wanda was gone, and Charlotte jumped out of bed and over the dresser. A pool of blood was forming under Gretchen's head.

Charlotte ran out into the hallway and yelled for help. Jared was the first to arrive. As he looked at Gretchen sprawled on the floor he asked, "Charlotte, what happened? You didn't do this, did you?"

"No, I didn't do this. Gretchen saw Wanda and fainted, hitting her head hard on the floor." One of the nurses came and was giving orders to get a stretcher.

"Jared, Wanda put Brooklyn in one of these rooms, and said she may need help."

Jared asked, "Charlotte, did you hit your head? You had a conversation with Wanda?"

"This isn't the time to question me. Let's just check these rooms."

The second door they tried was sealed shut. Charlotte tried pushing against it. "This must be it."

"Charlotte, Charlotte, you're too small to open the door." He gently picked her up by her waist and set her aside. He then slammed into the door with his shoulder. The door popped open, and there was Brooklyn curled up in a fetal position in the corner of the room. Charlotte ran over to her friend. "Brooklyn, are you all right?"

Brooklyn didn't answer; she just kept rocking back and forth saying, "I need a doctor. I need a doctor."

Jared picked her up, and Charlotte knew whatever scared Brooklyn had been bad. It would take an awful lot to scare a street rat. They moved quickly down the hall and caught up to the stretcher carrying Gretchen.

Charlotte asked, "Is Gretchen all right?"

Nurse Rogers scowled. "She'll live, if that's what you mean. What happened in your room anyway? Is this something I need to write up?"

Jared yelled, "No, Gretchen just slipped and hit her head."

The nurse turned and saw Jared. "Who are you carrying? I suppose she slipped too?"

Jared furrowed his brow. "No, we don't know what happened to her."

Charlotte stuttered. "We found Brooklyn like this."

The nurse gave the teens a stern look. "What's her number?"

Charlotte looked at Jared, and he gave her a nod. "It's 3899, but why do you need her number? Is she going to get into trouble?"

"No, it's just that when I make out an incident report, I want to notify any kinfolk."

Charlotte looked down. "Oh, she doesn't have any family or friends that would care about her."

The nurse looked at Jared, who shrugged. "She's a street rat."

"Okay, you two go about your business. I can handle this from here."

Charlotte said in a weak voice, "Will I see her again?"

The nurse looked at Charlotte. "That's a funny question. Why wouldn't you see her again?"

Charlotte mumbled, "I don't know. She just looks like a vegetable. Lying there, not moving."

The nurse looked at Brooklyn in Jared's arms. "Cadet, grab that wheelchair for number 3899, and let the nice guard's arms have a rest. You should be able to visit both of these young ladies tomorrow. Now, go. I've got to get these two patients some medical care."

As Charlotte watched her friend being wheeled away, she saw the chipped and faded orange polish on Brooklyn's nails. "I hope I see you tomorrow, Brooklyn."

Jared put his arm around Charlotte. "So, it looks like you've had a busy morning. Let's go somewhere private so we can talk."

"Yes, I need to talk to someone. I only trusted three people in this hellhole, and now two of them are in deep trouble. Jared, do you think Gretchen or Brooklyn will die?"

Charlotte began to snivel, and Jared drew her in close to his body as they meandered down the hall. Jared ran his free hand through his hair. "Charlotte, I don't know what's going on at Primevil, but you need to tell me everything you know."

As they walked back to Charlotte's room, some patients roaming the hallway yelled, "There's Wanda." This time Charlotte didn't tell them to shut up or leave her alone. She needed to sort through some things. She was exhausted. She rested her head against Jared's chest and trembled as he held her tight, reliving her morning adventure. Now the fortress of furniture looked ridiculous around the bed. After retrieving the kittens from the dresser, Charlotte climbed over the nightstand and into one of the beds. Jared leaped over with ease.

Charlotte brought the kittens as close to her as she could. "Jared, the cause of Brooklyn's and Gretchen's unfortunate deterioration today was caused by Wanda, and yet she told me things I'd have never have known on my own."

Jared checked Noon's leg. The little kitten's leg had scabbed over, so Jared removed the rubber band that was acting as a tourniquet. He massaged his neck and said with some skepticism in his voice, "What did she tell you?"

"I don't know if you'll believe me, but here goes. She told me that when we're born, we have a gel-like probe inserted into our brain, and when we turn sixteen that probe explodes, which is what sends teens into a netherworld, never to come out of their insanity. Then they remain at the asylums until it can be determined that they're not carrying any diseases. Once the teens are cleared, the probe is activated somehow, and the teens die a torturous death. Their bodies are sold to the meat-packing industry known as Blood Red Meats."

Charlotte looked at the grim look on Jared's face. He managed to say, "Do you think Wanda's telling the truth?"

Charlotte nodded and said softly, "Yes, Jared. That's how she died."

Jared hugged Charlotte close to his chest. "Why did she tell you all this?"

Charlotte shook her head. "I don't know—maybe because when she was alive, I resembled her. Or, maybe because she knows I haven't lost my mind like a lot of the others in this place. Jared, we still have most of our sanity and thoughts. I don't think she could have told a lot of these patients; her information would've fallen on deaf ears. The patients don't even have the foresight to be scared out of their minds when they are dragged to an asylum, let alone to save themselves."

The room fell silent. Nothing could undo what was just said.

They were wrapped in each other's arms and both finally fell asleep around three a.m.

19

Charlotte's Weekly Session

Jared held Charlotte throughout the night, and the next morning Charlotte woke looking haggard and sick.

She wiped the sleep from her eyes and removed the band restraining her hair. She brushed through her long locks with her fingers and twisted the band once again to make a tight ponytail. "What time is it?"

"It's not quite eight o'clock."

"I need to get to my weekly mandatory therapy session."

Jared engulfed Charlotte's tiny frame in his arms. "Charlotte, just blow off your weekly session with the doctor; you've missed so many, why worry about them now?"

"This time it's not to discuss my life and health issues, but I want to see if I can get some information out of Dr. Farrow about Dr. Oracle."

Jared lightly brushed Charlotte's cheek, with his hand. "I don't like the sound of this. It's not up to you to save the patients at Primevil—or anywhere else, for that matter."

"Jared, my mother always told me I was assertive, and I admit that I am. Look, I'm not going to get myself in trouble. I'm just going to ask a few questions. He won't even get suspicious. Dr. Farrow is basically harmless. He's a follower, not a leader."

Charlotte went into the bathroom and started brushing her teeth. Jared came up behind her. "I know I can't talk you out of your little plan, so I won't even try, but I want you to page me when you're done with the session."

Charlotte spit and rinsed. "Oh, and Jared."

"Yes, Charlotte."

"Can you feed the kittens this morning? I really have to run; it's late."

"Yeah, and don't forget to page me, the minute you're done."

She started for the door and stopped in front of him, only to give him a quick kiss on the lips. "Thanks, and after my session, I'm going to the hospital to see Brooklyn and Gretchen. Maybe we can go together."

"That'd be great. Just stay out of trouble."

Charlotte made it to Dr. Farrow's office early. She sat in the chair next to the door and thought, *If Dr. Farrow gets unnerved by my questions, I'll just fake a headache and make a quick exit.*

The minute the white coat flashed in front of her, the door slammed shut. The doctor pushed one of the chairs in the room right in front of her, making a terrible scraping sound. The white lab coat sat forcefully in the chair, and it was only then that Charlotte saw Dr. Oracle sitting in front of her.

"I see by your expression, number 3737—I think I'll call you Charlotte for this session—that you weren't expecting me. Dr. Farrow didn't think you'd show for your weekly session. Up to this point you've attended very few. I told him that I'd be taking over your medical care. He had no problem with that."

He leaned in close to Charlotte's face. "You don't mind, do you, Charlotte?"

She stammered out a few words. "I'm meeting Jared, right after this."

Dr. Oracle laughed and stretched back in his chair. "That's fine you've found a friend, but that's not what I asked you. Having a problem concentrating?"

"No, I'm focused on your every word, Dr. Oracle." She tried to sound intimidating, but it just came out pathetic.

Dr. Oracle stood up and locked the door. "Don't want any interruptions, do we?"

Charlotte sputtered, "I don't think you're supposed to lock the door." She remembered Gretchen telling Jared it was against policy to lock a patient's door. She was hoping the same policy applied to the doctor's office.

Dr. Oracle stroked his chin. "I see you've had time to read over Primevil's policies and procedures, but I don't think anybody will right the wrong in this situation and write me up for an infraction. Do you, Charlotte?"

Charlotte could feel her self-confidence dwindling as she shook her head no.

"Now, just a few harmless questions, and you can be on your way."

Dr. Oracle leaned forward and patted Charlotte's knees. "Let's begin. I'm not going to candy coat my questions, Charlotte. The first thing I want to know is, what are you up to?"

"I . . . I don't know what you mean."

"Sure you do, but unless I'm not making myself clear, let me rephrase my question." He poked the side of Charlotte's head. "What's going on in that brain of yours? I believe you and your friend Brooklyn have been in my lab, and before you deny this accusation let me show you something."

He dug in his pocket and pulled out a wadded-up piece of light-blue satin fabric. Charlotte could feel her legs start to tremble. "I can see by your reaction that you know this belonged to your friend's dress. Also, I hate to pile this on you, seeing the color has left your face, but I've heard from a reliable source that you caused the fire in the surgical suite where the lobotomies are performed."

She sat scared stiff. He continued, "I see the cat's got your tongue."

Charlotte's eyes became misty. Did he know about the kittens? Was he the one who'd hung them by their legs in Jared's room?

She didn't know why, but she blurted out something unrelated to the subject at hand. "Do you know Wanda?"

The expression on Dr. Oracle's face changed from that of someone in complete control to a man on the edge of insanity. His left eye started twitching, and his lip curled up. He started stammering. "What does she have to do with what I'm asking you?"

Charlotte found her confidence, and what little power she had returned. "The rumor at Primevil says she's come back from the dead to destroy you." Charlotte thought this might be true, but Wanda hadn't exactly told her that.

Dr. Oracle got up and paced the small office. He muttered, "Wanda S. Flesh."

Charlotte said softly. "Wanda's flesh."

Dr. Oracle heard Charlotte and spun around. He got a few inches from her face. "What do you know about Wanda? You look very much like her. Was she your relative?" He pointed to the corner of the room just above the desk and screamed. "Look—there she is!"

Charlotte looked where Dr. Oracle was pointing, and she could make out a ghoulish spirit. It was Wanda.

He started fumbling with the lock on the door. He was shaking so badly, he was having a hard time unlocking the door. He slammed the door open. "Get out of here."

Dr. Oracle flew in a rage and started tipping the chairs over. He tried to overturn the desk, but it was obviously too heavy for him. He was twirling around when his feet got tangled, and he hit the ground hard.

Charlotte was filled with fear, but she just stood by the open door and watched in horror. Dr. Oracle was lying on his back with his legs bent. His arms were flailing at his sides, as his bent legs started dragging him toward the door. Dr. Oracle's eyes rolled back in his head, and his tongue darted in and out of his mouth. Drool was running down the side of his face as he spit out a word.

"Kill."

That was more than Charlotte could stand to look at. The image before her was almost as bad as Wanda. She ran down the hall and ducked into the infirmary, out of breath.

Mrs. Bellow jumped. "You startled me." She came over to Charlotte, who was trembling, and put her arm around her. "Good heavens, what's the matter?"

Mrs. Bellow steered Charlotte to a chair. "Tell me what's going on."

Charlotte said in a shattered voice. "I'm fine. I just left my weekly session, that's all. Can you page Jared to meet me out along the beach? I need to get some fresh air."

Mrs. Bellow grabbed the back of Charlotte's chair. "Sure, I just need to sit down for a minute; the room is spinning."

"Mrs. Bellow, what's wrong?"

She steadied herself and paged Jared to come to the ocean side of Primevil. "I'm not sure. Ever since the day I received that doggone concussion, I've been having trouble with my balance. But I'm fine. At least, some color is returning to your face. Did Dr. Farrow have a tough lesson plan for you this week?"

Charlotte shrugged. "Yeah, something like that." She didn't tell Mrs. Bellow that Dr. Oracle had shown up instead, and that he had some type of mental breakdown. "I'll meet Jared on the beach, and if you want, I'll come right back to check on you."

"No, honey, you go do your thing with Jared. I'll be fine."

Charlotte opened the infirmary door and looked both ways. She ran down the hall and out the double doors of Primevil. As she stood outside inhaling the ocean breeze, she heard a wonderful soothing voice.

Jared grabbed Charlotte around the waist and gently kissed the back of her neck. "So, tell me, how was your session with Dr. Farrow?"

She turned and faced Jared, circling his neck with her arms. "Let's just say it was intense. Jared, let's go closer to the waves. I don't want anyone overhearing our conversation."

They walked down to where the water lapped at their feet and sat down. Charlotte loved digging her nine toes deep into the sand. It almost made her feel as if by doing this she could disappear. She laid her head against Jared, and waited a moment before talking.

"Jared, I think I've seen true evil today."

He didn't say anything, just looked at her. She could see and feel his burning eyes upon her. She explained to Jared what had transpired in the past hour.

He shook his head slowly from side to side. "This place gives me the creeps. Dr. Oracle is becoming unhinged." He picked up Charlotte's small hands in his. "We need to escape, soon."

She put her finger to his lips. "No, Jared. Not without Brooklyn, and Gretchen. Besides, what do you plan on doing—scaling the rock wall?" She pointed to the ocean. "Or swimming to freedom, only to be recaptured by the Collectors and dragged to Redwine Hill all over again?"

"That was plan B. The first option was to buy our way out. I've several hundred dollars stashed away, and that would be plenty to buy the silence of a few Collectors."

"Did your plan include Brooklyn and Gretchen?"

He looked out toward the vast ocean. "No. Just us."

"What would we do once we were free of Primevil? You know just as I do that once you've been registered insane, you can't erase that blighted bit of knowledge. We're marked for life."

"Yes, I know, Charlotte, but I've cousins—I believe they're still living in New York someplace. We could find them. They managed to barely escape the sixteenth-birthday curse that started ten years ago. They are twins who are twenty-seven years old now. Timothy and Terry—they'd hide us."

Charlotte's shoulders sank. "Not without Brooklyn and Gretchen. Let's go see how they're doing today."

Jared stood and helped Charlotte to her feet.

As the ocean wind ripped at their clothes, they walked in silence. Charlotte thought it would be nice to be free of this torturous place, but not without her friends.

20

The Mental Ward

Charlotte and Jared went to visit Gretchen. She was on the medical ward, whereas Brooklyn was on the locked mental ward.

As they walked into Gretchen's room, she was sitting up. Her hair was matted down with dried blood, and she had an IV infusing with a smaller bag of red blood cells dripping into the tubing. Charlotte sighed when she saw her friend would be okay. "Hey, Gretchen, you're doing better than I thought. "

Gretchen pointed to the red blood cells. "I guess I lost a bit of blood." She rubbed the back of her head and moaned. "Got nine stitches too."

Gretchen smiled at Jared. "I'll be out of here tomorrow, and then back to work."

Jared gave Gretchen a small fist jab to the shoulder. "Can't keep you down, huh, Gretchen? Are you sure it's okay to return to work so soon?"

"Yep, the doc gave me the all clear. Not that I'll be wrestling with any unruly patients or anything. I'll leave that up to you, Jared."

Charlotte sat on the bed as her stomach growled.

"Sounds like you need to head for the lunchroom."

"Yeah, I didn't have any breakfast this morning." Charlotte rubbed her stomach, as if she could calm her hunger pangs. "Gretchen, since you're going to work tomorrow, can I tag along to see how things are done when a patient comes to Primevil?"

"Yeah, I'd like some company." Gretchen then looked down and started rolling the sheets between her fingers. "Charlotte, can I ask you something about what happened yesterday?"

Charlotte got an uneasy feeling, but forced a small smile on her face. "Ask away."

"Who were you talking to? The person or thing on the bed next to you."

Jared sat next to Charlotte on the bed as she said, "Uh, that was, uh, Wanda."

Charlotte braced herself for the fallout. Gretchen shook her shoulders and made a disgusting face. "Don't worry, Charlotte. I'd seen her before, under my bed, that night I told you about. I was just surprised to see her sitting on your bed. I'm usually not that squeamish."

"Gretchen, you don't have to explain. Wanda is unnerving, no matter how many times you see her."

"Where's Brooklyn—she too busy to come visit me?"

Charlotte scratched her forehead and then looked at Jared. "Go ahead and tell her," Jared said.

Gretchen was trying to comb the tangles out of her matted hair with her fingers. "Tell me what? Did Brooklyn faint, also, when she saw the grotesque Wanda?"

"No. You were the lucky one, with just a head injury. Brooklyn's mind went into a dark place."

She picked a blob of dried blood out of her hair and flicked it on the floor. Charlotte grimaced as Gretchen said, "I don't understand."

Jared said softly, "Brooklyn went insane."

Gretchen yelled, "What!"

Charlotte got right in Gretchen's face. "Yeah, she went crazy, loco; she's a real nut ball."

"Okay, I get the point. She's like the other patients now. What can we do to help?"

Jared said, "The only things she's got going for her are her friends and time."

Charlotte tried to sound comforting. "We're going to go visit her now and see if we can bring her mental state out of wherever it is. Do you want to come?"

Gretchen swung her legs over the bed, and at the same time she quickly grabbed the back of her head. "Let me stabilize myself first. Just give me a minute."

Jared helped Gretchen stand while Charlotte quickly looked in the bathroom. "Do you want a wheelchair?"

"No, wheelchairs are for babies. They brought me into this room in one, but I'll have you know I protested the entire way."

Jared smiled at Gretchen. "Good for you."

Charlotte interlocked her arm with Gretchen's. "Let's go see if Brooklyn's made any improvement since yesterday."

Gretchen let out a small moan, and Charlotte looked at the sutures in the back of her head. "Your wound is oozing a bit between the sutures. Do you want to sit back down?"

Gretchen poked Charlotte's arm. "What do you take me for? A sniveler? I want to see Brooklyn, just like you two do. Now, come on. I bet I can make her laugh or at least come out of her stupor to punch me."

Charlotte gave a weak grin. "We can always hope."

They slowly walked toward the psych ward. The twelve asylums of Redwine Hill were in a circle, and in the middle was the one hospital the dozen asylums shared. Gretchen was on the medical floor, and there was also a surgical floor, a terminally ill floor, and a psych floor. The psych floor held the truly crazed patients. They used the elevator to get to the top floor of the hospital.

Charlotte was holding Gretchen's arm tightly. "Hey, Charlotte, loosen your grip. Seeing your friend can't be any worse than a visit from Wanda—and since we're on the subject, can't you tell your flesh-eating friend to ease up?"

Jared was now holding up the bulk of Gretchen's weight, and she turned and smiled her "rat teeth" smile at him. "Thank God you have muscles, Jared."

Charlotte could tell by the way Jared furrowed his forehead that he was stressed. "Yeah, this is what I've always had in mind when I was getting in shape."

Charlotte winked at Jared. "Anyway, Gretchen, I don't think Wanda meant to scare anybody, but since we don't know what happened in that room, and Brooklyn's not talking, we may never find out."

Jared adjusted Gretchen's leaning body. "Let's just see how she's doing before we count her out."

Gretchen leaned even further into Jared. "Count her out from what?"

The elevator doors opened, and they were all too horrified to speak. They shuffled out of the elevator in a group, sticking together, afraid to let go of each other for fear of becoming one of the lunatics in the hallway.

Charlotte shivered. "I think I saw a movie like this once, when I was around thirteen. I defied my mother when she told me not to watch this zombie movie. She said I'd be scared for weeks, but I didn't listen to her, and guess what? I couldn't sleep in my room. I slept down in the living room on the couch with the lights and television on. I didn't care even when the late show was over and the TV was filled with white snow. I couldn't be alone."

Gretchen squeezed Jared's arm. "Yeah, kind of like the night I saw Wanda under my bed."

Charlotte gave a loud sigh. "You know, if you can get past Wanda's looks, she's an all right disembodied spirit."

Jared shook his head. "Yeah, she sounds like a real genial ghost."

There, standing in the hallway, was every imaginable form a person could be twisted in. The garish looks on the patients' faces brought their appearance to monstrous, demonic states.

Charlotte squeaked out, "I didn't even know a person could contort their body like that." The majority were scantily clad, in not much more than thin stained pajamas. There was dried food on their clothing, face, hair, and bodies.

Gretchen snorted. "So much for hygiene. I guess that's the first thing to go. I hope Brooklyn doesn't look like this. I want to remember her like she was."

Charlotte pinched Gretchen. "Stop talking as if she's dead."

Gretchen mumbled, "She may as well be, if she's on this floor."

Jared looked up at a nurse who was coming down the hall. "Finally, something I recognize. A human being."

The nurse smiled as she stood in front of the three. "Visitors, on this floor? What a nice surprise, or did you end up here by mistake?"

Jared let go of Gretchen, who now heavily relied on Charlotte to hold her up. Jared shook the nurse's hand. "We've come to see 3899."

"Oh, yes, she's our newest patient." She pointed down the hallway. "She's way at the end of this hall. Her room is on the left."

The nurse got close and whispered, "She's not gotten any better since yesterday, so I fear her psychosis may be permanent."

Gretchen said in a snide voice, "We'll be the judge of that. You don't even know her."

Jared grabbed Gretchen's arm. "Nurse, thank you for your time."

As they slowly walked away, Charlotte nudged Gretchen. "I think the nurse is still looking at us."

Jared looked at Charlotte. "Just keep putting one foot in front of the other. Gretchen, you need to have a little decorum when it comes to dealing with the personnel at Primevil."

Gretchen spit out, "What does that mean, Jared?"

Charlotte patted Gretchen's arm. "It just means have a little tact, some manners. Haven't you heard the saying 'you can get more flies by using honey instead of vinegar'?"

"No, and that's a stupid saying. I'm not trying to catch flies, and who would anyway?"

They were standing in front of Brooklyn's door. The entire hallway smelled of urine and other things. Some patients rambled up to them, jerking and slapping their hands together. Jared gave a half smile. "If you take away their physical problems, they're just like us."

Gretchen snapped at him. "Speak for yourself."

Charlotte let go of Gretchen as she made her way toward the bed. "Brooklyn, it's me, Charlotte." The room was dark, and Charlotte could see Brooklyn was in some kind of four-point restraint with every extremity tied down. This frightened Charlotte, but she wouldn't let the others see how scared she was.

She leaned over the bed. "Brooklyn, we've come for a visit."

Brooklyn raised her head off the pillow and let out a blood-curdling scream. Charlotte grabbed at her chest and stumbled backward.

Tears welled up in her eyes, and Jared and Gretchen froze. A familiar voice came down the hall. It was Mrs. Bellow, and she was greeting the patients. "Good morning. I see you've combed your hair today. What a lovely day to be up and about." None of the patients responded back, but it was so good to hear Mrs. Bellow's voice. "Yes, that's a brilliant color for you. I believe the gray brings out your eyes." There were some guttural sounds coming from the patients, but nothing a person would understand.

The entire room was bathed in warmth from the voice coming from the hallway. Mrs. Bellow flicked on the light. "Brooklyn, we can't have you drowning in a sea of darkness. Oh, good morning, Charlotte, Jared, Gretchen. How's the patient doing?"

Charlotte patted her own chest with her hand. "See for yourself, Mrs. Bellow. Tell us what you think of Brooklyn's condition."

Mrs. Bellow leaned over Brooklyn, who once again gave that horrific scream. Mrs. Bellow didn't flinch.

Charlotte was impressed. "That didn't scare you to death."

Gretchen rubbed her belly. "It gave me a stomachache."

Mrs. Bellow turned and gently spoke. "What did you expect? At least she is responding to my presence. If she just lay there and did nothing, I would say she didn't have much of a chance for recovery, but since she knows I'm here, that tells me she's getting some information through to her brain. Be careful what you say in front of her. She can hear and see; it just doesn't seem like it."

Mrs. Bellow put her arm around Charlotte. "Think of it this way. So she screams. She saw something, God knows what, and is just now reacting to it. She's making progress. You know, it's funny—some of my best nurses were scared when they first started working here. They didn't understand how gory a person could look, especially when eating."

Charlotte looked at Jared. "No, I understand that, perfectly."

"Well, I never let a new nurse to Redwine Hill take on—how should I put this?—the nursing duties that are not for the faint of heart, should I say. Let them get familiar with the smells, noises, and unusual surroundings before having them deal with the patients. I learned that the hard way. Lost a lot of nurses at the beginning, throwing them into the mix too soon."

Mrs. Bellow leaned over the bed as Brooklyn let out several more screams. Mrs. Bellow just smiled and pulled at her ears. "You see, she sees me. It's hard on my ears though."

All four watched as Brooklyn licked her lips. Mrs. Bellow went and got the plastic water glass at the bedside table. "She'll tell you what she wants; you just need to watch and recognize the signs." She held Brooklyn's head up and put the glass to her lips. Brooklyn drank half a glass before it started dribbling down the sides of her face. Mrs. Bellow took a hankie out of her nursing uniform pocket and gently wiped Brooklyn's face. "See, Charlotte, don't be scared of her. She was just thirsty and didn't know how to tell you."

She brushed back Brooklyn's hair, and Mrs. Bellow's eyes became moist. "Brooklyn, you can call me anything you want. 'Mrs. B.' is just fine with me."

She slowly walked toward the door and then turned. "I'm going to get something to eat before the cafeteria closes. Should I tell the servers to wait for you three?"

Charlotte moaned. "I don't think I can eat anything."

Gretchen nodded. "Me either."

But Jared said without hesitation, "I'm starved; tell them I'll be down in just a few minutes."

Charlotte didn't know if she was more impressed with Mrs. Bellow and her compassion or Jared for being able to eat after what they just saw. Jared could eat anywhere or anything. She was definitely moved by Mrs. Bellow though.

Charlotte watched as Mrs. Bellow left the room and heard her talk to the patients in the hallway. She slowly walked over to Brooklyn. "Are you hungry, Brooklyn?" There was no answer, but no screaming either.

Charlotte sat on the bed next to Brooklyn. "I think I'm going to sit and talk with Brooklyn for a while."

Gretchen was leaning heavily against Jared. "Jared, can you take me back to my room? This head wound is beginning to sap my strength."

Charlotte looked over at them. "Gretchen, I think you're using your head wound to your full advantage. Jared, if I were you, I'd find the nearest wheelchair and plop Gretchen's sorry butt in it."

Charlotte looked back at Brooklyn, and she thought she saw a twitch of a half-smile cross her lips.

Gretchen yelled out, "Charlotte, you're just jealous that Jared is paying so much attention to me."

"Yeah, he has to; you're hanging all over him."

Jared propped Gretchen up. "Let's go find a wheelchair. I need to get to the cafeteria before they close down the line."

Charlotte didn't take her eyes off her friend. "I know you can hear me, Brooklyn. I swear I saw you smile."

Charlotte sat holding her friend's hand and doing her best, trying to feed her lunch. She was worn out. Two cadets came to get Brooklyn for a scan of her brain. Charlotte cried out, "Stop, please. You're using too much force to remove her restraints. I'll do it. Just be patient." As Charlotte looked at the leather straps, she could see the abrasions underneath. She held on to her friend's hand, leaned down, and whispered into Brooklyn's ear. "Brooklyn, I'll talk with the nurse about a doctor's order to get these restraints removed, but you need to do me a favor and not go ballistic once they're taken off."

She could feel Brooklyn squeeze her hand. Charlotte quickly but gently removed all four restraints, and watched as her friend was being wheeled out of the room on a gurney.

She tucked and straightened the sheets on the bed and went to find a nurse to ask about the restraints. As she walked the hallways, she didn't feel as threatened as she had when she came early that day. She found a nurse and explained how she thought Brooklyn was ready for the restraints to come off. The nurse was hesitant at first, but did agree to remove them once Brooklyn got back from her scan.

The nurse leaned against a patient's door. "We can certainly try to leave them off, but if your friend should act up or become enraged in any way, then the restraints will have to go back on."

"I understand." She walked down the hall feeling a little proud of herself for changing the way she felt about the severely mentally disturbed patients. She took advantage of this time, walking toward the elevator to compliment some of the patients. "What a lovely color you have on. Did you have a good night's rest? You remind me of someone I know." She didn't expect them to reply, but just talking to them made them more into people and not some deformity that she tried to avoid.

She waited at the elevator as one of the cadets saw her and came running toward her. "The doors are locked from this side, but you can come up to this floor without a key."

Charlotte smiled at the man, and she looked down the hallway. The patients were still moving about in the same way, but it was different. She saw their disabilities, but those were separate from who they were. She went to go find Jared.

Charlotte realized she was in a somewhat good mood. This had been an eye-opening day. Sure, Brooklyn was still in a coma of some kind, but it was promising to have her stop screaming, and for her restraints to come off.

Redwine hill

21

Registrar

The next morning, Charlotte was up early and went to visit Brooklyn, before going to see Gretchen. "Brooklyn, I can only stay a few minutes. I'm going with Gretchen today to register the incoming patients, but I'll come back later today." She bent down and kissed her friend on the forehead. Examining Brooklyn's wrists and ankles, Charlotte was pleased to see that the shackles were no longer in place.

She made it to Gretchen's room just as she was getting out of bed. She was slumped over, holding her head. Gretchen turned her head. "Charlotte, I think I did too much yesterday. I don't know my limitations. I'll get stronger, but I'm really weak right now. Could you get me a wheelchair?"

Charlotte was going to say something about her being a baby but decided against it. "Sure. I haven't eaten yet; are you hungry?"

There was a wheelchair just inside the en-suite bathroom. "I see they left your wheelchair." She wheeled it to Gretchen, who said, "I'm famished. After yesterday's show I didn't eat anything the rest of the day. What about you?"

She helped her friend into the rolling chair. "Actually, I had a nice long visit with Brooklyn yesterday, and I just saw her for a brief moment this morning. Her restraints have been removed. I think she's making some progress, and I don't think the patients on the locked ward are all that bad."

Gretchen moaned as she plopped down in the seat. "Okay, Charlotte, but let's not talk about them during mealtime. My stomach's still a bit queasy."

Charlotte rolled the wheelchair out of the hospital room and into the elevator. "Didn't they feed you anything this morning?"

"Yeah, they tried to serve me a tray with greenish oatmeal and some warm orange juice. I told them to pick it up. I just want a warm bun or toast, something mild in taste and appearance. No surprise colors."

They went through the line and got mostly bread products. Gretchen held up a roll. "Seems harmless. I think I can keep this down."

Gretchen held on to the tray while Charlotte found them a table.

Charlotte saw Jared coming with an over stacked plate. "Gretchen, do you think all guys have a cast-iron stomach or just Jared?"

She wiggled in the wheelchair. "Before I was dragged here, I did have a few male friends. Not a boyfriend, just friends." Charlotte got a pang of sorrow for calling Gretchen "Rat Teeth." Gretchen continued. "I dared a guy to eat a dead roach once and he did, without a grimace or anything. So I upped the dare. A snake skin, dried-out old pizza, and the real challenge—a suspicious looking moldy sandwich out of the garbage. He ate everything like he was sitting down at a buffet, all you can eat. He did get sick and have to be hospitalized, though. The sandwich had tainted meat, and he got very sick, but he had no problem eating it."

Jared put his tray down on the table, and Charlotte and Gretchen just looked at each other and laughed. Charlotte pointed to the tray. "Jared, did someone dare you to eat all that?"

He picked something off his plate and threw it in his mouth. "No, why?"

Charlotte waved her hand in the air. "Nothing, just sit and eat. I'm going with Gretchen after breakfast to log in patients."

"Are you doing this for entertainment or to find something out about the patients?"

Charlotte ate her last bite of toast. "Mainly to find something out, but hey, it could be entertaining."

Gretchen spread some butter over her second semi-warm roll. "You're going to be disappointed if you're going for any reason other than finding something out about Primevil. Nothing exciting happens down in holding. The patients come in, they're sedated and examined, and the rest is history. You might as well go and sit with Brooklyn and watch the flies circle around her mouth, betting on which fly will land first."

Charlotte wrinkled her nose. "Now you're just being gross."

Jared shook his head. "Gretchen, that was even crude by a guy's standards."

Charlotte stood and grabbed hold of Gretchen's wheelchair. "I'm ready."

Gretchen popped the rest of her roll into her mouth as Jared gently snatched Charlotte's hand away from the chair. His lips brushed against Charlotte's fingers. "Try to stay out of trouble."

Charlotte blushed and Gretchen said, "Yeah, she'll see you later. Pull it together, Jared. You're making a fool of yourself." She pointed around the cafeteria. "See—all these people are looking at you."

Charlotte looked around the room. She didn't want to make a spectacle of herself. Not a single person was staring at them. "Gretchen, you know if you tried hard to be pleasant, maybe you could get yourself a boyfriend."

"Yeah, do you have anybody in mind?"

Jared swallowed a bite of food. "Yeah, I think we can find you someone who walks upright and doesn't drag their knuckles on the floor."

Charlotte looked at Jared. "Who?"

"His name is Marty Keenley, and I think he'd be perfect for you."

Charlotte looked annoyed. "I was thinking he was more Brooklyn's type."

Jared chuckled. "Does it really matter? Street rat versus rat teeth—he's probably too old for them anyway. I think he's in his early- to mid-twenties."

Gretchen licked the butter from her fingers. "Sounds like a good catch."

Charlotte spun Gretchen's wheelchair around. "Let's go. I thought you'd go after another guard, like yourself."

"Since we're in here for the rest of our natural born lives, what difference does it make? Guard, patient, cadet—they're all the same. I think the percentage is about the same, males verses females."

Charlotte cut Gretchen off. "See you later, Jared."

He held his fork up and waved to them. "Yeah, I'll catch up with you later."

As they made their way to the holding area, Charlotte almost wished she were deaf. Gretchen continued on with her possibilities of a boyfriend. "He has to be taller than me, and clean shaven, not to mention have some seniority at Primevil. I guess he couldn't be a patient, because then we couldn't dance together at those ridiculous social events. I like blue eyes because they are mysterious and sexy, but brown eyes are strong and powerful. I don't care for dirt under the nails either, and you can tell a lot about a guy if he had a pet when he was on the outside. Men who like animals have a softer side, and I want a guy who respected his mother." Gretchen paused. "Does Marty Keenley have those qualities?"

Charlotte shook her head. "I can't say for sure. I can say he's taller than me, and clean shaven, but I can't even tell you the color of his eyes let alone any of that other stuff you were talking about."

They were outside the holding area. "Could you find out for me?"

"Yeah, I guess."

Gretchen punched in the code to the door, and Charlotte rolled Gretchen through the opening. Gretchen pointed to the table in front of them. "See, we already have a patient waiting for us. Looks like the nurse already jabbed her with a sedative." It was a fairly large room with eight tables but only one occupied.

Gretchen positioned her chair next to the exam table. "No coed stuff in the holding rooms. The female guards only exam the women, and male guards have another holding area for the guys." Gretchen poked Charlotte, who was standing next to her looking down at the girl on the table. "Too bad, I would've had a boyfriend a lot sooner if I'd been in the other holding area."

Gretchen snorted as she laughed, and Charlotte said, "Don't go down that road again about your ideal man; just show me what goes on in here."

Gretchen shrugged. "Okay, since you're standing and I'm not, start on the head first. We do a head-to-toe assessment. Check her hair for lice or nits. Pull open her eyelids; not many have anything wrong with their eyes. Some might have glasses, or had broken their glasses in the struggle. Some have contacts but no cataracts or deformities of the eyes."

Gretchen pointed to a small instrument attached to the wall. "Take that thing and twist the top and look in her ears, while I check her for lice."

Charlotte pulled the handheld instrument from the bracket. "What am I looking for in her ear?"

"Any malformations, bugs, dirt—anything that doesn't look like it belongs there. Also, you can tell if they have an infected eardrum by how taut the outer covering of the eardrum is."

Charlotte looked at Gretchen as she sat in her wheelchair, her hands gingerly going through the girl's hair looking for small bugs and eggs. "I didn't know you could tell so much by just looking at a body. Is this one of Jared's jobs, checking the male patients?"

"No, Jared doesn't register patients. He can look at things out on the floor, but they're nurses for that. Some days I can see up to forty patients, and the nurses are best used in other capacities, rather than checking a patient in at Primevil."

Charlotte was having a hard time getting the scope to work. She pounded it against the palm of her hand.

"Easy, Charlotte, you break it, you pay for it. Just turn the top part. Sometimes the connection isn't good, and the light will go out, but I promise it will work. If not, I blame it on the previous guard, and they have to pay for it."

"What's the light for anyway?"

Gretchen laughed. "Try to look in her ear without a light attached to that little instrument."

Charlotte tried to look in the girl's ear. "I can't see a thing. It's a very tiny tunnel, and completely dark inside."

"Okay, now twist the light and look."

Charlotte twisted the light on and bent down to look once again. "Oh, there's a bunch of golden-yellow stuff, but that's all."

"Don't worry, Charlotte; her earwax isn't contagious."

The red warning light went on. "We need to speed things up. Daytime is the busiest time in the holding area, and we don't want to get behind. If I have to ask for help, I'll be demoted."

"What does that flashing light mean?"

Gretchen continued her assessment of the girl in front of her, leaning against the table with her blood-streaked hair hanging down. "We're getting company."

A nurse burst through the door at the end of the room carrying a syringe. She opened the back door. "Hurry up—you caught me at a bad time."

Charlotte heard a man's voice on the other side of the door. "Did I interrupt your lunch hour?"

The nurse pulled something out of her pocket and snapped back, "Look, if you want your fee, shut your trap." She counted some money into a large tanned hand. "Now bring her in and put her on a table."

The Collector came through the door, dragging an uncooperative girl into the room. The nurse didn't bother plunging the syringe into a meaty part of the girl's body. She just slammed it into the lower arm. The nurse saw Charlotte looking at her. "Can't hit a moving target. I just plunge and hope I don't hit the Collector or myself."

The girl was emaciated and looked like she had been dragged through mud. She was covered from head to toe in filth and foul matter. The nurse pointed at Charlotte. "You're going to have to run this one under the shower first." Charlotte shivered as she thought about the day she had been brought to Primevil, kicking and screaming.

Gretchen gave an exaggerated sigh. "Charlotte, I'm almost done on this girl. If you could just roll that exam table into the shower; you don't have to stay in the stall, just push the green button and the water will spray down on her, clothes and all."

Charlotte rolled the gurney into the shower and quickly pushed the button. A spray of water came down, and Charlotte noticed the girl was jerking. She quickly ran into the room and turned the girl on her side. She figured she was going to drown her before her examination.

As Charlotte turned the shower off, the light went off again. The nurse came through with a handful of money and syringe in the other hand. Charlotte wheeled the extremely thin girl back in among the row of tables. Gretchen wheeled her way over to the table and started her exam. Charlotte saw that the nurse and Collector were having trouble. They were trying to drag two girls into the holding area.

The nurse yelled, "Don't just stand there—we need help!"

Charlotte went over and put her body on the one squirming around on the floor. "Don't fight them. Things will go a lot easier for you if you don't struggle. Trust me, I know. I'm a patient." She didn't know if the girl understood anything she was saying. She tried to remember back to that gory evening, with the Collector and his sidekicks dragging her to Primevil. Charlotte shuddered as the nurse plunged the needle deep into the girl's leg. It wasn't but a minute or two before the girl went limp.

The nurse wiped her brow and ran to get another syringe for the other girl. She yelled over her shoulder, "Where are your two hoodlum helpers?"

Charlotte looked up, and there slouched in front of her was the Collector who had brought her to Primevil. He leaned over, with enormous hands resting on his thighs, trying to catch his breath. "I guess they didn't want to make a couple of bucks. They said they had to meet with Dr. Oracle."

The nurse slipped out of the room and came back with another syringe. The Collector was stooped over picking up the cash from his own pocket, which had gone airborne in the struggle with the patients.

She jabbed the needle into the girl's arm and brushed her hair back off her forehead. "Some days I get a real workout." The nurse was sweating, and the girl Charlotte was sitting on wasn't moving. "Good lord, dear. Have you killed her?"

The Collector started yelling. "I still get paid for that one. She was alive when I brought her in."

Charlotte could feel the girl breathing; maybe she had taken her advice and stopped struggling. The nurse pushed Charlotte off. "You're in a heap load of trouble if this girl is dead."

Gretchen wheeled over. "She's not dead. I bet she's faking." Gretchen leaned over and pinched the girl hard. She let out a scream. "See—what'd I tell you?"

The Collector put his hand out. "Pay up."

The nurse pointed at Charlotte and the Collector. "Just put them on the table, and shut your trap. I'll give you ninety dollars for the both, since the one girl scared me half to death. I'd have had to fill out a ton of paperwork, if she died." She scowled at the Collector. "Something you know very little about—following rules."

He snatched the cash from the nurse's hand. "I have rules to follow—they just happen to be the ones I make."

The Collector and Charlotte carried the girls, straining to put them each on a table. His breath was just as bad this time around. She wondered if he recognized her, but from the way he was acting, the answer was no. He hiked up his pants and slammed the door behind him. Gretchen looked over at the door. "I hate that Collector; he's filthy, and he always smells funny."

Charlotte mumbled, "Yeah, rum and spoiled cheese."

"What?"

"Nothing."

The Collectors kept bringing in teenage girls. Charlotte hadn't found anything out, and Gretchen and she were exhausted. "You do this every day, Gretchen?"

"Yeah, but you get used to the pace after a while. When are you going back to work for Mrs. Bellow?"

"In a few days. I want to spend time with Brooklyn. My job isn't like yours. No rush."

There were only two girls that had lice, out of the twenty that had been dragged to the holding room. It was toward the end of the day, and she and Gretchen were tired. Gretchen gave a heavy sigh. "Just great—this girl has head lice. Charlotte, check the one you're looking at. Since these two came in together, I bet they both have lice."

Charlotte grimaced. "Yeah, she's got them too."

Gretchen pointed to a cabinet. "There are only two razors in this entire women's holding area, and one pair isn't worth the trouble. See the green one? You go ahead and use it first. I'll do the rest of the exam and come back to that."

"You want me to shave her head?"

Gretchen half-snorted a laugh. "Why do you think—these girls are going to go into modeling or something?"

Charlotte looked at her reflection in a mirror, which was mounted on the wall across the room. She pulled her ponytail around her shoulder and looked at the thick amber-colored hair. "No, but I'm just glad I didn't have head lice."

Gretchen looked up. "It's just hair; it'll grow back. And besides, if you don't watch where you're flinging your ponytail, you might end up with a few critters crawling up that golden mane of yours."

Charlotte immediately tucked her long, thick hair into her shirt. Gretchen laughed. "Now you look like some kind of hunchback."

Charlotte ignored Gretchen and began shaving the girl's head. "I'm not very good at shaving someone's head, but I did have to take a razor to my dog Jamie's fur, when she was sprayed by a skunk. I guess it's the same."

Gretchen was done with the exam of the girl on her table and wheeled to the cubbies. There were two small stacks of clothes. She tossed one of the stacks to Charlotte, which hit her arm, and the razor took a small gouge out of the girl's head. "Gretchen, now look what you've made me do."

Charlotte took her shirt and put it to the girl's scalp. Gretchen sneered at Charlotte. "I'm tired, and I need to lie down. Are you done with that razor yet?"

"Yeah, a couple more swipes with this razor, and she's free of bugs." Charlotte dabbed at the cut. They had undressed the patients as they examined them, and then clothed them in what the nurse had put in the cubbies.

As Charlotte dabbed at the small wound she had inflicted, she noticed a brown raised area the size of a pencil eraser toward the back of the girl's head. She thought back to what Wanda had told her about the probe that was inserted when babies were born. Like blood work, eye drops, or any other procedures that were mandatory on the maternity ward, the gel-like probe must now be part of hospitals' protocol. "Gretchen, come look at this."

"Charlotte, what is it?"

"Remember when you saw Wanda sitting on my bed and you fainted?"

Gretchen rolled her chair over. "Yeah, but I wasn't prepared for what I saw."

Charlotte waved her hand in the air. "That's old news. Wanda told me about a probe that's put into babies when they're born. Then when a teen turns sixteen, that probe ignites a blast in the brain, sending them into a downward spiral, never to recover."

Gretchen stood and leaned against the table. She slowly walked over to the girl she was examining and started shaving her head. "What's the purpose of that?"

"I don't know exactly, but it's something about using the teens to supply the meat industry."

"Wait! What did you say?"

"Yeah, you heard me right. The dead teens supply Blood Red Meats with a supply of meat products."

Gretchen was exhausted, and her breathing was labored. "Charlotte, you're vulgar. Is this why you wanted to come with me today? To find something incriminating?"

"Yep, I got a lot of information from Wanda, and I just wanted to see if I could find something on the incoming bodies. I was beginning to give up, but look—I found something."

Charlotte went over to the girl Gretchen had just finished on. She turned the girl's head and ran her fingers softly around the girl's shaved scalp. It took a while. She yelled out, "Look, Gretchen, here it is. It's not as dark in color, but it's about the same size." Gretchen came over and looked; she rubbed her finger on the small pea-sized shape. Charlotte pulled her rubber band off and started dragging her fingers through her own thick hair.

Gretchen stared, running her fingers through her blood-streaked hair. "Charlotte, you're not going to find anything on your head; your hair is too thick."

Charlotte yelled, "Get the cadet in here to transport these two, and get in your wheelchair."

"Where are we going?"

"We need to get Brooklyn and bring her out of her stupor. She'll end up on someone's plate as a steak or hamburger."

Gretchen plopped her body into the chair and yelled, "Hey, Cadet, get in here and do your job."

A sheepish young boy walked in. "I-I didn't know you were finished."

Charlotte looked at the preteen. "Don't worry. Miss Gretchen is just in a bad mood today."

He went over to the gurney and started wheeling it toward the exit.

Gretchen yelled, "Charlotte, speed it up. Not that I care that much about Brooklyn, I just wouldn't want her ending up as the main course on someone's kitchen table."

Charlotte pushed the wheelchair though the halls, running at times. As Charlotte wheeled Gretchen into the elevator, Gretchen's leg caught on the door. "Hey, Charlotte, slow down. I'd like to keep both my lower limbs, if you don't mind."

From the hallway came a familiar voice. "Charlotte, wait up." Jared was running toward them. He ran over and slipped into the elevator. "What's the hurry?"

Charlotte kept her composure. "Jared, you remember what I told you Wanda had said?"

"Yeah, but I don't—"

Before he could finish, Gretchen interrupted. "We had to shave a few heads in holding today, and found where the probe had been inserted, when they were born."

Charlotte looked at Jared. "I know Wanda's gross, but she tells the truth."

Jared ran his hand through his hair. Gretchen smirked, "Jared, you're probably not going to be able to feel your own protrusion on your scalp."

Jared looked at his arm. "I'm not trying to find any protrusion. I was just running my hand through my hair." Jared shook his head. "Anyway, what do you think is happening to Brooklyn?"

Charlotte said in a pleading voice. "Jared, I don't know. I just have this sickening feeling that Brooklyn is dispensable, and her time is up. Besides, did you see any young people on the locked ward?"

"Which means what?"

"That the patients up there are only for show, and that anyone young that gets admitted soon meets with death and gets transported to Blood Red Meats."

Jared blew out a slow breath. "I'd like to say you're crazy . . ." He looked away. "Sorry, I didn't mean to say crazy."

Gretchen scolded. "Jared, you're not going to hurt Charlotte's feelings. Just state what you have to say."

The elevator doors opened, and Charlotte expertly maneuvered the wheelchair through the patients in the hallway. Jared half-ran beside her. "I think you may be right about all this meat stuff."

As they were entering Brooklyn's room, a nurse yelled down the hallway. "If you're looking for your friend 3899, a cadet came and took her within the past thirty minutes."

Charlotte saw the room; someone had trashed it. The nurse stood beside the three. Charlotte said in a strangled voice, "Did Brooklyn put up a fight when she was taken?"

"No, this isn't from an altercation but from your friend going mad."

Charlotte tilted her head to the side. "What are you talking about?"

"The shackles were no longer on the patient's extremities, and I heard screaming and yelling. When I entered her room, she was thrashing around. All this damage—the mattress on the floor, side table smashed and broken, and her sheets torn to pieces—that was all done by 3899."

Jared cursed. "Where the hell have they taken her?"

The nurse said with little concern in her voice, "I guess for a lobotomy?"

Gretchen backed her wheelchair up and ran over the nurse's foot. "Thanks for nothing, Nurse."

Jared grabbed the chair, and Charlotte ran ahead trying to clear the way of patients. "Sorry, we're in a rush. Can you please clear the hallway?"

The patients didn't look up or try to get out of the way. Jared turned toward the nurse. "Please, come and unlock the elevator. We're in a hurry."

"I don't understand. She's just having a lobotomy for her outbursts."

Gretchen yelled, "Nurse, just get the doors unlocked."

The nurse was unnerved. She shook when she tried to put the key in the lock. "Dozens of lobotomies are preformed every day."

The elevator doors opened and they got in. Charlotte pushed the first-floor button many times.

Charlotte hissed. "I bet Dr. Oracle has something to do with this." If she wasn't so furious she would have dropped to her knees and cried. She raised her arm in the air and shook her fist. "Wanda, you better show yourself right now." She stomped her feet and screamed, "You need to help us."

Gretchen touched the back of her head. "Do we really need that ghoulish freak to help us?"

Charlotte rubbed her face. "I don't know, but it wouldn't hurt. Gretchen, just steel yourself for Wanda's appearance. Brooklyn's welfare is more important right now."

Thousands of ideas ran through Charlotte's head as the elevator doors opened and they ran down the hallway to the lobotomy suites. *What if we're too late? What if Brooklyn isn't getting a lobotomy? What if Dr. Oracle killed her and now she's in the morgue?* She sniveled and wiped her sleeve across her eyes.

Redwine hill

22

Wanda's Redemption

As they ran down the hall, Wanda showed herself. The handful of patients roaming the hallway went screaming and running for their rooms. Charlotte heard doors slamming, and Wanda growled out, "Brooklyn's not in the lobotomy suite. Dr. Oracle had her brought to his lab." Some fleshy items from Wanda's body fell to the floor and she said, "I'm on my way there, now. I'll meet up with you."

Charlotte saw a slimy mess that Wanda left behind. Gretchen waved her arms in the air. "You two go. Get out of here. I'm just slowing you down in this wheelchair. Go! Go!"

Jared took Charlotte's hand. "Come on, Charlotte. Brooklyn could be dead already."

They ran down the flight of stairs, and Jared pounded on the door outside. Charlotte yelled, "Jared, do something! No one's coming to the door."

Jared took his gun out. "Charlotte, get back." He gently but forcefully pushed Charlotte behind him and fired at the glass. Shards of glass went everywhere, and Jared put his hand through the open door and unlocked it. He grabbed Charlotte's hand and they went racing to find Brooklyn.

Dr. Oracle stood in shock. "Get out of here! What do you think you're doing?" He pointed to Charlotte. "I want you out of here. Now!"

Charlotte noticed Wanda was looming over something in the corner. Charlotte ran over, and Dr. Oracle yelled, "I told you to get out of here! I'll call the guards."

Jared sneered at Dr. Oracle. "I'm already here."

Dr. Oracle let out a primal scream and tore for the oversized door in the lab. He clawed at the iron handle trying to open the door. "God, there's Wanda. She's come to desecrate me."

Charlotte yelled, "Jared, I think Brooklyn's dead."

Jared hurried over to Charlotte. As they heard the sounds of the wooden door straining, moaning, and popping open, the smell of saltwater mixed with decaying flesh filtered into the room.

Jared grabbed his abdomen. "Charlotte, I feel I'm a manly guy, but Wanda's looks are making my stomach want to retch."

Charlotte was shaking Brooklyn. "Wake up. Brooklyn, wake up. Jared, just ignore Wanda."

There were two marks on Brooklyn's lower brow. "Jared. She's had a lobotomy."

Wanda huffed. "Brooklyn's fine. When Dr. Oracle inserted the long metal object, I held on tight and didn't let it puncture or do any damage."

Charlotte squawked out, "Sorry, Wanda, but I didn't know. Why isn't Brooklyn moving?"

Jared held his hand to his mouth. "I don't know if I can stand it in here much longer."

Wanda leaned close to Jared, and when she opened her mouth to speak, her tongue fell out. Jared bent over and held his hand to his mouth. "That's it. I've got to get away from Wanda."

Wanda slipped her tongue back in her mouth and smiled at Jared. Wanda slurped. "Okay, I put her in a vegetative state. She's fine. That hack, Dr. Oracle, thought he'd done a complete sectioning, but it wasn't for the lobotomy—it was to kill Brooklyn. He was going to ship her down the water corridor to the Blood Red Meats truck."

Charlotte got weak at the knees. "Wanda, if you weren't a ghost, I'd hug you."

Charlotte shook Brooklyn. "Wake up."

Wanda floated over Brooklyn. "Let me take care of her."

"But you're the one who did something to her mind to begin with."

"I didn't realize she was going to go into her mind that deep."

Jared came over and rested his hand on Charlotte's lower back. He grimaced at Wanda. "My stomach's stopped rolling."

Charlotte shook her small fist at Wanda. "Hurry up and get Brooklyn back to us."

Wanda bent over Brooklyn and whispered something into her ear. Brooklyn started to come out of her stupor as if she were being defrosted. Her extremities jerked, shook, quivered, and her joints snapped.

Charlotte scoffed. "What did you say?"

Wanda snorted. "I just said that if she didn't come to, I'd slaughter her."

Jared scowled. "You're a wretched dead person."

Wanda fiddled with her tongue. It looked as though she was trying to reattach it. "I'm not here to make friends. I'm trying to get revenge and inflict punishment due to my early demise. As long as you stay on my good side, you've nothing to worry about."

Charlotte rubbed Brooklyn's hand. She was slowly coming out of her mind-alternating state, with small twitches. "Where do you think Dr. Oracle went?"

Wanda stroked her long locks with her decaying fingers. "I suspect he's out butchering someone else."

The lab door opened, and Charlotte saw Mrs. Bellow wheeling Gretchen through the broken glass. Marty was at their side, and Gretchen wheeled forward. "I've brought reinforcements. Where's Dr. Oracle?"

The glass was crunching underfoot. Mrs. Bellow said, "Good Lord, what happened here?"

Brooklyn was coming out of her stupor. Charlotte let go of Brooklyn's hand. "I'm glad you're all here. We need to bounce some ideas around to stop Dr. Oracle and his madness."

Wanda held up her hand, while Mrs. Bellow and Marty grimaced as they looked in her direction. Wanda slobbered and said, "If any of you need to let go of your stomach contents, feel free so we can get on with our gathering."

Charlotte helped Brooklyn sit up. "Wanda, do you have some kind of plan?"

"Yeah, I do. I've been able to look around, and Primevil is not the solution to the problem."

Mrs. Bellow stated with an air of confidence, "Your looks don't have any effect on me. I've seen bodies in torturous conditions. I've worked in the medical field for over twenty years. What problem are we talking about?"

Marty looked away from Wanda as she spoke in a slurpy voice. "The teens of Boston and around the world are dying at an alarming rate."

Charlotte added, "Mrs. Bellow, the teens are dying to supply the world with meat."

Mrs. Bellow looked horrified. "What? I've never heard of such a thing."

Marty held his hand over his mouth. "I'm sorry but, Wanda, you look worse than I imagined. So what is this big plan of yours?"

Charlotte blurted out, "Gretchen and I found the markings on two new girls today. They looked like the markings Wanda told me about."

Wanda looked Charlotte in the eyes. "Did you think I was lying?"

Jared put his arm around Charlotte's waist. "Wanda. Just get on with your idea."

Gretchen rubbed the sutures on the back of her head. "Yeah, then we can take a vote if we like your plan, and no hocus-pocus, Wanda. I'm wise to your ways of doing things."

As Wanda rolled her eyes, one fell out and landed on Brooklyn's lap. She steeled herself as Charlotte got an ache in the pit of her stomach. She watched her friend lift the slimy round eye as her hand trembled. Brooklyn hissed, "Stop dropping body parts wherever you go. I'm not going to be the keeper of such gruesome things."

Wanda said with a snide tone, "I didn't ask you to pick my eye up. I've been picking up my parts since I was killed, and I'll continue to do it." She slipped her eye in place as it made a small goopy sound. "Where was I?"

Charlotte snapped. "Do you have a plan of some kind? I hope it's not some hodgepodge, useless scheme." Charlotte was still mad at Wanda for physically and mentally harming her friends.

"Oh, yes. I suggest we go to Dr. Oracle's residence. I didn't find anything at Primevil to help with any of the questions we all have."

Charlotte looked at the rest of the small, unimpressive group. "You know where he lives?"

"Just so happens I do. If we're going to find any incriminating information on the slaughtering of teens, I think that's where we'll find it."

Charlotte looked at her friends, Brooklyn and Gretchen. "They're in no condition to go traipsing around Boston. What if we wait several days, and leave early Friday morning?"

Mrs. Bellow placed her hands on her hips and let out a sigh. "I'll call in sick on Friday, and Brooklyn and Charlotte, I'll write an excuse for you."

Gretchen announced, "I'll plead out a headache from my injury."

Marty was nonchalant. "No one's going to miss me, so I'm in. Besides, it'd be good to get away from Redwine Hill."

Charlotte looked at Jared. "Can you get off work Friday?"

"Yeah, I'll just switch my day off with another guard."

Charlotte said, "Does Dr. Oracle live far away?"

Brooklyn asked, "How are we going to get there?"

Mrs. Bellow cracked down on a piece of candy. "Anyone care for a mint?" Brooklyn and Charlotte took a mint from Mrs. Bellow's hand. She continued. "I've a car, but it's not very big. I don't know if all six of us will fit, but we can try."

Charlotte looked at the group of six. "We'll just have to scrunch up together."

Jared crossed his arms. "Okay, that's it; we'll all meet at Mrs. Bellow's office Friday at six in the morning."

Brooklyn groaned. "Why so early?"

Jared went up to Brooklyn. "We need to be up and out before the patients start roaming the halls."

Gretchen shook her finger at Brooklyn. "I would've thought a street rat like you could wake at any hour of the day."

Jared looked at Gretchen. "Let's just get along. If you and Brooklyn are going to fight the entire time on Friday, then maybe one of you should stay behind."

Brooklyn crossed her arms in front of her. "I'm going. I didn't say anything. Gretchen always starts the arguments."

Marty defused the situation by taking the handles of the wheelchair and guiding Gretchen out of Dr. Oracle's lab.

Charlotte looked at Mrs. Bellow as she helped Brooklyn off the table. "Mrs. Bellow, can you page someone to replace the lab window and put the amount on my tab?"

Jared looked at Mrs. Bellow. "No. Mrs. Bellow, put any expense on my list. Charlotte already has too many things that she needs to work off."

"Charlotte, you and your friends run along, and don't worry I won't mention your name. I'll just say it was an accident. Dr. Oracle won't question me about the broken window."

23

Dr. Oracle's Manor

The next several days were uneventful. Charlotte asked around, but no one had seen Dr. Oracle at Primevil. He hadn't shown up since that day in the lab. Charlotte wondered if he'd gone completely insane.

The day before the field trip, Charlotte was beginning to get cold feet. She and Jared, along with Brooklyn and Gretchen, had a private meeting in Jared's room. Charlotte and Brooklyn were petting the kittens when Brooklyn held Noon up. "We can't leave these guys behind."

Charlotte said, "It's only for a day. Mrs. Bellow can't keep us out overnight. She told me that she can only sign us out for the daytime."

Brooklyn put Noon in Gretchen's outstretched hands. Charlotte stroked the kitten. "We could put enough food in the dresser to keep them satisfied for the entire day."

Gretchen sighed. "Or we can bring them with us."

Jared shook his head. "I don't think that's a good idea. They're still small, and the trip would definitely stress Noon out."

There was a loud noise in the hallway. Jared put his finger to his lips. "Shhh, I'll take care of this."

He pulled his gun from the holster and flipped the light switch. The room was deep in darkness as Jared slowly opened the door. He looked down the hallway and hesitated. "Roaming the hallways and leaving bits of yourself behind, Wanda?"

Jared flipped the light on. Wanda sneered with what was left of her lips. "Just scaring a new guard, that's all."

As Wanda floated into the room, Charlotte called out to her. "Can you please pull your hair forward, so it covers your face and body?"

Wanda flipped off the light. "No bother; now you can't see me."

Charlotte could feel her presence beside her on the bed. She pulled her arm away from Wanda's long tresses. She felt her ravaged hand groping for something. "Wanda, what the hell do you want?"

In a gravelly voice she said, "I was just trying to find the kittens."

Charlotte said quickly, "Gretchen, hand her Noon, so she can stop assaulting me."

Gretchen hesitated. "I-I don't want to touch you. No offense, Wanda."

Wanda snatched the kitten from Gretchen's arm. Gretchen snapped, "Ouch. Wanda watch what you're doing with those long claws."

"I can see in the dark, you know. Why do you think most ghosts haunt at night?"

Gretchen said with a bit of a laugh, "So, you're nocturnal?"

Jared's deep voice spoke. "Wanda, what do you want?"

"I've just come to tell you something I don't think you know."

The kittens were purring. Charlotte thought, *At least Noon likes Wanda.*

Charlotte said in a questioning tone, "You've found Dr. Oracle?"

"No, and I won't be going with you to his house. I gave Mrs. Bellow Dr. Oracle's address. Funny, though, she acted like she already knew where he lived. Her car's all gassed up and ready to go, tomorrow. She told me to tell you to be in front of her office at six a.m. sharp."

Charlotte said, "Why won't you be coming?"

"I'd love to come, but I only reside at Primevil. A ghost doesn't travel to different places. Stays put, in the place they died. I'd do anything to see the look on Dr. Oracle's face when you walk in and contaminate his house with your presence."

"Jared asked, "Does Dr. Oracle have any guns in his house? Is there any risk to us entering?"

"I've never been there, and like I said, I can't leave Primevil, but I doubt very much if he knows how to use a gun. He's not really the hunting type."

Charlotte massaged her temples. "Yeah, he'd rather torture and kill people."

The four fell asleep around two in the morning. Jared gently touched Charlotte as she slept. "It's time to wake up."

Charlotte stretched and looked around the room. Wanda was gone. "What time is it?"

"It's five forty-five."

Charlotte poked Gretchen and Brooklyn. "Get up. We can't be late. We've got fifteen minutes." Charlotte put the kittens in the bottom drawer. "Jared, can you get the little fur balls some meat from the cafeteria? Since it hasn't opened yet, I figure the ladies are so in love with you that they'd give you just about anything."

He was brushing his teeth. "Yeah, no problem. You three run and do whatever it is that girls do in the morning."

Brooklyn and Gretchen ran out the door, and Charlotte reached up and kissed Jared's cheek. Gretchen turned and ran to her bedroom, and Charlotte ran after Brooklyn. "Hey, wait up."

Charlotte and Brooklyn brushed their hair and teeth. After a quick change of clothing, they ran to Mrs. Bellow's office. Mrs. Bellow was looking at her watch. "You four are right on time. Where's Marty? I'll leave him behind. I'm not going to wait for him. Let's go."

Jared pointed down the hall. "Here he comes."

Marty half ran, half limped down the hall. He had a swollen left eye. Jared forcible yelled, "What happened to you?"

He touched his eye. "My roommate thought I was making too much noise last night. He tolerates very little."

Mrs. Bellow shook her head. "Come on. Follow me. I've already checked you all out for the day. I'll have to warn you, though, that I've got night blindness, and since it's still dark outside, I may drive a bit slow."

Jared put his hand out. "I've got a driver's license. I had a car and job before I got hauled into Primevil."

Mrs. Bellow flipped Jared the keys. "Now, if any of you plan on running away, let me just say that if you do, I'll lose my job. I need all five of you to return with me. I might even have criminal charges put on me, so don't let me down."

Charlotte looked over at the small group of individuals. The only one she didn't know was Marty, and he was an agent, sent here by the president. Charlotte looked down. "I didn't even think that, Mrs. Bellow."

Mrs. Bellow led the way to an employee elevator. She put her thumb on the scanner and the doors slid open.

When the doors opened again, they quietly walked outside toward a small security structure. Brooklyn pointed to a homemade sign, and Charlotte mumbled the words. "We shoot to kill."

There were three guards, with guns, crammed in the small building. Charlotte nudged Jared. "These guards aren't patients, are they?"

Jared shook his head. "No, I'm afraid not, and that sign isn't just for looks. Can't interrogate a dead person. They don't like any loose ends, so when they aim, you're dead."

Mrs. Bellow stopped, and all three of the guards came out. The guard in front said, "Let's see your identification."

Mrs. Bellow showed her ID. "Dwight, this is absurd. You know who I am."

He waved his hand in the air. "Yes, Mrs. Bellow, but I don't know any of these patients." The guard pointed at them and barked, "Line up."

They all bunched together in a tight line. "You're all lucky that Mrs. Bellow here already sent your pictures to us ahead of time."

The second guard opened the folder he was holding. He came up to Charlotte, who was first in line. He got close to her and whispered, "If you don't have a boyfriend, I just broke up with my girlfriend."

Jared must have heard. He was standing next to her. He grabbed the man around the neck. "Yeah, scum ball, she already has a boyfriend."

The three guards jumped on Jared and took him to the ground. Charlotte screamed and kicked at one of the guards. "Get off him."

Mrs. Bellow saw the others moving to join in the fight. She stepped in between the ones scuffling on the ground and the ones standing. Then she put her fingers in her mouth and let out an earsplitting whistle. "Gentlemen, stop. Stop this at once."

She pulled at two of the guards with her hands. "Get off! You can't go around abusing patients."

Marty helped several of the guards up. Charlotte thought she saw Marty wink at one of them. Charlotte helped Jared up. "Are you okay?"

"Yeah, I'm fine."

The guard Jared had by the throat stood and punched Jared in the face. Jared went reeling backward and landed on the ground. He quickly came to his feet and lunged at the guard, but instead ran right into Charlotte, knocking her to the ground.

"Oh, God, Charlotte, are you all right?"

She looked at Jared's eye. His lid was cut, and blood dripped down into his eye.

Mrs. Bellow bent down. "Maybe we should forget about this little excursion. Plan it for another day."

Jared helped Charlotte to her feet. Charlotte stammered, "No, I think we're both fine. Jared, you're okay?"

The guard pointed to Jared. "He put his hands on my neck first. I was just defending myself."

Mrs. Bellow gave the guard a wicked grin. "Well, I heard your question to the young lady, and it wasn't appropriate. Perhaps this man was defending someone in his life."

Brooklyn found her inner street-rat voice. She moved in close to the guards and poked one of them in the chest. "You weasel. You're the lowest of the lows. You think because we're patients that you can treat us like dirt. Most of us are just teenagers, and you are hell-bent on having bloodshed. You outweigh us by tons." The guard was trying to get away. "That's right, you just burrow your head into your stupid uniform shirt."

Mrs. Bellow came up behind Brooklyn. "Glad to see you're back to your old self, Brooklyn, but we really need to get going."

"Oh, sorry, Mrs. B."

The guards hurried through identifying the rest of the patients' photos. Two of the guards walked into the security building, and the other guard cleared his throat. "Mrs. Bellow, the only reason I'm not writing these patients up is you've always been nice to me. Giving me something for my headaches, bringing me breakfast in the security hut when the other guards called in sick and I couldn't leave to eat. Not turning me in when you caught me parking in the doctor's parking space."

"Well, in my defense, the parking space belonged to Dr. Oracle, and I don't care for him."

"Doesn't matter, Mrs. Bellow, I appreciate those things, so consider this whole fighting business over." He straightened his shirt and walked back into the hut.

Charlotte bent over and picked up Mrs. Bellow's car keys. She handed them to Jared. "You didn't have to go ballistic."

He snatched the keys. "Yeah, I did. Mrs. Bellow, where's your car?"

Gretchen grabbed Charlotte's arm. "What did the guard say?"

"He just wanted to know if I had a boyfriend."

Brooklyn and Gretchen watched as Jared walked to the parking lot. Brooklyn said, "Charlotte, you're so lucky; he's handsome and gallant."

Mrs. Bellow yelled, "Jared, it's the small white car in lot number 102. Come on, girls and Marty—let's get moving before something else happens."

Jared found the car and got in and turned the key. Mrs. Bellow came and sat in the passenger seat. "The four of you will just have to squeeze in the back together."

Gretchen yelled, "I'll sit on Marty's lap."

Brooklyn snorted. "Fine, go ahead. No one else wants that position."

Once they were all in and settled, Charlotte, who was sitting behind Jared, asked, "Marty, why didn't you help Jared when the guards lit into him back there?"

"I-I didn't want to make things worse."

Charlotte sneered. "Worse for who?"

Brooklyn snarled at Marty. "Charlotte, I think the answer is obvious—for himself."

Jared ran his hand through his hair and grabbed the wheel. "Where to, Mrs. Bellow?"

Charlotte could see Jared's hands clutching the wheel. She knew he must be upset about Marty. She reached her hand up and touched the back of his hair. He clasped her hand in his and gave it a squeeze.

Mrs. Bellow pointed her finger out the window. "Pull out of the lot and take a right. I've never been in this area before. I think it will take us at least thirty minutes to get there. I'm sorry, Gretchen, but try to make yourself as comfortable as possible. If the sun is out on the way home, I'll drive, and you and Marty can sit in the passenger seat. Stretch your legs out in front of you."

Jared cut Mrs. Bellow off. "Like hell he will. If anyone is going to be sitting in the front seat, it'll be Charlotte and me."

Charlotte was looking out the window. "Brooklyn, look isn't that Polo and Seed dragging that kid into Primevil?"

Brooklyn trembled. "Yeah, that's them. I wonder where the Collector is."

Mrs. Bellow changed the subject. "Jared, what kind of car did you have before you came to Primevil?"

"I had a jeep. It was all tricked out. I spent a lot of time and money fixing it up. It was a real chick magnet." Jared shook his head. "Sorry, Charlotte, I don't know why I said that."

Charlotte tapped him on the shoulder. "That's fine, Jared. I realize you had a life before coming to Primevil. I guess I should have figured out that the only reason you've taken an interest in me is there's not a lot to choose from."

Charlotte sat back in her seat and got quiet. Jared stammered, "No, Charlotte, that's not it. The two years I went to high school, I had a lot of friends, but not like you."

Brooklyn smacked Jared in the back of the head. "Way to go, Jared."

Mrs. Bellow changed the subject. "Jared, merge on to the highway, just up ahead. Look how things are changing."

Gretchen said, "Mrs. Bellow, what do you mean by changing?"

"I think I heard that we now have zero-population growth. The housing industry has bottomed out. There's a big chunk of the population that no longer needs housing. The teens that are dying in epidemic proportions don't need a house, a car, food—they won't have any babies of their own. It will only be a matter of time before eighty percent of the elderly no longer exist. You can't make it into your geriatric years if you die before you're twenty."

As the rest of them talked about the future of the world, Charlotte was silent. She was still thinking about the comment Jared made about his car being a chick magnet until Jared pulled up and stopped. Mrs. Bellow put her hand up to shield the sun, which was now rising, then she pointed to a huge mansion. "Well, this is Dr. Oracle's manor."

Charlotte sat up and looked out the window. "It looks like an entire mall, but gated. Mrs. Bellow, there aren't any attack dogs, are there?"

Mrs. Bellow shook her head. "Wanda didn't mention dogs."

Brooklyn smirked. "Yeah, leave it to Wanda to leave that little detail out."

Jared got out and opened Charlotte's door. She saw his beaten face and remembered he got that from a bit of jealousy. She smiled at him and ran her hand along his face. "Charlotte, I didn't mean how it sounded."

"I know, Jared."

Mrs. Bellow said sarcastically, "Where are all the gentlemen when you need them?"

Jared ran around and opened the passenger door and helped Mrs. Bellow out.

Gretchen wrenched her neck to look at the building in front of them. "Are you sure this is a house? I think it must be a storage company with all the gates."

Mrs. Bellow looked down at the piece of paper in her hand. "This is the address Wanda gave me. Actually, it's the only building on this entire street."

Jared went and took Charlotte's hand and walked to the front gate. The others followed and Charlotte said, "It's not like we can ring him and see if he'll answer the door."

On the huge mailbox was the verse engraved: "The Oracle will survive when all else perishes." Charlotte pointed to the mailbox. "Looks like Wanda was right. This has got to be his place."

Jared looked at the tall iron gates. "Now we just need to find a way past these gates and break into the house." Jared pointed to the code box. "Mrs. Bellow, did Wanda give you a security code to use?"

"No, I didn't write down anything like that."

Charlotte looked at Mrs. Bellow. "Can I see that piece of paper?"

Mrs. Bellow handed the paper to Charlotte and said, "There's nothing on there but the directions Wanda gave me."

As Charlotte looked at the paper, the address was written down so poorly it was illegible.

But in the corner of the paper were squiggly numbers: 71157. Charlotte looked closely at the numbers. "Jared, push 7-1-1-5-7 on the security box."

Jared pushed the numbers in, but nothing happened.

Mrs. Bellow yelled, "Eureka! I know what those numbers are. Dr. Oracle was born July eleventh. Jared, push 7 first, then space, then 11, space, and finally 57. When I first got here I didn't realize Dr. Oracle was so eccentric; he wanted to know my birth date. He's fascinated with the day people are born. Anyway, I told him to tell me his birthday first and he did."

Jared pushed in the numbers and there was a click. Charlotte pushed the gates open. The building towered over them. Marty immediately said, "When we get inside, we should break up into three pairs."

Brooklyn gave a snide remark. "Yeah, of course we should. No offense, Mrs. B., but I'd get stuck with a slightly overweight woman, while Charlotte and Gretchen each have a man, and Jared and Gretchen carry guns."

Mrs. Bellow started to say something, but Brooklyn continued, "Yeah, I know, Mrs. B., you were a muscle-builder back in the day, but those muscles have gone weak over the years."

Mrs. Bellow interrupted, "Brooklyn I wasn't going to say that at all. I was going to say I have a gun in my purse and I won't hesitate to use it."

Brooklyn looked away. "Oh, sorry, Mrs. B., and in case we get into a situation where you have to defend me with that gun, forget about the crack I just said about your muscles."

Charlotte nudged Brooklyn forward. "Let's just get inside and survey the entryway. We can decide what direction we need to go once we're not standing outside these gates."

They ran for the front door, leaving Mrs. Bellow behind. Mrs. Bellow was slightly winded when she reached the door. "Hey, if you want a ride home, you'll wait for me."

Charlotte eyes were scanning the enormous house. "I think we need to meet back here every thirty minutes."

Marty turned to look around. "You better make that every hour. This place covers a lot of ground. It'll take at least thirty minutes to make it to the other end of this place."

Charlotte and Brooklyn were the only two without a watch. Jared looked at his watch. "Meet back here at seven-thirty."

Charlotte said, "What do we do if everyone doesn't show up in an hour?"

Mrs. Bellow was the voice of reason. "Let's not think that way. We'll just meet back here to compare notes. We're not looking for sacrificial lambs; this is just a reconnaissance mission."

Charlotte and Jared headed for the stairs, Marty and Gretchen went to the left, and Mrs. Bellow and Brooklyn went to the right. Charlotte looked back at the rest of them. Jared said with confidence, "It'll be okay, Charlotte. Like Mrs. Bellow said—we're just gathering information."

Charlotte nodded. "I know, but Dr. Oracle is so crazy that he could kill us all and no one would ever know."

Charlotte was so nervous she could barely climb the steps. Jared squeezed her hand, and Charlotte smiled at him. "Okay, let's go find something incriminating."

24

Madman at Work

Charlotte and Jared crept down the hall on the second floor. As Jared turned the knob on the first door, Charlotte got an uneasy feeling in her stomach. The first room was uneventful, and she breathed a sigh of relief. It was stocked full of antiques and collectors' items from all over the world. Some items looked like they'd come from the Oriental market. Animal heads that had been stuffed by a taxidermist were mounted on the walls, along with horns and ivory from Africa. There were collectibles from Indonesia, wooden fertility statues standing on either side of the door, and all types of drums, expensive musical instruments, and artifacts. Each item had been meticulously labeled with origin and date of purchase. Charlotte went over and ran her fingers along a Stradivarius violin, which was sitting on the top of a grand piano. Jared rapped on the three-tiered drums.

"Jared, do you want Dr. Oracle to find us?"

"He's got some really expensive stuff, Charlotte. He must be very wealthy."

"Yeah, so let's keep it down. He won't think twice about disposing of us. Looks like Dr. Oracle cares more about material things than he does the living."

They left that room and went into the next. Charlotte's mouth hung open. "Now, this is a treasure."

"Yeah, if you like this kind of thing."

There were rows of dark mahogany tables lining the room, each covered in jewels and jewelry. "Look, Jared, there must be millions and millions of dollars just lying around for someone to take."

"You forgot that we broke into Dr. Oracle's house, and right now he's planning our death. It's not exactly lying around for someone to take."

They heard a whirring sound and saw a small wall camera turn in their direction. "See, Charlotte, what'd I tell you?" He gently put his arm around her and whispered in her ear, creating a tingling sensation on her neck. "Shh, I think Dr. Oracle's security camera has spotted us."

As they backed out of the room, the sound of a gunshot echoed though out the house.

"Let's go!" he shouted.

Jared picked Charlotte up and went running toward the steps. "Jared, I can run. Put me down."

He put her down before descending the stairs, and they both ran down. Looking both ways, they could see Mrs. Bellow and Brooklyn running from one direction and Gretchen running toward them from the opposite hallway. Jared yelled. "Gretchen, where's Marty?"

"I don't know. I fired a shot so you'd hear me. We were checking out the first rooms on this wing, and when I turned to say something to Marty, he was gone. Just disappeared. There wasn't a sound or a struggle."

Mrs. Bellow said, out of breath, "Gretchen, why on earth did you fire your gun?"

Gretchen still had the gun in her hand and was waving it around. "Mrs. Bellow, someone took Marty."

Mrs. Bellow patted her chest. "I'm too old for this kind of thing. Don't be ridiculous—how could anyone take Marty without a struggle? He must have walked away on his own."

Brooklyn said, "Did you call for him?" Brooklyn cupped her hands to her mouth and yelled, "Marty! Marty, you get your sorry butt out here."

There was no answer; the halls were quiet. Jared cut through the silence. "Did anybody find anything significant? The only rooms we had time to look in were filled with Dr. Oracle's treasures. In just those rooms alone there was millions of dollars' worth of stuff."

Charlotte said. "Brooklyn, there was every type of gem and jewelry anyone could possible want."

Gretchen was looking back down the hall. Mrs. Bellow patted Brooklyn's arm. "We only had time to inspect one room, and it was full of torture devices."

Brooklyn shivered. "Yeah, electric chair. guillotine, spiked ball and chain, brass knuckles, a scaffold for hanging. Everything was marked and labeled: the rack, nail chair, a lot of saws in different sizes, a tongue tearer, and thumb screws. It was all gross."

Mrs. Bellow said, "Don't forget the live rats and Gila monster."

Charlotte followed as Gretchen entered a room. Charlotte called out, "Gretchen, where are you going? Did you find something useful?"

Gretchen turned. "There has to be a trap door or hidden compartment somewhere in this room. Marty couldn't have just disappeared."

They walked into the large office. Jared said, "There doesn't seem to be anything here that would stand out."

Brooklyn sneered at Gretchen. "Maybe Marty just wanted to get away from you? I could clearly tell by the way he looked at you in the car that he didn't feel comfortable with you sitting on his lap."

Gretchen got in Brooklyn's face. "Oh, really? You could tell all this by his facial expression and body language? Brooklyn, I think you've missed your calling. Maybe you should become a mind reader at Primevil."

Charlotte said, "Shh, do you hear that?"

The security camera, pointed at the desk, turned in their direction. Dr. Oracle's voice and image came from a screen behind the desk. "I see I have some intruders. How about a little game of cat and mouse? I've already taken the liberty of locking all exterior windows and doors. I'm afraid this is going to be your final resting place."

Gretchen screamed, "What have you done with Marty?"

Dr. Oracle leaned in close to the screen. "Do I detect some emotional feeling for him?"

"So what if I care for him? Where is he?"

"I'm not going to comment on Marty, but you all need to either sit where you are and wait to die, or get up and see if you can find a way out of my beautiful manor." He let out a weird cackle laugh and the screen went black.

Charlotte whispered, "This is where we could really use Wanda."

Brooklyn poked Mrs. Bellow in the arm. "What do we do now, Mrs. B?"

She shook her head. "I guess this is no longer a fact-finding mission. We need to formulate a plan."

Charlotte said, "We can't formulate anything until we see what we're up against." She looked around the room and thought, *What have I gotten us into? Primevil is a disgusting place, but at least we were alive. Maybe someone will notice Mrs. Bellow is missing and come looking for her. She's the only one Primevil would care about. But no one knows where we are.*

Jared went over to the window. "The windows are barred. It wouldn't matter if we broke the glass. Charlotte, as tiny as you are, you still couldn't shimmy between the bars."

Mrs. Bellow just sat on the couch while the others went running down the hallways, checking doors and windows. Charlotte screamed and pounded on the front door. Jared came up behind her and gently grabbed her around the waist. "Charlotte, you're going to hurt your hands. Brute force isn't going to get us out of here."

Charlotte yelled at the others. "Did you find any way out?"

Gretchen shrugged her shoulders. "Look, Charlotte, if I'd found a way out, I wouldn't be standing here."

Brooklyn came out of the torture room wearing brass knuckles. "Hey, look what I got. If I get in a fistfight with anyone, they're going down. There are a lot of weapons in there; might as well help yourself."

Gretchen pulled her gun out of its holster. "Yeah, Brooklyn, anything better than a gun?"

Mrs. Bellow stepped into the hallway. "Come sit down. You're wasting your energy. There's no way to escape. Just wait to see what Dr. Oracle wants."

Jared and Charlotte talked quietly among themselves as they all headed for the study. Charlotte whispered, "Jared, do you think Dr. Oracle is going to kill us?"

"Yeah, Charlotte, I do. Why else would he lock us in his house?"

"Do we have anything Dr. Oracle would want, besides our lives, to bargain with?"

Jared sighed. "Let's just wait and see. I'm sure he'll make some demands on us very soon. He's not one to prolong death."

Charlotte scanned the hallways as they walked back to the room. They crowed together on both couches and waited for Dr. Oracle to make his move.

25

Charlotte's Unforgivable Surprise

They all sat huddled together. Mrs. Bellow, Brooklyn, and Gretchen squeezed together on a love seat, and Jared and Charlotte sat on the other one. The door was open, and they could hear what sounded like wheels squeaking in the hallway. Jared got up, and Charlotte followed him to the door. As they looked out, Charlotte turned and said to the others, "It's some kind of small laundry cart, and it's inching its way down the hall."

Brooklyn got up and looked out the door. She turned and said, "Gretchen, you don't think Dr. Oracle killed Marty and stuffed him in that cart?"

Gretchen and Mrs. Bellow got up to look. Gretchen whispered, "That's too small for a human."

Brooklyn said, "Not if he's cut into pieces."

Gretchen yelled, "Shut up, Brooklyn. You're making this worse."

Gretchen jabbed Brooklyn in the side with her strong fingernail and said, "Be a good friend and go out and look at what's in the bin."

Brooklyn pushed Gretchen out the door. "Gretchen, you go look. I've already been scared to death this past week, by Wanda. I've had enough."

The cart squeaked and inched toward the open door. Mrs. Bellow said, "Who's pushing that darn thing?"

Jared mumbled, "There's no blood dripping from the sides or bottom. I doubt if a body is in there, especially Marty's."

Charlotte's voice trembled. "Marty's only been gone a short time. Dr. Oracle couldn't have killed him and stuffed him in the hamper. It's got to be something else. Do you think he put a killing device in the cart? Maybe were going to die from an explosion."

Brooklyn said, "And ruin his beautiful house? I don't think he'd go that far."

Their eyes were glued to the small industrial-style laundry basket coming toward them. Charlotte felt her breath hitch in her chest when the cart stopped just a few feet away from them. She stood on her tiptoes to see what was in the cart. "It looks like a cart filled with laundry. I think it's a trick. Jared, come with me. I'm not going to stand here all day waiting for something to happen. It'll either kill us or it won't."

Charlotte grabbed Jared's elbow, and they crept out the few feet. She looked into the cart and screamed at the top of her lungs. She ran away, tears streaming down her face.

Brooklyn yelled, "Jared, who is it?"

He said in a fairly soft voice, "It's a dog. A small Irish Wolfhound."

Charlotte beat her hands on the walls. "Not just a dog. That's my dog—Jamie."

Mrs. Bellow tried to comfort Charlotte. "Honey, it could be anybody's dog."

Charlotte knew it was Jamie, but she slowly walked over to the cart. There, lying on a pile of dirty laundry, was her dog. There was no blood, but Jamie was clearly dead. Charlotte sniveled out, "See—she has her collar on." She screamed at Jared. "Look at the name tag—what does it say?"

Jared picked up the silver dog tag. "It says 'Jamie.' Charlotte, I'm so sorry."

She could hear the screen come on in the room they had just left. Dr. Oracle said, "Charlotte, I see you've found the little surprise I had for you. How do you like it?"

Charlotte snapped and lunged for the television screen. She jumped on the desk and tore at the screen violently. "Rest assured your dog went into death peacefully, but you and your friends . . . well, that's a different story. You'll have a torturous demise."

Charlotte tore the television screen from the wall, and Dr. Oracle let out an ear-piercing stream of laughter.

After turning over and trashing everything in the room, she was weary. She walked over to the cart and bent down, then took her beloved Jamie out. Charlotte kissed and stroked her as if she were still alive, then sat on the floor. "Jared, can you hand me a few items from the hamper so I can wrap her up?"

Gretchen said in a soothing voice, "Charlotte, we'll bury Jamie on the beach at Primevil."

Brooklyn sat next to Charlotte. "You can visit her every day. At least Jamie won't end up in the stew. We'll give her a proper burial."

Charlotte placed Jamie in the dirty laundry. "I always hoped Jamie had gone to live with my younger friends." Charlotte said a silent prayer, then went and put her companion under the overturned desk. She bent down and kissed her, then stood up. "Jamie, hopefully Dr. Oracle won't find you under there." When she got to the door, she looked back. "I'll come back and get you."

She went out the door and down the hall, screaming as tears ran down her face. "I hate you, Dr. Oracle. I'm going to find and kill you. I'll slice you into little pieces and feed you to whatever scavenger will take you." She pounded her hands against the wall until her knuckles were bleeding.

Brooklyn yelled, "Do something, Jared."

"And, what do you want me to do? She needs to get this out or she'll go crazy."

She went spinning around with her arms raised, shaking her fists until she fell to the floor in a heap. Jared ran over to her and knelt down. "We'll find Dr. Oracle and take care of him." He rested his head against her forehead. "Charlotte, I hate to hurry you, but I fear if we don't move on, Dr. Oracle is going to slaughter us."

Mrs. Bellow came over, and along with Jared helped Charlotte up. With half a smile on her face she said, "Come on, honey, let's go find that disgusting snake."

Charlotte wiped her eyes on her sleeve. "Jared, can you help me bury Jamie when we get back to Primevil?"

"Yeah, we'll find a nice place to put her to rest."

Gretchen said, "That's if we get out of here."

They slowly shuffled to the next door and Brooklyn said, "What's our mission now, anyway?"

Charlotte ground her teeth. "To find and mortality wound Dr. Oracle."

Jared coughed and stammered, "Let's just see what we find. I'm with you on cutting down Dr. Oracle, but we need to keep our safety in mind." He put his arm around her shoulder and turned the knob.

Charlotte was caught up in her hatred. At this point she didn't care if she was captured and killed. Was this life really worth living? She laid her head against Jared's shoulder. Charlotte wasn't accepting defeat just for herself but for her friends also. Since her mother died in a car accident she'd been on her own. She was tired and depressed about how the world turned out for her. She thought, *Maybe death would be a quick fix for all this mental misery.*

26

Take All Prisoners

The next half-dozen rooms they entered housed computers and monitors. Charlotte had tears coming down her face. How could Dr. Oracle kill a defenseless dog? Anything living had no meaning for him. Charlotte ran her hand along one of the enormous control panels. "What if we just flipped all these switches?"

Mrs. Bellow tried to comfort Charlotte. "I know you're upset about Jamie, but do you really want to bring down an evil burden on others? We don't know what any of this is for. You might start something we can't stop."

As Mrs. Bellow was patting Charlotte's hand, the lights went out. She could feel Mrs. Bellow being dragged from her grasp. She screamed. "Jared, someone is taking Mrs. Bellow."

The room filled with motion. A chair spilled to the floor, and Mrs. Bellow was trying to talk. There was a small thud as if someone hit something. Charlotte tried to listen for Mrs. Bellow.

"Where are you? Mrs. Bellow, make a noise. Anything, so I can tell where you are."

They heard the sound of someone being dragged from the room and out into the hallway. Charlotte yelled. "Jared, do something!"

Jared pushed the button on his wrist, and a beam of light came out of his hand. He and Charlotte ran out into the hallway. She saw the last part of Mrs. Bellow—her legs and feet—disappear behind a large door across the hall. Charlotte pounded on the door as Jared tried to force it open. "Oh my God, I hope Marty and Mrs. Bellow aren't getting murdered. Dr. Oracle said it would be a torturous ending. Maybe we should just surrender?"

Dr. Oracle's voice came over the hallway speaker. "Sounds like a great plan. It would make it so much easier on me."

Charlotte scowled. "You foulmouthed little weasel—you're the scum of the earth."

She took off running for the second floor, with Jared at her side.

"Charlotte, there's nothing but his possessions on the second floor.

"Yeah, I know."

She ran into the room with all the jewelry and started pushing everything onto the floor. Dr. Oracle screamed from the speakers. "You lunatic! I'll slaughter you before you have a chance to make it downstairs to your friends."

Jared followed her lead. "Charlotte, I think the only thing we're accomplishing is pissing him off, but that's fine by me." Jared shoved a bunch of jewels into his pockets. "Might as well fill our pockets with this stuff."

Once everything in that room was lying on the floor, she ran to the other room. She picked up the Stradivarius and swung her arm high in the air, and smashed it hard against the grand piano. Over the loudspeakers came a sniveling Dr. Oracle. "Noooooo!" Then in a loud cry, "You heathen."

It only took a few minutes to destroy or upend the contents of the two rooms. Charlotte looked at Jared. She sighed and her shoulders slumped. "That felt good." She patted Jared's chest. "You're a natural."

She stepped into the hallway and said, "Listen, do you hear anything?"

"No, do you think he's going to surprise us with one of his torture devices?"

Charlotte got a sick feeling in her stomach. "Why didn't Brooklyn and Gretchen follow us up here?"

They both ran for the steps, and Jared grabbed Charlotte's arm. "Wait, it could be a trap."

"They'd have been right beside us, smashing things, if they were able." Charlotte gave a shrill cry. "Brooklyn, Gretchen, are you down there?"

They slowly walked down the hallway. Charlotte squeezed Jared's arm as tightly as she could. She quietly called their names again, but there was no answer. When she walked into the room where she last saw her friends, she said, "Jared, were they in this room when you lit up your hand, or had they already been dragged away with Mrs. Bellow, and we just didn't notice because of my tirade?"

Jared stammered, "I don't know. We ran out into the hallway. Maybe they were in the room and maybe they weren't."

Charlotte voice cracked. "I just know they're all dead."

"Don't think that way. If they were already dead, Dr. Oracle would've put them on some kind of display for us."

"You're right. There's no reason to kill them if he isn't going to inflict severe pain on us by showing us their bodies. He's probably mourning the death of his inanimate objects."

There was an odd odor floating in the hallway. "Do you smell that?" she asked.

Jared started coughing, and Charlotte's eyes began to burn. "Yeah, I hope Dr. Oracle isn't making a big pot of human stew," he said.

"Let's follow the stink. I bet we'll find Dr. Oracle."

Jared looked at Charlotte. "You're not going to cry and get upset about your friends?"

"I'm spent. I don't have anything left of my emotions. That part of my brain has literally turned itself off. We need to concentrate on stopping Dr. Oracle. He was a fool to lock us in; now we have to expose him for the freak he is. When we find Mrs. Bellow, she can tell us how to contact the Validator. Shut down and investigate this entire curse of the sixteen-year-olds."

"That is, if we find Mrs. Bellow still alive."

"Jared, is your brain buzzing?"

"Yeah, but I get that from time to time. It's just a little more intense right now though."

Charlotte put her shirt between her teeth and tore a strip off. "You want a tension bandage?" She tied the strip around her head.

"No, I'm good. I don't think that really helps anyway."

The odor was becoming intense. Charlotte said, "I've a keen olfactory sense. My mother use to have me smell different unlabeled cans of meat and vegetables, to make sure they hadn't gone rancid. I only made a mistake once. But that one time kept our stomachs rolling for weeks."

Jared followed Charlotte to the other side of the mansion. She pointed to a door straight ahead. "The smell is coming from behind that door. Give me your gun."

"I'm not giving you my gun. The last time I did, you shot me in the leg. Let me go ahead of you."

Charlotte stood her ground. "Look, Jared, I'll be in front of you. There's no way I could shoot you. You've got muscles to defend yourself—at least let me have something."

He looked at how petite Charlotte was and handed her the gun. "Okay, I'm ready, but don't shoot anyone we like."

Jared turned on his wrist light and put his other hand on Charlotte's shoulder. He gave a long sigh. "Let's see what's on the other side of this door."

She turned the knob with her left hand and kept a death grip on the gun with the other. She first opened the door just a couple of inches, and then all the way. "Jared. Jared, what happened to your wrist light? Where's the light? I can't see a thing!"

She grabbed his hand on her shoulder, but it wasn't Jared's hand. It was a deformed corpse bouncing up and down, jiggling around. Her hands fumbled trying to find the light switch. She finally found the switch and flipped it on. The carcass danced around—by what, she didn't know; there were no strings. The most terrifying part was Jared was gone. She aimed the gun at the corpse and shot. *Oh God, where's Jared? This gun isn't going to kill a cadaver.*

Charlotte slammed the door shut on the decayed hand. She slowly backed up aiming the gun at the door. "This is some kind of sick, demented joke. Dr. Oracle thinks I'll go insane, but I won't."

She steeled herself and looked around the room. "I'm in the kitchen." There was a large pot on the stove. It wasn't big enough to hold an entire body but it could hold body parts. The steam was coming up from the caldron. This was the putrefying smell that she'd noticed in the hallway.

Charlotte crept over to the stove. *Do I really need to look in the pot? Whatever Dr. Oracle threw in here, I don't need to see. It'll just scare me out of my mind.*

She walked away, patting her chest. She started pulling out drawers looking for something she could use to help find the rest of the gang. She tucked the gun into the waistband of her jeans and grabbed a carving knife. Her plan was starting to come together when she saw a mop in the corner of the room.

Charlotte had no idea if this plan of hers would work, but it was the only hope she had of finding Dr. Oracle and her friends.

Redwine hill

27

Charlotte's Plan

Charlotte rummaged through the cabinets. She took out several bottles of cleaning supplies and read the labels. She decided on one that read "flammable." She put the mop head in the sink and ran the liquid cleaning substance over it. Not soaking it, but just enough to make a torch. She pulled out several of the bristles from a broom she also found in the corner, then lit them on the stove burner. She hurried over to the kitchen sink and held the mop upright, then lit the mop. It became a blaze of fire. She ran out of the kitchen screaming like a banshee.

She held the mop over her head and ran down the hall and into every room. The loudspeakers crackled. "You fool. Charlotte, you can't burn this place down. It's been built with very few flammable materials, and it has a watering system that will put it out."

She yelled, "You're a low-life piece of garbage. I'll find you. Oh, and I'm not trying to burn the place down." The sprinklers popped out of their stationary positions and burst into a forceful stream of water.

Charlotte headed for the stairs before the water could extinguish her torch. She ran into his precious rooms filled with his mementos he'd collected throughout his travels. She yelled, "All this stuff was bought from blood money. You sold the bodies of teens for their meat."

The sprinklers spurted and spit out the water. She ran back downstairs and tried to set off as many sprinklers as she could. She spotted Dr. Oracle running down the hall, holding his head. He didn't even acknowledge her, just ran past her screaming, "My things, my wonderful, beautiful things."

He was pulling at the few remaining hair follicles he had on his head. When he got to the top of the stairs she could hear him run into the first room. "She's killed you, my Stradivarius."

The water was pulsating out of the sprinklers. The cloth bandage she had tied around her head was soaked, and the torch was spurting out. She made one last stop in the room that Brooklyn and Mrs. Bellow had described: the torture room. She gasped when she saw all the ruthless devices. She had to wave the mop over the sprinkler head several times before it burst forth and drenched Charlotte and the last remaining flame from the torch.

She ran down the hall toward the door that Dr. Oracle had exited. It was locked when they tried to save Mrs. Bellow, but now it was ajar. She stopped just outside the door and tried to find her courage. She could hear popping and sizzling, and knew the large control panels in the rooms on the first floor were being damaged by water. Once her hands stopped shaking she peeked in, then slowly pushed the door open.

She knew Dr. Oracle wasn't going to be in there, but she was afraid she would see her friends hanging from hooks attached to the ceiling. There in front of her was an enormous panel that covered most of the room. It looked pretty with all its lights blinking. It wasn't until she looked past the panel that she saw the large cage with iron bars. Jared was lying on the floor along with the rest of her friends. He struggled to sit up and leaned against his arms. "Charlotte, get us out of here."

By the looks of his injuries, Jared was the most severely beaten. The others rallied, and shuffled or crawled over to the gate. "How?" She tried shaking the bars with her hands, but they were solid and not going to give an inch. She yelled, "Jared, how do I open this cage?"

Jared's voice was forced. "Go over and look on the control panel—there must be a button or something."

Charlotte ran and stood behind the control panel. It was very intimidating. "I don't know what button or lever to push."

Brooklyn screamed, "Just push them all."

Jared yelled, "No. That could destroy any hope of getting out of here. Charlotte, isn't there anything labeled on the panel?"

"No, there isn't."

Charlotte watched as a Monarch butterfly fluttered around the terrifying control panel and landed on a button at the far right. "Serenity, is that you?"

Brooklyn called out, "She's gone insane. Charlotte, who are you talking to? Snap out of it."

"No, Brooklyn, there's a Monarch butterfly over here, and it landed on this amber-colored button."

Gretchen blurted out, "So you think that butterfly is Serenity, and she's come to your rescue? Jared, talk some sense into your girlfriend."

Brooklyn said, "Shut up, Gretchen. Don't you think it's a little weird that there'd be a butterfly in here?"

Gretchen bellowed, "I don't get the connection."

"Yeah, I know. It's just something between me, Charlotte, and Serenity. The only thing that Serenity left behind when she died was orange Monarch Butterfly nail polish."

Before Jared said anything, Charlotte could hear Dr. Oracle coming. She was sweating and shaking so badly so could hardly see the never-ending buttons. Charlotte screamed, "What do you want me to do, Serenity? "

She jabbed the amber button with her index finger, and the heavy iron door opened. Charlotte mumbled, "Thanks, Serenity."

Gretchen and Brooklyn started pushing each other to get out, and Mrs. Bellow stepped in. "Girls, we have bigger problems. Save your energy for something productive. We'll iron it all out later about bug spirits and things. Charlotte, come here and help me support Jared."

Charlotte immediately came to Jared's side. "What happened to all of you?"

Jared was swaying back and forth. "Let's just say Dr. Oracle isn't a stranger to inflicting pain."

Mrs. Bellow said, "Jared got the worst of it. He put up a fight, while the rest of us took a few smacks from Dr. Oracle's goons."

Charlotte looked at Mrs. Bellow. "What goons? Did you see who beat up Jared and whacked the rest of you?"

Mrs. Bellow waved her hand in the air. "That's all behind us now, but how did you think Dr. Oracle captured us?"

"You mean we have to worry about a couple of muscle goons, as well as Dr. Oracle?"

"Honey, don't worry about Dr. Oracle's sidekicks; they don't have enough brains between the two of them to do anything on their own. Dr. Oracle is the real threat."

Charlotte furrowed her brow. "How do you know this?"

Brooklyn said, "Charlotte, it doesn't take a mental giant to know the guys that smacked us around were feebleminded cretins. They thought Gretchen and me were guys."

Gretchen blurted out, "They didn't think I was a guy. They just didn't care who they beat up."

Jared ran his swollen, bruised hand through his hair. "Yeah, they were both princes. They weren't against hitting women."

Mrs. Bellow patted Jared's arm and then touched the small cut above her eye. "I'm a tough old broad. You know I use to be a bodybuilder."

Brooklyn said, "Mrs. B., let's not bring up the good old days." She gasped. "Look—he's at the door."

Dr. Oracle stood at the door to his control room and hissed. "Charlotte C. Carrion, you're a vile animal. We'll see who wins this fight. You might have won this round, but nobody gets away with ruining my things."

Charlotte let go of Jared and leapt at Dr. Oracle. She screamed, "You worthless, vulgar piece of trash."

Dr. Oracle slammed the door just as Charlotte lunged for him. She bounced off and collapsed to the floor. Jared hobbled over to Charlotte and groaned as he bent down. "Charlotte, are you all right?"

She adjusted the strip of material around her head. "I'm fine." She lifted her hand to stroke Jared's bruised face. "I'm sorry."

"There's no reason to say you're sorry. You didn't beat me."

She sat up. "I know, but if I hadn't been so self-righteous and always trying to right the wrongs of Dr. Oracle and Primevil, you wouldn't be in this condition."

Mrs. Bellow said, "Honey, it's too late to go back. Now that we know what's going on, we need to move forward."

Gretchen and Marty walked over. Charlotte looked at Marty and said, "Hey, Marty—how did you manage not to get your face used as a punching bag like Jared?"

He stammered, "Uh, I guess I didn't see the need to fight back."

Jared said, "Yeah, Charlotte. You were still out there. I wasn't going down without a fight."

Charlotte gave Jared a soft smile. As she looked around the room, she had time to take in her surroundings. The entire length of the room was lined with metal, housing the keypads and monitors. The colored blinking lights looked haphazardly mixed in, and the oversized computer was humming and clicking. Each of the screens was labeled with the continent and time zone for each monitor. Closest to Charlotte was the cage that had held her friends, and not much else was in the room.

As Charlotte cradled Jared's head in her lap, Marty stood. "I guess this is where I shine."

Jared started coughing and spit out blood from his split lip. "What do you mean—this is where you shine?"

Marty walked over and sat in one of the half-dozen chairs. "Has anyone else had any computer classes?"

Charlotte positioned Jared's head on Brooklyn's lap, who gave a big smile. Charlotte said, "Easy, Brooklyn, it's just temporary." She turned to Marty. "I had classes in my freshman and sophomore year in high school. Does that count?"

"Yeah, I think we can pull this off. This monitor is somewhat different than the one I practiced on with the group that was assigned to investigate the undoing of teens. I just never thought I'd see the control panel. It's a lot larger than I thought it would be. Come over here, and I'll instruct you on what to do."

As Charlotte walked over to him, he leaned in to her and whispered, "Sitting in front of this control panel is every operative's goal, but I never thought I'd be the one to help find it."

As Marty closed his eyes deep in thought, there was a crackling, hissing sound coming from the one large screen above the monitors. The screen flickered off and on, finally spitting out an image of Dr. Oracle. He was soaked, with his comb-over hair drenched and hanging down in his face. His lab coat was wet and smudged with dirt. He held his fist in the air and seethed with furry. Spittle came out of his mouth.

"Charlotte C. Carrion, you will not be lucky enough to escape my revenge. You will die many times. For the rest of you, I don't think your torturous death would benefit me in any way, shape, or form. So you'll all die a fairly quick death."

Dr. Oracle smeared the hair hanging in his face over to the side of his head and licked his lips. "Charlotte, I thought about having your body stuffed so I could enjoy looking at your face grimacing in pain when you died, but I couldn't pass up an opportunity to have a good meal."

Brooklyn spit out, "What a whack job. Shut up."

Gretchen held her hand to her mouth. "What's wrong with that dude? He's some kind of freak."

Charlotte was frozen at the gruesome sight on the screen, and she felt the gun being pulled out of her back waistband. A shot rang out, and the screen that had Charlotte mesmerized with fright went black. She turned to see Jared fall back on his heels with the gun in his hand.

She slipped out of her chair and onto the floor. "Jared, please just rest. Don't use your energy on Dr. Oracle. He's a madman. He has no emotional attachment to anyone other than himself."

Brooklyn came over and coaxed Jared to rest on her lap. He was short of breath, and seemed winded from firing the gun.

Charlotte said, "Okay, Marty. I see all the monitors are interconnected, and they all represent different parts of the world. What is it we need to do?"

Marty breathed out a long breath. "I can't work on all these monitors by myself, so why don't you take the half down at that end, and I'll stick with these."

Charlotte rolled an office chair, pushing the other chairs out of the way. Marty continued. "This entire room contains all the data on everyone that has been born, has died, or has been hospitalized throughout the world. The only thing saving some of these countries is the fact that—I don't know if I should call them lucky—they're a Third World country. These people aren't born in hospitals, and they don't go buy their meat in stores. They still hunt animals for food. They're not caught up in Dr. Oracle's scheme for wealth and power like the rest of us are. Dr. Oracle has come up with a way to eliminate the animal-meat industry by slaughtering teens, not caring that the economy would take a turn for the worst. No one graduating from high school or college; the only couples having babies are in their late twenties and early thirties, and pretty soon that won't even be the case. The housing market is dwindling along with every other job. Dr. Oracle didn't think ahead. You can't have fresh human meat if there are no babies to grow up into strapping teens ready to supply Blood Red Meats."

Charlotte's mouth was dry, and her tongue was stuck to the roof of her mouth. She stared at Marty. "I'll tell you now, Marty. I thought you were some goon of an operative when you first told me, but now I can see you've been a great actor."

"Yeah, just like Serenity."

Jared let out a moan. Charlotte looked at him on the floor. "Mrs. Bellow, what's wrong with Jared?"

"Honey, he took quite a beating. I'm sure Jared has some internal injuries."

Charlotte's eyes were filled with salty tears. She wiped her noise on her shirtsleeve. "Marty, hurry up—we need to get Jared back to the hospital."

Marty cleared his throat. "Type on each of the keypads the password I'm going to give you. It will get us into each of these computers: 'E-L-C-A-R-O-R-D.'"

Charlotte started typing and Marty said, "If you forget, it's very simple. It's 'Dr. Oracle' backwards."

Jared mumbled, "And to think I thought Dr. Oracle was a buffoon, and here he is controlling the world's entire meat industry from his house."

Marty was finishing typing the code word into the computers he had assigned himself. "In all fairness to you, Jared, he has no people skills whatsoever. He's suspected of having some kind of mental illness. I guess he continually had some very disturbing thoughts as a kid. Charlotte, everything logged in?"

"Yeah, Marty, now what?"

"I want you to hit, in sequence, the combination of the letters and numbers I give you." Marty rattled off: "11021956ALPHA."

He added, "Quickly, all the computers need to be programmed within just few seconds of each other."

"Yeah, well I said I took a computer class. I didn't say I took typing or memory games."

"Listen, they're only six lines to put in. Just hang in there."

Charlotte's hands were shaking. "What if this doesn't work?"

"Don't waste your concentration on talking."

Marty rattled off another row of letters and numbers. "01161985DELTA."

He quickly shouted out another line. "05051991LANDI." And another. "11201956GAMMA."

The sweat was rolling off Charlotte's face, and her palms were sliding on the keys. She was concentrating so hard her head felt like a bag of worms. She heard a lot of commotion on the other side of the door. It sounded as if the door was being pried open. Metal was groaning and screeching under some type of pressure; someone or something was using force to get into the room.

Charlotte looked over at Marty. "Hurry up."

He was holding his head and spitting out the next line. "04171985CHI."

Charlotte quickly typed the number into the three pads in front of her. "Marty, what else?"

"Uh, uh . . . I'm not sure." His hands were now clenched around his head. "11021956ALPHA."

"No! That was the first one. Think—what's wrong with your head?"

Marty stood and screamed out, "Oh God, no! My head is tearing open."

She looked on in horror and disbelief. She cried out, "What's wrong? Give me the last set of numbers."

He slumped to the floor in a heap. Gretchen ran over to him and felt his chest for any signs of life. "He's dead, Charlotte."

There was a small indentation in the metal door. Brooklyn ran to the door and tried to hold it shut. She yelled, "Gretchen, get off your butt and either help Charlotte or come help me hold this door shut."

Jared crawled over to Brooklyn. He was in no shape to help her, so he just sat and rested his back against the door.

Gretchen was in some kind of trance. She didn't move from her position.

Brooklyn cried out, "Mrs. B., Dr. Oracle is coming through the door. Now would be a good time to put those muscles you keep talking about to work."

A light shone through, and Dr. Oracle savagely yelled, "Hurry, you idiots, before they ruin my entire life's work."

Jared still had the gun in his hand, so he crawled over to the small opening that Dr. Oracle's thugs had made and shot several times. Dr. Oracle cried out, "You fool. If you kill me, this will be your tomb. There's no way out."

Mrs. B. sat next to Jared. She was sitting as if nothing was going on.

Charlotte felt hopeless, but then Brooklyn yelled, "Look—it's your little friend, Serenity."

"What? Brooklyn, what do you mean?"

The Monarch butterfly was floating over one of the keypads. Charlotte shrieked, "Gretchen, I'm sorry, but you don't have time to grieve. Get in Marty's seat and type out these numbers."

Charlotte felt foolish watching the butterfly fluttering and then landing on a number 1. "Gretchen, type in 1." They watched as the floating wing-bug went and landed on 11021956ALPHA. Charlotte croaked out, "No. We already used that code."

It was too late—they had already typed in the combination of letters and numbers, and smoke curled up from the underside of the monitors. Charlotte yelled, "It worked! Thanks, Serenity."

Jared said in a weak voice, "Charlotte, get back."

The smoke looked like gray snakes, curling and twisting as small flames lapped at the keypads. The rumble started on the floor and rose to the walls and ceiling. The walls started shaking, and bits of the ceiling came down. Charlotte looked at the monster of a computer as it gulped and sizzled into a full burn. The butterfly landed on one last colorful button. It was a dark rich-orange color. Charlotte pushed the button, and the huge metal door screeched and scraped open.

Charlotte saw Dr. Oracle running down the hall. His two sidekicks must have taken off when Jared fired at them. She grabbed Jared's gun, which was lying on the floor, and ran after Dr. Oracle. She fired off a few shots, hitting the walls.

Brooklyn yelled, "Charlotte, forget him. We need to get Jared to the hospital."

Gretchen knelt next to Marty and stroked his face. "Thank you, Marty. If I survive, I'll let everyone know you helped save the world from this epidemic."

Charlotte and Mrs. Bellow tried to get Jared up. As Brooklyn went over and gathered up Gretchen, she said, "I'm sorry, Gretchen.

I know you thought Marty would've made a good boyfriend, but it's time we got the hell out of here."

Gretchen wiped the tears from her eyes with the palms of her hands and looked at Brooklyn. She stood and went over to take Mrs. Bellow's place in supporting Jared. Gretchen quickly looked over her shoulder. "Bye, Marty. Mrs. Bellow—what happened to him?"

Charlotte said, "I think it's fairly obvious, Gretchen. The gel probe in his brain exploded."

Mrs. Bellow patted Charlotte's arm. "Honey, let's just get out of here. We can worry about Marty's death when we're safe. Besides, the only thing that comes to mind is that his probe didn't fully burst when he was younger. Dr. Oracle must have manually done something to make it go off now."

The four women half-carried Jared down the hallway. As Charlotte tucked the gun back in her waistband, she heard Dr. Oracle ranting about his stuff. "My beautiful things. That girl has no guilt over destroying my precious items."

She let out a long sigh as they headed for the front door.

They left Dr. Oracle's house and shuffled to the car. Mrs. Bellow walked around to the driver's seat. The huge manor was rumbling and shaking. Brooklyn and Gretchen jumped in the back, and Charlotte eased Jared in the front passenger seat. He put his head back on the headrest, and Charlotte jumped in the back. She sat hunched over between the front seats, on the console, as she stroked Jared's hair. Mrs. Bellow turned the key and Charlotte yelled, "Stop, Mrs. Bellow. Don't go. I forgot Jamie."

Gretchen grabbed Charlotte's arm. "Look, if I could leave Marty behind, you're going to have to leave your dog behind."

Charlotte pushed Gretchen's hand off her arm and jumped out of the car. She ran past the open gate and through the doors. She saw Dr. Oracle coming down the stairs trying to carry an armload of his precious belongings, as much as what could fit in his greedy arms. He didn't even look in her direction as she ran down the hall and into the room where she'd left Jamie. She saw the bundle of laundry on the floor and bent down. As she picked Jamie up and ran out, the mansion crumbled around her.

When she got to the car, the entire manor was crashing down. Brooklyn put her arms out, and Charlotte passed Jamie to her, then got in. "Sorry, Gretchen. I couldn't leave her behind."

Gretchen just looked out the window. "I know. We barely got Jared to the car. I don't think we could've dragged Marty out too."

The dust and dirt was waffling through the air to the car. Jared started coughing up blood. Charlotte tapped Mrs. Bellow on the shoulder. "Mrs. Bellow, step on the gas."

"Charlotte, honey, the sun has set, and I don't drive well at night. I've got night blindness, remember?"

Charlotte jumped out. "Okay, you're in the back."

They heard sirens going off all over Old Boston. Mrs. Bellow got behind Charlotte. "Do you have a driver's license?"

"No, but that doesn't mean I don't know how to drive. Considering the circumstances, I don't think that anyone is going to stop us."

As they pulled away, something in Charlotte's head popped. She brought her hand to her head, several inches above her left ear. "Did anyone else just feel a crazy sensation in their head?"

Gretchen said no, but then stammered, "Ouuuuch." She rubbed her head.

Brooklyn said, "Gretchen are your stitches bothering you?"

"No."

Charlotte could see Gretchen in the rearview mirror. She watched her pull something gel-like that was about one inch long from her head. "What's that, Gretchen?"

Charlotte's head was buzzing, and she massaged her head where she'd felt the pop. She swerved and Brooklyn said, "Charlotte, let Mrs. Bellow drive. Two hands on the wheel."

"Gretchen, can you feel right here on my head?" Charlotte said.

Gretchen took the rubber band out of Charlotte's hair. "There's a button or something sticking out."

"What! Where?"

"Yeah, right where you were rubbing your head."

Gretchen had a hard time pulling the probe out of Charlotte's thick hair. She held it in the air as Brooklyn screamed, "Gretchen, check my head."

As Gretchen checked Brooklyn's head, Charlotte pulled over and stroked Jared's scalp. "Gretchen, I've found Jared's probe—pull it out."

Gretchen said, "Sorry, Brooklyn, I don't feel anything." She reached over and slowly pulled the nub out of Jared's head. It had tiny specks of brain tissue attached to it. "Charlotte, I don't think Jared's came out as clean as ours did."

Brooklyn was still holding Jamie and pleaded, "Mrs. B., please check my head. It has to be there. I don't want to have that thing in my head forever."

Mrs. Bellow just sat and looked out the window. "Brooklyn, my dear, this is not the time. Charlotte needs everyone to be quiet, so she can keep this car on the road. Unless you all want to be quadriplegics and suck soup through a straw for the rest of your lives from an accident caused by Charlotte's distractions, then I suggest you all pipe down."

Jared had his head back and his eyes closed. He was quiet with the exception of the moans he'd let escape his lips when the car hit a pothole. Charlotte's eyes were misty. "I'm sorry, Jared. I'm trying to avoid anything in the street that would cause the car to bounce and make you feel uncomfortable."

Still with his eyes closed, he gave Charlotte a half smile. "I'm not worried about the bumps. I think you better drive as fast as you can." His words faded out. "I don't feel right."

Charlotte drove slowly past the emergency vehicles, which were surrounding the demolished manor. She then floored the gas pedal and rubbed Jared's arm gently. "Brooklyn, let's just worry about getting medical help for Jared, and then we can find the entry point of your probe."

Gretchen snorted. "Maybe Street Rat doesn't have a probe. She's probably insane on her own."

Brooklyn jabbed her elbow into Gretchen. "Shut up, Rat Teeth. At least I'm not ugly like you."

Gretchen hit Brooklyn in the shoulder. Mrs. Bellow said, "Girls, stop! I don't think Jared's breathing."

They pulled into Primevil's parking lot. Charlotte blared the car horn.

Dwight came running, yelling, "Mrs. Bellow, what's up?"

Charlotte yelled out the window. "Get some damn medical help out here."

Charlotte screeched the brakes next to the security hut. Dwight was running while pushing a wheelchair. Mrs. Bellow yelled, "No, Dwight, get a gurney, and I mean STAT."

Dwight looked confused. "What."

Mrs. Bellow waved her hand in the air. "STAT is just a nursing term for as fast as those legs can carry you."

Within seconds Dwight had a gurney and was helping Charlotte carry Jared's limp body. He swung Jared up and onto the gurney as the other guard called for medical help. There was a flurry of activity, and Charlotte watched as Mrs. Bellow ran after the rest of the staff yelling, "He's not breathing. Get an ambu bag."

Gretchen gave Charlotte a quick pat on the arm. "Charlotte, let the medical personnel do what they do best. Let's go bury Jamie."

Charlotte watched as the medical staff rushed Jared into Primevil. She looked around and Brooklyn yelled, "My probe popped. Gretchen, pull it out."

Gretchen groped around where Brooklyn pointed. Gretchen had to twist it around a bit, but it came out. Brooklyn rubbed her head as Charlotte gently picked Jamie's body up off Brooklyn's lap.

Brooklyn jumped out of the car and grabbed the unoccupied wheelchair. "Here, Charlotte, sit. You can't carry Jamie all the way to the beach. We'll go down and bury her, so you can visit her every day."

Charlotte plopped into the chair. She brought Jamie in close and dropped her head. Her shoulders shook with sadness as Gretchen rubbed them, then she pushed the wheelchair into Primevil.

Brooklyn sighed quietly. "I guess there isn't any reason to run away. All my friends are here at Primevil, but this would be perfect opportunity to do so."

The three girls wound their way through Primevil and out to the beach. Charlotte finally looked up with a tear-stained face when Brooklyn softly said, "Charlotte, we need to carry Jamie the rest of the way. The wheelchair won't roll through the sand."

Charlotte strained as she stood. Gretchen put her arms out. "I'll take her."

Charlotte said, "No, Gretchen, this is something I have to do."

The three walked slowly toward the beach. Charlotte went to a spot she thought would be perfect—far enough from the tide so as not to wash Jamie away. Charlotte plopped herself down on the sand still holding on to her dog. Brooklyn and Gretchen started digging with their hands. They were working up a sweat, but didn't stop until the hole was several feet deep.

Brooklyn came over to her friend. "Charlotte, it's time."

Charlotte kissed Jamie one last time, then gently put her little wolfhound in the sandy grave. She quietly cleared her throat. "God, I don't know if you care for animals up there, but I'd like to think Jamie's in good hands." She scooped up a handful of sand and gently sprinkled it over the small body. Brooklyn and Gretchen followed Charlotte's lead. Once the sand was piled over Jamie, Charlotte just stared out into the ocean.

Brooklyn put her hand out. "Come on, Charlotte. Let's go see what's happened to Jared."

Charlotte hung her head in grief as the three made their way back to Primevil.

Please, don't let Jared be dead.

28

The Fallout

There was a lot of hoopla going on around the world. Charlotte was requested, several times a day, to speak on television or give advice. It seemed that the Validator and the president had given Charlotte a special award, and a special team had dug through Dr. Oracle's house piece by piece and found Marty under the rubble. The president was going to have a statue made, honoring Marty, BT, and Serenity. No one found any treasure or collectors' items among the demolished building, and Dr. Oracle was never found.

Dr. Farrow and thousands of others were arrested, just in Boston alone. There was a severe shortage of doctors, nurses, technicians, and anyone else involved with, or thought to have had anything to do with, the murder and cannibalism of teens. They were incarcerated until things could be sorted out.

It was reported that the president had sound evidence that Dr. Oracle owned all the Blood Red Meat industries.

Charlotte watched the continual barrage of information flooding the news. She never heard one thing about his millions of dollars in material possessions. She figured Dr. Oracle must have had them hauled out of the building before or after its collapse.

Charlotte was resting in a bed next to Jared's in the intensive care unit of the hospital portion of Primevil. Tubes and IV bags hung at his side, and in the past week he remained in critical but stable condition.

Charlotte didn't want anything to do with reports or awards. She sat or slept in Jared's room during this time. When he had been brought in to ICU, the doctors and nurses didn't let her stay but a few minutes. It was only in the last few days, when the nurses saw improvement in Jared's condition, that they pulled some strings and got Charlotte a bed in his room.

Gretchen had her sutures removed from the incident in which she fainted after seeing Wanda. Brooklyn and Gretchen were quickly becoming best friends. They knocked on the ICU door and quietly walked in, carrying Midnight and Noon. Brooklyn said, "Charlotte we're going to see the male patients coming out of surgery. Do you want to come?"

Charlotte knew that the surgical staff was working overtime getting all probes removed. The damage had already been done to most, and those patients would need to stay in an asylum for the rest of their lives, but there were some who'd seemed to flourish once the probe was removed. Everyone not quite sixteen years old throughout the world was having their probe removed before it burst. Gretchen and Brooklyn leaped at the chance to snag a boy.

"You know," Charlotte told them, "the only time I leave Jared's room is to visit Jamie's grave. I even have my food brought in. But don't let me spoil your good time."

They walked over to Charlotte and leaned over and kissed her forehead. Charlotte took the small kittens and cuddled with them. Brooklyn picked up Jared's limp hand. "How's he doing today?"

Charlotte sighed and quietly said, "No change."

Gretchen leaned over Jared and whispered, "Jared, if you don't wake up soon, Charlotte's going to find another boyfriend. You know she's the prettiest girl at Primevil—or for that matter, throughout the Boston area."

Jared tried to clench his fist. Charlotte said, "Shut up, Gretchen, you're getting him upset."

"Well, I'm just telling him the truth. It's up to him to come out of his coma and sweep you off your feet, or someone else will."

Charlotte was disgusted. "Gretchen, I think Jared's in a drug-induced coma so he doesn't feel the pain. You're making him think too hard when he should be resting and recuperating."

Brooklyn said, "Come on, Gretchen, we've probably missed some of the best-looking guys already. You know how those other female patients are always squeezing us out."

They took the kittens from Charlotte and walked out of the room giggling. Charlotte thought back just a short time ago how mentally handicapped Brooklyn had been, after her encounter with Wanda. She smiled and whispered, "How Brooklyn's changed. Just the thought of her getting a boyfriend has just changed her entire outlook."

There was a television in Jared's room, but Charlotte never listened to it. Mrs. Rogers walked in and clicked on the TV. "Charlotte, I thought you might want to see something on the screen."

Mrs. Rogers flipped to a national station. "I wanted you to see why Mrs. Bellow hasn't been around."

Charlotte sat up when she saw Mrs. Bellow. She watched the screen as Mrs. Rogers turned up the volume. "Why is Mrs. Bellow kissing the Validator?"

"That's her husband. Anyway, I wanted to show you that she is accepting an award for your little group of do-gooders."

"Mrs. Rogers, did you know the Validator was her husband? She told me her husband was dead."

"I didn't know that, but it's been all over the news. I guess you don't watch much TV. He had taken his wife out of retirement to investigate Redwine Hill. She's been traveling all across the world collecting stuff for you. Awards, presents, accolades— she's not camera shy."

Charlotte said, "So she was a spy."

Mrs. Rogers became uneasy. "I guess you could call her a spy."

Mrs. Rogers went over and checked Jared's intravenous bags. "He's scheduled to have another bag of antibiotics hung. I'll be right back."

Charlotte turned the volume up and sat at the bottom of her bed, glued to the television set. She watched as Mrs. Bellow held the Validator's hand affectionately and smiled at him. He was in his late forties, husky, with a full head of deep-brown hair. The caption on the screen read "Validator at the White House," and there were a dozen or so microphones attached to the podium. He was dressed in a dark suit, and as the camera scanned the gathering of the media, there was Mrs. Bellow. She no longer wore her nurse's uniform but had on a nice beige satin dress and jacket. Charlotte heard the Validator say, "Charlotte C. Carrion has saved thousands of teens from a gruesome demise."

Charlotte looked over at Jared. "Yeah, but I didn't do a very good job helping you."

Mrs. Rogers came in with a small bag and piggybacked it into the main IV. "Charlotte, did you know that on one of the stations the newscaster said that Mrs. Bellow had been a bodybuilder in her younger days? Can you believe that?"

Charlotte smiled. "Yeah, she told me that; in fact ,she told me that several times."

About thirty minutes after Mrs. Rogers left, a nurse came in. "Good news, 3737. I mean Charlotte. Jared's blood work came back, and he no longer needs the antibiotics. Looks like his body is finally strong enough to fight off the infection." The nurse went over and took the small bag off, then looked at it. "Huh, it's not expired. Even if it was, it wouldn't be a cloudy color with bits of stuff floating around."

Charlotte jumped out of bed and walked over to the IV stand. "What are you asking me? I never touched Jared's fluids."

The nurse shook her head. "No, I didn't say you did. It just looks like there's something else in this bag. It looks like the bag is contaminated, that's all. I'll have to report this and make an incident record." She bent down and looked at the infusion site. "Hmm, looks okay. No redness or swelling. You'll let me know if he complains of a burning sensation in his arm, won't you?"

"Yes, absolutely. Can I ask you something?"

"Sure, but if it's a medical question, maybe you should ask Mrs. Rogers. She seems to know everything, and I don't mean that in a bad way."

"Yeah, I know, but everyone seems so busy. Do you have time to tell me about Jared's injuries? I'd like to know the full extent of what happened to his body."

Charlotte walked back to her bed, and the nurse sat down. "All I know is what I read in his chart."

"Which would be?"

She pursed her lips and blew out a long sigh. "Let's see, he had several broken ribs, and one punctured his lung. You see that tube draining reddish vicious fluid coming out his upper side? That's keeping his lung open. Then there was his severe concussion. It actually helped that he had a hole in his head from the removal of his probe. His head was swollen, and the doctors needed to drain the excess fluid buildup. He had a lot of bruised internal organs and a ruptured liver. They couldn't repair the damage to his liver, so they removed a portion of it."

The nurse stopped. "Do you want to hear any more?"

Charlotte felt the color leave her face. "There's more?"

The nurse picked up Charlotte's hand and tears filled her eyes.

Charlotte croaked out in a weak voice, "Tell me."

The nurse fiddled with the small antibiotic bag in her hand. "I don't think I should tell you. I'll go get Mrs. Rogers."

Charlotte grabbed her elbow. "Please, tell me."

The nurse stammered, "The doctors think he's blind."

Charlotte screamed, "What! Why do they think that?" She jumped into Jared's bed.

The nurse said, "Oh, be careful not to pull his chest tube out. It's sutured into place, but jumping on it could pull it out so it's no longer draining fluid."

Charlotte backed up and stretched her hand over to Jared's face. She brushed back his hair so she could see his beautiful brown eyes that were closed. "Why do they think he's blind?"

"Look, I shouldn't have said anything. He hasn't been conscious since he came in. The doctors fear that when he stopped breathing, or when they cranked up the oxygen in the emergency room, that they damaged his eyes while trying to save his life. To little or too much oxygen can affect a person's eyes."

Charlotte started crying, and the nurse continued. "It's not a given. It's like when a neurologist sees a comatose patient and runs his pen on the bottom of his foot. The patient may flinch, but until he wakes, no one really knows for sure what the extent of the damage is."

Charlotte screamed and ran out of the room. She ran down to the beach and fell in the sand on Jamie's grave. "I couldn't even save my boyfriend—what kind of person am I?" She sat and sobbed for a long time. She was covered in sand, and when she finally sat up and brushed it off, she saw Mrs. Rogers talking to two deformed individuals. She wiped the sand-mixed tears off her face and blinked her eyes several times to clear the sandpaper feel out of them. She focused on the two thin males. "That's Polo and Seed. What are they doing talking to Mrs. Rogers?"

Charlotte turned when she heard Brooklyn and Gretchen running toward her. Brooklyn said, "Oh, Charlotte, I'm so sorry."

They both hugged Charlotte as she said in a whisper, "Don't say 'sorry' to me. I didn't lose my sight. I can't believe Jared may not be able to see."

Gretchen said, "Does that really bother you? Would you break up with him for that reason? And if the answer is yes, I'd love to be his girlfriend."

Brooklyn said, "Yeah, Gretchen, you're a perfect girlfriend for a blind man."

Charlotte yelled, "Shut up. Shut up! I'm not going anywhere." She looked up just as Mrs. Rogers and the two goons were pointing in her direction. Charlotte watched as the small group of three quickly split up. Mrs. Rogers headed back toward Primevil.

Brooklyn said, "Charlotte, come back inside. We'll sit with you and Jared."

Gretchen interlocked her arm with Charlotte's. "We'll play cards or something quiet."

Charlotte smiled a weak smile. "You'll be happy to know Mrs. Rogers confirmed that Mrs. Bellow used to be a bodybuilder."

Brooklyn said, "Yeah, I heard that on one of the stations—could have fooled me, though."

Gretchen kicked some sand with her toes as they walked back to the asylum. "Mrs. Bellow is quite an actress. You know, when she first arrived at Primevil, I was the one to show her around. I think if I had known she was the Validator's wife, I'd have schmoozed her more. The Validator has always been so private. I've heard he rarely goes out in public. He's a really very secretive, as far as publicity goes."

Brooklyn sneered. "Yeah, you're such a suck-up, Gretchen."

"Listen, Brooklyn, it wouldn't hurt for you to put in for a job around here."

"I don't want to work at Primevil. As soon as they clear us of any insanity issues, I'm out of here."

Gretchen said, "What about you, Charlotte? Are you going to stay and work in the infirmary?"

"I don't know. I'll wait and see what kind of condition Jared is in before I decide what to do."

Brooklyn said, "I'm hooked on all the media hype. I'm like a junky, can't get enough."

Gretchen laughed, "You just want to catch a glimpse of yourself on TV."

Brooklyn smirked at Gretchen. "Maybe so, but I heard the Validator isn't quite sure about reopening the universities yet. He said until all the evaluations on the afflicted were performed, he wouldn't know how many of them could attend college."

Charlotte gazed out at the ocean. "Yeah, I heard that also. Most of the teens whose probe had already been activated are still damaged. Once the brain has been injured, it's hard to come back. Mrs. Rogers told me it was like having a stroke. We all just got lucky when our probes fizzled out before they could destroy a large portion of our brains." She rubbed the back of her neck. "Have you heard what happened to Blood Red Meats?"

Gretchen got excited. "Yeah, I saw video of the employees and managers being hauled off to jail. All over the world they were being pulled out and put in handcuffs. The news said that they'd sort out who was guilty and who wasn't once they gathered all the information."

Brooklyn snickered. "Most of the employees looked like deer caught in headlights. They had a look that showed they had no idea what went on at Blood Red Meats, but come on—the bodies came into the factories in human form. They had to know something. Even if they thought the bodies died of natural causes, that was wrong on so many levels."

Charlotte looked down at Jamie's grave. "At least everyone younger than sixteen is getting the gel probe removed. Hopefully that will expedite the opening of eleventh and twelfth grade again."

Brooklyn picked up a fairly large stick that had washed ashore. She threw it into the ocean and watched as the waves lapped at it. "Charlotte, you can probably have any type of job you want, now that you're a hero and everything."

Charlotte remembered the day she thought Serenity's bloated arm was a stick, floating in on the tide. "Who knows—maybe I'll go back to high school and graduate."

She thought about her dog Jamie, and how nice it would be to have her here, now.

The three girls looked up to see a cadet standing just outside Primevil waving his arms and screaming. The words were taken by the ocean roar. Charlotte stopped and pulled back. "I'm not going in. The cadet is saying something about Jared. I heard his name, and I'm not going in."

Gretchen and Brooklyn tried to pull Charlotte forward. Gretchen said, "You can't stay out here for the rest of your life."

Brooklyn got right next to Charlotte's ear. "It's probably good news."

Charlotte shook her head and cried, "No. It's always bad news at Primevil."

Charlotte watched as the cadet ran toward them. "Oh, please, no, God. Please, no."

As the boy got within a few feet of Charlotte, she could see he was smiling. "Miss Charlotte, your boyfriend is coming around. The doctors stopped the drugs that put him in a coma; said he was stable enough to heal on his own."

"What about his sight? Can he see?"

"Oh, I don't know. The nurse didn't say anything about that."

The boy ran back toward Primevil.

Brooklyn said, "See, you won't have to get another boyfriend. He's alive."

Gretchen looked at Charlotte, who had tears in her eyes. "Are you crying out of sadness, or are you so ecstatic that you can't move your damn legs to go see Jared?"

"It's my fault that he's lying in that bed. Sure, he's beating insurmountable odds, but what if he's blind? I can't bear looking into his brown eyes wondering if I did this to him."

Brooklyn said, "What are you talking about? You didn't beat him. Besides, you would've been impressed with Jared; he put up one hell of a fight. He was trying to get to you, Charlotte."

"See, that's what I'm saying. He should have just been like the rest of you. He shouldn't have put up a fight, for me."

Gretchen said, "I think it's kind of sexy that he cared for you that much. I can't even get a guy to get me a free cup of coffee in the lunchroom—too much trouble crossing the room or something."

Brooklyn wiped the tears off Charlotte's face with her sleeve. "Now look, Charlotte C. Carrion, you take that butt of yours and march it right in to see Jared like nothing's wrong. It's not his fault he loves you more than you love him."

Charlotte scowled. "That's not true. I just can't stand to see him in such a horrible state. It tears out my heart to see him lying there. I wonder if he'll even know me. What if he has brain damage; what if he is blind? I'm just not good at showing Jared my true feelings. It's a protective mechanism I've used my whole life."

Brooklyn said, "So what if he's blind or mentally slow? It seems to me that there's no difference between a person not caring and person not showing their emotions. It's the same thing. Don't be coldhearted."

Gretchen and Brooklyn started dragging Charlotte toward Primevil, and Brooklyn said, "There's only one way to find out."

Charlotte jerked herself free of her well-meaning friends. "I can walk by myself, thank you."

Brooklyn said, "That's okay. We're walking in that direction anyway."

Gretchen pinched Charlotte. "Yeah, we're going to visit Jared, whether you are or not."

The three girls stood outside Jared's room. Charlotte could see that he had his arm bent and lying across his face, covering his eyes. Brooklyn gave Charlotte a slight push.

"I'm going," Charlotte said.

She silently tiptoed over to his bed and stood there, too scared to say anything. She knew she'd love him whether he was blind, mentally handicapped, or anything else the nurse hadn't told her, but in the next moment she'd know for sure whether Jared would be calling an asylum home. She didn't think she could take care of Jared on her own.

Brooklyn tapped her on the shoulder. "Charlotte, go on, talk to him."

Charlotte turned and started to walk out with Brooklyn trailing her. "I need to talk with Jared on my own. I'll catch up with you later."

Brooklyn started to protest, but Gretchen grabbed Brooklyn's elbow and they walked down the hall. Brooklyn was pleading her case for staying in the room. "What if she runs out on him? What if she doesn't go in the room at all?"

Charlotte turned when she heard Jared speak. He lifted the arm that was lying across his face and said in a very weak voice, "Hey, beautiful. Don't be scared of my appearance." He pointed to the chest tube and IVs. "All this is just temporary."

Charlotte walked over to the bed. She bit down so hard on her bottom lip that she tasted blood. She didn't want to cry. "You can see me?"

He slowly pulled the covers back. "Come here. Yes, I can see you. My vision isn't what it was. The doctor tested my vision, and it's nothing that glasses or contacts won't correct. How do you feel about a guy in glasses?"

Charlotte ran around the foot of his bed and crawled into his arms. "I think you'd look very distinguished."

Her tears flowed onto his bare chest. She could feel the small puddle of saltwater drops collecting on his chest.

He brought her in close and whispered in his strained voice, "Did you hear that Mrs. Bellow is married to the Validator? She's been making a lot of personal appearances in your behalf. I guess she used her maiden name when she came to Primevil."

Charlotte rubbed his chest with her hand, content being in Jared's arms. "How do you know all this?"

"I heard everything said in my room."

He was fading into sleep. Charlotte clung to him as if he would leave her if she also slipped into slumber. She whispered, "Jared, I love you."

She wasn't expecting a reply, but Jared said, "Yeah, I know."

He cradled her in his arms and brushed his lips against hers. It was a soft, sensual kiss, but it didn't last long. He was soon asleep.

29

Getting Back to Normal?

Jared's physical wounds were healing, and Charlotte, Brooklyn, and Gretchen were on the emotional mends. Jared's chest tube was out, and he was getting his strength back. It had been about two weeks since Jared came out of his drug-induced coma, and Charlotte had to update him on everything that had happened at Dr. Oracle's manor. He'd forgotten about Jamie's death, his beating, their escape from the mansion, and the demise of the enormous estate.

Charlotte yawned and stretched. "I can't wait to get out of here. I think the Validator is going much too slow on relocating the patients that are able to leave."

Brooklyn said, "Yeah I saw him on the news yesterday and he looked almost green. I think he's sick or overwhelmed with all the things that need to get done. I asked Mrs. Rogers about foster homes last night and she just gave a little laugh and said I shouldn't hold my breath."

Gretchen poked Brooklyn. "You really think people are going to bust down Primevil's door planning to foster the mentally insane?"

Charlotte said with a snip in her voice, "Gretchen, we're not mental patients. We're perfectly normal."

Gretchen snorted. "Yeah, Charlotte, try telling that to eligible families looking for a teenager to make their family complete. You think they'd believe we weren't damaged goods living at Primevil?"

They were in Jared's hospital room, playing cards, and Brooklyn had just finished polishing her toes with the Monarch polish and was painting Gretchen's fingernails.

Brooklyn held the bottle of polish in the air. "It's almost gone. I wonder where I can get another bottle this same color."

Gretchen said, "Do you think that Monarch butterfly in Dr. Oracle's mansion had anything to do with Serenity?"

Charlotte said, "Sure. That place was locked up tighter than a tomb. There was no way a butterfly could ever get in."

Charlotte put her cards down on the bed. "I won." She started laughing. "That's three in a row."

Jared looked at Charlotte. "I almost forgot what your laugh sounded like."

Mrs. Bellow walked into the room in street clothes. The girls all yelled. "Mrs. Bellow!" Brooklyn said, "Good to see you out of your uniform, Mrs. B."

Mrs. Bellow looked around the room. "Charlotte, I see you got all your awards I sent you. You really should give a few interviews. You're such an enigma, and everyone wants to know all about you. There're at least two dozen different media groups outside Primevil waiting to talk with you, Charlotte. It's almost impossible to get in or out without getting barraged by someone wanting to know your feelings on this entire escapade."

Charlotte waved her hand in the air. "I'm not much for gloating. Once Jared gets well enough to be discharged from the hospital, I'll do a few interviews, but right now I just want to be with him."

Gretchen said, "Come, sit and play cards with us."

"I wish I had the time, but as you all know, I'm not bashful, and I'm off to give another interview. Charlotte, what they really want to know is if you and Jared are serious."

Jared started laughing, and then grabbed his side. "Side still tender. Out of all the things they could ask, that's what they want to know? Tell them yes, of course we're serious about each other."

Charlotte could feel her face warming. "Mrs. Bellow, just tell them 'no comment.'"

Jared smiled at Charlotte and she said, "Don't they want to know more about the gel probe, which eluded medical personnel for ten years?"

"Not really. That's too technical. They'd rather hear about your love life."

Brooklyn laughed. "You mean lack of a love life."

Jared repositioned himself on his bed. "Brooklyn, our love life is just fine. She's sixteen and I'm seventeen. What's the rush?"

Mrs. Bellow said, "Should I tell the media that?"

Jared said, "Go right ahead. Leave them guessing."

Mrs. Bellow did a quick spin. "What do you think of this dress?"

Brooklyn said, "I was just going to tell you it looks fabulous, Mrs. B."

Gretchen held up the Monarch polish. "Would you like me to paint your nails to match your multicolored dress?"

"I'll pass. No time. I've got more media interviews."

As Mrs. Bellow was leaving the room, Brooklyn said, "Hey, Mrs. B. I saw the picture of you on TV, when you were a bodybuilder." Brooklyn let out a low whistle. "Pretty sexy."

"Girls, that was when I was much younger. Actually, that's where the Validator and I met. He was a judge in one of those contests." She sighed. "Enjoy your youth; I know I did."

Charlotte said, "That was quite an accomplishment, Mrs. Bellow. Have fun on your interview."

"Oh, I will."

"And, Mrs. Bellow?"

"Yes, Charlotte?"

Charlotte looked at Jared and gave him a shy smile. "You can tell the media that Jared and I are an item."

Mrs. Bellow clapped her hands together. "Fantastic. See you girls next week."

Charlotte leaned over, and Jared gave her a soft kiss on the lips.

Brooklyn frowned. "Enough mushy stuff. Charlotte, order us a pizza from the cafeteria. Since you've become somewhat of a champion, they don't deny you anything. Tell them to have a cadet bring it here."

"How about a vegetarian pizza?"

Jared groaned. "I'd like a little meat on the pizza."

Charlotte crinkled her nose. "After everything you know, Jared, you still want meat?"

He shrugged his shoulders. Charlotte said, "That's okay, I'll order two pizzas."

The girls laughed and played cards late into the night. Jared went to sleep right after he ate. Charlotte said, "That pizza was the best food I've had at Primevil."

Brooklyn said, "Hey, Charlotte–is this what it's like to have a slumber party?"

She looked at her friends. "Yeah, this is what it's like."

Charlotte thought about all the horror that filled the walls of Primevil. She knew if she hadn't been surrounded by her friends, she would've gone insane like her great-grandfather did, after the war. She surveyed the three around her, knowing they would always be a permanent fixture in her mind. She pursed her lips and blew out a breath of air as her eyes got misty. She softly said, "Thanks, guys."

Brooklyn wiped her pizza smile on her sleeve. "Thanks for what?"

Gretchen dealt the cards and Charlotte said, "Thanks for always being around."

Brooklyn said, "Like we had a choice."

Charlotte grinned at Brooklyn. "You didn't have a choice to come to Primevil, but you had a choice whether to be my friend or not."

Brooklyn patted her chest. "Yeah, things turned out for the best. I've never had friends like you two. Charlotte, the day we met I thought I'd have to mop the floor with you. If it wasn't for your overly developed bodyguard over there, I'd have had you begging for surrender." Brooklyn let out a loud burp.

Gretchen said. "That's just utterly gross, Brooklyn. Once a street rat always a street rat."

Charlotte rearranged the cards in her hand. "Let's just play some cards and accept the differences between us. We don't need to be alike."

Brooklyn picked up her cards. "Yes, finally a winning hand. Gretchen hurry up, you go first."

Charlotte leaned over the bed and picked up Jared's hand and gave it a squeeze. He opened his eyes and gave her a slight smile. He brought her hand to his lips and brushed his lips over her fingers. "Night, Charlotte."

He fell fast asleep. She swept the hair off his forehead. "Night, Jared."

Redwine hill

30

The Unwelcomed Guest

In the weeks that followed, buildings were being demolished. The lobotomy suite was torn down, along with Dr. Oracle's lab and morgue at Primevil. Jared's outer appearance had healed, but his internal organs were still suffering from his beating. It would take time for him to feel completely normal. Charlotte, Brooklyn, and Gretchen played cards every night in Jared's room. Charlotte heard all about the eligible males that were worthy of her two friends' attention. Brooklyn and Gretchen spent every waking moment prowling the halls of Primevil looking for any male patients that would give them the time of day. Evaluations were still being done on the patients in order to decide who could leave Primevil and who would become a permanent resident at the asylum. It was a slow process. The medical staff was running on a skeleton crew. A lot of the personnel had to be locked up for taking bribes and payments to supply Blood Red Meats. Even the ones who just did nothing but turn a blind eye to what was happening got fired, or incarcerated.

Gretchen said, "Brooklyn, did you see the way the guy in the light-blue button-down shirt looked at you."

"Yeah, I think he's cute. I think I'll talk to him tomorrow."

Charlotte said, "What about you, Gretchen? Any prospects?"

Jared said, "You mean victims."

"Jared if you weren't still suffering from your beating, I'd smack you for that comment. No, I didn't see anyone that even gave me a second look. I think it's these darn teeth of mine.

Charlotte looked at Jared, who gave a sheepish grin. "I'm sure it's not your teeth, but if you want, I can request for you to have some dental work."

Brooklyn almost yelled. "Yeah, Charlotte can request just about anything and she'll get it."

Gretchen ran her tongue along her teeth. "Do you think the dentist could really do something with my smile?"

Brooklyn said, "Rat Teeth, I don't see why not. Charlotte, will you make a request for Gretchen?"

"Sure, first thing in the morning." Charlotte paused. "What do you all think about us getting a four-bedroom condo together? We can finish high school and then decide what we want to do from there."

Jared said, "I'd like to ask a favor, but I don't know what the rest of you would think."

Charlotte gave Jared a soft smile. "What, Jared? You've been through so much. What's your favor?"

"Well, since no one else in this room has living parents, can I ask that my mother live with us, as our guardian? I haven't seen my mother since I was brought here, but I'd like to find her and have her be a part of our lives."

Brooklyn crossed her legs, Indian style, on the bed. "I'd love having a mother watching out for me."

Charlotte said, "I think that's a very nice solution to moving out on our own. I think I can get the Validator to give us a condo on the nice side of town, but what do we do for monthly income?"

Gretchen got excited. "We could all get jobs, and go to school."

Brooklyn's shoulders drooped. "I wasn't a very good student—that is, when I did go to school. I don't think I could go to school, do homework, and get a job."

Jared got up and went to his dresser and dug around. "I don't think we'll need to worry about getting jobs." He pulled a black sock out of his drawer.

Gretchen said, "I don't think a sock will pay for anything."

Jared dumped the contents of the slightly worn sock out on the bed.

Charlotte screamed and hugged Jared. "Those are the jewels from Dr. Oracle's house! I forgot you took a handful."

Brooklyn slipped a ring on her finger. "Look at this. I've never seen such exquisite jewelry before. This ring alone must be worth a fortune."

The lunch lady brought the evening pizza into the room as Brooklyn dove across the jewels.

Charlotte went and took the pizza. "Thanks."

Brooklyn sat up when the woman left the room. "Whoa, that was a close one. Can't let anybody know you have this."

Gretchen picked up a fairly large jewel. "Jared, you could get killed if someone knew you had these. It would certainly change someone's life for the better."

Brooklyn opened the pizza box. "Charlotte, I'm surprised the Validator didn't offer you a reward of some kind. What a cheapskate."

Charlotte waved her hand in the air. "No need. Besides, he probably has enough on his mind."

Gretchen pulled a blob of cheese off the lid and popped it into her mouth. "I don't know about being busy. I'm with Brooklyn. You deserve a lot more than a handful of awards and a thank you."

Jared patted Charlotte's thigh. "I agree, but maybe he's just waiting for things to calm down first. You know—a proper ceremony and everything. Mrs. Bellow wouldn't forget you, Charlotte."

Just as they each took a piece of pizza, in floated Wanda.

In her slurping voice she said, "Charlotte, we need to talk."

Brooklyn groaned and Gretchen said, "Get out, Wanda!"

Jared sat up and sighed. "We can't deal with you. Every time you come around it sets terrible things in motion."

Charlotte held her stomach. "Not now, Wanda. We just got our food, and your looks are making my stomach upset."

"I've kept out of the way this entire time, but I need to talk with you, Charlotte."

Wanda brought out a cellophane bag and started eating something. Charlotte yelled, "No. get out. You're grossing me out."

Wanda sucked the muck off one of her ravaged fingers. "I just thought we could all sit and talk over dinner."

Charlotte held her stomach. "Get out! Get out! Get out!"

"Okay, don't go getting hysterical on me. I'll come back in thirty minutes."

Brooklyn yelled, "Wanda, don't come back at all."

Wanda ignored Brooklyn and floated out of the room crinkling her bag of goodies.

Charlotte grimaced. "I can't eat."

Jared picked up a piece of pizza and handed it to Charlotte. "Come on, Charlotte, don't let Wanda spoil your dinner. I know she didn't think twice about ruining our meal. Put that image out of your mind."

Gretchen said, "Let's play cards." She dealt each of them a hand.

As they played some new game Gretchen had just made up, Charlotte nibbled on her slice of pizza. By the time she had one full slice down, Wanda was back.

Jared grumbled, "What do you want?"

"I've come to ask a favor."

They all yelled at the same time. "No!"

"I'm not leaving until you hear me out."

Charlotte looked at Wanda. "What is it?"

Brooklyn got as close to Charlotte as she possible could. "Are you crazy? She's nothing but trouble."

Charlotte spoke with a confidence she didn't know she had. "We should at least hear what she has to say. She was a big part of taking down Blood Red Meats and Dr. Oracle."

Charlotte leaned against Jared's chest and sighed. "What's so important?"

Wanda sat between Gretchen and Brooklyn on the bed. The kittens were softly curled up on the comforter, where they always were.

Charlotte looked at Wanda cellophane bag. "Wanda, no eating in front of us."

Wanda rolled up the bag. "Fine. First, I want to say kudos to all four of you, but Dr. Oracle is still out there."

Charlotte held up her hand. "Wanda, we've all matured past our biological years in this place. I've grown up a lot, and it's not because I wanted to but because I was forced to. I don't think it's up to us to find Dr. Oracle."

Brooklyn said, "Yeah, I had less stress when I was a street rat living by myself than I've had in here."

Jared got disgusted. "Look we all almost lost our lives, and Marty did. Just let the authorities find him."

Wanda's voice was raspy. "The only problem with waiting around for the authorities to find him is that all four of you are on Dr. Oracle's hit list. As a matter of fact, you're the only ones on his hit list."

Brooklyn said sarcastically, "So you've seen this list?"

Wanda picked up Noon and looked at the kitten's stump. "Not exactly, but I know he's planning something for the four of you. So if you don't get him first, he'll get you."

The room fell silent. Charlotte finally said, "We don't even know where he is."

"Listen, I'm not a mind reader, just a ghost. He'll find you, but you need to be prepared. Jared, maybe you and Gretchen could show Charlotte and Brooklyn how to shoot."

Jared shook his head. "Guns really didn't help us at Dr. Oracle's manor."

Wanda put up her decayed hand. "Fine, you figure out the details of protecting yourself. I'm just here to warn you. He's not going to let you live as long as he's alive. You destroyed everything he worked his entire life for. He could have kept doing his evil for years to come. The hard gel probe had been undetected." She put Noon down and continued. "With the following he has, Dr. Oracle could start everything back in motion. He's a brilliant man, and his IQ is off the charts. It's too bad he didn't use it for good."

Charlotte asked, "Wanda, why are you still roaming the halls of Primevil? Haven't you done what you set out to do? Let the world know how teens were dying and being used to supply the meat industry?"

"I'd like to think I could rest now, but I need to get revenge for my death, and there's only one person who was responsible for that. I'm not going anywhere until I see Dr. Oracle in a morgue or six feet under."

Charlotte watched as Wanda opened the bag she was holding and dug down to the bottom, pulling the last piece of innards out and popping it into her mouth. Then Wanda left the bed and floated out the door.

Jared looked at Charlotte and shook his head. "Charlotte, you can't possibly be thinking of bringing Dr. Oracle to justice?"

"We're just teens." Brooklyn sounded deflated.

Charlotte rubbed her forehead. "I don't want to think about any of this now. I know Wanda's right. She may look horrific, but she's never lied. I just don't know if this small group has what it takes to find and capture Dr. Oracle. I wouldn't know where to start looking." She got off the bed. "I'm going out to visit Jamie's grave. Anybody else want to go for a walk?"

Gretchen grabbed Brooklyn's arm. "Let's go see who's in the lounge." They each picked up one of the kittens and started talking about who they'd run into in the teen lounge.

Jared was up and out of bed. He wrapped his arm around Charlotte. "Finally, a respite from Pete and Repeat."

Charlotte laughed. "They're a bit intense, but they're on a mission to find themselves boyfriends."

As they walked out Primevil's doors, the ocean wind was blustering. Charlotte grabbed her ponytail and held on to her hair. They sat in the sand by Jamie's grave. Charlotte said, "I like this place for Jamie's resting place. No one ever comes over this way. It's peaceful."

Jared said in a sensual voice, "Yeah, a secluded spot."

Charlotte took her shoes off and dug her nine stubby toes into the sand.

Jared gently turned Charlotte's face and kissed her passionately. She let go of her hair and put her arms around his neck. Her stress level disappeared, and she melted into him.

31

Suspicion about Mrs. Rogers

Jared pulled away from Charlotte. She said, "What's wrong?"

He held his hand to his lips. "Look along the rock wall. Is that Mrs. Rogers?"

Charlotte put her finger to her lips and whispered, "Yeah, and she's talking to those two goons who dragged me to Primevil. I think their names are Polo and Seed."

"What's she up to?"

"I can't say for sure, but we need to keep an eye on her. I've seen Mrs. Rogers out here before with those two. And when she hung a small bag to your IV a few weeks back, the night nurse said the liquid in the bag looked funny. Don't worry, Jared—you didn't get much of that cloudy stuff."

"Let's go in and find Brooklyn and Gretchen. We need to be very careful around Mrs. Rogers. There is no reason for her to be out here talking to a Collector's sidekicks."

When they entered Primevil, they saw Brooklyn and Gretchen down the hall, talking and giggling with some teenage boys. Charlotte smiled and skipped into Jared's room. "Isn't that great? They each found someone who's interested in them."

Jared ran his hand through his hair. "Do you have Mrs. Bellow's phone number? I think we need to inform her about Mrs. Rogers's mysterious behavior. She needs to have her husband check her out."

"Yeah, I agree." She dug in her jeans pocket and pulled out a wad of crumpled paper.

"Love your filing system."

"I'll be right back. I'm going to find a phone."

Jared jumped off the bed. "Not without me."

They walked to the cafeteria, and Charlotte asked the only lunch lady left, "Can I use your phone?"

"Honey, they have a phone in the infirmary."

Charlotte didn't want to use the clinic phone. She didn't want to run into Mrs. Rogers.

Jared picked up some fruit and distracted the lady so Charlotte could talk with Mrs. Bellow without anyone listening in. "If it wouldn't be too much trouble, those beef sandwiches you used to fix me sound great."

The large woman blushed. "I'll get right on it."

Jared was eating his sandwich when Charlotte came back to him. With a mouthful of food he said, "So what'd she think?"

Charlotte shrugged. "She was very concerned, and wanted to get to the bottom of this. I hope we don't get Mrs. Rogers fired because of our overactive imaginations."

"Here, sit and have a sandwich."

"Is it a meat sandwich?"

"Yeah, what else is there?"

Charlotte crinkled her nose. "No thanks. Anyway, Mrs. Bellow wants us to go to some kind of party, here in town. She thinks we should go and put in an appearance. She said people are beginning to think the teens who flushed out this demented scheme of Dr. Oracle's are a figment of everyone's imagination."

"Who cares if no one believes we exist? That's even better for us. We can fly under the radar, so to speak."

Charlotte twisted her fingers. "I told her we'd all go, including you. Before you protest, I don't want to go without a date, so you're coming."

"Well, since you put it like that, how can I refuse?" He put the last piece of sandwich in his mouth. "So when is this big party?"

"Two weeks from this Friday. Mrs. Bellow is out of town right now, and she said she wanted to make the party special."

They headed out of the cafeteria and back to Jared's room. Brooklyn and Gretchen were sitting on the bed playing with the kittens. Charlotte said, "I've got good news for both of you."

They both asked, "What."

"It's not all that exciting. Mrs. Bellow is throwing us a party to do a meet and greet. I told her we'd all be there. It's in a few weeks."

Gretchen smiled. "Oh, Charlotte! Can you please call a dentist tomorrow and schedule me an appointment for my teeth?"

"Sure, but do you think a dentist can do anything for your teeth in such a short time?"

Brooklyn laughed. "Hey, I think you should leave the big rat teeth in front. Maybe there'll be a guy there that likes that kind of thing."

Gretchen said, "Well, Brooklyn you're no looker, either. As I recall at the patient dance, you looked rather garish with all that makeup on."

"I did not. Mrs. Bellow wiped most of it off. Charlotte, did I look bad?"

Charlotte quickly changed the subject. "The best part is that Mrs. Bellow is going to get the dresses and Jared's tuxedo for us. So we can do each other's hair and makeup."

Brooklyn screamed at the top of her lungs, "This is going to be the best night ever."

Gretchen joined Brooklyn and yelled, "Dancing, music, and guys."

A cadet came running into the room and looked at the two girls screaming. "Is everything all right? Should a get a nurse? Mrs. Rogers is just down the hall."

Charlotte answered, "No, don't do that. Everything is fine." She pointed to Brooklyn and Gretchen. "They're just excited to be going to a dance, that's all."

Brooklyn said, "Not just any dance—a dance where we're the main attractions. If I can't get a boyfriend out of this, I might have to give up."

The cadet looked at Charlotte as Brooklyn and Gretchen danced around the room. "Cadet, everything is fine," Charlotte assured him.

"Are you sure?" He pointed to the two dancing and bouncing around the room. "They seem a bit crazed to me."

Charlotte shook her head. "No, they're fine. They're just boy crazy, that's all."

Gretchen and Brooklyn left Jared's room. Gretchen looked over her shoulder. "Charlotte, don't forget to call the dentist tomorrow. I'm sorry I'm always asking you for a favor, but nobody is going to do anything special for me. My only claim to fame is knowing you."

Brooklyn jabbed Gretchen in the side. "Come on, you can show me how to put on makeup."

Charlotte got off the bed and went and stood at the door, watching her friends skip down the hall, arms interlocked. "Gretchen, you could ask for anything too; you just don't think you can. We're a team, remember?"

Brooklyn turned back to look at Charlotte. "I'm going to try on a little bit of all the makeup that Mrs. Bellow gave us. You don't mind, do you? I know I put it all in my dresser drawer, but some of it belongs to you."

"Of course not. You go right ahead. Knock yourself out."

Charlotte went back over to the bed, and Jared smiled. "You really think that's going to come out all right? Leaving her in the hands of Gretchen for supervision on decorating their faces? I'd hate to be the mirror looking at that mess."

Charlotte laughed. "Yeah, Brooklyn thinks more is best, but I think if she just used a little blush and a more natural color lipstick she'd be fine."

"I don't know, Charlotte." He shook his head. "Too much, not enough—what's the difference? The outcome is the same. Unless a guy is visual impaired, it's not going to end pretty."

Charlotte grabbed Jared's hand. "That reminds me. Did you make an appointment to get your eyes checked?"

"Yep, so you don't mind going to the party with a guy wearing glasses?"

"Nope, and I figure if any guy wants to make fun of your 'four eyes,' your muscles will quickly stop any of that kind of conversation."

His smile landed on her lips, and she watched as he stretched out on his bed. She asked in a soft voice, "Do you want to play cards?"

"I'd love to, but I can't seem to keep my eyes open tonight. I'm exhausted, but you go right ahead."

Charlotte was somewhat disappointed; she loved talking with Jared even more than she liked talking with her two girlfriends. Since the beds were pushed together, she leaned over and gave him a quick kiss on the cheek. "Night, Jared."

He was already in slumber land. *I wish I could fall asleep that fast.*

She spent the next several hours tossing and turning. *I hate parties, and accolades. Brooklyn and Gretchen thrive on this type of thing. Jared could take it or leave it. Whatever I wanted, Jared would do for me, but it always makes me feel so uncomfortable. I'm sure the dresses Mrs. Bellow picks out won't be too hideous.*

Redwine hill

32

Betrayal

Jared had gone to his eye appointment and now wore glasses. When he walked into the room with his new specs on, Charlotte looked up. "You look distinguished. Do you feel any smarter?"

"No, if anything, it's going to take a while to get use to them. I don't think my physical attributes and glasses are a good combination."

"Well, I think you look handsome, even cute, in your glasses."

"Cute was not the look I was going for. Hey, where are Gretchen and Brooklyn today? Another dentist's appointment?"

"Yeah, they're both super happy with the work the dentist is doing on their smiles. This is the last day, for the final touches. I think they both actually look pretty now. They'll be able to get a boyfriend now, for sure."

Jared groaned. "Unless the dentist did something with their personalities, I still don't think they have a chance in hell to snag a boyfriend."

The day of the party Brooklyn and Gretchen were buzzing with excitement. Charlotte had her trepidations about the evening, but she wouldn't spoil this for her friends. Mrs. Bellow walked in the girls' room with her arms full of beautiful dresses. Brooklyn and Gretchen jumped off the bed, waking Noon and Midnight. Brooklyn screamed as she grabbed one of the dresses out of Mrs. Bellow's arms. "It's beautiful, Mrs. B. Is this one mine?"

"Yes, Brooklyn, the light blue is for you. Remember when you got your blue dress stuck in the door and I used my scissors to cut you loose? I told you I'd get you another dress, and here it is."

Brooklyn hugged Mrs. Bellow. "Thank you, Mrs. B." She ran toward the bathroom. "I'm trying it on."

Mrs. Bellow handed Gretchen a pale-yellow dress. "This will look good with your skin color."

Charlotte was still sitting on the bed. "Charlotte, I got you a light-green dress. It will go beautiful with your amber hair."

Charlotte said in a weak voice, "Thanks, Mrs. Bellow, but are you sure I can't stay here at Primevil? I'm not much for crowds."

"You'll be fine." Mrs. Bellow gave Jared his tuxedo, and handed all of them their matching shoes.

"How'd you know my size?"

"Simple, that came from the admissions notes. I just took the measurements to the dressmakers and tuxedo store, and voila! I hope they fit. Jared, nice glasses, by the way."

"Thanks, Mrs. Bellow."

"Now, you all meet me at the clinic by five thirty."

Mrs. Bellow left, and Brooklyn and Gretchen yelled after her, "Thank you."

Charlotte felt uneasy and was fiddling with her dress. "I'm not sure if we should go. What if Dr. Oracle shows up?"

Brooklyn scowled. "Are you crazy? Gretchen, grab Charlotte's arm. If we have to drag you to the party, you're going."

Gretchen said, "Dr. Oracle isn't going to show his face with all the media attention that will be there."

Jared smiled at Charlotte. "It's just one party. We'll dance a few songs, meet a few people—might be fun."

Charlotte had never danced with Jared. "I guess I wouldn't mind dancing with you."

Gretchen said, "I knew you'd change your mind."

Jared leaned over and gave Charlotte a kiss on the cheek. "Charlotte, I'll see you later."

"Bye, Jared."

Brooklyn had her dress on. She held on to the matching shoes with one hand and Charlotte with the other. "I get to use the makeup first."

Gretchen said, "I think you better take a shower first."

Charlotte was the last to get cleaned up. Brooklyn already had two coats of makeup on and was starting with a third. Charlotte went over and took the eye shadow brush away. "Brooklyn, less is more."

Brooklyn stuck her tongue out at Charlotte. "That's a stupid saying. Less is just less."

Gretchen said, "Well, Brooklyn, in this circumstance, I'm on Charlotte's side."

Charlotte brushed out her long, thick hair. This was the first time she'd gone anywhere without her ponytail. Once they zipped each other up, they stood in front of the mirror. Brooklyn said, "We're all a vision. If only any of my foster parents could see me."

Charlotte gave each of them a squeeze as Jared walked in. He looked at Charlotte. "Whoa, you look ravishing, Charlotte."

Brooklyn sneered at Jared. "What are Gretchen and me—the beastly girls?"

Jared came over to Charlotte and kissed her softly on the neck. "I didn't mean to offend you. Brooklyn, Gretchen—you look wonderful."

Brooklyn said, "Thanks. What do you think about my face?"

"Why, what's wrong with your face?"

Brooklyn said, "See, Charlotte, Jared thinks my makeup looks good."

"Uh, I didn't exactly say that."

Gretchen said, "Come on. Mrs. Bellow will probably leave without us if we're not there at the clinic by five thirty. You know how she is about being punctual."

Brooklyn and Gretchen walked in front of Jared and Charlotte, bouncing, skipping, and giggling down the hallway.

Some of the patients came out of their rooms to see what was going on. Gretchen poked Brooklyn. "Hey, isn't that the guy you were talking to a few days ago?"

Brooklyn stuck her tongue out at the teenage male patient. "Yeah, the one that didn't bother to look me up."

Gretchen squeezed Brooklyn's elbow. "Just play it cool. Like we get dressed up like this all the time."

Brooklyn gave a slight wave to the teen. 'Have a nice evening. We're going to an awards party."

Brooklyn and Gretchen started laughing, and Gretchen snorted. Brooklyn turned to look back at the boy and said, "That wasn't me who snorted. I have manners."

Gretchen was laughing so hard she was snorting all the way to the clinic. When she got her composure, she said, "Brooklyn, now look what you've done. I'm sure I've streaked my makeup with laughter tears."

Charlotte didn't want to delay the inevitable any longer. "We'll fix it when we get to the party."

"You've brought makeup with you?"

Charlotte held up one of the kitten bags. "Yep. I've got everything in this bag but the kittens."

Gretchen said, "Shhh, there's Mrs. Bellow.

Mrs. Bellow tapped her watch. "Right on time. Let's get going."

Brooklyn said, "Mrs. B., you haven't said how good we all look."

"Oh, I'm sorry. You all look presentable. Now let's get going."

Charlotte looked at Jared and mouthed the word presentable.

Jared shrugged his shoulders. "She's probably trying to keep her cool." He pointed to Brooklyn and Gretchen. "I bet she thinks they'll say something to embarrass her."

Charlotte adjusted the bag on her shoulder. Jared asked, "Do you want me to carry that thing? It doesn't exactly go with the dress."

"No, I'm fine. I'm not there to impress anyone, anyway."

They got to the security hut, but this time there were no security or guards coming to inspect them.

Mrs. Bellow got in the car and turned the key, while Jared helped all the girls into the backseat. He jumped into the front passenger seat, and they took off.

Mrs. Bellow was being exceptionally quiet. Charlotte leaned forward. "Mrs. Bellow, are you feeling all right? Usually you're talking up a storm."

Mrs. Bellow shook her head. "I'm just tired. Such a whirlwind of activity lately. After tonight I'll get some rest."

They hadn't gone far when they pulled up to a grand house. Charlotte leaned over Gretchen and looked out the window. "Who lives here? It doesn't look like a party to me."

Mrs. Bellow didn't wait for Jared to open her car door. She popped it open and said, "Follow me."

They all jumped out and followed Mrs. Bellow to the front door. Charlotte was rearranging the bag she was carrying. She thought she'd have time, but instead of Mrs. Bellow knocking on the door, she just opened it. There was an old, thin butler standing there. He quickly locked the door once they had all passed the threshold and said, "Welcome home, Mrs. Bellow."

Charlotte stomach was becoming upset. "This is your house, Mrs. Bellow?"

She said in a curt tone, "Yes. I live here."

Jared leaned into Charlotte. "I don't like this."

Charlotte whispered, "Me neither. My stomach hurts."

They followed Mrs. Bellow into a large room that looked like the study.

Two large men that looked like bodyguards stood on either side of the door. Mrs. Bellow turned and locked the door.

Charlotte said in a weak voice, "Is this where the party is?"

Mrs. Bellow snapped, "There is no party. Why don't you all have a seat? I want to tell you a story."

Brooklyn said, "Mrs. B., I'd rather go to the party. We can talk some other time."

Mrs. Bellow yelled, "Shut up. One more sentence from you and I'll have my two friends here take care of you. Brooklyn, you really don't know about social graces, do you?"

Charlotte scanned the room, and on the desk beside the couch was a picture of Mrs. Bellow, the Validator, and Dr. Oracle. She gasped.

Mrs. Bellow said, "I see you've noticed my picture." She walked over and picked it up and showed it to the others now scrunched on the couch. "You see, this picture was taken many years ago when I was a bodybuilder. My husband and Dr. Oracle were two of the five judges. That's how we all met. We've been very close ever since. I wasn't married at the time, but after a year of dating I got married. I continued to use my maiden name, mostly for professional purposes, and my husband climbed the political ladder."

She looked at the picture sweetly and said, "Now, where was I. Oh, yes. Dr. Oracle was a genius, and he had a lot of extra money.

Let's just say my husband's career took off shortly after making a deal with Dr. Oracle."

Charlotte stammered, "I-I don't understand . . ."

"I really was pulled out of retirement, but not how you think. My husband wanted me to find and suppress who was stirring up trouble. So I started working at Primevil. I called Dr. Oracle that night Serenity came down with a high fever. She was talking out of her mind from the drugs I gave her—not from a fever. Once she figured out my identity, she tried to escape. I saw my chance when she was standing by the ledge. I crept up behind her and pushed her over. I didn't know her arm was going to catch on the fence and float into shore, but that worked out in my favor."

Mrs. Bellow smiled at Charlotte. "I knew Serenity was an operative, and I can't take all the credit for BT's death. When Marty came to my office, as he did so many times, I knew who he was, so I would pretend to have a conversation on the phone about BT and his accusations. Marty got scared and anonymously turned him in to Mrs. Rogers for a lobotomy. Marty was the one who pulled the trigger, but I put the idea in his head."

Brooklyn was sweating profusely and looked pale and distraught. Gretchen was no better off. She was twisting her fingers to the point of making her knuckles pop and turn white. Jared's jaw clenched, and his hands curled into fists.

Charlotte cried out, "You're sick. Did you know who Marty was when you had me dance with him at the patients' dance?"

"Of course. Didn't mean I couldn't have a little fun along the way at your expense."

Charlotte stood. "We're not staying here."

"Sit down, Charlotte, or my bodybuilding friends will tear you apart."

Jared grabbed Charlotte's hand.

"Yes, Jared, calm your girlfriend down," Mrs. Bellow said.

Mrs. Bellow cleared her throat. "I killed Marty also. Remember, I had my purse with my gun in it. I was going to shoot him and then blame it on one of you, but things didn't work out that way. I couldn't have any witnesses."

She went over and took her purse out from behind the desk and pulled a small device out. "The only way I could incapacitate him was to blow up the gel probe in his brain. I just reached in my purse, programmed his number in, and pushed the button. Bam, he was dead. It's a shame I can't use this to click you four dead. Since you've had your probe removed, I'll just have to think of another way. Marty was twenty-five and worked for the president. He loved his job. He was one of the lucky ones that could function once the probe went off when he was sixteen."

She glared at the ceiling, tapping the clicker against her chin. "I believe the probes had gotten so much more advanced since the first ones ten years ago."

Charlotte's voice shook. "What about when you got your concussion from the rioters?"

"I never had a concussion. Those animals did go berserk for some reason. Dr. Oracle was trying to tweak the probes, but it backfired. He tried that a couple of times a year."

Brooklyn said in a weak, almost inaudible, voice, "You were so convincing."

"I thought so. I majored in nursing, but I have a minor in theater. I can't take any credit for Wanda though. She is a ghost that haunts Primevil."

"I was the one that put something in Jared's antibiotics, not Mrs. Rogers. But, Charlotte, when you called me about your suspicions, I had to do something about the four of you."

She looked at them squeezed on the sofa. "Oh, one other thing. I was the one who tied your precious kittens by their legs to the ceiling."

Brooklyn leaned back on the couch. She stammered out in a whisper, "I think I'm going to faint."

Gretchen gritted her teeth. "You better pull yourself together, Brooklyn. I'm not going to carry you out of here if you black out. Charlotte, think of something?"

Jared leaned into Charlotte and whispered, "I can't take down those two goliaths guarding the door by myself."

Charlotte thought this had to be a bad dream.

There was a tap on the door. Mrs. Bellow went to see who it was. She turned and walked behind the desk. "While we wait for Dr. Oracle to show up, let me show you something—or should I say someone. Here's an operative that I didn't know about until you pointed me in her direction."

She pushed a button and a screen came down. There on the monitor was Mrs. Rogers. Her hands and feet were tied together, and she dangled over a pit. Mrs. Bellow smiled. "You can't see them in the monitor, but there are several alligators ready to tear Mrs. Rogers to pieces. The picture in front of you has been made available by Dr. Oracle, who will be joining us shortly."

There on the screen popped two familiar faces. It was Polo and Seed. Mrs. Bellow screamed, "Those idiots. What are they doing?"

They pulled and yanked Mrs. Rogers to safety, then untied the knots. The noise above Mrs. Bellow's house grew louder. Charlotte yelled, "They're helicopters."

Mrs. Bellow seethed. She picked up her purse and had her gun halfway out. "It's too late for you."

Charlotte let go of Jared's hand and reached into her bag. She tried not moving the top part of her body while she fished around in her bag.

As Mrs. Bellow aimed her gun at the couch, she said, "Brooklyn, don't look so surprised. Remember when you and I were partners in Dr. Oracle's house? I told you I carry a gun."

Charlotte pulled out Jared's gun that she had put in her bag.

Mrs. Bellow laughed. "Charlotte, you forget that I know what a good shot you are. You shot Jared in the leg, remember? You can't aim and shoot that thing."

Charlotte didn't blink or hesitate. She fired all the rounds at Mrs. Bellow. Most of the bullets didn't meet their mark, but two hit Mrs. Bellow in the chest, and she went flying backward.

One of the bodybuilders almost took the doors off their hinges when he ripped them open to escape. The guards ran down the hall while Charlotte got up and ran over to Mrs. Bellow.

Charlotte's tears flowed down her face and onto her dress. They mixed with the blood on Mrs. Bellow dress. "Why did you do this?"

She spit out blood. "Simple, Charlotte. For greed."

Mrs. Bellow's eyes fluttered shut. Brooklyn knelt by Mrs. Bellow and shook her shoulders. "You were like my mother. Why! Why!"

She started screaming and crying, pounding on Mrs. Bellow's chest. The blood splattered up onto Charlotte and Brooklyn. Brooklyn yelled, "I hate you, Mrs. B. I hate you."

She laid her head on Mrs. Bellow's chest and squeaked out, "Why?"

Gretchen and Charlotte picked Brooklyn up. Charlotte said in a quiet voice, "Come on, Brooklyn. There's nothing we can do for her now."

Jared picked Brooklyn up as she went limp in his arms.

Suddenly, Mrs. Bellow's home was crawling with emergency personnel.

Charlotte went to talk with them. "You'll find Mrs. Bellow inside the study, dead. How did you know?"

The police captain said, "We got a call from the president. He'd been contacted by Polo and Seed, told that Mrs. Rogers had been kidnapped."

Charlotte pulled her hair back. "Is Mrs. Rogers all right?"

He nodded. "She's fine. Let me get a unit over here to take you home."

Charlotte said, "What about the Validator, and Dr. Oracle?"

"Well, the Validator has been arrested, but Dr. Oracle has slipped away."

The police cruiser pulled up, and Jared put Brooklyn in the front seat and the three of them crawled in back.

The ride back was silent. No one could think of anything to say.

When they arrived at Primevil, there was a messed-up Mrs. Rogers to greet them. She didn't say a word; she just gave each of them a big hug. Her wrists and ankles were bruised and bleeding, and she had a black eye and a cut on her cheek.

Charlotte mumbled, "Mrs. Bellow is dead."

Mrs. Rogers said, "I know. I'm sorry."

Charlotte looked at Mrs. Rogers. "I almost got you killed. I thought you were one of the bad guys."

"Honey, don't worry. I'm an operative, and I'm used to this. You're just sixteen years old."

Brooklyn was awake but unstable. Jared picked her up and carried her into Primevil. Jared called out, "Charlotte, you coming?"

Charlotte ran to Jared's side.

Jared waited outside the girls' room as they changed out of their party dresses. Brooklyn took her beautiful dress off and threw it in the trash. She slowly put her pajamas on and crawled under the covers.

Gretchen took Noon and Midnight out of the dresser drawer. She handed Noon to Brooklyn, who quickly brought the kitten to her chest.

Gretchen slid under the covers of the other bed and snuggled with Midnight.

Charlotte left the room and walked with Jared up to his room. She said, "Jared, tomorrow we find a house to move into."

Jared nodded and wrapped his arm around her. He went into the bathroom and came out with his pajama bottoms on. Charlotte was already under the covers. He slipped under the sheet and comforter and put his arms around her. He gently brushed his lips against her hair.

Charlotte was trying not to cry, but she couldn't hold back. She sobbed for several hours before she was completely exhausted and cried out. Her brain was numb, but finally she drifted off to sleep.

33

Getting On with Life

The next day Mrs. Rogers stopped by to talk with Charlotte and Jared. She knew of a house they could live in. Jared had taken enough jewels from Dr. Oracle to keep them well provided for several years. Jared said, "Mrs. Rogers, it needs at least five bedrooms. I'd like to find my mother and have her live with us."

Charlotte said, "We're all going back to high school."

Mrs. Rogers smiled. "Good for you. I'll look into finding your mother. I'll be leaving in a couple of days. The house I rented with Polo and Seed has enough bedrooms for all of you."

Charlotte grimaced. "Polo and Seed work for the government?"

Mrs. Rogers laughed. "I know, looks can be deceiving, but they're the best agents we have. They don't really have polio or scurvy, and their names aren't Polo and Seed."

Charlotte sat up and stretched. "But those two were the ones that dragged me to Primevil."

"They had to be believable or they wouldn't fit in," Mrs. Rogers said. "Jared, I'll find your mother, and then I'm off to my next assignment."

Charlotte said, "Bye, Mrs. Rogers. I'm sorry, again, for getting you in danger."

Mrs. Rogers wrote down the rental house address and the phone number and handed it to Charlotte. "The house is paid for an entire year. You can move in as soon as you want. Our Secret Service committee falls under the purview of the president of the United States. The Validator didn't have any control over our department. You'll be safe from Dr. Oracle. I was told that someone will be watching over you at all times."

Jared said, "Thanks for the house, Mrs. Rogers."

The next day the teens left Primevil by way of taxi cab. They had very few personal items. Charlotte put Noon and Midnight in her bag. Before they got into the cab, Charlotte looked back at the creepy building and shivered. She looked at Jared and her friends and whispered, "I can't say it was all bad."

Jared jumped in the front, and the girls clamored into the backseat. The cabbie said, "Where to?"

Charlotte handed the man the piece of paper.

"Oh, Craig Place," he said. "That's in a good part of town." He handed the piece of paper back to Charlotte.

In the safety of the cab and knowing they wouldn't have to return to Primevil, the four teenagers talked openly about the recent events.

Gretchen said, "I wish I'd had a camera when Brooklyn was crying the other night. Her cake-packed makeup reminded me of clown. You've got to cut back on that stuff."

Brooklyn held her bag up. "Since Charlotte put both kittens in her bag, I had room for all my cosmetics." Brooklyn bowed her head. "Maybe I should have left them behind. It'll just remind me of Mrs. Bellow."

Charlotte said, "She was a part of our lives. It was good until the very end."

Brooklyn swallowed hard. "Yeah, but it was all a lie. She never cared about us."

Charlotte pulled Noon out of her bag and handed the kitten to Brooklyn, and she took Midnight out. "At least we got two adorable kittens out of Primevil. Not many can say that."

Gretchen said, "You know, I never thought I'd say this, but I can't wait to get back to high school."

Brooklyn said, "I didn't think you were a good student."

"I wasn't, but at least the guys will be normal."

Brooklyn said, "Just because the teen guys aren't living at an asylum doesn't mean they'll be normal."

Charlotte reached through the front seats and patted Jared's arm. "A lot of teens won't have any-place else to live if they're orphans. Jared just happened to have taken a handful of jewels from Dr. Oracle's private collection so we can afford things."

As they pulled up to a nice two-story light-yellow house with black shutters, the cabbie said, "Here we are."

Jared counted out the money for the fare, then jumped out of the car and yelled. "Mom!"

There was a petite dark-haired woman sitting on the steps to the house. He gave his mother a hug and yelled, "Charlotte, this is my mother." He didn't let go of his mother. "Mom, this is. . ."—he blushed—"my girlfriend. Charlotte."

Charlotte put her hand out to greet Jared's mother, but she scooped Charlotte up in her arms. Tears were still streaming down her face and onto her shirt. She said through sobs, "It's nice to meet my son's girlfriend. You are quite fetching."

Charlotte was almost speechless from the compliment. "Thank you. It's nice to meet you."

Jared placed his hand gently on his mother's shoulder. "Brooklyn, Gretchen, this is my mother, Denise Walker."

She released her hold on Charlotte and wiped her eyes with her fingers. "I never thought this day would come. I went to the asylum many times, but they wouldn't let me in to see Jared. I guess they thought I was some reporter who just wanted to get a story for the media. I showed them my identification, but that wasn't enough. Before this all happened, I had no idea where Jared was or if he was still alive. With my other two kids, the Collector came to the house and took them. I knew where they were, but Jared had been at work when he turned sixteen. I begged him not to go to work that day, but he's very stubborn. He's always been a hard worker. Wanted money to fix that stupid run-down jeep of his."

Charlotte looked at Jared, who shrugged his shoulders. She asked Denise, "Have you been waiting long?"

"No, I just got here." She gave all the girls another hug, and gave Jared a kiss on the cheek. He saw her constant never-ending stream of tears and tore a section of his shirt off. He handed it to his mother as she dabbed at her face.

Noon and Midnight popped their heads out of the bag Charlotte was carrying.

"What darling kittens," Mrs. Walker said.

Gretchen grabbed Noon, and Charlotte cuddled with Midnight. Mrs. Walker stroked Noon. "Oh what happened to that one's leg?"

Jared winked at Charlotte. "Mom, it's a long story. We can get caught up once we get settled in."

They walked up the steps, and Charlotte unlocked the door.

Charlotte said, "Mrs. Rogers told me that there's one master bedroom downstairs, and four smaller bedrooms and two baths upstairs."

Jared said, "Mom, would you like the master bedroom?"

She smiled and shrugged her shoulders. "That sounds fine to me."

Everything was already set up in the house. The four teens walked up the steps to the second floor. Charlotte looked in her bedroom and one of the bathrooms. "Mrs. Rogers thought of everything. Look—even toothpaste and toothbrushes."

The rest of the day they became familiar with their surroundings; they even walked to the high school they'd be attending. As nightfall settled over the house, everyone got ready for bed.

Jared said, "Charlotte, since my mother lives here, I don't think we can sleep in the same bed, even though we've always had our clothes on. I'll just lie down in here with you for about an hour." Jared's mother had already said her "good nights" and went to her room.

Brooklyn and Gretchen bounced into the room, and Gretchen said, "Do you two want to play cards?"

Jared had his arm behind his head and the other one wrapped around Charlotte. "I don't. Charlotte, do you?"

Charlotte said, "Thanks, but I'll pass."

Gretchen and Brooklyn went into Gretchen's room and gently shut the door.

Charlotte snuggled into Jared's chest, and the darkness filled the room. "Jared, did you hear that?"

He yawned. "Hear what?"

"There it is again. You don't hear anything."

"No, just a few crickets. Why, what do you hear?"

Charlotte wasn't about to tell Jared that what she heard scared her to death: "We Willy Wanda crippled and deformed, you count your sanity while I count mine." She thought maybe Wanda had followed them to the house, even though Wanda said she couldn't leave Primevil.

She relaxed some when she heard Brooklyn and Gretchen laughing. She figured they were playing a prank on her.

Jared yawned. "Charlotte, you don't mind if I go back to my room, do you?"

"No, go right ahead. I think I'll just stay up and play cards with Brooklyn and Gretchen."

Jared walked her across the hall and took her in his arms. He gently brushed her lips with his. "Charlotte, this is where we start our new life together."

Charlotte crinkled her nose. "Yeah, I know."

She watched Jared shuffle into his room and looked over at her own room. She got a chill and quickly opened Gretchen's door. She ran and landed on the bed, scattering the cards.

Gretchen handed Midnight to Charlotte. "Now we'll have to start all over. Hand me the cards, and I'll deal them out three ways."

Charlotte couldn't shake the feeling that everything wasn't going to be all right. The house was pleasant enough; that wasn't it. She just had a strange feeling, and she couldn't place what it was. Maybe she was crazy. After all, Jared hadn't heard anything. But maybe it hadn't been her friends singing that rhyme.

As they played cards late into the night, at around two a.m. Charlotte heard it again. It was coming from downstairs. "We Willy Wanda, crippled and deformed, you count your sanity while I count mine."

A chill ran up Charlotte's spine. There is something in this house. She strained her ears to listen, but didn't hear anything.

Brooklyn poked Charlotte. "Snap out of it. If you're not going to pay attention, we'll deal you out."

"I'm paying attention." But she still couldn't shake the way her stomach felt. She said to herself under her breath, "This is a new beginning. Do you hear that, Charlotte? A new beginning."

The End

Made in the USA
Charleston, SC
24 October 2012